Luke & Lara

Poornima Manco

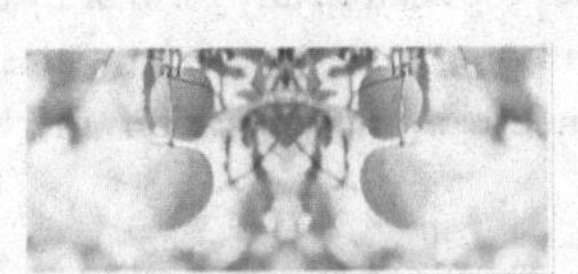

*To those who wait, who wander, who remember—may friendship be
your compass and love your shore.*

What is a friend? A single soul dwelling in two bodies.
— Aristotle

Us

Buoys

"When did we get so old?" she groaned, tugging at a silver strand on her head as if it had materialised overnight.

"Old? Speak for yourself, darling. I'm still a spring chicken," he grinned, winking in that same boyish way that had not faded with time. Perhaps the only thing that hadn't.

She rolled her eyes, but when their gazes met—hers filled with mock exasperation, his with that ever-familiar twinkle—something electric sparked between them. Something that had always been there, dormant but never extinguished.

The silence stretched between them, thick with the weight of decades, of inside jokes that needed no explanation, of unsaid words that hung in the air like ghosts, of shared laughter that had carved lines around their eyes, and heartbreaks too deep to name. Their history sat between them, unmovable and undeniable.

Then, as if on cue, they burst into laughter, the sound bubbling up from somewhere primal and true, light and effortless, wrapping around them like a warm embrace against the chill of time's passage and the sadness of what lay ahead.

They had always been each other's lifelines, buoying one another through life's deepest waters, steadying each other through every storm that threatened to capsize them. Their hands, now weathered and mapped with veins that told stories of their own, still found each other with the same certainty as they had decades ago.

And no matter how strong the currents became, they would hold on.

Always.

Lara (May 1980)

Drowning

Drowning was beautiful. It was a strange thought, but it struck her unexpectedly as she sank to the bottom of the pool. White, translucent bubbles danced upward, spinning like ethereal ballerinas, their grace mocking her panic. The deep blue of the water wrapped around her like a velvet shroud, heavy and unyielding. Her chest burned as the water invaded her lungs, each desperate gasp meeting only the cold, suffocating embrace of the pool.

Was she dying? Her mind was strangely clear as the chaos in her body began to ebb. A peculiar calm washed over her and she stopped struggling, surrendering to the numbness in her limbs and the pull of gravity. She let herself drift downward, weightless and resigned.

Just a moment ago, she had trusted Lexi with her life. Foolish, really, but Lexi had seemed so confident, so relaxed and at home in the water. The blonde girl had laughed as Lara splashed in the shallow end, making her feel silly, her laugh cutting deeper than any insult.

"You're like a baby," Lexi had teased with a casual cruelty.

Lara had flushed, hot shame rising through her. She had watched

Lexi sprint toward the diving board, her lean body arcing through the air in a perfect dive. She had sliced through the water like a blade, emerging moments later with a triumphant grin, droplets glistening like jewels on her sun-kissed skin. Then she had turned to Lara, her eyes sparkling with challenge. Lara had looked away, her stomach knotting. She didn't belong here, among these dolphin-like children, with their confident laughter and effortless grace. She had been content to paddle in the shallows, waiting for the day her mother would teach her to swim.

Get comfortable with the water first, Zinia had said. *Learn to understand it, to become one with it.*

Neither Lara nor Zinia had expected this gaggle of American kids, loud and boisterous, taking over the pool like it was their kingdom. This was Delhi, after all, and the pool was only frequented by the adults who worked in the adjoining offices, and that too, after office hours. These, could be their children, visiting from the U.S., Zinia surmised.

"You could make friends with them, Lara," Zinia had suggested earlier, her voice hopeful but tinged with a shadow of doubt as she looked at Lara, silently conveying her dismay.

But Lara hadn't wanted friends like them. Their lithe bodies, their wild energy, their laughter—it all intimidated her. They belonged to a world she couldn't touch, a world that made her feel small and clumsy. And yet, when Lexi had extended her hand, her voice teasing but oddly inviting, Lara had felt a surge of boldness. Maybe she could prove herself just this once. She had grasped Lexi's hands and let the older girl guide her into the deeper water. Slowly, hesitantly, she had kicked her legs, loosening her grip, believing that maybe, just maybe, she could do this. That's when Lexi had let go.

The laughter came first—sharp, bright, and merciless. And then Lexi had swum away, her golden head breaking through the surface like an exultant seal. Lara had sunk instantly. Panic seized her, her arms thrashing, her legs kicking wildly, swallowing mouthfuls of chlorinated water as she tried in vain to claw her way to the surface.

Now, as the fight ebbed out of her, the pool swallowed her whole, its silence deafening. Above her, the world shimmered like a mirage, tantalisingly close but hopelessly out of reach. Below, the darkness beckoned, soft and final. Lexi's laughter echoed in Lara's mind one last time before it faded into the stillness, leaving only the quiet rhythm of the water pulling her in deeper.

A body broke through the distant surface, strong arms wrapping around her, pulling her upwards. For a fleeting moment, she resisted. It had been so calm down there, so peaceful. The quiet depths had felt like an escape. But then her body betrayed her, instinct taking over, and she surrendered to the upward pull, her legs kicking weakly.

When they broke the surface, the air stabbed her lungs like knives, and her breaths were ragged and desperate. She was guided to the pool's edge, her limbs limp and trembling with exhaustion. The sharp taste of chlorine lingered as she retched water into the drain, her body heaving with the effort. Her eyes burned, her throat ached, and hot tears blurred her vision.

"Hey," a voice said gently, cutting through the ringing in her ears. "Hey, are you okay?"

She squinted upward, the sun blinding her. When her vision cleared, she saw him. A boy, nut-brown skin glowing in the sunlight, his dark, wavy hair dripping water onto his face. His eyes were soft, kind, and filled with worry. She couldn't answer. Her teeth chattered uncontrollably, and her chest still heaved as she clung to the pool's edge. From the corner of her eye, she noticed Lexi and her friends huddled together in the shallow end, where she had been safe not long ago. They watched her, their faces pale, their confidence drained. The boy stayed close, steadying her trembling form. Was it he who had saved her? She didn't have the strength to ask.

The lifeguard came rushing over, his face a mixture of panic and guilt. "Lara, baby, what happened? I just stepped away for a moment..."

She barely registered his words. Her limbs felt like lead as she dragged herself out of the pool, wrapping her towel tightly around her slight frame. She sat on a nearby chair, her body shaking with the aftershocks of fear. The boy followed and sat beside her, his voice gentle but firm. "I'm Luke," he said. "I saw what Lexi did. She'll be dealt with, I promise. But first, are you okay? Do I need to call someone for you?"

His kindness was too much. Lara's chest hitched, her heart constricted, and then the tears came. She could handle Lexi's laughter, even the betrayal, but this unexpected kindness from a stranger? It unravelled her completely. Through her sobs, she barely noticed the lifeguard on the phone. Then, suddenly, Zinia was there, her arms warm and steady, wrapping around Lara's trembling body. She rocked her gently, whispering, "It's okay, baby. Mummy's here now. It's okay."

Lara buried her face in her mother's shoulder, shutting out the world. She refused to look at Lexi or Luke, their faces swimming in her mind like unwelcome ghosts. All she wanted was for this day to end, for the sun to set and take her humiliation and fear with it.

Her tenth birthday had been an unmitigated disaster.

"Why are you pushing her, Zin? The poor child's had a fright." Yash's voice was steady, but exasperation simmered beneath.

Zinia let out a sharp breath. "If she doesn't get back in now, she never will. It's like riding a horse—"

"Neither of us has ever ridden a horse," Yash interrupted, unimpressed.

"You know what I mean."

"You mean well, but she needs a break."

"You're too soft on her."

"And you're too hard."

"She's our child," Zinia snapped. "I love her, but she needs to toughen up!"

"She will. In time."

A pause. Then, softer, Zinia asked, "Do you think she's awake?"

"Let her rest. It's Sunday."

Lara lay curled in bed, listening. The balcony which wrapped around the living room and her bedroom was usually a space for morning tea and newspapers, but it had become a battleground right now. She squeezed her eyes shut, willing their voices away, but they pressed on.

"How can I ask for an apology, Yash? She's my new boss's daughter."

"Well, if that boy speaks up, maybe she'll be forced to give one."

"That boy is also her brother," Zinia said, bitterness underlining her words.

"Half-brother."

"Half, quarter—what does it matter? Family sticks together."

"Even with these Americans?"

"Don't be ridiculous. They're people, not aliens."

"Their values aren't like ours."

And there it was. The old argument. The West, tradition, marriage, morals. Lara had heard it all before.

Yash, a staunch Hindu, held fast to tradition like an anchor in a storm. To him, life meant the sanctity of marriage, daily prayers, and an unwavering respect for elders. Zinia, a Goan Christian with a love for Western music and a liberal mindset, and a stubborn refusal to give either up, was just as firm in her beliefs. Their ideologies clashed in a way that felt both familiar and exhausting, a reminder of how different they were, and yet, how deeply they loved one another. After all, they had fought the odds to marry despite every objection from their families.

Lara felt pulled between them, stretched thin, torn between worlds. Today, more than anything, she just wanted some quiet. She burrowed deeper under her coverlet. Just a few more minutes before she had to face the day.

"It's not that bad," Renu said, licking the sides of her ice cream cone with precision, her eyes twinkling. "You could have drowned to death on your birthday."

Lara let out a startled laugh, the sound bubbling up despite herself.

"I nearly drowned!" she spluttered.

"Yeah, but you didn't," Renu said with a shrug. "And anyway, you were rescued by a gorgeous boy."

"I didn't say he was gorgeous!" Lara frowned, the heat rising in her cheeks.

"He sounded gorgeous," Renu countered, unflinching, as she kept licking her cone, making sure not a single drop escaped.

Lara rolled her eyes. Renu had recently started devouring Mills & Boon novels, which meant she now saw romantic heroes everywhere. Lara had just graduated from Enid Blyton to Agatha Christie. She much preferred her heroes with twirling moustaches, egg-shaped heads, and a knack for solving murders like Monsieur Poirot.

"Anyway," Lara muttered, "Mummy wants to take me back to the pool on Saturday, and I don't want to go."

"Why not?"

"Haven't you been listening?" Lara asked, exasperated.

Renu gave her a sly look from under her lashes. "Yeah. But... what if *he*'s there?"

"I still don't want to go!" Lara snapped, turning away in a huff. "And Mummy won't take no for an answer. She said she'll get into the pool with me and teach me this time."

"So, what's the problem? Once you learn, you can show that horrible girl you're not afraid of her anymore."

"I'm NOT afraid of her," Lara shot back, crossing her arms and pouting.

"Okay." Renu popped the last bite of her cone into her mouth and crunched down with a loud, satisfied chomp. "Now, can we go back to yours for some more cake?"

School passed in a blur that week, each day melting into the next with little excitement. Classes went on as usual, and Anjali, her friend at school, gifted her an Agatha Christie book for her birthday. It was a Miss Marple mystery. Lara felt a pang of disappointment—it wasn't Poirot—but she smiled and gushed over it, anyway. Anjali had meant well, and Lara didn't want to seem ungrateful.

She avoided talking about the pool, her near-drowning, or her rescue. The memory remained tucked away, the trauma of it still too recent to ignore entirely. Zinia's resolve to take her to the pool on Saturday still loomed over her, but Lara ignored it, hoping Zinia would forget but knowing deep-down that she wouldn't.

Sports Day arrived on Friday. Lara was part of the relay race, and the thought filled her with a mild sense of dread. She wasn't particularly sporty, and all she wanted was to avoid embarrassing herself. Unlike her athletic classmates, Lara had no dreams of glory. She simply hoped not to trip like some hopelessly uncoordinated classmates, who always seemed to stumble over their own feet.

In the end, the race wasn't a disaster. Her team finished a respectable third, earning her a small wooden bowl as a prize.

"What's this for, then?" Yash teased when she brought it home. He held it up, pretending to inspect it. "Is it a begging bowl? Will you be out on the streets, asking for alms now, hey?"

Lara laughed, setting the bowl aside. It wasn't much, but she was glad the day was over. She retreated to her favourite nook, the Miss Marple book in hand, and let herself sink into the comforting world of crime-solving. So when Zinia dangled the promise of lunch at The Centre after a swim, Lara, still foggy from her reading, absentmindedly said yes before realising what she'd done.

Trapped!

At least there was a lunch of fish and chips to look forward to.

The morning at the pool wasn't as bad as Lara had feared. The place was empty except for the lifeguard, who gave her a sheepish smile. Zinia's tense shoulders relaxed as she and Lara stepped onto the damp tiles.

Lara hesitated at the edge, curling her toes over the smooth lip. She dipped one in, stomach tightening.

"Come on, baby," Zinia coaxed, her voice soft but edged with impatience. "No one's watching." When Lara still didn't get in, Zinia scowled. "If you don't get in this instant, I will come out and drag you in," she warned, her voice sharp enough to make Lara move.

Lara slid into the water without another word, the chill shocking her skin. She paddled quickly over to where Zinia stood, eager to avoid further scolding.

"Good," Zinia said briskly. "Now, hold on to the side and kick."

At first, Lara clung to the edge like it was a lifeline, her kicks hesitant and awkward. But bit by bit, her fear ebbed away. Zinia was patient, guiding her gently, and soon Lara was blowing bubbles in the water, her kicks growing stronger. By the end of the hour, she could semi-float without clutching the side. The only thing she refused to do was venture into the deep end.

"It's alright," Zinia said with a sigh, brushing a stray strand of hair from her face. "One step at a time."

Later, as they sat at The Centre, eating fish and chips, Zinia's tone softened. "I wish I could teach you properly, darling," she admitted, her fork prodding at a piece of fish. "But I just don't have the time. One boss is already breathing down my neck, and now there's the new one." She paused, staring thoughtfully into the distance. "Maybe I'll ask Nangia," she mused. "He brings his daughters to the pool every Sunday. Perhaps he wouldn't mind teaching you."

Lara didn't answer, letting the pleasant heaviness in her limbs anchor her to the moment. She gazed around The Centre, soaking in its serene luxury. Here, the world outside—hot, dusty, and teeming with chaos—felt like a distant memory. The quiet hum of air conditioners, the plush sofas, the soft carpets, and the pad-footed waiters created a haven of calm. Conversations were murmured, not shouted, and everything seemed cocooned in layers of order and ease. Lara thought she could live here forever, especially if her favourite vanilla ice cream with hot chocolate sauce was always on the menu.

"Zinia! *Dikri*! It's been too long!"

A booming voice shattered the moment. Mrs. Jijibhoy, round and swathed in a cream saree, descended upon them. She launched into a monologue, barely pausing for breath. Ordering a coffee, she talked incessantly about herself, with Zinia opening and closing her mouth like a fish, trying to get a word in.

Lara tuned out, swirling her ice cream into a perfect chocolate-vanilla mix, sneaking sideways glances at her mother's captor, until the woman's attention turned to her.

"What is it, young lady? Do you have something to say?"

Lara hesitated, then blurted at Mrs Jijibhoy, "Why are you called a boy when you're a girl?"

The woman's chin quivered. "Well! I never!" She left in a huff, her coffee untouched.

Zinia exhaled sharply, her initial glare at Lara softening into laughter. "Thank you, darling," she said between giggles. "That was a much-needed rescue."

Lara grinned, her chest warming at her mother's approval. She wasn't entirely sure what she'd done, but whatever it was, it had turned out just right.

"Excuse me," a voice called softly, followed by a head peeking out around the corner. "Are you Zinia Seth?"

Zinia blinked, startled. For a moment, she just stared, then managed a nod. "Yes, that's me. Do I know you?"

A striking woman stepped fully into view, her short, curly hair framing a sweet, smiling face. "Not yet," she said, her voice smooth, "but you've met my husband—your new boss, Jim Brown. I'm Christine. And this," she gestured beside her, "is my son, Luke. I believe you've met him too?"

Lara's breath caught as her eyes darted to the boy standing beside the woman. It was him—the one who had pulled her from the water, the one whose face had been a blur except for his soft brown eyes, which she hadn't forgotten. Now he stood there, solid and real, his kind eyes meeting hers in a frank stare.

———

"It's a strange setup, but who am I to judge?" Zinia said lightly, spooning more curry onto her plate. Lara caught an edge in her tone —curiosity, maybe judgment.

Yash frowned, lowering the TV volume. "So Christine is his second wife, and Luke is hers?"

"Yes. And Lexi and her brother are from the first marriage. They're just visiting."

"Complicated," Yash muttered.

Zinia cast a glance at Lara, who was busy tearing her *chapati* into tiny pieces. "The boy has beautiful manners. Christine's British, so no surprise there."

"And our little princess?" Yash tugged Lara's plait, his teasing tone cutting through the tension.

"She was mostly quiet. Except when she asked Mrs. Jijibhoy why she was called a boy."

Yash chuckled. "Did you at least thank Luke?"

Lara shook her head, guilt creeping in.

"I did," Zinia said, rescuing her. "I was thinking of taking them Jude's bebinca as a thank-you."

"But I like that cake!" Yash protested.

Zinia rolled her eyes, passing him another *chapati*. "We'll get more when we visit." Then she raised her voice. "Valli, don't make any more! There's plenty."

Yash turned the TV back up. The news droned on about an

attempted assassination. The room tensed. Lara tuned it out, letting her mind drift.

Then Yash snapped off the TV. "This country is going to the dogs."

"Oh, come on, Yash," Zinia scoffed. "Just because the Janata Party lost—"

"Lost? After what she did during the Emergency? And now she's back in power? That man who attacked her... he's not a criminal, he's desperate."

"You can't be serious! Nothing justifies attempted murder."

"Assassination," Yash corrected.

"Whatever! It just stings, doesn't it? Watching a woman run this country better than those imbeciles ever could."

"You can't call them imbeciles! Morarji Desai—"

"Yes, yes, very respected, and half his cabinet quit under him. What about that?"

Across the room, Valli met Lara's eyes. "Baby, do you want to go to bed?"

Lara nodded quickly, grateful for the escape.

Lying in bed, she picked up her book, but Luke's warm brown eyes kept intruding on her thoughts. Sitting next to Luke at lunch had been strange, a novel and unsettling experience. Boys were a mystery, whispered about in hushed giggles at her all-girls' school. Anjali once said having a boyfriend meant holding hands, as if that simple act cemented everything. Lara frowned. She didn't want to hold hands with anyone. Not Luke. Not anyone.

Marriage? Even worse. Marriages meant arguments, long silences, and closed doors. What she wanted was freedom—luxurious hotels, plush carpets, nights spent reading without a care. Just like Uncle Jude. Just like Aunty Roxanna used to.

Would her dream ever come true?

Floating

Uncle Jude chuckled and reached out to ruffle Lara's hair. "You'll be swimming like a fish in no time," he said, tapping ash from his cigarette into the ashtray with a practiced flick.

Lara gazed up at him, her eyes full of pure adoration. To her, Uncle Jude wasn't just an uncle, he was a hero. Tall and effortlessly charming, every detail about him felt larger than life. His trousers had a crease sharp enough to cut paper, his shoes gleamed like polished obsidian, and he always smelled incredible—spicy, musky, and distinctly Uncle Jude. Much as she loved her father, he didn't have the same flair, the same effortless magnetism that made Uncle Jude seem like he'd stepped out of the pages of a novel.

"How long are you in town this time, Jude?" Zinia asked, expertly peeling the long white radish into a steel bowl. She was making *mooli parathas*, his favourite. It was a fussy task, grating the radish and squeezing out the water to avoid ruining the dough, but Zinia always did it without complaint when Uncle Jude visited. Lara knew this, because she'd overheard Zinia grumble about it when he wasn't around.

"Just the usual 24 hours. My flight to Bombay's tomorrow evening," Jude replied.

"How's Roxy doing?"

"She's fine. Busy with the church, as always."

Yash brought over a glass of whisky and handed it to Jude. "How was the flight from London?"

Jude leaned back, taking a sip of his drink before answering. "Fine, except for this arrogant fool in First Class."

At this, everyone leaned in closer. Uncle Jude was a flight purser and his inflight stories were always the best.

"Spoiled film industry brat got drunk and caused a scene. I had to threaten him with handcuffs before he finally behaved."

"Would you really have handcuffed him?" Yash asked, raising an eyebrow.

"Of course," Jude said with a grin. "With the captain's permission. Not that I'd get it. Most of those guys are too busy being starstruck. But the passenger didn't know that. All he could picture were his name and face splashed across the front pages of every newspaper. Works like a charm."

"Who was it? Someone famous?" Zinia asked, pausing mid-grate.

"Roshan Kapoor, no less."

"What?!" Zinia gasped. "He always seems like such a gentleman!"

"They all do when the cameras are rolling," Jude said with a wink. "In real life, they're just a bunch of—"

Yash nudged him with an elbow before he could finish.

Jude smirked and turned his attention to Lara, his eyes twinkling. "So," he said, leaning forward conspiratorially. "What's new in Laraland?"

Lara grinned, her cheeks warm with delight. When Uncle Jude was around, it felt like the entire world leaned in just to listen.

Long after the *mooli parathas* had been devoured and the whisky drunk, the room settled into an easy warmth. The adults, loose-limbed and relaxed, began talking in low voices about everything and everyone. Lara nestled into Zinia's side, her head resting against her shoulder as Zinia stretched her legs out on the sofa.

"I've tried with Pedru," Jude said, his voice tight with frustration. "But he won't return my calls. He's bleeding our parents dry and banking on the idea that once they're gone, he'll inherit the ancestral home."

"He knows that's not happening!" Zinia snapped, her tone sharper than usual. "We all have an equal share in that house, and Ma and Da are only in their sixties. They're hale and hearty—touch-wood—and have plenty of years ahead of them. He's delusional if he thinks otherwise!"

"When was the last time you visited Goa, Zin?" Jude's jaw was set, his voice cutting. "You haven't seen what he's done to them. Ma and Da are shadows of themselves because Pedru's a parasite. He even sold Grandma's antique silver box to fund his drinking!"

Zinia's frown deepened. "I speak to them every week, Jude. They haven't mentioned any of this."

"They wouldn't," Jude said bitterly. "They don't want to burden you. But believe me, things are spiralling out of control over there."

Yash, who had been listening quietly, leaned forward. "Maybe you should both go together. See if you can talk some sense into him."

"It's too late for sense," Jude said with a bitter laugh. "But we can try to convince Ma and Da to evict him. He's a grown man—thirty-five years old! It's time he stood on his own two feet."

Lara's eyelids grew heavy as she listened. She had vague memories of meeting Uncle Pedru once, long ago. A tall man with a wide grin and hands that felt too large when he'd shaken hers. But her grandparents' house in Goa was etched in her mind with vivid clarity: a sprawling maze of rooms filled with hidden treasures and quiet corners perfect for hiding. The garden was her favourite, with its swaying palms and sturdy trees she loved climbing.

"I miss that house," Lara murmured sleepily, more to herself than anyone else.

Zinia looked thoughtful. "What if we all went down for Christmas?" she suggested, turning to Jude. "You, Roxy, Alex, and us—me, Yash, and Lara. If we go as a family, it won't feel like an intervention. It'll just seem like a holiday."

"I'm not sure your parents would want me there," Yash said gloomily. "They've never really warmed to me."

"Nonsense, Yash," Zinia said, dismissing the idea with a wave of her hand. "After all these years? You and Jude get along just fine. Ma and Da are just... formal with you because they don't want to say the wrong thing. But they know I'm happy, and that's all that matters."

Lara opened her eyes briefly, her curiosity piqued. "Are we going to Goa?"

"Not just yet, darling," Zinia said, patting her head. "Valli, take baby to her room."

Lara rose reluctantly, her limbs heavy with sleep. She hugged Uncle Jude tightly, holding on a little longer than usual, unsure when she would see him next. The thought of Goa filled her mind as Valli led her to bed—climbing trees, playing hide and seek with Alex, and rediscovering the house's every nook and cranny. With those happy visions, she drifted off into a deep, dreamless sleep.

The next evening, Yash came home early—something so unusual it stopped Lara mid-sentence as she worked on her homework at the dining table.

"Why are you home so soon, Papa?" she asked, looking up from her books.

"I wasn't feeling too well, Lara. Had to shut the shop early."

Lara froze. Most of Yash's customers came in the evening. His stationery shop was busiest after office hours. For him to close it early... She studied his face. He looked pale, his movements slower than usual, as if exhaustion had settled into his very bones.

"Shall I call Mummy?" Lara asked as Valli appeared with a glass of water.

"No, no," Yash said, waving the idea away. "She's busy in a meeting. I'll just lie down for a bit."

That made Lara sit up straight. Yash never lay down. Even on Sundays, he was always doing something—fixing a broken fan, reorganising the shop accounts, or catching up on the news.

As soon as Yash disappeared into the bedroom, Lara's fingers trembled as she dialled Zinia's office.

"Nangia uncle?" she stammered when the voice on the other end answered. "Can you... can you put me through to Mummy?"

"Is that Lara? Of course! But first, tell me, young lady, are we still on for swimming lessons this Sunday?" Nangia uncle's jovial voice boomed through the receiver.

Lara swallowed the lump in her throat. "Yes, but please, Uncle, can you call Mummy?"

There was a long wait before Zinia came on the line, and her tone was clipped. "What is it, Lara? Couldn't it have waited?"

"Mummy," Lara's voice quivered. "Papa isn't feeling well. He shut the shop and came home. He's lying down now."

The line went quiet, and when Zinia finally spoke, her voice had changed—brisk and efficient, but threaded with something unspoken. Was it fear?

"Yash came home early?" she said, sounding more startled than concerned at first. "He never comes home early. He even works Sundays."

"That's why I called," Lara said softly, hoping her tone conveyed the urgency she couldn't quite put into words.

"I'm coming home right now," Zinia said.

After the call, Lara sat at the table, her pencil abandoned. She stared out of the window, watching a sparrow hop from branch to branch. Yash had never been ill before. Her thoughts turned dark. What if he was like the woman down the road, who had wasted away until she was gone? What would they do without him? Would they have to leave Delhi? Live in Goa? Or worse, with Yash's parents in Indore?

"Sahib is sleeping, baby," Valli interrupted, her voice kind. "Do you want a sandwich?"

Lara nodded, her stomach growling. She took small bites of the sandwich, but thoughts—gloomy and heavy—kept swirling in her mind.

A car door slammed outside. The sound jolted her, and she set the sandwich down as the doorbell rang. Zinia walked in, and behind her was a stocky man with startling blue eyes.

"Hello, Lara," Zinia said quickly. "This is Jim, my boss. Is Papa in the bedroom?"

Before she could answer, Zinia hurried toward the room, leaving Lara alone with the foreign man. Jim smiled down at her. "I brought your mother home as soon as I heard. She was worried sick, and I didn't want her flagging down an auto rickshaw to get here."

Valli appeared with a tray and offered Jim a glass of water. "*Chai,* sahib?"

Jim looked puzzled.

"She means tea," Lara translated. "Would you like some?"

"Ah," Jim said with a grin. "No, I'm more of a coffee person. Still learning the lingo here."

Lara carefully wiped her hands on a napkin, avoiding his gaze. She didn't know what to say to this strange, overly cheerful man.

"You can tell your mother the car is ready to take them to the hospital," Jim said, his voice soft. "But there's no need to rush."

Before Lara could reply, Zinia emerged, supporting Yash. He looked pale but managed a weak smile at Jim. Without another word, they helped Yash into the white foreign car waiting outside.

Lara ran to the balcony, her heart pounding as she watched the car pull away. It gleamed in the evening light, a stark contrast to the dusty street. The neighbours were watching too, their expressions a mix of curiosity and disbelief. A white man and a foreign car in their neighbourhood—it was the kind of story that would be whispered about for weeks. But Lara didn't care about the neighbours. She cared only about the pale, tired figure being whisked away inside that car.

"Diabetes!" Zinia exclaimed, throwing up her hands in exasperation. "I should have guessed. No more *aloo parathas* for you, Yash!"

Yash lowered the newspaper he was reading and met her gaze calmly. "The doctor said if I watch my diet and start exercising, I could reverse it."

"Reverse it?" Zinia retorted, her voice dripping with scepticism. "Like your mother has? Face it, Yash—you come from a family of food lovers. Your 'good intentions' will last a week, maybe two. And then it'll be right back to the *parathas* and *jalebis*." She turned toward the kitchen. "From now on, I'm instructing Valli to avoid making starchy foods altogether."

Lara, sitting quietly nearby, let out a small, inaudible sigh of relief. It was only diabetes. Yash's mother had lived with it for twenty years, and she was fine. This wasn't some terrible illness, and for now, that was all that mattered.

"Anyway," Zinia continued, brushing invisible crumbs off her hands as if to punctuate her decision, "I was thinking that we should visit the Browns this evening. They've been so kind to us. I'll take them some flowers and the bebinca cake."

"Not me," Yash groaned, shifting uncomfortably in his chair. "It's stock-taking day. I've called Raju in to help with it."

"Fine," Zinia muttered, the irritation in her tone barely concealed. "I'll take Lara with me. But don't forget your medication, Yash. I've already reminded Valli."

"I won't, Zin," Yash said, with a twinkle in his eyes. "You're always looking out for me. What would I do without you, my heart?"

"Oh, stop your nonsense!" Zinia snapped, though the faintest blush crept up her cheeks. Her eyes flicked briefly to Lara, and her voice softened. "It's my job, as your wife."

Lara stood up, pretending to fetch something from another room. She knew better than to linger. This was her parents' moment—a fleeting, unspoken tenderness that rarely surfaced in their busy lives.

She didn't want to intrude, but as she stepped away, a small smile danced on her lips. Then it was wiped off with the horror of having to visit the Browns' residence. Oh no! She would have to meet that boy again, and his family. Would the horrid Lexi be there? Would she have to be all *nice-nice* to her? Lara wanted desperately to wriggle out of the visit, but she knew there was no escape. Zinia would tolerate no protest, especially since she was convinced they owed the Browns a debt of gratitude. And, if Lara was being honest, albeit begrudgingly, she couldn't deny the truth of it. Zinia's boss had gone out of his way to help Yash, taking him to the doctor, waiting with him, making sure he got home safely, and even dealing with the insurance. As for the boy... yes, he made her squirm, but he *had* saved her from drowning. She still hadn't thanked him properly, and that nagging sense of unfinished business gnawed at her. It was only fair they went.

When the evening brought a slight coolness to the air, Zinia handed Lara a hairbrush with a firm, "Tidy yourself up," before they set off to the taxi stand. Taking a taxi was an event in itself, a rare splurge reserved for special occasions like trips to the railway station or the airport. Most families in their neighbourhood didn't own cars. The Sahais down the street had one—a boxy Ambassador—but for everyone else, it was scooters and motorcycles. Yash's pride and joy was his Bajaj scooter, and Lara secretly loved being wedged between her parents on rides to the cinema or family visits. But Zinia didn't know how to ride a scooter, so on their own, they were at the mercy of auto-rickshaws, or, like today, the slightly more reliable taxis.

At the stand, Zinia haggled over the rate with one of the Singh brothers, who both dressed in khaki uniforms and wore identical blue turbans. The only difference between them was the small mole on one's face, but to make things even more confusing, they were both called *Sardarji* by everyone in the locality. Lara could never tell them apart. As Zinia's sharp tone cut through the evening air, Lara shifted on her feet, staring at the battered taxi that would carry them to this dreaded visit. How long would they have to stay? How long before she could escape the awkwardness of polite smiles, forced conversations, and that boy with his kind but unreadable eyes? The knot in her stomach tightened as Zinia signalled the deal was struck, and one of the Singh brothers started the car. There was no turning back now.

The drive wasn't long, and before Lara knew it, the taxi pulled up in front of an imposing grey house in Vasant Vihar. A cascade of vibrant pink bougainvillea spilled over the high fence, framing the gate where a chowkidar leaned idly on his post. His casual demeanour vanished as soon as Zinia stepped out of the taxi; he snapped to attention and offered her a crisp salute.

"Jim *sahib andar hain?*" Zinia inquired, her voice brisk and polite.

As the chowkidar responded, Lara's gaze wandered over to the house. It was the sort of home she'd only seen in glossy magazines—spacious, meticulously maintained, and exuding quiet opulence. On the way over, Zinia had explained how expats like her boss were granted such prestigious accommodations, complete with staff, cars, and chauffeurs. This, she'd said, was part of the allure that brought them to India. Lara felt a pang of awe mixed with curiosity. The manicured surroundings, the hushed wealth of the neighbourhood—it was a world far removed from her own.

After a brief exchange, the chowkidar swung the gate open, and they stepped into a garden fragrant with flowers. Before Zinia could even ring the bell, a maid appeared at the door, her hands folded in a polite *namaste*. She ushered them in with practiced ease.

The interior of the house was cool and quiet, the air conditioner humming softly in the background. Somewhere deeper inside, a faint thump of Western music echoed. Lara's heart sank slightly—was it Lexi blaring that awful racket? She bit the inside of her cheek, willing herself to stay calm.

Christine rushed into the room. She stopped short when she saw Zinia, her face flushing with surprise.

"Oh," she exclaimed, a little breathless. "I thought Jim had come back!"

Zinia's brows furrowed slightly in confusion. "I...I'm sorry to intrude. We just wanted to drop off some flowers and a cake to say thank you. I hope it's not a bad time. We have a taxi waiting outside, so..."

Christine let out a small laugh, placing a hand on her chest. "Oh, no, no! I must seem like such a scatterbrain—it's been one of those days." She sighed, then motioned towards the sofa. "Please, Zinia, do sit down. I've been so frazzled I forgot my manners entirely. It's just been a madhouse here today!"

"What happened?" Zinia asked, her tone soft and curious.

Christine sank into an armchair, shaking her head. "Steve and Lexi were leaving for the US today, and Jim—bless him—decided to put their passports somewhere 'safe'. Three weeks later, of course, he couldn't remember where that was! The entire house turned upside down looking for them."

"Did you find them?"

Christine threw her hands up. "Just in the nick of time! And you'll never guess where..."

Zinia tilted her head, eyebrows raised in silent inquiry.

"With his golf clubs, no less! Honestly, who *does* that?" Christine exclaimed, her voice tinged with exasperation and amusement. "Husbands, I tell you!"

Both women exchanged knowing smiles, shaking their heads in unison as they laughed, the tension of the moment easing into camaraderie.

"And I haven't even said hello to this young lady yet!" Christine turned her warm gaze to Lara, her smile kind. "Lara, isn't it? How are you, dear?"

Lara managed a small, shy smile, her relief almost tangible. She was secretly glad that Lexi had left before they arrived. If luck was on her side, she would never have to see that girl again.

"Shilpa," Christine called out to the maid, "bring some *chai*, please."

Zinia stood up, shaking her head. "Really, Christine, that's not necessary. We just came by to drop off the flowers—"

"I know, and thank you." Christine's smile was genuine. "They're beautiful. It's such a thoughtful gesture, Zinia. But I insist you stay. It's been a chaotic day, and I could use a moment of peace, and good company. Please?"

Zinia hesitated for a moment, then nodded graciously. Her eyes flicked to Lara. "Actually, if your son is around, Lara would like to say something to him, too."

"Luke?" Christine's gaze shifted to Lara, and in that moment, Lara couldn't help but notice how much her eyes resembled the boy's. "Let me call him."

Lara's heart sank. She stared at her feet, willing him not to answer. But moments later, she heard the soft pad of footsteps entering the room.

"Hello," came his quiet voice.

"Luke, you remember Mrs. Seth, your dad's secretary? And Lara?"

"Yes, of course," he said, his tone polite but warm. "How are you?"

Lara dared a fleeting glance at him from beneath her lashes.

"Lara?" Zinia's voice nudged her gently.

She drew in a breath and blurted, "Th-thank you for saving me from drowning." Her words wavered, and she kept her gaze firmly on the floor.

"That's okay," he replied simply. Then, after a beat, his voice brightened. "Hey, do you want to meet my pet tortoise? His name's Arthur Conan Doyle."

Lara's head shot up, startled. "Like the author?"

"Yes!" Luke's face lit up, his enthusiasm contagious. "Have you read any Sherlock Holmes? I've got the complete collection. Want to see?"

For the first time since arriving, Lara felt a flicker of curiosity overpower her discomfort. "Okay," she murmured, her shyness momentarily forgotten.

"He's twelve, and he loves reading. He even let me borrow a few of his Agatha Christie books."

Renu hopped into the final square of the hopscotch, balanced for a moment, and spun around to hop back. "So you're not scared of him anymore?" she asked, her voice teasing.

"Scared? I was never scared of him!" Lara's face flushed as she pouted. "I was just... well... unsure. I didn't know how to talk to him or what to say."

"Are you in love with him now?" Renu asked, her eyes sparkling with mischief.

"No, Renu! I'm not in love with a boy!" Lara exclaimed, hands on her hips. "He's just a friend."

"A boyfriend?"

"Not like that!" Lara huffed. "Yes, he's a boy, and yes, he's my friend. I like him, okay? But only because he's kind and nothing like his horrible sister."

Renu plopped down on the edge of the hopscotch grid, letting Lara take her turn. "Why do his brother and sister live in America?"

"They're his half-brother and half-sister," Lara explained, tossing her pebble into the first square.

"What's that supposed to mean?"

"They have a different mother. She's American."

"Isn't he American too?"

"No, he's part British. He was born in London and lived there until he was ten. Then they moved to America."

"He told you all that?"

"No, his mum told my mum."

Renu shook her head, frowning. "It's all so confusing."

Lara shrugged. "I guess. But I'm just glad we can talk now. He said I could come back and borrow as many books as I wanted, as long as I took care of them and didn't dog-ear the pages."

"What does that even mean?" Renu asked, puzzled.

"It's when you fold the corner of a page to mark your place."

"Oh, I do that all the time," Renu declared. "How else am I supposed to remember where I stopped?"

"You use a bookmark, silly!" Lara said, leaping off the last square with a flourish. She grimaced, thinking about the sorry state of Renu's books—dog-eared, food-stained, and barely holding together. She was relieved that Renu didn't care for crime novels.

"Are you still going to Goa for Christmas?" Renu asked as they wrapped up their game of hopscotch and strolled toward the park, badminton rackets swinging at their sides.

"Yes, that's what Mummy said when Uncle Jude visited last week. It'll be fun to celebrate Christmas with Granny and Grandpa there."

"Do you, like, go to church and everything?" Renu asked, tilting her head curiously.

"Yes, that's what they do, so I suppose we will, too," Lara replied casually.

"Do you go to church here?"

"Not really, unless it's for something at school," Lara shrugged. "Mummy's not very religious."

"But your Papa is, no?"

"Religious?" Lara considered this for a moment. "Yes, I guess so. He prays every day in the *mandir*. Sometimes I join him."

Renu stopped abruptly, turning to face Lara with an expression of genuine puzzlement. "Are you Hindu or Christian?" she asked, the question landing as though it had just dawned on her.

"Uhh, I don't know," Lara said after a beat, her voice uncertain. "I suppose I'm a bit of both. Why do you ask?"

"Dunno," Renu replied, her brow furrowing for a moment before she suddenly skipped ahead, the question discarded like an afterthought. Lara followed, her thoughts lingering on an answer she couldn't quite pin down.

At home, Zinia's favourite record played softly, filling the air with nostalgia. She was in an unusually cheerful mood.

"You know," she said for what felt like the hundredth time, her eyes sparkling, "you were named after this song."

Lara's Theme from Dr. Zhivago. Lara nodded; she knew the story by heart. It was Zinia's favourite movie—the one she and Yash had gone to see when they first held hands in a darkened theatre. It was the moment she had realised she loved this skinny, awkward Hindu boy who had been courting her so cautiously. Lara had heard it all before, yet it still warmed her to see the joy on her mother's face as she hummed along, pruning her beloved plants.

"Did you have a good day at the office, Mummy?" Lara asked, watching her closely.

"Yes, I did," Zinia said, turning to her with a radiant smile. "Christine took me out to lunch at The Centre. I think we could really be friends."

Lara raised an eyebrow. This was unusual. Zinia always kept her work life and personal life meticulously separate. To her, colleagues were colleagues, not friends. But Christine, it seemed, had crossed that line.

"Christine barely knows anyone in Delhi," Zinia went on, almost talking to herself now. "She says she feels isolated. It would be nice to get to know her better. Did you know her mother is Anglo-Indian?"

"What does that mean?" Lara asked, tilting her head.

"It means she has Indian blood," Zinia explained.

"Oh," Lara murmured, trying to grasp the significance.

Zinia paused, glancing at her plants as though lost in thought. "It means we might have more in common than I realised. But I'm sure your Papa will have something to say about it."

"Why?" Lara pressed, sensing there was more to this than Zinia was letting on.

Zinia sighed softly. "He'll probably say that since she's my boss's wife, I should keep my distance."

"Why?" Lara asked again, genuinely curious.

But just as suddenly as the mellow moment had begun, Zinia snapped out of it, as though realising she'd shared too much. Her voice grew brisk. "Come on now, wash up and start on your homework. You don't want to fall behind, do you?"

The conversation ended, but Lara couldn't shake the feeling that she'd glimpsed a deeper part of her mother, one that rarely surfaced.

"Now, remember everything I taught you—let your body relax in the water, take a deep breath in, and blow the bubbles out gently," Zinia instructed, her voice steady but distant, as though her thoughts were already elsewhere.

"Mummy, why can't you come into the pool with me?" Lara's gaze flickered up to her mother's face, her stomach churning with nervous anticipation.

"Darling, I told you, I have to catch up on some work."

"On a Sunday?"

"Your papa works on Sundays too," Zinia replied with a casual shrug, smoothing her saree.

Lara's eyes dropped to her feet, toes curling against the rough tiles. She wished Nangia Uncle wasn't the one teaching her. He was kind enough, but his presence felt strangely detached. And his daughters, with their sleek ponytails and brightly coloured swimsuits, had been splashing and racing earlier, ignoring her entirely. They seemed to belong in the water in a way Lara didn't, their laughter and confidence a world apart from her hesitance.

"Listen, Lara," Zinia said gently, crouching slightly to meet her daughter's eyes. "I'll only be gone an hour. Nangia Uncle is just going to help you practice the basics—nothing scary, I promise. No deep end today. Just stay in the shallow water and do your best. Okay? Now go rinse off before you start."

Lara nodded reluctantly, clutching her towel tighter. She stepped into the shower, the sharp smell of chlorine mingling with the rush of cold water as it spilled over her. It was a scent that pulled her in two directions: the excitement of learning to swim and the quiet dread of failure.

Wrapped in her towel, she followed Zinia out to the poolside. The sun climbed higher, scorching the pavement, and a shiver rippled down her back despite the heat. Yash had said the mercury would reach 40 degrees today. She hoped they'd be home by then, safely out of the sweltering sun, far away from the uneasy feeling knotting her stomach.

"Okay, baby, I'll see you later," Zinia said, brushing a kiss on Lara's forehead before walking away.

"Come in, Lara," Nangia Uncle called from the pool, his voice warm and encouraging.

Lara dipped a toe into the water, then stepped in fully, forcing herself to breathe evenly. It's going to be alright, she told herself. Nangia Uncle was kind, patient even. He would teach her gently. But he wasn't Zinia. Her muscles refused to relax, her limbs stiff as she clung to the pool's edge and kicked half-heartedly. Despite her efforts, the anxiety buzzing in her chest wouldn't let up.

"Look, child," Nangia Uncle said, his tone tinged with a gentle admonishment. "If you stand up, the water barely reaches your waist. There's no need to be scared. Take a deep breath and try floating on your stomach if the back is too tricky."

Lara nodded and gave it another shot, but panic took over each time, her feet instinctively finding the bottom before she could even begin. After a while, Nangia Uncle's daughters distracted him, and he left Lara to practice alone in the shallows. She didn't want to disappoint him, so she tried again, first on her stomach, then on her back.

Zinia's voice echoed in her mind. *Just let go, Lara. Look up at the sky, breathe, and relax. Imagine you're lying in bed, safe and weightless.* She closed her eyes and willed herself to let go. For a moment, Uncle Jude's face surfaced in her thoughts, his booming laugh and warm pride. She imagined how happy he'd be when she could finally swim. But the image shifted, replaced by Lexi's mocking laugh, sharp and cruel. It pierced through her confidence, unravelling her calm. Her body tensed, sinking further into the water. Panic flared—she was going under. Suddenly, firm hands pressed against her back, steady and reassuring. They lifted her gently, holding her afloat. Her eyes snapped open, an apology already forming on her lips, but instead of Nangia Uncle, she saw Luke. He was grinning down at her, his hair wet and glinting in the sun. His skin was only two shades lighter than hers, and suddenly the bit about Christine being part Indian made sense. Luke could pass for Indian except for when he spoke. That's when he sounded like a foreigner.

"I saw you struggling," he said, his tone light and teasing. "Figured you could use a bit of help."

This time, instead of embarrassment, Lara felt a quiet reassurance. Luke was her friend. He was a steady and safe presence. Besides, he had helped her before, and she allowed herself to trust him now.

"How long have you known how to swim, Luke?" she asked as he handed her a float and urged her to kick.

"Since I was a baby," he said with a smirk, an unruly curl falling on to his forehead. His brown eyes glinted with mischief. "Mum claims she tossed me into a pool and just waited for me to figure it out."

"Really?" Lara's eyes widened, equal parts horror and awe.

He laughed, his grin lighting up his face. "Not really. I started lessons when I was three."

Before she could respond, Nangia Uncle swam over, his brow furrowed with concern.

"It's alright, Uncle," Lara said quickly. "This is Luke Brown, Mummy's boss's son."

"Ah, Luke!" Nangia Uncle's face relaxed into a warm smile as recognition set in. "Yes, of course. Are you here for a swim?"

Luke nodded, his gaze drifting momentarily to the deep end, where Nangia Uncle's daughters were splashing and laughing. For a fleeting second, Lara's heart tightened, a sharp pang of unease cutting through her. Would he leave her to join them?

But then Luke turned back, his focus entirely on her, his tone steady and kind. "Alright," he said, "shall we work on your breathing now?"

Time seemed to dissolve as Lara relaxed into the rhythm of learning. The once-daunting task of floating on her back now felt effortless, a minor triumph that filled her with pride. Floating on her front still made her heart race, but Luke reassured her with his calm confidence. "You'll get there," he promised, and for the first time, she believed him. Between Luke's patient guidance and Nangia Uncle's firm encouragement, swimming no longer seemed like an insurmountable skill that kept escaping her grasp. Someday, Lara thought, she too would glide through the water like the girls slicing across the deep end.

When Zinia arrived with Christine in tow, Lara felt a pang of disappointment. Could an hour really have flown by so quickly?

Zinia leaned down by the poolside. "Would you like another twenty minutes? Christine and I were thinking of grabbing a cold coffee."

"Yes, please, Mummy!" Lara beamed, her face aglow with excitement.

Zinia turned to Luke with a warm smile. "Thank you for looking after Lara."

"It's no problem, Mrs. Seth," Luke replied, waving casually at his own mother, who was busy on the phone placing an order for coffee for Zinia and herself, and french fries for Luke and Lara.

As the two mothers settled at a poolside table, their laughter fading into the hum of a lazy afternoon, Lara and Luke played on—splashing, trading stories about books and about Arthur, Luke's beloved tortoise. The day shimmered, golden and unhurried, as if it might stretch on forever. In Luke's company, Lara felt something rare: an unfiltered joy. She felt safe as he took her hand, gently leading her into the deep end, then back to the shallow waters with the same quiet care. Somewhere deep inside, she knew Luke wouldn't let go. Not like Lexi had.

When Yash appeared unexpectedly, the spell was broken. At first, Lara thought his arrival was just another surprise on an already perfect day. But one look at his face told her otherwise. His expression was tight, his jaw set, and he went straight to Zinia, leaning in to whisper something in her ear. Lara watched as the colour drained from her mother's face. She stood up quickly, nearly knocking the table over. Something was wrong. Something was very wrong.

Later, bundled into a taxi with no explanation, Lara turned to her mother, her voice small but insistent. "What happened? Why did we leave like that?"

Zinia's lips pressed into a thin line. Her voice was flat when she finally answered. "Uncle Pedru's been arrested."

Luke (May 1985)

Drifting

Happy Birthday! Fifteen, huh? I can't believe it. I still remember that wide-eyed kid petrified in the pool, and me feeling like some kind of superhero when I pulled you out. And look at you now—quite the swimmer! Mr. Nangia tried his best, but you wouldn't go near the deep end until I held your hand. I felt like a hero then, too.

How are you celebrating? Back in the pool, conquering fears? Or has Zinia planned something extravagant? I can practically hear your laugh reading this.

By the time this letter (and my gift) reaches you, May will probably be over. I'm trying to convince Dad to send it via CoMail, but you know how he is—"Good things take time, Luke." Let's hope he listens for once.

This year's book is 'Perfume: The Story of a Murderer'. It's weird and unsettling but impossible to put down. Trust me. And before you complain, it's payback for 'Salem's Lot'.

39

Since when are you into horror? That book had me checking under my bed for weeks. I might owe you nightmares for life.

In other news, Steve and Lexi are visiting. And no, Lexi hasn't magically become less awful. If anything, she's doubled down. I don't know where she gets it from. But Steve? He's great. You'd like him. Dad's spitting image—blue eyes, sandy hair—the whole deal. He's also a quarterback now, which I know means nothing to you, but trust me, it's a big deal.

Are you still playing basketball? Never thought you'd get tall enough to dunk. Ha! Kidding. I'm proud of you especially as you always claimed you weren't sporty enough. It's cool seeing you find something outside the pool, though swimming will always be my first love (basketball comes close).

On a more serious note—how's everything with your uncle? Is he still in prison? I'll never forget the look on your mum's face that day—like her entire world had cracked open. My mum still talks about how she kept apologising, as if any of it was her fault. She says that moment made her realise what a strong and kind person Zinia is. I'm glad they stayed close. It's why we have, too.

Now, for the girlfriend update. No one special yet. Cindy keeps dropping hints, though. Might take her to a movie on Friday and see where it goes. What about you? Still swooning over Poirot, or has a real-life hero finally caught your eye?

Anyway, I've gotta go. If this is late, I'm sorry, but know that I'm thinking of you today. Hope it's an amazing one, Lara. You deserve it.

Love,
Luke x

"Still writing to that skinny brat in India, Luke?" Lexi's voice was syrupy sweet, but the edge in her words cut through like a blade. She perched on the arm of the couch, swinging one leg idly, her manicured nails glinting as she twirled a strand of perfect blonde hair.

Luke clenched his jaw and kept his focus on Jim, who was looking over the package. What was the point of responding? Any comeback would just give Lexi more ammunition.

"Luke, I'm not using CoMail," Jim said with a slight shrug. "But I'll head to USPS myself and send it Priority Express. It'll get there as fast as humanly possible. Sound good?"

Luke nodded, though he wasn't convinced. Even with Priority Express, the Indian postal system was notoriously unpredictable. "Maybe I'll ask Mum instead," he mumbled.

"Oh, absolutely," Lexi chimed in, her grin widening. "Christine would love to jump through hoops for her darling boy. How could she say no?"

"Lexi," Jim warned, his voice sharp enough to make her smirk falter.

Luke grabbed the package and headed back to his room, letting the door click shut behind him. He tossed it onto his desk and exhaled, running a hand through his hair. He couldn't wait for Lexi to leave. At eighteen, she was undeniably beautiful—ice-blue eyes, flawless skin, a smile that could dazzle anyone who didn't know better. Most people overlooked her nastiness, chalking it up to some kind of charm or just "teenage attitude". But Luke and Christine saw her for who she really was. If she couldn't charm you, she'd make your life miserable.

He collapsed onto the bed, eyes fixed on the ceiling, as if it might offer answers. Since returning to the U.S., life had slipped into a different rhythm—more hurried, more contained. Gone were the small indulgences of their days in India, the ease they'd once mistaken for normal. Texas felt both vast and strangely narrow, as though space had grown while something essential had shrunk.

Luke often felt stretched thin across three continents: the one where he was born, the one where he'd grown up, and the one he now called home. Each held a piece of him, but none held him entirely. He floated somewhere in between, not rooted, not drifting—just suspended. Always wondering where, if anywhere, he truly belonged.

Steve and Christine had gone out for groceries hours ago. What was taking them so long? If he had to endure another second in Lexi's company, he might actually lose it.

"Hellooo! We could use some help here!" Christine's voice echoed from the front door, saving him from his spiral of irritation.

Luke sprang up and headed out, meeting Steve in the driveway, whose arms were full of grocery bags.

"What took you guys so long?" he asked, grabbing a few bags.

"The lines were nuts," Steve said, grinning. "And Christine, being Christine, helped this sweet little old lady, then made me carry all her groceries to her car."

Luke laughed. "Sounds about right."

Steve shook his head in mock defeat.

As they hauled the bags inside, Steve glanced toward the living room where Lexi was sprawled on the couch, skimming through a magazine. "How's Lexi been?"

"Like a caged lion," Luke muttered. "Pretty sure being stuck at home is her personal hell."

Steve chuckled knowingly. "Yeah, she's never been good at sitting still. She'd rather be out, centre stage, soaking up the attention."

There was a note of fondness in Steve's voice, but Luke wondered if his older brother truly saw Lexi for who she was, or if he, too, was blinded by love, the way Jim was.

Later that night, as they gathered in front of the television watching Miami Vice, Lexi sighed dramatically, draping herself across the couch like a soap opera heroine.

"Don Johnson is soooo handsome! I wish I had a boyfriend who looked like that."

Jim glanced at her, opening his mouth to reply, but Christine cut in, her voice calm but edged with steel.

"Looks aren't everything, Lexi. Character is what counts."

Lexi turned her head slowly, fixing Christine with a pointed, icy gaze. She looked her up and down, her lips curling into a mocking smile.

"Well, clearly, or Daddy wouldn't have left Mommy for *you*."

Everyone froze.

Christine's face paled, and before anyone could respond, she stood abruptly, her chair scraping against the floor. She left the room in silence, but the hurt in her eyes was unmistakable.

"Chrissie!" Jim called after her, rising to follow.

Luke shot up too, following them out, but Jim put out a hand to stop him. "No, Luke. Let me handle this."

Luke hesitated, the anger roiling inside him like a storm. He didn't want to go back into the room with Lexi, so he lingered in the hallway, just out of sight.

From the kitchen, he could hear Christine's trembling voice.

"You never correct her, Jim! Why can't you stand up for me? Just once?"

"Chrissie, listen to me," Jim's voice was low and steady, the way it always was when he was trying to soothe. "She's acting out. You know she's never gotten over the divorce, and she's looking for someone to blame."

"Then why not blame you? You're the one who left!"

"Because blaming me would mean losing me," Jim said, his voice soft. "She's scared, Chrissie. She's always been daddy's little girl, and now she resents the fact that I've built a life without her and her mother in it."

"Steve doesn't act like this," Christine countered.

"Steve is more mature. He's always been the peacemaker."

Christine let out a long, shaky breath. "It's just a few more days. I'll survive."

"Thank you," Jim said. "It will get better. She just needs time to understand that some relationships run their course. Things with Holly and me were broken long before I met you. Falling in love with you wasn't something I planned; it just happened."

Luke slipped away before they noticed him, his chest tight.

Back in the TV room, Steve's voice cut through the air like a whip.

"That was completely out of line, Lexi. Christine's been nothing but kind to us. Why are you always so nasty to her?"

"If she hadn't stolen Daddy away—"

"She didn't!" Steve's voice rose, uncharacteristically sharp. "Dad met her during a work project in London, and nothing happened until after the divorce."

"You're so naïve, Steve!" Lexi snapped. "Luke is only a year younger than me. Do you seriously believe they weren't already involved before the papers were signed?"

Steve's tone softened. "What does it even matter, Lexi? People fall out of love. Dad is still here for us, and Mom's moved on in her life. Why can't you?"

Luke cleared his throat as he reentered the room. Lexi looked up, her fury flashing briefly before morphing into something else entirely.

When Jim and Christine returned moments later, Lexi's face crumpled as if on cue. She bolted to Jim, burying her face in his chest, her sobs loud and theatrical.

"Sorry, Daddy!"

Jim's voice was firm, but his hand stroked her hair in that comforting way that made Luke's stomach churn.

"You owe Christine an apology too."

"Sorry, Christine," Lexi murmured, her voice small, her eyes darting up briefly to gauge Christine's reaction. Christine nodded, her face impassive, but Luke could see the strain behind her composed expression. As the tension dissipated, Lexi's sobs subsided, her head still nestled against Jim's chest. Luke clenched his fists. Once again, Lexi had twisted the situation to her advantage, her crocodile tears washing away her cruelty.

The morning after Steve and Lexi left for North Carolina, Luke found his mother in the sunroom, her feet resting on the little footstool. She cradled a steaming mug of coffee, her eyes following a squirrel darting across the garden.

"Cute little fellow, isn't he?" she said, glancing at Luke as he came to sit beside her on the sofa.

"Yeah," Luke murmured, his gaze flickering to the squirrel before turning to her. "Mum, can I ask you something?"

Christine shifted, her smile softening. "Of course. Anything."

He hesitated, then took a breath. "Is it true that Dad was still married when you met him?"

The question hung in the air. Christine stilled, her mug poised halfway to her lips. Slowly, she lowered it onto the coaster and folded her hands in her lap. "Why do you ask?"

"Something Lexi said the other evening," Luke admitted, his voice steady but tinged with unease. "It's been bothering me."

"You know better than to let Lexi get under your skin," Christine said gently, though her tone carried a hint of warning.

"Still," Luke pressed, meeting her eyes. "I need to know."

Christine's expression softened further, though a shadow of hesitation crossed her face. "Alright," she said, her voice deliberate. "Yes, it's true. I met your dad while he was still married to Holly. But Luke, their marriage had been broken for years before I came along."

Luke nodded, absorbing her words, but he wasn't done. "Was there any overlap? Between it ending and... you two beginning?"

Christine paused, the silence stretching as she seemed to search for the right words. Finally, she met his gaze, unflinching. "There may have been," she admitted quietly. Then, leaning forward slightly, she added, "Does that make me a bad person, Luke?"

Luke held her gaze, his own eyes steady and sincere. He shook his head. "No, Mum. It doesn't. I just wanted the truth, and I'm glad you gave it to me."

Relief flickered across Christine's face as she reached out, her hand warm as it enveloped his. She gave his hand a gentle squeeze. "Thank you, sweetheart," she murmured.

Luke offered her a small smile, and they sat in comfortable silence, watching the squirrel scurry through the garden.

Christine sighed, leaning back into the sofa. "You know, when I was your age, I used to think life was black and white. Things were either right or wrong, good or bad. But life has a funny way of teaching you that there's a whole lot of grey in between."

Luke tilted his head, intrigued. "What do you mean?"

Christine's lips curved in a faint smile. "When I was seventeen, I had a best friend named Claire. She was brilliant—top of the class, kind-hearted, the sort of person everyone admired. But one summer, she got caught up in something messy, and everyone turned on her. They didn't care about her side of the story. They didn't care why she did what she did. She became 'the bad one' overnight."

"What did she do?" Luke asked, leaning in.

"She dated a teacher," Christine admitted, her voice low. "It was wrong, yes, but it was complicated. She thought she was in love, and he made her believe it was mutual. I stood by her when no one else would, because I knew her heart. I knew she wasn't a bad person, just someone who'd made a mistake."

Luke thought for a moment, his expression thoughtful. "Did she ever forgive herself?"

Christine gave a small nod. "Eventually. But it took time and people who didn't give up on her. That's why I'm telling you, Luke— sometimes good people make choices that aren't perfect. It doesn't define who they are. What matters is how they move forward."

Luke absorbed her words, then said, "That's why you could build a life with Dad, isn't it? You didn't let the judgment or guilt define you."

Christine smiled, her eyes glistening. "You're smarter than I give you credit for, you know that?"

Luke grinned. "I learned from the best."

Christine chuckled softly and ruffled his hair. "You're a good kid, Luke. I hope you know that."

"I do, Mum. And for the record," he added, his tone teasing, "I'm glad Dad found you. You're the glue that keeps us all together."

Christine's hand lingered on his shoulder, and she gave it a gentle squeeze. "Thank you, sweetheart. That means more than you can imagine."

They sat there for a while, watching the squirrel dart from tree to tree, no further words needed between them.

"She's already left?" Marty's face fell, the disappointment unmistakable.

Luke leaned against his dresser, arms crossed. "Yep. Packed her bags last week and *sayonara*." He tried to sound indifferent, masking his relief that Lexi was gone, along with her drama.

"Damn, man," Marty muttered, shaking his head. "She's a stunner."

Luke snorted. "So you've said. About a hundred times."

"Well, she is," Marty insisted, eyes wide like Luke had just committed blasphemy.

"Alright, Romeo," Luke said, glancing at the clock on his nightstand. "How about a jog? Work off some of that... frustration."

"What? Now?" Marty's eyebrows shot up.

"No better time than the present," Luke grinned, already pulling on his sneakers.

Five minutes later, they were pounding the pavement, Marty

huffing beside him. "So... I hear you're taking Cindy to the movies," Marty managed between breaths.

Luke raised an eyebrow. "Did she tell you that?"

"Well, she implied it." Marty flashed him a sheepish grin.

Luke rolled his eyes. "Then I guess I am."

"She's a catch, man! Pretty, popular... The guys are gonna be dying of jealousy."

"Yeah," Luke said, the word landing flat.

Marty glanced at him, frowning. "You don't sound too excited."

"It's not that. I'm just not sure we have much in common."

Marty let out a bark of laughter. "Dude, who cares? It's not like you're picking a life partner. You don't need common ground to have a little fun."

Luke didn't respond right away, his gaze fixed on the road ahead. He wished he could share Marty's carefree outlook, but something in him baulked at the idea of spending time with someone just to impress others. Or worse, to meet expectations he didn't fully understand himself.

"Maybe," Luke said finally, his tone neutral. "Guess I'll find out on the day."

Marty clapped him on the shoulder. "That's the spirit! Trust me, man, you'll have a blast."

Luke forced a grin but couldn't shake the uneasy knot in his stomach. As they turned the corner back toward his house, he wondered if Cindy—like Marty, like Lexi—saw only the surface. And if anyone would ever bother to look deeper.

That night, as Luke stared at his Chemistry homework, the equations blurred into meaningless lines on the page. He set down his pen, leaned back in his chair, and rubbed his temples. The problem wasn't the formulae; it was the nagging sense of detachment he couldn't shake. Why did he always feel so out of place? In America, he had always stood out—first for his accent, and then for his skin, which darkened quickly in the sun, giving him the nut-brown complexion of someone with Spanish or Italian heritage. The idea of admitting his Indian heritage never sat comfortably with him. His Granny had been Anglo-Indian, but she never spoke about it, her history buried under layers of silence.

Yet, during those brief years in India, something had shifted. Living there had felt like returning to a home he hadn't known he was searching for. There was a warmth, a quiet acceptance in the way people treated one another. Perhaps he was lucky because his father's expat lifestyle had buffeted him from the average person's experience. Christine had certainly argued that both colourism and classism existed in India, even though she loved the country just as much. Luke had never encountered it, and as a result, felt a strong connection to the land he had spent his first few teenage years in. For the first time, Luke had felt seen—not for his looks, but for his essence.

Then there was Lara. The memory of her tugged at him, unbidden and bittersweet. Beneath her quiet, reserved demeanour, she'd surprised him—a sharp wit, a quirky humour, and a heart so open it made him feel unworthy. She wasn't just a friend, she was like the sister he'd never had, barring Lexi—although she had never really been a sister to him. But Mum had once hinted, half-jokingly, that Lara might have a crush on Luke. The thought had made him squirm. He didn't want her to see him that way. What he wanted was their easy camaraderie—their shared jokes, debates over books, and her lopsided smile that could brighten his worst days.

Here, in America, girls swooned over him for reasons that baffled him. Dark and dashing, they called him, as if his genetics were some achievement to brag about. But Luke knew better. He hadn't earned those looks—they were pure accident, the legacy of mixed bloodlines he barely understood. And because he hadn't earned them, he felt they weren't truly his. What he had earned—his sports accolades, his place on the track team—felt hollow, too. None of it filled the gnawing void inside him. His academic performance was lacklustre, and no subject stirred the spark of curiosity he so desperately craved. Dad had already started dropping hints about colleges, but Luke had no answers. No direction. Nothing to cling to except an overwhelming sense of drifting.

His friends, Marty, Craig, and Ed, didn't seem to share his turmoil. Their ambitions were uncomplicated—girls, cars, and the carefree pursuit of fun. They lived in the moment, deferring the future to some far-off abstract afterwards. But Luke couldn't share their ease. Somewhere in the back of his mind, the question loomed: What do I want? And the silence that followed terrified him.

———————

Two nights later, Christine's delighted whoop jolted Luke from his focus. He tossed his pen aside and wandered into the kitchen, where she paced, the cordless phone pressed to her ear, eyes bright with excitement.

"Yes! Absolutely! Jim won't mind—why would he?" she laughed. "August? Perfect timing!"

Luke leaned against the doorway, arms crossed.

"How long?" she asked, then frowned. "Just a week? Not nearly long enough! But, I'll take it!" Her grin widened. "Yes, yes! He's right here. Hang on!"

She turned, waving Luke over. "Well? Do you want to talk to Lara or not? It's an international call!"

His heart lurched. "Lara?"

"Yes! Hurry!"

Luke practically lunged for the phone. "Hello?"

"Luke! Hi!" Her voice was clear, warm, but rushed. "Mummy said I could say a quick hello. It's so good to—"

The line cut off. Luke froze, the dial tone ringing in his ear.

"Damn it," he muttered.

Christine sighed. "International calls can be tricky. But wasn't it nice to hear her voice?"

Luke nodded, jaw tight. Something about hearing Lara stirred a longing he hadn't expected.

At dinner, Christine casually announced, "Zinia's visiting in August."

Jim, mid-bite, barely registered it. "This is amazing, Chrissie. What's in this sauce? Wait, who's visiting?"

Christine huffed. "First of all, Jim, I didn't make the pasta. Luke did."

Jim raised an eyebrow at his son.

"And second, Zinia, your former secretary from Delhi?"

"Oh! Zinia!" Jim perked up. "She's visiting?"

"Yes," Christine sighed. "Her brother got her a ticket."

"The one who—"

"No, Jim, not the one in prison! The flight purser one."

Jim grinned. "Hard to keep up."

Luke smirked, but Christine shot Jim a glare.

Jim turned back to Luke. "Wait, you cooked this? Should I be worried?"

"Worried about what?" Luke shot back. "That I might be better than you?"

"Touché."

Christine cut in. "And what exactly is wrong with him enjoying cooking, Jim?"

"Absolutely nothing," Jim said, raising his hands in surrender. "Luke, you're doing great."

He turned to Christine. "So, should I make myself scarce when Zinia arrives?"

Christine rolled her eyes. "She's coming to see all of us, Jim. She'd find it rude if you vanished."

"Man, I'm striking out tonight," Jim muttered, grinning.

He turned to Luke, who was absently pushing pasta around his plate. "So, buddy, thought more about college?"

Luke shrugged, gripping his fork. "Not really. I guess I still have time."

The table fell quiet for a beat.

"Well," Jim said gently, "whenever you're ready, I'm here."

Luke nodded, mumbling a quick "Thanks," but his mind was already elsewhere, caught between the past, the future, and the uncertainty of his place in both.

Sinking

The sun was warm on Luke's skin as he reached the basketball court, laughter cutting through the hum of the neighbourhood. Marty, Craig, and Ed were already warming up, sneakers squeaking against the asphalt. Nearby, kids shrieked on the swings, bikes whirred past, a dog barked in the distance. Luke dropped his bag at the edge of the court and tilted his face to the sun. For now, life felt uncomplicated.

"Finally!" Marty called, spinning the ball on his finger. "Thought you were gonna bail. You ready to get schooled?"

Luke grinned. "Let's see what you've got."

They split into teams—Luke and Marty against Craig and Ed. Simple stakes: losers bought sodas. The game kicked off fast, Marty cackling as Craig missed an easy shot. Luke dribbled down the court, the ball an extension of himself. For a fleeting second, he thought of Lara. Did she feel this same rush when she played back in India? He shook off the thought and pivoted, sinking a flawless three-pointer.

"Seriously?" Craig groaned.

The court pulsed with the rhythm of their sneakers, the sharp thud of the ball, the occasional jeer—"Airball!" "Weak!" Luke played with precision, weaving through defenders. When he dunked, the rim rattled, Marty whooped, and Ed muttered, "Showoff," grinning despite himself.

Then Ed tugged off his T-shirt to wipe his sweat. Luke's breath caught. He swallowed hard and looked away.

During a water break, Ed tossed him the ball. "Man, you're unstoppable today. Steve been coaching you again?"

The mention of his half-brother sparked a warm flicker of pride. "Yeah. Last time he was here, he wiped the floor with me. Said my defence was trash."

Ed laughed. "Well, looks like you fixed that."

Luke smirked, but a pang of longing hit. Steve's visits were always too short, leaving behind lessons that lingered. Maybe tonight, he'd call and tell him about the game.

Back on the court, the game hit a fever pitch. Craig and Ed clawed back to tie the score, but Luke and Marty answered with equal intensity. With seconds left, Craig attempted a desperate pass. Luke read it perfectly, stole the ball, sprinted, and leapt—smooth layup. The ball swished cleanly through the net.

"Game!" Marty roared, arms in the air. "Sodas on you, losers!"

Laughing, he clapped Luke on the back. "Superstar moves, man."

As the others grabbed their bags and headed to the corner store, Luke lingered, dribbling the ball. The court was nearly empty now, but Steve's voice echoed in his mind, "Basketball's like life, Luke. Don't just react, think ahead. Set up your next play before the ball's even in your hands."

Luke smiled. Maybe life wasn't that simple. But for now, he'd hold on to this small win. He jogged after his friends, the ball tucked under his arm, stretching the moment just a little longer.

"Well, that was some movie!" Cindy exhaled as they stepped out of the theatre into the warm evening air. "I don't think I've breathed normally since the first explosion!"

Luke nodded, a polite smile on his face. He thought about how tightly she had clung to his hand during the film. Maybe it was the tension of the action, but deep down, he wasn't convinced. *Wasn't Rambo: First Blood II a terrible choice for a first date? What had made him pick this movie?*

At the ice cream parlour, Cindy leaned forward across the table, her chin resting on her hands. "Sylvester Stallone is just so..." she trailed off, her eyes dreamy.

"Chiselled?" Luke offered, one eyebrow raising slightly. He couldn't deny Stallone's physique. After all, he was the kind of man that gym posters were made of. He'd often lingered over Sly's pictures, too.

"Dreamy," Cindy corrected with a wistful sigh. "And those eyes..." Her gaze flicked to Luke's. "Yours are pretty gorgeous too, you know."

Luke shifted uncomfortably, dropping his eyes to the napkin in his lap.

"I've been waiting forever for you to ask me out," she said with a playful pout. "If I hadn't 'accidentally' dropped my book in front of you last month, I don't think you'd have even noticed me!"

Her accusation was half-joking, but it hit its mark. Luke's throat tightened as he fumbled for a response. "I, uh—"

"Never mind," she interrupted with a bright smile. "That's history now. So... where are we going next Friday?"

Cindy's voice bubbled with excitement, but Luke's thoughts drifted. Around them, other couples filled the booths, their laughter and quiet whispers blending with the clinking of spoons and hum of the parlour. Luke couldn't help noticing how they leaned into one another, their connection palpable. *Why don't I feel that?*

Cindy was still talking, her hands animated as she shared her dreams of being a fashion designer. "Someday, models will walk down the runways in Paris and Milan wearing my designs. Just wait and see!"

She paused, her eyes narrowing as she studied him. "Actually... you'd make a great model. With your height and those cheekbones? Perfect."

Luke laughed, the tension breaking. She had no idea who he really was. She was crafting a version of him that fit into her fantasy—a hero, a muse, someone he didn't recognise.

Just then, Craig and Heather strolled in. "Hey, man!" Craig called, grinning as they fist-bumped.

"Come join us," Luke said quickly, ignoring Cindy's fleeting frown. More people meant less pressure, and that suited him just fine.

As they sat and joked about the movie, Heather teased, "Cindy, you're a trooper! No way Craig would get away with taking me to an action movie for a first date."

Cindy giggled. "Yeah, next time I'm picking. No explosions or guns allowed!"

Luke leaned back, his eyes on Cindy as she laughed easily with Craig and Heather. She was sweet, no question about that, her energy bright and infectious. But no matter how hard he tried, something felt... off. His thoughts drifted to Lara, to the effortless connection they shared. With her, he didn't have to explain himself—she just understood. They had grown up side by side during Jim's years in Delhi, spending endless weekends by the pool, swapping books, and building a bond rooted in trust and shared moments. Lara made him feel safe, seen, and entirely himself.

Cindy was different. She was new and unpredictable. Everything about her felt like uncharted territory. Maybe time would smooth the edges, make things clearer. Maybe.

Walking Cindy home that evening, he held her hand, feeling the smoothness of her palm, but there was no spark, no electricity. When they stopped at her door, he leaned in to kiss her cheek, because that's what he was supposed to do. But Cindy had other ideas. She turned her face just in time, her lips brushing his, lingering as her body pressed lightly against his. Her kiss was warm and eager, her tongue darting shyly before retreating. As she pulled back with a playful wave, Luke stood frozen, her perfume lingering in the air. He raised a hand to his lips, feeling a strange hollowness settle over him. *Why does it feel like I'm going through the motions?*

Alone in the dim light of the streetlamp, he sighed and started walking home, the darkening day pressing down on him.

At home, Luke found Jim on the patio, gazing out at the yard with a beer in hand. The sky was ablaze with hues of pink and orange, midnight blue slowly encroaching upon twilight. Grabbing a soda from the cooler, Luke dropped into the chair beside him.

"Back already?" Jim asked, a grin on his lips. "How was the date with Cindy?"

Luke shrugged. "It was fine, I guess."

"Just fine?" Jim chuckled. "Doesn't sound like fireworks." The teasing tone softened as Jim looked closer. "What's on your mind, kiddo? You look like you're carrying the weight of the world."

Luke hesitated, swirling the soda in his hands. "I don't know, Dad. College, sports, girlfriends—it's like everyone expects me to have all the answers. I just... don't."

Jim took a long sip of his beer before setting it down. "Here's the thing, Luke. Nobody has it all figured out. Least of all at your age." He leaned back, his gaze drifting to the horizon. "They say hindsight's twenty-twenty. There's plenty I'd have done differently if I'd known where it would have led."

Luke tilted his head, intrigued. "Like what?"

Jim chuckled again, brushing off the question. "Let's just say there's a list. But let me tell you something—you're not the first to feel this way. I had a similar talk with Steve when he was your age. Looked just as lost as you do now."

"Steve?" Luke blinked, surprised. "He's always seemed so sure of himself, like he had everything figured out."

Jim smiled, shaking his head. "That's what you saw. But he came to me once, worried he'd let everyone down if he didn't follow the path people expected. I told him what I'll tell you now: life isn't a straight line. It's trial and error, lots of it. You don't have to know everything right now."

Luke studied his dad, searching for the right words. "Dad?"

"Yeah, buddy?"

"If no one has all the answers, then why do you keep pushing me about college?"

Jim raised an eyebrow, taking another swig of beer. "Ah, there it is." He exhaled, setting the bottle down with a soft clink. "Luke, here's the thing. You've got this knack for overthinking. You'll analyse something into the ground rather than make a choice. I've been there. And let me tell you, that kind of hesitation? It can cost you." Luke started to object, but Jim held up a hand. "Wait, hear me out. I'm not saying you don't act or decide in other ways. But with the big stuff? You freeze. I know, because I was the same. I let life push me into choices I wasn't ready for. That's why I'm on your case—to shake you out of this waiting game you're stuck in. Do you get it?"

Luke stared at his father, the weight of his words settling over him. He nodded slowly. "Yeah, I think I do."

"So, listen," Jim said, "Steve called earlier. Said he missed your last call. He's home tonight, so if you want to ring him..."

Luke nodded, though he didn't move. He wanted to call his brother, but he also wanted to stay right here on the porch. Moments like this with Jim didn't come often. Growing up, Mum had been his go-to for worries and questions. Jim had always been kind, sure, but distant—a figure on the periphery of his emotional life. Lately, though, Luke craved something different. He wanted a man to guide him, someone he could look up to and didn't feel a disconnect from, someone who could relate to the turmoil within him. Steve fit that mould, but being so far away in Raleigh made those moments fleeting. Could he and Jim, sitting together now under the fading evening sky, find a way to bridge the quiet distance between them?

"Dad?" Luke asked hesitantly.

"Yeah?" Jim turned to him, his expression curious.

"Do you miss Steve and Lexi?"

"What makes you ask that, Luke?"

Luke shrugged, his voice careful. "I was just thinking... If I only saw you a couple of times a year, I don't know how I'd feel about it. I guess I can understand why Lexi acts out sometimes. I don't think I'd be too happy either."

Jim sighed, setting his beer down and leaning forward. "Life's messy, kiddo. And no, I wouldn't have wanted things to turn out the way they did. But this is where we are. We live in Texas. Steve and Lexi are in North Carolina. Would I rather have us all together? Of course. But careers, circumstances... they've kept us apart. I'm doing my best for them and for us. Always have." He paused, his eyes reflecting the waning light. "As for Lexi... She's a complicated kid. She's always been high-strung, even when she was little. And yeah, she didn't get as much of me as Steve did. I was around more when he was growing up." Getting up, Jim walked to the cooler and pulled out another beer, cracking it open with a sigh. "The truth, Luke? We don't get to choose all the cards life deals us. All we can do is play them the best we know how."

Luke sat silently, watching Jim take a long sip. He'd never thought of him as someone burdened by regrets. But maybe that was just another thing he didn't fully understand, another part of the gap they had yet to cross.

Later, after hanging up from his chat with Steve, Luke leaned back in his chair and closed his eyes. One by one, the faces of the people in his life came to mind—Christine, with her gentle wisdom, Jim, with his quiet strength, Steve, always steady and sure, his friends, full of laughter and camaraderie, and Lara, his anchor through so much of younger years in India. He had more love and support than most could ever hope for. Why then did this gnawing ache of loneliness cling to him like a shadow he could not shake off?

———

Luke rifled through his locker when Marty and Ed strode up, grinning.

"You won't believe what went down in Science," Marty said, barely holding back laughter. "Jake mixed the wrong chemicals on purpose—boom! Green foam everywhere!"

"Geller's face, man," Ed wheezed. "Looked like he got slimed."

Luke grinned. "Jake's lucky he didn't blow the place up."

"Maybe," Marty shrugged. "But if you'd been there, Geller would've laughed it off. Everyone knows you've got that golden touch."

Luke shook his head, smiling. "Pulled my share of stunts, too."

As they headed to history, Marty's words lingered. Did charm really buy him a free pass? The thought vanished the moment Mrs. Anderson handed out a pop quiz.

What year did the Boston Tea Party occur?

Luke stared at the question. 1773? 1774? He chewed his pen, scribbled a guess, and pushed through the essay question with vague sentences. When Mrs. Anderson reviewed the answers, each correction felt like a blow. Then she called on him.

"Luke, why was the Boston Tea Party a turning point?"

His stomach sank. "Uh... taxes? And tea?"

Laughter rippled through the class. Mrs. Anderson smoothly redirected, but Luke slumped in his seat.

After class, she pulled him aside. "I know you're capable of more. What's going on?"

Luke hesitated. "I just can't keep the facts straight."

She studied him. "Do you like stories?"

"Yeah, I guess."

"Then stop memorising history. Instead, see it as a story. Real people, real choices. Try that."

Her words stuck with him. Could history come alive that way?

At lunch, Marty smirked. "Hey, Luke, want some tea for our resident expert?"

Luke rolled his eyes but grinned. "Hilarious."

Then his gaze landed on a bespectacled boy at the next table, hunched over a book, looking lost.

"Who's that?" he asked Marty.

"New kid," Marty shrugged, already cracking jokes with someone else.

Luke hesitated, then stood and walked over. "Hey, I'm Luke. What's your name?"

The boy blinked up, startled. "Uh, Eric."

"Wanna sit with us?"

Eric's face lit up. "Yeah. Sure."

As they joined the table, Marty snickered. "Luke's got himself a sidekick. Bet we'll never shake him off."

Cindy shot him a glare. "Don't be a jerk. Luke's decent, and that's why people like him."

Marty smirked. "Bet he lectured Eric on the Boston Tea Party on the way over."

"Careful," Craig added, grinning. "His half-British side might still be salty about all that wasted tea." He mock-marched like a Beefeater, sending Cindy into peals of laughter.

Luke just shook his head, smiling. Let them tease. He hadn't done it for attention. His parents had taught him to do what's right, not for praise, but because it mattered. If there was one voice worth listening to, in all the surrounding chatter, it was the quiet one inside.

When Luke got home that evening, he found Christine sitting cross-legged on the living room rug, surrounded by a sea of photo albums.

The golden glow of the setting sun filtered through the curtains, casting a warm light over the room. She was flipping through the pages of an old album, her face sad.

Dropping his rucksack by the door, Luke wandered over and sat down beside her. "What's all this, Mum?"

Christine looked up, startled, a glazed expression in her eyes. She smiled faintly. "Oh, Luke. I didn't even hear you come in."

He reached for the album in her lap, gently sliding it from her hands. The first photo was of him as a baby. His chubby face lit up in a grin that mirrored hers. As he turned the pages, fragments of their shared life spilled out: Steve and Lexi flanking him in a stiff pose, him splashing in the pool with Lara, their family standing in front of the Taj Mahal, Mum and Zinia laughing over coffee. Each picture was a portal to a memory from a time gone by.

He closed the album and set it aside, then cupped her chin lightly, tilting her face toward his. "What's going on, Mum?"

Christine sighed, her wistful smile returning. "I thought I'd pull out some albums to show Zinia when she comes in August."

Luke frowned. "Mum, it's only May."

"I know." Her gaze dropped to her hands. "I just wanted to get organised."

"Then you started feeling sad."

"Not sad," she corrected after a pause, her voice soft. "Just... nostalgic. Time moves so fast, Luke. It feels like yesterday you were that little boy in the photos. I just want to hold on to every moment before it slips through my fingers."

Luke leaned back against the sofa, her words settling into him. "Mum, do you ever have regrets?"

Christine blinked, surprised. "Regrets? Why do you ask?"

He hesitated, searching for the right words. "Just wondering. When you look back, do you ever feel like you could've chosen differently?"

Christine shifted closer, her eyes searching his. "Luke," she said, her voice gentle but firm, "any choice that brought you into my life is a choice I would make a thousand times over. No regrets there, what-soever. You are the best decision I ever made." She pulled him into a hug, his head resting on her shoulder. "You're my heart, Luke. Always."

They sat like that, the silence stretching comfortably between them, broken only by the soft ticking of the clock. Luke closed his eyes, comforted by the steady rhythm of her breathing. Then the phone rang, shattering the moment. Christine rose to answer it and held out the receiver a moment later. "It's Steve," she said, her expression curious. "He wants to talk to you."

"Steve?" Luke asked as he took the phone. "Hey, bro! What's up?"

"Lukey!" Steve's voice was unusually upbeat. "Just checking in. How'd that date with Cindy go?"

Luke frowned. They'd spoken just a few days ago, and he was sure he'd mentioned the date then. This wasn't like Steve. "It was fine, nothing special. How about you? Everything alright?"

"Good. Just heading out with some friends," Steve replied, his voice muffled by background noise. "Thought I'd call while I had a minute. Hey, you should come visit. Check out the university—it might be a good fit for you after high school. Plus, I miss hanging out with you, little brother."

"Uh, sure," Luke said, his confusion growing. "Everything okay with Lexi? Your mum?"

"They're fine," Steve said quickly, brushing off the question. "Why?"

"No reason, just... never mind."

A burst of laughter echoed in the background, and Steve's voice turned hurried. "Gotta go, bro. Let's talk soon, yeah? Maybe plan that visit."

Before Luke could respond, the line went dead. He set the phone down, his brow furrowed.

Christine looked up from her album, her eyebrows arched. "What was that about?"

Luke shrugged. "Honestly? No idea. He invited me to his college to check it out. Said he wants to spend more time together."

"Really?" Her eyebrows climbed higher. "Are you planning to go?"

"I haven't even thought about it," Luke replied, laughing softly.

"Oh!" Christine suddenly clapped a hand to her forehead. "I almost forgot—a letter came for you from India. I'm guessing it's from Lara." She smiled up at him. "I left it on your bedside table."

Luke leapt to his feet, a flicker of excitement replacing the confusion. "Thanks, Mum! I'll see you at dinner."

He hurried to his room, the anticipation building as he spotted the envelope waiting for him. Lara's letters were more than correspondence—they were bridges across time and space, binding them together. He tore it open and began to read, her words leaping off the page, vivid and alive. For a moment, it felt as if she were right there beside him, chatting and laughing, sharing her secrets, closing the miles with every stroke of her pen.

Dear Luke,

It's so hot here in Delhi! The temperature's already hit 40 degrees Celsius. I have no idea what that is in Fahrenheit, but trust me, it's unbearable. Mummy finally gave in and switched on the air conditioner. Even she couldn't handle it anymore, though Papa keeps grumbling about the electricity bill. He's on a mission to switch off every single light the second I leave a room. Parents, I tell you!

Birthday plans are going to be the usual—nothing too exciting. Renu wants to come swimming, but since she can't swim, she'll just splash around in the shallow end while I do my laps. I'll join her after, of course. Mummy's promised to take us to The Centre for lunch, and yes, you guessed it, ice cream with chocolate sauce for dessert! Anjali might drop by later for cake and a movie. Papa's planning to rent a VCR, and if we're lucky, we'll get E.T. Fingers crossed the video parlour has a copy!

I'm reading 'The Shining' now. It's so good, even better than 'Salem's Lot'! You really should give it a shot, though I know you probably won't. Renu thinks I'm crazy for loving horror novels. She's still stuck on her Mills & Boon books and, get this, has a massive crush on that new boy who moved into our neighbourhood. Poor thing, she doesn't know he already has a girlfriend. I've seen them walking his dog together. I haven't had the heart to tell her yet. Should I?

Speaking of dogs, I'm still begging Papa for one. He almost gave in this time—he says I'm finally old enough to take care of it properly. The problem is Mummy. She keeps insisting she's "allergic" to dog fur, but I know she's just making excuses because she doesn't want the extra mess. I've promised to handle everything, but she's not convinced. Don't worry, I'm not giving up. I will have a dog by the end of 1985. Mark my words!

Oh, and guess what? Mummy's planning a trip to the US! Uncle Jude's sorting out her ticket, and Aunty Roxanna will go with her. They're planning to visit New York and Washington, and after that, Mummy will come to see you for a while when Aunty Roxy goes to Denver to visit her folks. Isn't that amazing? I so wish I could come too, but you know how it is—we just can't afford it. But I've told her she has to bring me back a Walkman. Please make sure she gets a good one!

How are things on your end? How's school? And your friends—Marty, Craig, and Ed? You've written so much about them I feel like I know them already.

I'm sure our letters will cross in the post again, just like last time. So, in advance, thanks for whichever book you're sending me. I really hope it's not another weird one.

When are you coming to India next? I miss you, Luke. It feels like it's been forever, and I hope we can meet again soon.

Lots of love,
Lara xx

Luke set the letter down, a grin on his face. He was certain—absolutely certain—Lara would hate 'Perfume', but that only made him chuckle loudly. Expanding her reading horizons, whether or not she liked it, was his own little mission. He missed her more than he cared to admit, and with each letter, that ache grew sharper.

The last time he'd seen her, she was on the cusp of thirteen—wide-eyed and quick to laugh, with her gangly limbs and boundless energy. But from the sound of her letters, she had blossomed into someone even more vibrant—funny, confident, and full of life. When would he see her again? He doubted his parents would return to India soon. Maybe, after university, he could finally take off and travel. Surely they'd grant him that freedom once he had checked all their boxes—graduated, found a respectable career path.

The thought of being tied down straight after finishing his studies filled him with a quiet dread. He wanted to see the world first. Travel through Southeast Asia, maybe even make it to Australia and New Zealand if his savings allowed. India, of course, would be his first stop.

He carefully tucked Lara's letter into his book, planning to reread it after dinner. Her words carried so much of her. He could almost see her chewing on her pen, twisting a strand of hair around her finger as she figured out what to write next. It was in the way she rambled about books, complained about the Delhi heat, and dreamed of getting a dog with such fierce determination. Their monthly correspondence had become a lifeline, a steady thread that connected their two worlds. He loved writing to Lara; he loved hearing from her. And in a way he couldn't quite explain, he felt responsible for her.

There was an old belief, he'd read somewhere, that if you saved someone's life, you were bound to them forever. If that was true, he didn't mind. In fact, he welcomed it. He would gladly look out for Lara for the rest of his life.

That night, as Luke drifted into sleep, he dreamed of water—of him and Lara in a vast and endless blue pool. They splashed and laughed, their voices echoing in the still air. Droplets clung to their hair, their faces lit with a carefree joy that felt so real he could almost taste it. The water shimmered, cool and inviting, wrapping around him like a memory he never wanted to leave.

Then. "Luke." A hand on his shoulder, firm but trembling. His mother's voice, something strange within it.

He blinked awake, still half-drenched in the dream, the blue of the pool lingering somewhere behind his eyes. But Mum's face shattered the image instantly. She looked as if the world had collapsed beneath her feet.

"Luke," she whispered, choking on his name. "Steve's gone."

"Gone?" The word tumbled out of him, sluggish and disorientated. "Where?"

Mum swallowed hard, her voice barely holding together. "He... they... there was an accident." Her hands twisted together, knuckles white. "The boy driving... he was over the limit. Two of them were injured. The other two..." Her voice broke completely. "Steve... he's gone, Luke."

He stared at her; the words dissolving in the air between them, weightless and meaningless. Gone? How could Steve be gone? They'd spoken just a few hours ago. He could still hear his voice, could still feel the warmth of their conversation, the strangeness of his words, his invitation to visit... This was a mistake. She was wrong.

"You're lying," he whispered.

But the way she looked at him—eyes wide with unshed tears, lips trembling—made something inside him crack.

No.

No!

How?

Why?

The questions pounded through him, relentless and cruel. How could someone be here one moment and just... be gone the next? It didn't make sense. It couldn't make sense. But the way Mum reached for him, the way her arms wrapped around him, holding on like she was afraid he'd slip away too, made it all too real.

Lara (May 1990)

Tides

"Twenty, Lara! A whole new decade!" Shweta nudged her playfully. "You're officially old now."

"I am not old," Lara shot back, flicking her freshly layered hair with casual precision. She'd spent hours agonising over the cut, ensuring each feathered strand framed her face just so—just like Pooja Bhatt's. It was more than a haircut; it was a quiet rebellion against the softness she was ready to shed, a step away from the girl she'd been, toward the woman she was becoming.

Change was everywhere. The country was stirring, opening itself to the world, shedding old skins in favour of something shinier, riskier, freer. And Lara felt it—felt it in her bones, in her reflection, in the flutter of possibility. A new decade had arrived. And with it, perhaps, the promise of her own transformation.

A shadow in her peripheral vision made her stomach sink. Karan, sauntering toward them, a red rose twirling between his fingers.

"Uh oh," Shweta muttered. "Here comes trouble."

Karan stopped in front of Lara, flashing his signature grin. "Happy birthday, beautiful."

She accepted the rose with forced politeness, already dreading his next question.

"What's the plan tonight?" he asked, leaning in.

Before Lara could deflect, Shweta answered. "Movie night. Madhuri and Renu are coming too."

Karan smirked. "Which movie?"

Lara cut in quickly. "We haven't decided." If he knew, he'd just show up.

Madhuri jogged up, breathless, holding two samosas. She faltered at the sight of Karan. "Oh."

Karan turned the full force of his charm on her. "Is one of those for me?"

Madhuri blushed and handed him one without hesitation. Lara sighed inwardly. Another one falling for the act. She turned to leave, but Karan fell into step beside her. "Let me take you out for your birthday."

"You really don't have to," she said briskly.

"I don't have to," he grinned. "But I want to."

Lara quickened her pace, slipping into class and sinking into her seat beside Sandeep. Karan wouldn't dare bother her here. He hated Sandeep.

Dr. Girdhar's lecture on John Donne droned on, but Lara's attention drifted as Sandeep doodled a heart, an arrow piercing through it.

"Who's that for, Sandy?" she teased.

He grinned. "Who do you think, Lara-lu?"

She pretended not to know. His quiet, persistent crush had been there since their first year, unspoken and safe. With a flourish, he added a "Happy Birthday" above the heart and slid it over.

Lara smiled. "This is lovely, Sandy." She tucked it into her book, carefully avoiding the flicker of disappointment in his eyes. From across the room, she could feel Karan's glare boring into her back.

As class ended, Madhuri waved from the lawns. Lara nodded, grateful for the escape. As she walked outside, a familiar ache settled in her chest. She missed the simplicity of her all-girls' school, where life had been free of the exhausting dance of unwanted attention. The boys here were a problem. If they had brains, like Sandeep, they lacked charm. If they had charm, like Karan, they lacked substance. None of them had the perfect mix she was looking for.

No one except Luke, a quiet voice in her mind whispered. But she shut it down as quickly as it came. It was pointless to dream of the impossible.

Unlike her friends—like Madhuri, who seemed willing to settle for the first boy who showed her attention—Lara had higher expectations. Zinia often said it was all about self-worth: those who valued themselves too little would accept far less than they deserved.

Zinia opened the door, her face lit up with a rare smile. "I've just had a letter from Christine!" she announced, waving it triumphantly.

Lara dropped her bag to the side. "What does she say?"

"Things are looking up. Her parents helped with the house, so they've finally moved to a two-bedroom place in..." Zinia paused, scanning the letter. "Egham."

"Egg and ham," Yash quipped from across the room, grinning.

Zinia shot him a withering look that shut him up instantly.

Lara ignored the exchange. "How's Jim? And... Luke?" Her voice faltered on his name, a habitual hesitation she couldn't quite shake.

Zinia's smile dimmed, replaced by a softness in her eyes. "Still nothing from Luke?"

Lara shook her head, the familiar ache tightening in her chest.

Zinia sighed and set the letter down. "Jim's on medication now. He's doing... okay, I suppose. Christine doesn't say much, but I can tell. The depression hit him hard. That's why they left the States. Too many memories."

Lara swallowed the lump in her throat. "And Luke?"

Zinia hesitated, choosing her words carefully. "She says he's doing that hotel management course. Seems to be enjoying it, at least.

For a while there... he was lost. But now, it's better." She looked Lara straight in the eye. "Don't give up on him, sweetheart. Keep writing. One day, he'll write back."

Lara's voice cracked. "It's been five years, Mummy. Five years. I've tried everything. He won't even pick up the phone."

Zinia reached for her hand, squeezing it gently. "I know, darling. But it's not just you. He's shut everyone out—Christine, Jim, his friends... Grief does that. Some people run from it, some drown in it. Luke... he chose to disappear. Don't blame him for it. Just keep being the friend you've always been. Sometimes, that's all we can do."

Lara nodded and walked to her room, her thoughts heavy. When had everything gone so wrong? She reached for the keepsake box tucked away in her drawer—the one that held all of Luke's letters, each one a relic of a friendship that had once felt unbreakable. She traced the edges of the last letter he had sent, the one that came with that odd book, 'Perfume'. Lara had read it countless times, clinging to his words as if they could bring him back.

The accident had happened not long after. Zinia had spoken to Christine briefly, her voice hushed and sombre. Lara had sent a condolence card, scrawling words that felt empty, inadequate. And then, they had stepped back, letting the family grieve in silence. At fifteen, Lara had tried to imagine what it would feel like to lose her cousin, Alex, or Zinia and Yash, but her mind had refused to go there.

Back then, loss was just a distant, abstract idea. Something that happened to other people, in other places. But as the years passed, it had carved its way into her life with cruel precision. Losing Luke— her Luke—was not sudden or irrevocable like Steve, but it was just as devastating. Slowly, relentlessly, grief had stolen him from her, leaving a void where their easy laughter and midnight-penned letters used to be.

When Zinia had returned from the States, from that difficult visit with Jim and Christine—insisted upon despite the tragedy—she had come back with a sadness Lara had never seen in her before.

"They're not the same," Zinia had said, her voice thick with sorrow. Jim had sunk into a deep depression, abandoning his high-flying job and retreating into himself, living off savings and old memories. Christine, ever practical, had thrown herself into work, taking on more projects just to keep their home afloat.

And Luke... Luke had become a shadow of the boy she once knew. Gaunt, withdrawn, his once-bright eyes vacant and hollow. He had barely spoken two words to Zinia during her visit.

"It was too soon," Zinia had sighed, regret etched into every line on her face. "I should have cancelled the trip."

Even the sleek, silver Walkman that Zinia had brought back for her—a gift she had longed for—couldn't fill the void left by Luke's silence. No reply to her letters, no acknowledgment of the memories she tried so desperately to hold on to. This quiet, invisible erosion of their bond was loss, and it ached in a way she had never imagined possible.

Now, as she penned yet another letter to Luke, Lara knew deep down that this one, like all the others, would go unanswered. She had long stopped expecting a reply, yet something within her refused to let go. Writing to him had become less about hope and more about habit—a ritual, a lifeline to a past she couldn't bear to lose, even as it drifted further beyond her reach. Each word she wrote felt like a whisper into the void, an echo of what once was and what she feared would never be again. And yet, she wrote. She wrote because she couldn't do otherwise, because to stop would mean admitting that he was truly gone. The bond between them had been forged in the heat of that long-ago summer. On the day his hand had pulled her from the depths of the pool, saving her life. In that moment, something unspoken had tethered them together—an invisible thread that, no matter how frayed, she couldn't bring herself to cut. So she kept writing, sending out words like prayers, clinging to the faint hope that somewhere, somehow, he might still be listening.

———

"It's a prestigious competition, Lara, and we want you to represent our college," Dr. Girdhar said, peering at her over the rim of her glasses, her voice carrying both authority and expectation.

Lara took the pamphlet from her, scanning the details with trepidation. Elocution competitions had always been her forte—her crisp enunciation, poised delivery, and impeccable choice of material had earned her accolades before. But this... this was the renowned St. Thomas College. The best of the best. The thought of standing there amongst other equally top-notch competitors sent a ripple of nervous energy through her.

She remembered how it had all begun—a casual whim in her first year, stepping onto the stage with little more than a love for words and an instinct for storytelling. She could hold an audience captive, weaving them into the fabric of whatever piece she chose. Lately, she'd been enamoured with Tennessee Williams, his lyrical prose and conflicted characters offering a depth she loved to explore. Could his words help her win here, too?

"No, Lara," Dr. Girdhar said, as if sensing her thoughts. "This time, they'll hand you the piece just ten minutes before you go on stage. That's all the time you'll have to prepare before facing the judges and the audience. But I believe in you."

Lara swallowed, nodding. The North Campus of Delhi University loomed large in her mind, an unfamiliar territory filled with towering expectations. She couldn't afford to falter. Failure wasn't an option—not here, not now. She had to prove she was worthy of being sent as a contestant to St. Thomas and, more importantly, worthy of bringing home a win.

Shweta and Madhuri were practically buzzing with excitement, perhaps even more than Lara herself.

"We're finally going to step inside the hallowed halls of St. Thomas!" Shweta squealed, clutching Lara's arm. They had all dreamed of studying there at some point, but whether because of grades, distance, or sheer bad luck, it had never materialised. Still, visiting, even just for a day, felt like a minor victory, a chance to see what made it so legendary.

Lara, however, gnawed at her nail, doubt gnawing right back at her. "I don't know if I can pull this off. I've always had days to prepare, sometimes weeks. But ten minutes? That's insane."

"Oh, come on, Lara," Shweta scoffed, nudging her playfully. "You read stuff out in class all the time without even glancing at it beforehand. This is second nature to you. Now, if it were me..." she trailed off with a dramatic eye roll.

"Or me!" Madhuri chimed in, her voice rising to a pitch. "I'd be shaking so hard I wouldn't be able to stand. Dr. Girdhar wouldn't have picked you if she didn't think you could do it."

Lara forced a smile, but inside, a familiar unease stirred. Did they have any idea how much effort it took to appear confident? How often she battled the sinking feeling of not being good enough? She'd mastered the art of hiding it, presenting a polished, unshakable front —but deep down, she wondered how long she could keep fooling everyone, including herself.

The day dawned bright and blistering, the heat already pressing down on the streets as Lara, Shweta, and Madhuri climbed onto the crowded DTC bus bound for North Campus. The journey would take at least an hour, or probably more, but Lara barely registered the rickety swaying of the bus as she focused on steadying her nerves. She popped a cough drop into her mouth, letting the cool menthol dull the growing anxiety in her chest.

That morning, both Zinia and Yash had wished her luck—Yash pressing a tiny idol of Ganesh into her palm, and Zinia reminding her to carry the small crucifix she'd given her when she turned twelve. Now, they sat together in her pocket, symbols of faith intertwined, just like her whispered prayers—half Hindu chants, half fragments of the Lord's Prayer, a tangled, desperate plea for courage. She crossed her fingers, hoping, above all, not to embarrass herself.

When they finally arrived at North Campus, which was miles away from her own college in the South Campus, they stepped off the bus, hot and sweaty. Lara took a deep breath, fanning herself and gulping down water to regain composure. The imposing façade of St. Thomas's College loomed ahead, and with one last deep breath, she led the way inside, flanked by Shweta and Madhuri.

The hall was already bustling with students from various colleges, a sea of strangers with keen eyes and quiet confidence. As Lara registered at the desk, Shweta and Madhuri slipped into the audience, leaving her alone among the contestants lining up along one side of the room. A quick headcount made her stomach tighten—at least thirty-five competitors. Her palms grew clammy. Could she really do this?

She shifted uneasily, then caught sight of a slim, elegant girl chatting with an exceptionally handsome boy who leaned lazily against the wall, exuding an effortless charm.

"That's Kalyani Menon, the St. Thomas's entrant," a girl beside Lara whispered conspiratorially. "Everyone's betting on her to win."

Lara swallowed hard. "And him?"

"Sushil Nair. Her boyfriend. His mother reads the English news on Doordarshan."

Lara watched them, mesmerised by their calm confidence, their quiet certainty that they belonged. They were St. Thomas Students. Of course, they belonged because of their intelligence, their charisma, and their impeccable credentials. For a moment, doubt clawed at her chest—how could she possibly compete against people like that? But then, something shifted within her, a quiet determination settling in her bones. She would not back down. Not now. She would not let nerves dictate her performance at this stage. With renewed resolve, she squared her shoulders and strode towards the table where the sheets of paper were being handed out, ready to face whatever lay ahead.

. . .

Later, as they spilled out of St. Thomas, giddy with excitement, Madhuri clutched Lara's arm, her eyes sparkling. "Lara, did you see their faces when they announced you as the winner? The St. Thomas crowd looked like they'd been slapped! They thought Kalyani had it in the bag."

"Just goes to show—never assume anything's a sure thing," Shweta added, a triumphant smirk tugging at her lips.

"How does it feel?" Madhuri asked, tilting her head curiously.

Lara forced a smile. But inside, the victory felt hollow. The exhilaration had faded the moment she'd overheard one judge murmur to Kalyani, *"If it were up to me, you'd have won."* Those words had drained the win of all its sweetness.

Before she could respond, a baritone voice cut through the chatter. "You deserved to win today. You were very good."

Lara turned, stunned, her breath catching as she met Sushil Nair's gaze. His dark eyes held hers for a fleeting second—steady, knowing—before he turned away, his stride unhurried, his posture effortlessly self-assured. He moved toward Kalyani, who waited with an expression Lara couldn't decipher.

For a moment, she stood frozen, the world around her fading into a blur. His words lingered in the air between them, weightless yet powerful, bestowing upon her the unexpected gift of validation.

In the days that followed, Sushil lingered in her thoughts like a tide—sometimes gentle, other times crashing with force, pulling her under. She couldn't understand why two fleeting seconds, a passing compliment, had etched themselves so deeply into her being. It wasn't the words he'd said, but the way he'd said them—like he truly *saw* her. Not since Luke had anyone looked at her like that, as if she were made of glass, her innermost thoughts and feelings laid bare.

While slicing through the water during her weekly swim, she tried to recall his face. But it was the memory of his effortless grace that surfaced—the way he had leaned against the wall and the lazy elegance of his long strides as he'd walked away. Her heart thundered in her chest, a mix of yearning and resignation. This was ridiculous, she told herself. Sushil belonged to another world, one that was far removed from hers. He was in a top-notch college, destined for greatness, his way paved by his lineage and his intellect. And even if she could briefly imagine stepping into that parallel universe, he belonged to someone else. Was she destined to fall for people who were as unattainable as stars in the night sky?

That evening, during her usual walk around the block with Renu, her troubled thoughts must have betrayed her.

"What's going on with you?" Renu asked, struggling to keep pace with Lara's brisk strides. "You look... preoccupied."

"I..." Lara hesitated, grappling with the strange mix of feelings that she couldn't quite name. Renu had been her confidante since they were five—through scraped knees, whispered secrets, and every embarrassing crush. But this... this felt different. The ache in her chest wasn't just longing. If she had to name it, it might have been desire. A raw, unfamiliar pull, tangled with the wish to be seen and wanted in a way that made her feel both exhilarated and exposed. Finally, she exhaled. "I met someone."

Renu's eyebrows shot up. "Who?"

"A boy."

The flood of questions began, relentless and teasing. "Where? Who is he? Do you like him?"

Lara laughed, shaking her head. Saying it out loud made the whole thing feel absurd. It was just a silly infatuation—a fleeting crush, no different from their shared swooning over Salman Khan or Aamir Khan, film stars who graced the silver screen.

Still, Renu looked visibly relieved. "Thank God!" she exclaimed, throwing her hands up dramatically. "Finally, someone to take your mind off Luke! I honestly thought your epic crush on him would never die."

"Luke?" Lara's voice rose in surprise. "Luke is just a friend. A really good friend."

Renu rolled her eyes. "Oh, please. Don't act like I haven't noticed. You used to light up every time his letters arrived. Yeah, you didn't see it, but it was obvious to everyone else."

Lara let out a dry laugh, shaking her head. "Okay, first of all," she said, ticking points off her fingers, "I used to dissect his girlfriends with him. Not exactly the stuff of romance. Second, what's the point of crushing on someone I can't even get within a mile of? And third—just in case the universe needed another cosmic joke—Sushil already has a girlfriend. So yeah, dead end."

Renu frowned, then broke into a grin. "Fine, but at least you've got options. It's not like there's a shortage of boys chasing after you in college."

Renu's own reality, an all-girls' college devoid of eligible suitors, hadn't yet delivered on her romantic fantasies. But dreams were safer than reality, Lara realised. They were a playground for possibilities, untethered to the messy truths of life.

As the days went by, the memory of Sushil and that fleeting moment of connection receded into the background, like a tide retreating from the shore. Some dreams were meant to stay as dreams, ephemeral and weightless. Reality, on the other hand, demanded her full attention. Exams loomed large, and this year was proving to be far more challenging than the last. Her love for literature had always been her compass, guiding her effortlessly through coursework. But now, the texts felt heavier, their layers more complex. From Sophocles to Donne, from Romanticism to Existentialism, each area of study required her to dig deeper, think harder.

On evenings when her legs dangled over the armchair, nose buried in a book, Yash would pass by and chuckle softly.

"Studying, are we? Or just finding an excuse to read another novel?"

She'd look up, grin, and dive back into the text. Yash, with his businessman's mind, saw little value in the worlds she explored. Rupees and *paise*, profit margins and ledgers—they were his language, his poetry. How could she explain to him that a single line of verse, beautifully wrought, could reveal more about the human condition than a lifetime of numbers? She didn't have the heart to try. Zinia understood, even if only partially. Having been taught by Irish nuns at a convent, her English was strong and her appreciation for books was genuine. But even she had struggled to comprehend the insatiable appetite Lara had for stories.

"You need to join a library, Lara," she had said years ago, exasperated, after the birthday books she'd carefully chosen were devoured within a week. "You don't read books—you inhale them."

That love of reading had grown into a hunger to uncover the roots of English literature. Lara thrilled at the way those roots stretched back millennia, all the way to Greek tragedies, Roman epics, and Biblical parables. Each text was a doorway, connecting her to minds that had pondered the same questions of existence, love, and loss centuries before her. How remarkable, she thought, that words written by the long-dead could still resonate, still move her.

Reading transported her to worlds far beyond her own—distant lands she longed to see, languages she dreamed of speaking, foods she imagined tasting. The urge to spread her wings and step into those imagined landscapes struck her with a force so intense it left her breathless.

But for now, those desires remained suspended, like a bird pausing before flight. She picked up her book again, allowing herself to be drawn back into the story. She didn't know what the future held, but in these pages, she found solace and wonder. For now, she was content to journey through the minds and worlds of others, immersing herself fully, waiting for the day when she could write her own story in faraway places she had only dared to dream about.

Uncle Jude's and Aunty Roxanna's visits were always an event, filled with stories, laughter, and the lingering scent of imported chocolates and perfumes they brought as gifts. This time, there was an added thrill—Alex was coming too. Only six months younger than Lara, he had been vacationing in London with his parents, and they had decided to stop over in Delhi for a few nights on their way back to Bombay.

The house buzzed with the frenetic energy that only last-minute preparations could bring. Zinia was in a whirlwind of cleaning, barking orders as she flitted between rooms. She and Yash had given up their room for Jude and Roxanna, while Lara was expected to do the same for Alex. That meant all of them—Lara, Yash, and Zinia—would cram into the living room for the next few nights. With Valli already sleeping on a mat there, it felt like solving a jigsaw puzzle just to figure out how four people could fit into the living space.

Lara was excited, though she couldn't quite suppress the small pang of irritation at leaving behind the sanctuary of her room. Gone were her late-night reading sessions. With Zinia, Yash, and Valli all in the same space, there would be no way to keep a lamp on past bedtime. Her comfortable routine was about to be upended, but what did that matter? Uncle Jude, Aunty Roxanna, and Alex were coming!

It had been nearly five years since she had last seen them. Though Uncle Jude often passed through Delhi on his flights, Roxanna and Alex hadn't visited in what felt like forever. From the last photo she had seen, Alex had shot up to six feet—an unimaginable height in her world of more petite girlfriends, where at five foot eight, she often felt like a giant. She couldn't wait to see if they still had that effortless childhood camaraderie they had once shared on their sun-drenched vacations in Goa.

Zinia had given them all strict instructions for the morning of their arrival. "They'll be exhausted after the night flight. No unnecessary noise in the house, okay? Let them sleep it off."

Duly warned, Lara busied herself with preparing her room. She stripped off the bed linen as Zinia had instructed and replaced it with crisp, freshly laundered sheets. Only when she was done, did she step back and truly look at her space through fresh eyes.

What would Alex make of it? The mandala-patterned maroon bedspread, the towering bookshelf overflowing with novels, the large black-and-white posters of Marilyn Monroe and Madhubala watching over the room like silent sentinels? Those luminous faces had always made her feel cocooned and safe, their beautiful smiles bestowing the room with a benign luminosity. But now, as she surveyed the space, she realised that to an almost-grown-up boy, her room might seem... strange, oddball even. Then again, why should she care? Alex was family. He'd take it, or leave it, without a second thought.

When they arrived, Aunty Roxanna gave Lara a stiff, perfunctory hug, while Uncle Jude swept Zinia into a bear hug that nearly lifted her off the ground. His warmth, as always, was expansive, an easy counterpoint to his wife's cool reserve. But it was Alex who unsettled Lara the most. He looked exhausted and withdrawn. He spoke only when spoken to, and even then, his replies were brief, almost grudging. He barely met her eyes.

Where was the boy who had once spent entire summers climbing trees with her, who had been her partner in hide-and-seek and their shared childhood conspiracies? This wasn't the cousin she had known. This was a tall, brooding stranger, and she wasn't sure what to do with him.

Zinia and Papa, perhaps sensing the awkwardness, were overly effusive in their welcome, filling the air with chatter and laughter. Valli brought out steaming cups of *chai*, and Uncle Jude launched into a lively recounting of their travels. It was only when he mentioned Stratford-upon-Avon, Shakespeare's birthplace, that Lara leaned in, eager to hear more.

"Lara's studying Shakespeare in college," Zinia offered helpfully.

"Oh?" Aunty Roxanna turned her gaze to Lara. "Which play?"

"Macbeth."

"Predictable," she remarked, before turning away, the disinterest in her voice sharp enough to sting.

Lara sat back, momentarily stunned. Had she always been this dismissive? Or was Lara only now picking up on the undercurrents that had long existed?

She had overheard snippets of conversations over the years, whispers about how Aunty Roxanna had opposed Zinia marrying a Hindu man. She was deeply religious, and to her, anything outside of Christianity was little more than a misguided path. But now, after years of polite restraint, it seemed that hidden animosity was seeping through the cracks, tainting what should have been a joyful reunion.

"She was just tired," Zinia murmured later, as she smoothed down an imaginary crease on her saree. "They all were. Once they've rested, they'll be fine."

But the worry line between her brows told another story. She had felt it too—that subtle, suffocating air of disapproval. And despite Uncle Jude's boisterous attempts to keep the mood light, the weight of it hung over them, heavy as a storm cloud refusing to break.

In the days that followed, as everyone settled in and exhaustion gave way to routine, the atmosphere lightened, at least on the surface. Conversations grew warmer, laughter more frequent, and for a while, it seemed like Zinia had been right. But beneath the polite smiles and carefully measured words, Lara sensed something brittle, something forced. Now and then, the veneer cracked. A sharp remark. A lingering glance, heavy with judgment. A tension so subtle yet pervasive, it made Lara feel as if she were tiptoeing through a minefield. She had never felt the need to be cautious around family before, but now, around Aunty Roxanna and Alex, she weighed her words, bracing for an unseen blow.

Alex, in particular, remained a mystery. Sullen and withdrawn, his moodiness was brushed off as typical teenage angst. But Lara wasn't so sure. She attempted to pull him into conversation—books, movies, football, even the music she remembered him loving as a child—but his responses were clipped, his eyes distant, as if he were counting the days until he could escape. And when that day finally came, when they packed their bags and left for Bombay, Lara felt the weight lift. A silent, collective exhale passed through the house. She caught the way her parents' shoulders dropped, the unspoken relief settling into their bones. Something had shifted over the years, something none of them had the courage to name.

What had happened in those five years to turn family into strangers?

Waves

Her book was gone.

The last book Luke had ever sent her—'Perfume'—had vanished without a trace. It had never been her favourite, but that wasn't the point. It was his last gift to her, a relic of their shared past. And now, as she tore through her room, pulling open drawers, rifling through shelves, a cold, sinking feeling spread through her chest. It wasn't just missing. It had been taken.

Alex.

The realisation settled like a stone in her stomach. He must have taken it. But why? And why hadn't he asked? She would have gladly lent it to him. He couldn't have known the book's significance, but surely, Aunty Roxanna had taught him the same thing Zinia had drilled into her—*you don't take what isn't yours.*

Her pulse pounded with frustration as she strode toward Zinia's room, determined to ask Zinia how to handle this. But just as she reached the door, voices from inside made her pause.

"Roxy has just become more bitter over the years," Zinia murmured.

"Why, Zin? She's got a good life, hasn't she?" Yash's voice was low, measured. "They are well-off. Jude earns a hefty salary and gets foreign currencies as his allowance. They travel the world, they live in a swanky apartment in Juhu. So why the bitterness?"

"She never recovered from having to give up the job."

Lara's breath caught.

Aunty Roxanna had once been an air hostess, just like Uncle Jude was a flight purser. They had met in the sky, fallen in love mid-flight. But back then, the airline had a strict rule that married women couldn't continue flying. They had kept their relationship a secret for years, even married quietly, just so she could keep her job. But when she got pregnant with Alex, her wings had been clipped.

"She knew what she signed up for," Yash countered.

"Yes, I know." Zinia sighed. "But that's not all. It's the constant comparison. Our family versus hers."

"Our family, as in?" Yash's voice tightened.

"Not just you and me. Maybe you and me too. But mostly Pedru and his prison sentence. Her brothers are high-fliers. One's a doctor in the US, and the other an IAS officer. And then there's Jude. The rest of us? We don't measure up. So she looks down her nose at us."

"That's ridiculous, Zin. We may not be up to her standards, but we have a good life. And tell me, which family doesn't have its skeletons, hey?" A chair creaked as Yash shifted. "It's poisoning the boy, you know that? Did you notice how closed off he was? That's not the same Alex from years ago."

Lara stood frozen outside the door. The missing book, Aunty Roxanna's coldness, Alex's brooding silence—it all clicked into place. It wasn't just a stolen book, although that did sting. This was a boy acting out, a boy drowning in the weight of his mother's resentment. How was she going to handle this? Was it even worth confronting?

Then she thought of Luke's last letter—the teasing way he had written about the book, the care he had taken in choosing it for her. It wasn't just 'Perfume'. It was his last gift to her. And that made it worth it. She squared her shoulders, marched to her parents' room, and knocked once, sharply, before pushing the door open.

"Alex took my book."

Zinia and Yash looked up, their faces mirroring the same startled expression.

"I've looked everywhere. It's gone. And I want it back."

Silence. A flicker of surprise, then hesitation.

"Are you sure...?"

"Well..."

Both started speaking at once, then stopped, exchanging a glance. Then Zinia patted the bed beside her. "Come here, Lara."

She hesitated, then sat.

"Was it one of Luke's presents?" Zinia's voice was soft, knowing.

Lara nodded. The tightness in her throat caught her off guard. Before she knew it, tears burned behind her eyes. *What is wrong with me?* Zinia reached for her, smoothing her hair like she had done when Lara was a child. "I'll call Jude tonight. Ask him to check. I'm sure it's just a misunderstanding, sweetheart. You'll get it back, I promise."

Lara exhaled, leaning her head against Zinia's shoulder, allowing herself, for just a moment, the luxury of feeling small, of not having to be a grown-up. As her mother stroked her hair, their voices faded into a hum, blending into the hush of the evening. Some days, she wished she could stay here forever, wrapped in the quiet comfort of childhood, where books were an escape and not reasons for strife, and the hardest decision was which story to lose herself in next.

Ten days later, the book arrived in the post accompanied by a brief note of apology.

I'm sorry, Lara. I started reading it and I couldn't stop. I should have asked before borrowing the book. Alex.

Lara turned the book over in her hands, her fingers tracing the splotch on the cover, the dog-eared pages. A sigh escaped her lips. Before Alex had stolen it, the book had been immaculate, just as Luke had given it to her. Now, it was marred. She placed it back on the shelf, stepping back to take in the collection she had built over the years. Stories that had shaped her, words that had been her refuge. Her gaze settled on the books Luke had gifted her, each one carrying the weight of his presence. Without hesitation, she pulled them all from the shelf, stacking them neatly into an empty shoebox. Then, with a firm push, she shoved it under the bed—out of sight, out of reach.

No one would take them from her again.

On Sunday afternoons, Zinia and Yash had taken to napping, a habit they'd never indulged in before. Lara was understanding, in a quiet, unsettling way, that her parents were growing older. Both were now in their forties. Yash, always lean, had grown thinner, his body worn down by diabetes. The disease gnawed at him from the inside, affecting organs in ways they could only guess at. He wavered between restraint and indulgence—one day swearing off sugar, the next drowning in a bowl of *kheer*. Lara had joined the chorus of voices urging him to take better care of himself, though she wasn't sure how much weight her words carried. Zinia, still a force of nature in so many ways, now showed her age in the tiredness of her eyes, in the fine lines that deepened across her forehead. She still argued, still fought her battles, but more often than not, she let them go before they reached their natural conclusion. Increasingly, she spoke of homesickness, of leaving Delhi behind for Goa, away from the city's relentless noise and thickening smog. Even Valli, who had been a constant in their lives, had talked about returning to her village in Tamil Nadu. Lara couldn't imagine their home without her—the small, sharp-eyed woman who had been a quiet anchor in her life.

It felt like something was shifting, like the world she had always known was tilting ever so slightly, waiting for the inevitable moment when everything would change.

When she looked at herself in the mirror, she often felt a strange disconnect. Outwardly, she was tall and slim, attractive by some standards—enough to draw attention, sometimes the kind she didn't want. But inside, she was still figuring things out. A dreamer who found refuge in books, who longed to explore the world but still keep a safe distance from it. Her humour swung between childish and sharply sarcastic, her sense of self still unformed in so many ways. And yet, through it all, she knew she wasn't ready to let go—not of her parents, not of Valli, not of the security their presence provided. She needed them as she stood at the edge of something unknown, trying to gather the courage to step forward.

Her future was a topic she rarely discussed with her parents. Choosing to pursue a B.A. in English Honours had been her quiet rebellion, one her father hadn't fully approved of. He had wanted her to follow a more practical path, to study commerce and accountancy as she had in her final years of school, a decision made at his behest. Though he never said it outright, she knew he had harboured dreams of her joining his business, maybe even taking it over someday. Lara didn't have the heart to tell him that balance sheets and profit margins were not her calling. Those final two years of school had been a slow agony, her mind rebelling against the sterile language of ledgers, the suffocating logic of numbers. If not for a kind-hearted teacher and the patience of a few friends, she might not have even passed.

She was grateful that Zinia had stood by her when she had fought to study literature. From the moment she had stepped into her first class, it had felt like coming home. These last three years had given her something she had never experienced before: the sheer joy of learning. For once, she wasn't struggling to keep up; she was thriving. And for the first time, the attention she received wasn't for her looks, but for her intellect. Yet a question lingered in her mind—what next?

The possibilities stretched before her, endless and uncertain. The only thing she truly wanted was to stay among her books, to lose herself in the worlds of the writers she admired, to understand why they wrote what they did, to uncover the circumstances that shaped their words. How had Joseph Conrad, who only learned English in his twenties, written something as powerful as 'Heart of Darkness'? How had Virginia Woolf harnessed stream-of-consciousness to carve entire universes out of thought?

She had begun to consider pursuing her Master's degree. Maybe she was simply postponing the inevitable, delaying the moment she had to step into the real world. But if staying steeped in academia meant she could keep chasing the questions that set her mind on fire, then perhaps, for now, it was exactly where she was meant to be.

———

Preparatory leave began quietly, without ceremony.

On her last day of college, Karan made one last attempt, swaggering over with his usual lazy grin, hoping she'd finally agree to a date. Lara met his gaze with polite indifference, turning him down once again, without hesitation or guilt. She knew Karan well enough to see the pattern. He scattered his attention like seeds in the wind, hoping something would take root. Some girls had fallen for his charm; others, like her, had refused to be swayed. It wasn't Karan she worried about. It was Sandeep.

"You'll keep in touch, won't you, Lara?" he asked, his voice tinged with quiet desperation. His glasses, perpetually askew, slid further down his nose as he peered at her, willing her to promise.

"Of course I will, Sandy! And we'll see each other at the exam centre. It's not goodbye yet."

But they both knew it was.

Their farewell party had been a blur of laughter and tears, nostalgia wrapping around them like a familiar shawl. When Shweta and Madhuri had pulled her into a tight hug, Lara had felt her throat close up. They had been her world for three years, but now that world was shifting. What lay ahead for them?

Sandeep had his sights set on journalism. Shweta was stepping into the workforce as a receptionist at her father's firm. And Madhuri

—Madhuri's parents were already scouting for a suitable husband. Her days of carefree singlehood were numbered.

Sandeep fidgeted, then blurted out, "Can I finally have your phone number? I've been asking for three years!"

Lara scribbled the digits onto a scrap of paper and slid it across the desk.

She hesitated. Should she warn him? Should she tell him that her father still clung to the idea that boys who called the house had only one motive? That the only exception had ever been Luke, because Luke had been there from the beginning, woven into the fabric of her childhood? But she said nothing. Instead, she smiled and watched as Sandeep carefully tucked the slip of paper into his notebook, as if it were something precious.

They spent most of their last day of college holed up in the cafeteria, escaping the relentless summer heat. The air was thick with the mingling scents of *chai* and frying *samosas*, the clatter of trays and chatter of students filling every corner. Madhuri returned from the counter, balancing three plates of samosas drenched in tangy *chutney*, plopping into her seat with a dramatic sigh. As they half-heartedly discussed coursework, their conversation meandered in all directions—floating between frustration, resignation, and the bitter-sweet awareness that this was the end of an era.

"Papa wants me to start working immediately after exams," Shweta groaned, tearing a *samosa* apart with unnecessary force. "I asked for just a few weeks to relax, maybe even travel, but he won't budge! And Mama? She won't say a word in my defence. So while the rest of you will be enjoying your freedom, I'll be stuck in an office before our results even come out."

Madhuri gave her a sympathetic pat before launching into her own grievances. "All the *rishtas* my parents have shown me so far? All moustached men. I don't like moustaches! But when I told my mother that, she looked at me like I'd insulted the entire family lineage. *Why are you so concerned with appearance?*" she mimicked in an exaggerated voice. "She didn't even see my father's face until after they got married! She says I'm lucky to have a choice."

Lara murmured something meant to be reassuring, but in truth, she barely had to deal with such pressures. She glanced at her friends and felt a quiet gratitude settle over her. Unlike them, she wasn't being rushed into the next stage of life. There was no looming job to take up, no impending marriage to prepare for. Her parents, practical as they were, never made her feel like a burden or an obligation to be offloaded. While an extra income would certainly help, and marriage would be one less mouth to feed, neither of them saw her as a problem to be solved. For now, she still had time. No guillotine hung over her head just yet.

From somewhere deep in her thoughts, Luke's face surfaced. Where was he? What was he doing at this precise moment? It would be early morning in the UK. Was he rolling out of bed, heading to his course? Or was he sleeping off a hangover from the night before? She wished she knew more—more than the occasional scraps of information Zinia relayed from Christine's increasingly infrequent letters. Across the table, Madhuri and Shweta were still talking, but Lara's mind drifted further. Would he ever write back? Would she ever see him again?

They straightened instinctively as Dr. Girdhar approached their table, her sharp gaze scanning them with the same authority that had commanded their attention in class. But today, there was something different, a rare softness in her expression, a quiet pride that tempered her usual severity. "I just wanted to wish you girls the very best in your exams," she said, her voice measured but sincere. "I have no doubt you will do well." Then, her eyes landed on Lara, holding her gaze with an intensity that sent a shiver down her spine. "I expect great things from you," she said, her tone firm, almost prophetic. "Someday, I want to be able to say, *I taught them. They were my students.*"

And just like that, she turned and walked away, leaving them rooted to their seats—stunned into silence, her words echoing in their minds much after she had gone.

———

Zinia's conference in Cochin was an unwelcome disruption to Lara's carefully curated study leave. It was only the second time Zinia was leaving for an extended period—the first had been her international trip with Aunty Roxanna—but the timing of this one felt particularly cruel. Lara needed everything in its place, her world balanced, the household moving in its usual rhythm.

"Do you have to go, Mummy?" she asked, hoping that some trace of desperation in her voice might make her mother reconsider.

Zinia barely looked up as she packed. "Of course I have to go, Lara. Both my bosses will be there—they need me." Her tone was firm, edged with impatience. "How can I say no?"

Even Yash shook his head at Lara, as if to say, "You know better than this."

Lara did know better. But knowing didn't change the fact that, despite being twenty years old, she still felt tightly tethered to her mother's presence. As if, without her, the threads holding her world together might unravel. Yash and Valli were part of the home, of course, but they were adjuncts—Zinia was the centre. The fulcrum around which everything revolved. Who would remind her to go to bed on time instead of poring over her books till dawn? Who would check in to see if she was actually revising and not just staring blankly at the pages? Who would ensure the household moved with the quiet efficiency that made it feel whole?

Zinia paused, watching the storm of emotions play across Lara's face, and her own expression softened. "I'll only be gone a week," she said, her voice gentler now. "It's not that long, Lara. And besides, it's time you started functioning as an adult. There will come a time when you'll have to take full responsibility for yourself and your choices. Why not start now?"

Lara said nothing, just nodded and left the room.

That night, as they sat at the dining table, Yash cleared his throat and looked at her with a thoughtful expression. "Would you like to go to Singapore for a holiday after your exams, Lara?"

Lara's head snapped up. The only vacations she had ever known were family trips to Goa or, on rare occasions, to Indore to visit her paternal grandparents. She had never travelled abroad, never even thought of it as a possibility. Their finances had always been carefully managed, every expense accounted for. Even Zinia's last trip to the US had been a strain.

"Are you serious, Papa?" she asked, wide-eyed.

He exchanged a smile with Zinia before turning back to her. "We've been thinking about it for a while," he said. "You've worked hard, and we figured you deserved a treat. Since you never got that puppy you've wanted all these years, this is our way of making it up to you."

Lara sat still, her mind racing. She had long given up hope of getting a dog, knowing full well that neither of her parents had the time or patience for one. Instead, she had found comfort in Renu's Alsatian, soaking up whatever scraps of affection the dog had to spare for her. But this—this was a surprise beyond anything she had imagined. The sting of Zinia's departure dulled instantly, replaced by a bubbling excitement. A trip. A real trip. She could hardly believe it.

Subconsciously, Lara had always imagined that her first trip abroad would be to London, to see Christine and Luke. But that dream had always belonged to the realm of fantasy. She knew that Uncle Jude could only arrange discounted tickets for Zinia, his sister. Neither she nor Yash qualified. But this? Never in her wildest dreams had she imagined that her parents would take her to another part of the world. The excitement bubbled inside her, threatening to spill over.

"You lucky thing!" Renu exclaimed, her voice full of equal parts joy and envy as Bosco, her Alsatian, tugged impatiently at his lead. She tightened her grip, sighing. "When are you going?"

"Papa was thinking September," Lara said, barely able to contain her grin. "That way, we have enough time to sort out visas and tickets."

"Just Singapore?"

"No, Bangkok too! Can you believe it?"

Renu groaned dramatically. "You lucky thing," she repeated, shaking her head.

"I wish I could take you with me," Lara said, meaning it.

"Someday," Renu smiled wistfully. "Someday, when we're older and rolling in money, we'll go on holiday together."

"Yes," Lara agreed, clasping her friend's hand briefly. "We absolutely will."

They walked on, their laughter mingling with the warm evening air, speaking of futures they could only dream of, making promises neither could know if they would keep. Ahead of them, Bosco stopped, hiked his leg against a lamppost, and took a long, unbothered piss. The future could wait. For now, there was this moment—full of possibility, full of hope.

With May slipping away and exams looming, Lara drifted from one spot to another—the balcony in the cool hush of early mornings, the dining table cluttered with notes, the living room couch where she read until her eyes blurred, and finally, the sanctuary of her bedroom. No matter how much she studied, the more she felt she didn't know.

"It's just pre-exam jitters, Lara," Yash reassured her, his eyes crinkling with warmth. "You'll do fine."

But she didn't want to do fine, she wanted to excel. Dr. Girdhar's words echoed in her mind, filling her with both determination and doubt. Was she truly as capable as her professor believed? Or was she merely reaching for something just beyond her grasp?

Meanwhile, with Zinia away, Yash had declared open rebellion against dietary restrictions. It started innocently enough—a box of pastries from Cake House—but soon escalated to *rosogullas*, *gulab jamuns*, and an ever-growing stash of biscuits. Valli clucked disapprovingly, Lara scowled and tried to throw them away, but without Zinia's watchful eye, Yash was unstoppable.

"Papa, I swear I'm telling Mummy when she gets back," Lara threatened, hands on her hips.

Yash only grinned, placed a finger to his lips, and popped another syrupy sweetmeat into his mouth.

One evening, as Yash joined her on the balcony, Lara watched him prop his feet up on the wrought-iron table and sigh deeply, as if shaking off the weight of the day.

"Why are you being such a rebel, Papa?" she asked, narrowing her eyes at him.

Yash smiled, the corners of his lips twitching with mischief. "Lara *beta*, I've always believed that no matter what we do, whatever is written in our destiny will happen."

Lara sat up, intrigued. "Are you saying we don't have free will?"

"Not exactly. We make choices, yes, but only in the small things. The big decisions... those are made for us."

"By whom?"

"Well, by God, of course."

"Which God?"

"Whichever one you believe in," he said, waving his hand dismissively. "The point is, our paths are already mapped out. We may take detours, we may stumble, but eventually, we all end up where we were always meant to be."

Lara studied him carefully. "And this... grand philosophy of yours—how does it justify you sneaking sweets and defying Mummy's rules?"

Yash chuckled, patting his belly. "Ah, my dear child, I simply want to live before I die. If I'm denied my few pleasures, then what's the point? It would be like dying a slow death every single day."

"But Papa..." Lara began, knowing full well his logic was riddled with holes.

"No buts, *beta*." He leaned back, hands folded behind his head. "Let me have these few days of freedom. Once your mother returns, I promise I'll go back to being a good boy."

Lara shook her head, but she couldn't help the smile tugging at her lips.

A strange new rhythm settled over the house in her mother's absence. Yash, freed from Zinia's watchful eye, became almost boyish in his indulgences, sneaking sweets and staying up late with the television volume far too high. Valli, ever the silent presence in the background, seemed to step forward, fussing over Lara as if she were the lady of the house now. And Lara... Lara felt unmoored, drifting in a way she had never experienced before. How would she manage on her own in the world?

She knew that in the West, children left home as early as sixteen, carving out lives independent of their parents. But here in India, that wasn't the norm. Moving out only happened under two circumstances—work in another city or marriage. The thought unsettled her. Was she ready for either?

Had Luke moved out? The question surfaced unbidden, and with it came the weight of everything she had been avoiding. It had been over a month since she had last written to him. She told herself it was because of exams, Uncle Jude's visit, the farewell party. But deep down, she knew there was another reason. She understood that to move forward she had to loosen her grip on the past. Luke belonged to a world she no longer had access to. He was a childhood memory, a cherished but distant part of her story. What was the point of holding on to someone she no longer knew? She had decided. After her exams, she would write him one last letter—a quiet, dignified farewell.

Just then, Valli appeared on the balcony, wiping her hands on her saree, a bundle of envelopes tucked under her arm.

"Sahib, *chitthi aaya*," she said, handing the stack to Yash.

Yash flipped through the letters, pausing when he found one

addressed to Lara. He held it out, distracted by the bill in his other hand. "This one's for you."

Lara's breath caught. The handwriting—the familiar, looping scrawl—made her pulse quicken. Luke. Without a word, she sprang to her feet and hurried to her room, her heart pounding. Inside, with trembling fingers, she tore open the envelope.

My dearest Lara,

'This is the dead land
This is cactus land
Here the stone images
Are raised, here they receive
The supplication of a dead man's hand
Under the twinkle of a fading star.
Is it like this
In death's other kingdom
Walking alone
At the hour when we are
Trembling with tenderness
Lips that would kiss
Form prayers to broken stone.'

I have no doubt you recognise these words. You must be studying T.S. Eliot by now.

Why, after all these years, am I writing to you, quoting 'The Hollow Men'? A valid question. Allow me to explain.

My life in the last few years has felt just that—hollow. Steve's accident stripped everything of meaning. Plans, dreams, ambition—what are they worth if everything we build can be reduced to dust in an instant? We humans rush from one milestone to another, chasing success, collecting friends, striving for love, competing, conquering, believing we are invincible. But in the end, we are nothing more than specks—specks that can be wiped away in a heartbeat.

I've read a lot since then. Poetry, philosophy, anything that might offer an answer. I've tried to be a good son to Mum and Dad, but my aimlessness, my inability to feel anything beyond this ache, hasn't helped. You know Dad—his grief swallowed him whole. He retreated into silence, into his own darkness. Mum, poor Mum, became the one holding everything together. She kept us from sinking completely, but at what cost?

I didn't write to you, Lara, because I couldn't, not because I didn't want to. I had no words for what I was feeling, what I am <u>still</u> feeling. I function because Mum needs me to. She can't bear another person falling apart while her world collapses around her.

And now, another blow. Dad has asked for a divorce. He's leaving for North Carolina to be near Lexi. He says he owes her that much. I don't even know what I feel anymore. Anger? Resentment? Relief? He's been absent for so long, yet it's Mum who is suffering the most. After all the sacrifices she made to keep us together, to keep us afloat, he's simply... letting go. And she, in her heartbreak, doesn't even have the strength to be angry.

I know I have no right to ask anything of you, not after the silence I've given in return for all your kindness. But if you could—if you could—please ask Zinia to write to my mum? And if there is any way she could visit, I know Mum would draw strength from her. She needs a friend, someone who won't judge, who won't say I told you so. Zinia is that person.

Lara, I have read your letters over and over again. Your

words have kept you alive in my mind, even in my silence. In the emptiness, they bring me something close to joy—small, fleeting moments where I feel connected to something real. Through them, I have shared in your world, in your triumphs and tribulations, in you.

I haven't said it in many, many years, but Lara, you mean the world to me. I wish for you a life filled with light, untouched by sorrow, filled only with laughter, love, and endless possibility.

Love,
Luke x

Luke (1995)

Currents

"Who's this, then?"

Sue picked up the photograph that had slipped from between the pages of his book, examining it with mild curiosity.

Luke took it from her fingers, slipping it back between the pages as though it had never left. "Just Lara," he said, his voice deliberately casual.

"Just Lara?" Sue repeated, her tone teasing but observant. "What an interesting name."

He didn't respond, just turned away, pulling more shirts from the wardrobe.

"You've never mentioned her before," she pressed, watching him closely.

"Not much to mention." He folded a shirt with precise movements. "We were childhood friends. More like pen pals now."

Sue let out a laugh. "Pen pals? It's 1995, Luke! Who still has pen pals?"

Luke smiled but didn't answer.

"She's pretty," Sue mused, tilting her head, studying him as much as the photograph.

"I suppose so," he muttered, rummaging through the wardrobe. "Hey, have you seen my navy trousers? The ones with the piping on the side?"

Sue tapped her chin. "Did you take them to the dry cleaners?"

Luke groaned, smacking his forehead. "Damn. I forgot."

"I can pick them up for you," she offered.

"And come all the way to Egham just to drop them off? That's too much, Sue. I wouldn't ask that of you."

"Hey, I don't mind! Besides, it'll give me a chance to meet Christine. You still haven't introduced us."

Luke grabbed his toiletries from the bathroom, avoiding her gaze. Sue was right, it was long overdue. A perfect opportunity, really. And yet, something inside him resisted. He didn't want to give his mother the wrong idea. And he wasn't sure why.

"Umm, I think I'll stop off at the dry cleaners before I take the train."

He kept his voice light, but Sue wasn't buying it. Her expression shifted, the teasing glint in her eyes fading.

"Luke?" She studied him, a crease forming between her brows. "Are you ashamed of me?"

His stomach twisted. "What? No! What makes you say that?"

Sue folded her arms. "You've never introduced me to your mother. We never hang out with any of your friends. And now, you're heading off to the U.S. for six weeks, and you don't even want to spend your last weekend here with me."

Luke sighed, stepping closer. She looked up at him—curly blonde hair piled on her head, freckles dusting her cheeks, her usual bright-eyed warmth dimmed by doubt. "Sue," he said, wrapping his arms around her and pressing a kiss to the top of her head. "You're reading this all wrong. I will introduce you to Mum, when the time is right. I just... I haven't seen her in over four months, and I want to spend some time with her before I go. Besides, she lives much closer to Heathrow. She's driving me there with all my luggage."

Sue shifted in his embrace, still unconvinced.

"And my friends? You know I don't have many. But when Mark gets back from Germany, I promise you'll get to meet him. You can interrogate him as much as you like."

She giggled despite herself.

Luke cupped her face, forcing a smile. "I'm going to miss you, you know."

"Not as much as I'll miss you," she murmured. "I wish I was going with you."

His chest ached at the sadness in her voice. "I know, honey. I wish you were too. I thought you'd get hired—"

"They didn't want me." Her voice was quiet, tinged with hurt.

When the U.S. airline had come scouting for flight attendants, they had both applied, hoping to take on the adventure together. With all her experience, Sue had been sure she'd be a shoo-in. But somehow, they had only picked Luke. And now he was leaving her behind.

He could still remember the first time he'd met Sue, onboard one of his earliest flights, fresh out of his hotel management course, still finding his footing in an industry he hadn't quite planned on joining. She had teased him then, just as she did now.

"Why are you flying when you could be managing hotels?"

Luke hadn't known how to answer. Was it the endless hours sweating it out in the kitchens? The managers rolling up their sleeves to cover for absent staff, the relentless grind of a profession that never truly clocked out? Or was it simply the slow realisation that, despite all his training, the hotel world wasn't for him? The airline industry wasn't much different—crazy hours, sleepless nights, a lack of routine —but here, at least, the view changed. The people changed. The destinations, however small, were constantly shifting. Cardiff and Leeds, Dublin and Manchester—it wasn't glamorous, but it gave him a sense of movement, a fleeting taste of something bigger. And that was enough, for now.

Sue had attached herself to him early on, fascinated by what she called his 'Heathcliff looks,' a brooding intensity she claimed reminded her of her favourite hero from *Wuthering Heights*. He had laughed at that. Unlike the girls he had dated in the past, Sue at least read. Maybe not as much as he did, but enough to understand why he preferred a quiet evening with a book over a night out. More importantly, she never tried to change him. She rarely complained about anything.

Could he see a future with her? He wasn't sure. Christine, of course, had started dropping hints. *You're twenty-seven now, Luke. By your age, I was married and expecting you.* But something inside him hesitated.

It had taken years to piece himself back together after Steve's death and Jim's quiet defection to the U.S. Years of unravelling and rebuilding, of pulling himself out of the void grief had left behind. Now, he tread carefully, wary of making choices he couldn't undo. He had seen what hasty decisions could do to a person, how easily the wrong path could pull you under. And if there was one thing Luke had learned, it was this—he wasn't ready to sink again.

———

Christine yanked the door open before Luke had even finished knocking, as if she'd been waiting. A second later, she wrapped him in a fierce hug.

"My darling boy," she murmured. "I've missed you."

Luke held her close, noticing how small she felt. When they pulled apart, he took in the flat—familiar, yet faded. Dust on the photo frames, wilted flowers in the vase. She looked older, too. More tired.

"Tea?" she asked, too brightly.

"Always."

In the kitchen, she moved with her usual efficiency, arranging cucumber sandwiches and opening a pack of Mr Kipling cakes. He knew better than to help—this was her ritual, something she could control. But he saw it: the heaviness in her shoulders, the slow drag of her hands.

"How've you been, Mum?"

"Oh, great!" she said too quickly. "Work's busy. I can barely keep up." But as she poured the tea, her smile wavered. "Sometimes, though, the silence at night can feel... oppressive."

Luke swallowed hard. "Any news from Dad?" he asked.

Christine stirred her tea. "Not for a long time. But that's okay. It's how it should be." Her eyes met his. "And you? Has he reached out?"

Luke exhaled. "Yeah. An email. I meant to reply, but... I didn't know what to say."

Christine set her cup down. "You should write back."

He let out a humourless laugh. "Why? He made his choice."

She sighed. "Luke, it wasn't about choosing her over you. He was drowning in guilt. Going back was his way of atoning. It was never about love, or a lack of it."

Luke scoffed. "And you just accept that? You were the one left picking up the pieces."

Christine held his gaze. "I had many wonderful years with him. Some people don't even get that much. I refuse to be bitter."

His throat tightened.

"You can't live in the past forever," she said gently.

"Neither can you, Mum." He leaned forward. "You don't have to be alone."

She laughed. "At my age? Don't be ridiculous."

"I'm serious."

Christine tilted her head knowingly. "And you? Anyone special?"

Luke hesitated. "No one serious."

She studied him. "I hope your dad and I haven't made you afraid of love."

Luke swallowed. Then, forcing a smile, he said, "Actually... there is someone. Sue. Met her flying out of Gatwick."

Christine's face lit up. "Oh, Luke! I was beginning to think you'd never find someone."

He chuckled. "I did date, Mum."

"Yes, but not seriously. Not someone you truly let in."

As they talked about Sue and his new job, a thought nagged at him. Had his mother ever envisioned more for him? Something grander, more intellectual, more in keeping with her and dad's ambitions? If she had, she'd never let it show. Christine had always been his biggest supporter. His unwavering champion. He owed her more than he could ever say.

As she cleared the table, she glanced over her shoulder. "Write to your dad, Luke. He'll want to see you while you're in the States. You owe him that much."

Luke exhaled, rubbing the back of his neck. *Did he?*

———————

Dinner was lasagne with a crisp green salad. His favourite.

Luke took a bite, sighing in satisfaction. "I'm going to miss this when I'm in the U.S."

Christine chuckled, ladling more onto his plate. "You'll get good food there too. We didn't exactly starve in Texas, did we?"

"No, I mean *this* food. Your food. Nothing beats home cooking, Mum."

Her face softened. "Which is why I made it for you," she said simply.

They ate in companionable silence, Christine sipping her wine, watching him with quiet satisfaction. He could feel it, that motherly contentment of seeing her son home, even if just for a short while.

"So," she asked, swirling the stem of her glass between her fingers, "are you excited? This new training—will you be flying everywhere now?"

"A lot of routes to the U.S. and Europe," Luke said between mouthfuls. "But guess what? They fly to Delhi too."

Christine's brows lifted. "From London?"

"From Heathrow," he confirmed.

A flicker of excitement crossed her face. "Does that mean you'll be living closer?"

Luke nodded, smiling at her reaction. But a moment later, he saw the shift—the way her expression changed as the meaning of his words sank in.

"Delhi," she repeated, her voice quieter, almost wistful. "You could see Zinia. And Lara."

Luke grinned, unable to hide his excitement. "Yeah. I haven't told them yet. I want to finish my training first, and then, when I finally get assigned a trip there—I'll just show up and surprise them. I can't wait to see Lara's face!"

Christine's eyes shone. "She'll love that, once she gets past the shock," she murmured, smiling and nodding. "They're such a wonderful family, aren't they?"

"I know," Luke said, leaning back in his chair. "I mean... Zinia dropped everything to come be with you when Dad left."

Christine's expression turned thoughtful. "I can't even begin to thank her for that. She was my rock, Luke. She even helped Jim pack up his things. And not once—not once—did she say anything cruel, though I know she was seething on my behalf."

She set down her fork and looked at him, eyes sharp with curiosity. "But there's one thing I've always wondered. How did she even know? I hadn't written to her."

Luke cleared his throat, pushing his food around his plate. "It was me," he admitted. "I wrote to Lara. I asked if Zinia could come over. I figured you needed someone in your corner, and... I—I was pretty useless back then."

Christine exhaled slowly, her gaze softening. "I thought so," she said, her voice quiet. Then she hesitated, as if debating whether to say what was on her mind. "Did you know they sacrificed their family trip to Singapore so Zinia could be here with me?"

Luke's fork froze mid-air. "What?! Lara never said a word!"

Christine nodded. "I had to pry it out of Zinia. That's just the kind of people they are, Luke." She studied him for a long moment, as if weighing something in her mind. Then, with a quiet gravity, she said, "All this to say, don't let Lara down, honey."

Luke frowned. "Let her down? What do you mean?"

Christine leaned forward, searching his face. "I mean... if there's any part of her that's hoping for something more, you need to be the one to set things straight. Unless, of course, you feel the same way?"

Luke's chest tightened. The air between them suddenly felt heavy. Christine waited, her eyes gentle but unwavering, watching for the answer he wasn't sure he even had. Luke swallowed hard, his words faltering as he tried to put his feelings into something that made sense. "Mum... I—I don't feel that way about Lara," he said, stumbling over each syllable. "She's special to me... always has been. But that bond... I can't ruin it by turning it into something else." He exhaled sharply, running a hand through his hair. "I don't know how to explain it. I need her in my life, but not as a girlfriend."

Christine tilted her head, studying him. "As a sister?" she asked gently.

Luke hesitated. "A sister," he echoed, but even as he said it, the word didn't sit right. He shook his head. "No... not exactly. I used to think that's what it was, but now... I don't know. It's deeper than that. We're two souls who just get each other—like an unspoken understanding. Like... two people tied together by something bigger than definitions." He let out a breath, frustrated at his own inability to articulate it. "God, I don't know how to explain it."

Christine reached across the table and patted his hand. "You don't have to, not to me. But maybe Lara needs some kind of clarification." She paused, watching the way his jaw tensed. "She's twenty-five, Luke. And, as far as I know, there's no one in her life. No boyfriend, no mention of anyone special."

Something twisted uncomfortably in Luke's stomach. Had he been leading her on without realising it? When he had finally broken his silence and written to her again after all those years, it had been like a floodgate opening. They had poured themselves into their letters, reconnecting, making up for lost time. He had rediscovered Lara. And through her, rediscovered himself. But had she seen it differently?

Surely she understood that with all these years and miles between them, the only relationship they could ever have was one of deep, abiding friendship. Nothing more.

"I'll talk to her, Mum," he said at last. "Whenever I see her. But, hey—she might just be keeping a boyfriend under wraps. Her dad's still pretty strict about that kind of thing, right?"

Christine smiled, though it didn't quite reach her eyes. "Maybe," she said lightly. Then, with a glance at his half-eaten plate, she nudged it toward him. "You've got enough on your plate—literally and figuratively—so finish up and get some rest. We've got a busy few days ahead."

Luke hesitated, then said, "I need a favour, Mum."

Christine's fork hovered midair. "Anything," she said, her brows knitting together.

He hesitated for a fraction of a second before continuing. "Could you post Lara's gift for me?"

Christine lowered her fork and studied him. "Another book?" she asked.

Luke nodded. "One I think she'll like." He ran a thumb over the edge of his napkin. "It's called 'A Fine Balance' by Rohinton Mistry."

Christine took a sip of her water, her gaze never leaving his. "That's not exactly light reading."

"No," Luke admitted with a wry smile. "But Lara doesn't do light reading anymore."

Christine chuckled, shaking her head. "No, I suppose she doesn't —what with that Master's degree." Then, softer, "You really do know her, don't you?"

Luke exhaled, leaning back in his chair. "Yeah," he murmured. "I suppose I do."

The last few days before his departure passed in a blur of movement —sorting through documents, ensuring he had enough clothes (and matching socks) for six weeks, fixing all the things Christine had long stopped noticing. The broken lightbulb, the leaky tap, the letterbox that hung off its hinges.

Luke didn't mind. He enjoyed keeping his hands busy. He liked, more than anything, spending time with his mother. Christine had always been his anchor, the steady, unwavering presence in his life. She had been there through his worst moments, through the hollow years after Steve's death, through Jim's quiet, unceremonious exit. She had never asked too much of him, never demanded more than he could give. And now, as he prepared to leave, he felt that familiar, almost childlike need to make her proud.

On his last morning at home, he stretched at the breakfast table, nursing a mug of tea. The sky outside was dull and grey, but the kitchen was warm, filled with the soft clatter of Christine peeling potatoes.

"Mum, I'm heading to the leisure centre for a swim. Need anything from the shops?"

She barely looked up. "Just a bulb of garlic. I'll make that chicken you like tonight."

He smiled, reassured by her predictability.

As he swam later, cutting through the cool water in steady strokes, his thoughts drifted. A new job. A fresh start. The prospect of it sent a current of nervous excitement through him. It was the feeling of stepping into the unknown—both thrilling and unsettling.

Would he reconnect with his childhood friends—Marty, Craig, Ed, and all the other boys who had once been in his world? He had once half-heartedly tried to track down Cindy, but grief had dulled his efforts before they could take root. Had she ever thought of him? Or had she moved on as effortlessly as he had convinced himself he had?

And then there was Jim. And Lexi.

His half-sister remained frozen in his memory, the same spoiled, entitled teenage girl he had barely tolerated. But had she changed? Had she, too, been reshaped by loss? Was it her pleas that had pulled Jim back to the States, to the life they had all left behind? He didn't know. More importantly, he wasn't sure if he even wanted to.

What he did know was how much he had changed. He was no longer the boy with the easy laugh and guileless charm. He had become quieter, heavier somehow, as if carrying the weight of something he couldn't quite name. He over analysed every decision, every interaction, as if preparing for unseen disasters. He stayed in the background more, listening rather than speaking, watching rather than acting. And yet, people still gravitated toward him. Sue. His colleagues. The friends he had gathered along the way. He didn't understand why. What did they see in him—a man who, when he looked in the mirror, still felt like he didn't quite fit in his own skin?

What was he searching for? What piece of himself had been lost along the way?

When he returned home that afternoon, Christine was standing by the window, a letter in her hand. She turned as he entered, holding it out to him without a word. He took it, already knowing who it was from. Jim's handwriting. His mother watched him as he read, her gaze gentle but probing, waiting for his reaction. He gave her none. Years of practice had made him an expert at concealing his emotions.

Jim's words were what he had expected—pleas for reconciliation, assurances of love, regret edged with justification. He missed him. He wanted to hear his voice. He wanted Christine to convince Luke to reach out. The decision to leave had been difficult, but necessary. He was still settling into his new/old life in North Carolina, still figuring things out.

Luke set the letter down carefully, smoothing out the creases with his fingers. Then, without a word, he walked into the kitchen and switched on the kettle.

Christine followed, lingering in the doorway. "Let me," she offered as he pulled out two mugs.

"No," Luke said, reaching for the tea bags. "I want to."

She didn't press him. Instead, she watched in silence as he moved through the familiar motions, his hands steady, deliberate. When he finally set a mug in front of her, she wrapped her hands around it, absorbing its warmth. Then, finally, he spoke. "Alright, Mum. I'll call him."

Christine exhaled softly, a slow, measured release, as if she had been holding her breath all this time. She reached across the table, covering his hand with hers. "I'm glad, Luke," she said simply.

That night, their last night together before he left, they played Scrabble, just as they had when he was a child. The board was worn; the edges frayed with time, but the game felt the same. They laughed over old memories, reminisced about the days when life had been simpler. Then, as they sat in the quiet warmth of the living room, Christine looked at him, her eyes glistening. "I love you so much, Luke."

He swallowed past the sudden tightness in his throat. "I love you too, Mum."

She hesitated, then took his hand. "Promise me something," she said, her voice quiet but firm.

He frowned slightly. "What?"

"Promise me that you will live a full life. A life without lies or pretence. A life where you are honest—not just with others, but with yourself. Especially with yourself."

For a long moment, he held her gaze. Then, slowly, he nodded. "I promise," he whispered. And he meant it.

The next morning, they rose before the world had fully woken. The air was crisp, the streets still cloaked in the hush of dawn. Luke loaded his bags into the boot while Christine locked up the house behind her, the sound of the key turning in the lock echoing in the stillness.

They drove in silence, the low hum of the radio filling the quiet space between them. The roads, usually so relentless, so clogged with commuters, felt momentarily subdued, as if they, too, were holding their breath. The street lights flickered past in a golden blur, and for the first time in weeks, Luke allowed himself to simply exist in this in-between space—half here, half already gone.

Then Christine spoke. "I was younger than you when I first met your father." Her voice was soft, almost distant, but steady. She wasn't just reminiscing, she was leading him somewhere.

Luke stretched, still heavy with sleep. "Yeah, Mum," he murmured, stifling a yawn. "I think you might have mentioned it once or twice."

She smiled faintly but didn't take the bait. "He was older. More experienced. He had already lived a life before me. At first, I found him overwhelming—this loud American with his big ideas and boundless energy. He talked too much, too fast. But when he turned his attention to me..." She exhaled, the breath thick with memory. "When those bright blue eyes landed on me, I couldn't look away."

Luke sat up a little straighter. He had heard fragments of their story before, but never like this, never with this raw openness.

"I fell in love, Luke. Me, the shy wallflower no one ever noticed. I fell in love with his intelligence, his conviction... and with the idea of life being an adventure." Her hands gripped the wheel just a little tighter. "I thought we would travel the world together, that nothing could touch us." She fell silent as the traffic lights ahead flickered from amber to green. "What we built, what I believed would last forever, didn't." She turned to him then, her smile sad. "But from it, I got something irreplaceable."

Luke held his breath.

"You."

Her hand reached across the console, resting on his arm for a brief moment—warm, steady, grounding. "Whatever you do, Luke, don't be afraid to go after the life you really want. Whether it ends in happiness or heartbreak, at least you will have truly lived."

Something in his chest twisted. He wasn't sure if it was longing, fear, or that old ache he had never quite been able to name.

"So much advice, Mum?" he said lightly, forcing a grin. "What's gotten into you?"

Christine chuckled, but there was something wistful in the sound. "I'm going to see less and less of you, Luke. Your life is leading you far away from me, and that's how it should be. But I want to say everything I need to while I still have the chance."

His throat tightened. He nudged her playfully, trying to shake off the weight of her words. "Don't be like that, Mum. I'll come straight to you after training, alright? And I'm not disappearing to another continent. I'll be right here, maybe even living close by, if I can afford it." He shot her a grin. "So no getting all maudlin on me."

She laughed, and the moment eased, the weight lifting just enough for him to breathe again.

When they pulled up outside Terminal 3, Christine turned to him fully, her expression unreadable for a moment. Then she said, "One last thing, Luke." He met her gaze. "I don't say it enough," she murmured, her voice fierce with love. "But I am so, so proud of you."

The words hit him like a fist to the chest. He felt the familiar prickle of tears but swallowed hard, pushing them down. Instead of speaking, he leaned over and kissed her cheek, lingering for just a second longer than usual. Then he stepped out of the car.

Above him, a Boeing 747 roared overhead, slicing through the sky, its metal body catching the first glint of morning sun. Luke tilted his head back, watching the silver streak disappear beyond the clouds. For the first time in a long time, something stirred deep within him. A feeling he hadn't let himself believe in for years. Excitement. Possibility. Hope. With a small, almost boyish grin, he exhaled, squared his shoulders, and thought, *Life, here I come.*

Undercurrents

"You're twenty-seven? No way. I'd have guessed younger."

Luke barely glanced at Andy, the Filipino guy slouched beside him, before turning back to his notes. There was something about Andy—too sharp, too observant, as if he enjoyed stripping people down to their rawest selves. It put Luke on edge.

"Not much of a talker, huh?" Andy pressed, his voice loud enough to turn a few heads.

Luke resisted the urge to sigh. Of all the people in class, why had he ended up next to the one person he instinctively disliked? He had hoped for Samantha, the redhead with the easy smile, but instead, he got Andy, brash and full of opinions on everything.

It was only their first week at the training centre in New Jersey, but two classmates had already disappeared. One had failed her first test, the other had been dismissed for something as minor as unpolished shoes. No goodbyes. No explanations. Just gone. It was a silent warning: step out of line, and you're out.

Luke had expected everyone to tread carefully, but not Andy.

Andy swaggered through training like he owned the place. His wit was sharp, his remarks just shy of being cruel. He made people laugh, but there was something under his humour—something knowing. Something that made Luke's hackles rise.

That evening, Luke hesitated before sitting down in the cafeteria. There were other trainees, people from different courses, faces that seemed friendlier, but he knew it was smarter to bond with his own group. He had five more weeks with them.

He set his tray down next to Samantha, who gave him a quick smile and scooted over.

"So, Luke," Timothy, one of the older trainees, leaned forward. "You're gonna be based out of Heathrow, right?"

"Yeah," Luke nodded, taking a sip of his water.

"You met Jason and Peter yet? They're in the class ahead of us— also Heathrow-based."

"No, not yet," Luke said, interested. He was the only one in their batch headed there. The rest were bound for bases in the U.S.— Washington, Chicago, Houston.

"I'll introduce you later," Timothy said, before turning to chat with someone else.

Luke pushed the food around his plate, eating more out of obligation than hunger. The cafeteria meals had lost their novelty days ago. Now, each bite felt mechanical, a routine to keep his body moving while his mind drifted elsewhere.

Samantha let out a dramatic sigh. "I wish I hadn't eaten that pie. Now I feel gross and fat."

Luke glanced at her. "You're not gross or fat."

"Oh, I know," she grinned, "but if I keep eating like this, I will be. Everyone says the first year of flying is the worst—trying out all the onboard meals. Not that I'll see the good stuff. I'll be stuck on domestic routes."

The conversation flowed easily after that. Luke relaxed as the table filled with chatter and laughter.

Timothy was in his forties, this being his second career. "I used to be a cop," he said with a shrug. "Figured I might as well see the world while I've still got some good years left."

Samantha was fresh out of college, full of excitement about flying.

They joked about the course, the trainers, the strange rules that made no sense.

"One trainer told me today that we might lose more people before the course is over," Kevin, Luke's roommate, said, lowering his voice. "Said they're watching us. If they think you're slacking, even a little, you're done."

Luke nodded, then tensed as someone dropped into the seat beside him.

Andy.

"Come on," Andy drawled, stretching out in his chair. "You gotta be real dumb to get kicked out. This isn't med school. Just show up, keep your uniform neat, and do the work. How hard is that?" He nudged Luke's elbow. "Right, man?"

Luke managed a tight smile before swallowing his last bite and standing.

"You done already?" Timothy asked, surprised.

"Yeah, I'm going to turn in early," Luke said, grabbing his tray.

"Wait up, I'll come with you," Kevin said, pushing his chair back. Luke was glad Kevin was his roommate. He was easygoing, no drama.

"That Andy," Kevin muttered as they walked out. "He's just so..."

"Annoying?" Luke supplied.

"You feel it too?"

"Oh yeah."

Kevin shook his head. "Don't know what it is, but the trainers seem to love him."

Luke smiled. "That's because he never shuts up. Teachers love a know-it-all."

"Well, he doesn't know it all. And he better watch out—he could be next." Kevin laughed before veering left.

"Where are you going?" Luke frowned. "Our room's that way."

"Going to see Joanne," Kevin winked. Then he disappeared through the double doors.

Luke shrugged and kept walking.

He had already noticed it—the casual way some of the guys talked about "playing away from home." It was an open secret. Some had girlfriends, fiancees, even wives, yet here they were, making plans with whoever was available.

He had been invited to join in, to "live a little." When they had joked that this was the best profession for a straight man, that it was "a numbers game," Luke had walked away.

He thought of his mother. Of Lara. Of Sue. There was no way he would ever become the kind of man who disrespected the women who loved him.

Lara's letter was a pleasant surprise. Christine had enclosed it with her own. Luke tore open the large envelope holding both letters.

He opened Christine's first.

Dear Luke,

I'm so glad to hear you're enjoying training and settling in. Like I said before, this is the start of something new and exciting. Make the most of it, Luke. These moments don't come around often.

Life here is fine, just busy. Work is good and keeps me engaged, which is always a good thing. Your father has been reaching out more frequently, asking me to convince you to call him. I've told him you're swamped, but Luke, maybe it's time. Just one call.

I'm not saying you owe him anything, but... maybe you owe yourself some closure.

We have a new neighbour—Frank Godfrey, a widower, I think. We've had a few chats in passing, and he's asked me to the pub this weekend. I don't know, Luke. Should I go? I don't want him getting the wrong idea, and if it's awkward later, well... we still have to share a landing. What would you do?

Also, I'm enclosing a letter from Lara. Have you not given her your U.S. address? I had an email from Zinia last week—Yash is seriously thinking about selling the business. Honestly, I hope he does. His health isn't what it used to be, and he needs to slow down. I'll update you on everything when you're home.

How's Sue? Are you keeping in touch? I'm looking forward to meeting her once you're back.

Lots of love & big hugs,
Mum X

Luke set the letter down, his gaze drifting beyond the window. Outside, the evening light cast long shadows across the lawns, where a few people strolled, their laughter carrying faintly through the air. He was grateful that Kevin was with Joanne—he needed this moment alone.

His conversations with Jim had always been strained, their exchanges growing more infrequent as the years stretched on. But despite everything, despite the silence and the resentment, Luke couldn't deny that a part of him still missed his father. In those bleak months after Steve's death, when grief had turned them all into strangers, Jim had still been there. A presence, even if a distant one. And then he wasn't.

His leaving had shaken Christine, but Luke had seen it coming. Steve's accident had hollowed his father out, drained the light from him. The man who had once been larger than life, whose energy had filled every room, had become a ghost of himself. When he finally left for the U.S., Luke hadn't felt anything. Not even sadness. Just a quiet detachment.. His loyalty had always been to his mother—the one who had stayed, who had held their family together even as it threatened to collapse.

But now, it was Christine, the woman who had every right to hate Jim, who was asking Luke to find some compassion for him. If she could, why couldn't he?

Luke exhaled sharply, rubbing a hand over his face. Then, with a shake of his head, he picked up Lara's letter. A photograph slipped out, fluttering onto his lap. He studied it closely. Lara stood between Zinia and Yash, their arms looped together in a way that spoke of effortless closeness. But it was their faces that caught his attention.

Yash was thinner than Luke remembered, his frame almost gaunt, his presence diminished. Zinia, too, had changed—grey now threaded through her dark hair, and there was a soft roundness to her that came with middle age. And yet, despite the visible markers of time, there was something undeniably whole about them. They looked happy. Solid. A unit. Luke swallowed, an unexpected flicker of envy rising in his chest.

Then his gaze landed on Lara. She looked beautiful, as always, but there was something else there too—something weary in the way her shoulders sat, in the faint shadows beneath her eyes. She had thrown herself into her job, the long hours at the PR firm wearing her down bit by bit. He could see it now, in the slight tightness of her smile. He set the photo aside and unfolded her letter. And then he began to read.

Dear Luke,

I'm sorry it's taken me so long to write back. Life has been non-stop. Early mornings, late nights—I feel like I'm constantly running on empty. I know you told me to take time for myself, but honestly, it feels impossible. Being in a start-up means wearing a dozen different hats, and while it's exhausting, I don't really mind. It keeps me occupied, and I'm learning so much. But some days... some days, I wonder if this is really what I want.

Papa is seriously considering selling the business now. His diabetes has worsened, and it's affecting everything, including his eyesight. I used to think diabetes wasn't a big deal, just something manageable, but I was so wrong. It's insidious, eating away at him little by little. You'll see it in the photo—he's lost so much weight.

Mummy keeps him in check, of course, hovering over him, making sure he follows all the rules. But the truth is, the damage is already done. And yet, he laughs. He jokes about it, shrugs it off, never lets on if he's scared. It drives Mummy mad, but we both know she wouldn't have him any other way.

Thank you for the birthday book. 'A Fine Balance'! I was thrilled to get it and I've been meaning to read it. When is another matter entirely! My bedtime routine? Non-existent. These days, I collapse into bed already half-asleep and wake up feeling just as tired. Can you believe it? Me, not reading before bed.

Some days, I wonder if I'm in the right profession. I never wanted to teach, and journalism never felt quite right.

either. So when this job came along, I thought—why not? Maybe it would be my thing. Maybe it still could be. But if Papa does sell the shop, we'll need the extra income, so any big career decisions will have to wait.

Have you left for training already? If you have, you'll probably only read this once you're back. I hope it was everything you wanted it to be, and that this job gives you everything you're looking for.

And Sue? You still haven't sent me a picture.

Give my love to Christine, and keep some for yourself, too.

Love,
Lara xx

In the weeks that followed, training became even more rigorous—long hours, gruelling emergency drills, and constant scrutiny. Grooming inspections turned into daily rituals, where even a stray wrinkle or an unpolished shoe could spell disaster. They lost three more classmates —one for being five minutes late, the other two for what seemed like trivial infractions.

"This job is about timekeeping!" one instructor barked. "The aircraft won't wait for you to stroll in whenever you feel like it. In this industry, punctuality isn't just important, it's everything."

Exhaustion became their constant companion. Even Luke, with his prior experience in aviation, struggled to keep up. The sheer scale of this airline's fleet dwarfed anything he had known before, and the endless drills—CPR repetitions, evacuation commands drummed into their skulls, emergency scenarios that had to be executed without a second's hesitation—left no room for error.

The pressure stripped away distractions. Even the budding romances that had sparked in the early days fizzled out as coursework took precedence. Most nights, trainees collapsed into bed, too drained to do anything but sleep.

Luke found his strengths in the practical elements—customer service, first aid—but when it came to public speaking, he faltered. He wasn't shy, never had been, but standing in front of his classmates, delivering announcements in a controlled yet engaging tone, took effort. He wasn't alone—Samantha, usually self-assured, turned crimson every time she stumbled over a phrase.

Andy, of course, was effortlessly charismatic, revelling in every moment the spotlight found him. He preened when instructors praised him, basked in his own confidence, and made no effort to endear himself to anyone. His arrogance was grating, his smirk ever-present. Worse, he had taken to calling Luke "Heathrow"—a nickname that was as mocking as it was persistent.

"C'mon, Heathrow," he'd drawl, leaning too close. "Crack a smile. You look like you're heading to a funeral, not a flight."

It grated on Luke's nerves more than he cared to admit.

Then came the fire drill. They had to take turns donning their PBE hoods, navigating through simulated smoke, and using a Halon extinguisher to combat a staged onboard fire, which was a cardboard cutout of a real fire. And, as fate would have it, Luke was paired with Andy.

Andy hovered close as Luke adjusted his grip on the extinguisher. When Luke hesitated, Andy's hands wandered over his, steadying the metal canister.

"Relax," Andy murmured, barely audible over the surrounding chaos.

"We're supposed to be fighting a fire, in case you haven't noticed," Luke shot back, his words edged with sarcasm.

Andy's lips quirked into a knowing smirk. He leaned in just enough for Luke to feel the heat of him, the whisper of his breath against his ear.

"Some fires," Andy said, voice low, "aren't worth fighting."

Then he was gone, sauntering away as if nothing had happened, leaving Luke gripping the extinguisher with unsteady hands, his pulse a beat too fast, his mind spinning with the weight of something he didn't quite understand.

By Friday evening, the pressure had reached its peak. A week of relentless drills and looming exams had left everyone wound tight, and the group was desperate to cut loose. Plans for drinks and a club quickly took shape—one night to let go before the grind resumed. Luke declined without hesitation. A night out was the last thing he wanted. A quiet evening with a book sounded infinitely better.

As the others cheered and clapped each other on the back, he felt Andy's gaze on him.

"I'm out too," Andy announced.

Luke's stomach twisted. Of course. Now he'd have to deal with him all night.

They fell into step as they walked back toward the dorms. The evening air was thick with the scent of cut grass, the sky darkening into that in-between moment before night fully took over.

"So," Andy said, voice smooth, measured. "What's the plan for your wild Friday night?"

Luke kept his tone light. "Oh, you know. Calling my girlfriend back in London."

Andy's stride faltered for half a second. "You have a girlfriend?"

Luke glanced sideways. "Yeah. Why?"

Andy opened his mouth, then shut it again. He shook his head, stuffing his hands into his pockets. "Doesn't matter." His voice had lost some of its usual sharp edge. Then, without another word, he veered off toward his dorm.

Luke let out a slow breath, the tension draining from his shoulders. That was... weird. He upped his pace, suddenly eager to get inside. Maybe it *was* time to call Sue. He had been so buried under training that he'd let her letters and calls go unanswered. Sue never nagged, never demanded more of him than he was willing to give. But even she had limits. She deserved better than silence.

In his room, he pulled out the card that allowed him to make international calls. Then he entered the code and the number and pressed dial.

———

The phone rang for so long that Luke nearly hung up. Just as his thumb hovered over the button, Sue's voice crackled through the line.

"Hello?" She sounded groggy.

"Sue? Sorry, were you sleeping?"

"Luke?" Her tone sharpened, sleep instantly forgotten. "My goodness, I was about to send a search party to New Jersey! Why on earth haven't you answered my calls?"

Luke exhaled, rubbing the back of his neck. "It's been brutal here, Sue. Nothing like our training back home. That was a walk in the park compared to this..."

"Really?" The irritation in her voice faded, replaced by curiosity.

As he detailed the intense weeks of training—the relentless drills, the exhaustion, the pressure of constant evaluation—he felt himself relaxing. This was Sue. Familiar, steady, grounding. Talking to her stripped away the tension that had coiled in his gut since his last encounter with Andy. Then he finally paused and asked, "And you? What's new? How's work?"

"It's fine," she said, though there was a slight hesitation. "I've been doing a lot of Cardiffs—there and back. Early starts, but at least I'm home early, so I make it to the gym in the evenings. And I've caught up with Sheila and the girls for drinks a few times."

"That's great. How's Sheila?"

Sheila had mentored them both when they first started flying, guiding them through the early days.

"She's good. Doing what she does best—taking all the newbies under her wing. They adore her, just like we did."

"Just like we *do*," Luke corrected, grinning.

"Yes, but Luke..." Her voice wobbled slightly. "It's not the same without you. I keep thinking, what if I'd gotten the job too? We could've been doing this together."

Luke tensed. The easy flow of conversation screeched to a halt. He'd let himself forget, just for a moment, that Sue saw them as a team. That she still saw him as part of her future. But did he? He stumbled through some vague reassurance, but the warmth in his voice had drained. He knew it. She knew it.

"You *do* miss me, right?"

"Of course I do," he said quickly. Too quickly. He forced a chuckle, tried injecting something real into the words, but even to his own ears, they sounded hollow. Desperate to shift the conversation, he told her about the group heading out for drinks, how he'd chosen to stay behind and call her instead. That seemed to soothe her, and she laughed, chatting as if nothing had changed. But Luke could feel it. A shift. A widening gap between them that neither of them wanted to name.

Then she asked, "Have you written to your father yet?"

Luke inhaled slowly. "Actually, yeah. Just a brief letter. Told him I was here on training, and if he wanted, we could catch up over the phone." He hesitated. "He hasn't called."

"Oh, I'm sure he will," Sue said, ever the optimist. "Maybe the letter hasn't even reached him yet?"

"Maybe."

"Well, you'll find time to talk, won't you? It's important too."

"Yeah," Luke murmured, though he wasn't sure if he meant it.

The conversation wound down. He was already bracing for it when Sue said softly, "I love you."

His stomach clenched. He knew he should say it back. That was the expected response. The normal response. Instead, his voice came out stiff, unnatural. "Talk soon, yeah?"

A pause. Then, quietly, "Yeah."

Luke ended the call and stared at the ceiling, his heart pounding for reasons he didn't fully understand. What the hell was wrong with him?

Sunday was the only day they could sleep in—no early drills, no instructors breathing down their necks, no reminder of all they had yet to prove. So when the phone rang, slicing through the silence in their room, Kevin groaned and yanked the pillow over his head with enough force to tear the seam.

Luke, half-suspended in that fragile space between dreams and consciousness, reached blindly for the receiver, knocking over the alarm clock. It clattered to the floor, a small avalanche of sound in the quiet room. "Hello?" His voice was rough, thick with sleep and the remnants of a half-forgotten dream.

The second he heard the voice on the other end, he jolted upright, his spine straightening as if an electric current had passed through it. That voice. The one he'd spent years trying to forget.

"Everything okay, bud?" Kevin peeked out groggily from under the pillow, one eye squinting against the intrusion of morning light.

Luke cleared his throat, already pulling on his sneakers, muscle memory taking over while his mind raced ahead. "Yeah," he muttered, the lie bitter on his tongue. "Yeah, it's fine." But it wasn't.

Running a trembling hand through his hair, he grabbed a clean T-shirt from the back of his chair, splashed cold water on his face, and left the room before his roommate could see the storm brewing in his eyes.

Jim was standing with his back to him when Luke arrived at reception ten minutes later, shifting his weight from one foot to the other like a man waiting for his sentencing. He looked smaller than Luke remembered—not in stature, but in presence. The broad-shouldered giant of Luke's childhood had diminished somehow. The stockiness of his youth had given way to a soft, almost slumped frame. A bald patch now shone at the back of his head, catching the morning light like a halo.

Luke swallowed hard. "Dad?" His voice came out hoarse, unprepared for this confrontation.

Jim turned, and for a moment, there was raw uncertainty in his eyes. Then his weathered face broke into a wide smile, revealing new creases around his mouth that Luke had never seen before. "Lukey boy! I've missed you."

Before Luke could react, Jim pulled him into a bear hug, his grip strong, almost desperate. The familiar scent of his father's aftershave crashed over Luke like a wave, triggering a cascade of memories he'd carefully locked away: pancake Sundays, fishing trips, his father's rare but booming laugh that filled the entire room.

Luke stood stiff in his father's arms, his body unyielding. He wasn't ready—wasn't sure if he'd ever be ready—to give Jim the validation he so clearly needed. The cost was too high, the betrayal still too fresh despite the years that had passed.

Jim pulled back, studying him with eyes that mirrored his own. "You look good. Grown up."

"I am grown up. I'm twenty-seven, or have you forgotten?" Each word carried the weight of birthdays uncelebrated, milestones unmarked, years spent constructing a life around his father's absence.

Jim's smile faltered, but he nodded, absorbing the blow with the quiet dignity of a man who knew he deserved worse. "No, I haven't forgotten." He held up a paper bag, grease already seeping through the bottom. "Figured you wouldn't be eating well here. Brought you some real barbecue. Your favourite."

Luke hesitated, then took the bag from his hands, their fingers brushing briefly. "Thanks, Dad." The word felt foreign on his tongue, disused and dusty.

They walked outside to a bench by the small lake, the water shimmering under the morning sun like shattered glass. Ducks floated lazily across the surface, oblivious to the years of silence stretching between father and son.

Jim exhaled, running a hand over the stubble on his jaw. "I took the red-eye to get here. Figured I'd see you before you head back to London."

"You could visit me there, too." Luke's voice was sharper than he intended, barbed with unspoken accusations. "It used to be your home once."

Jim sighed, rubbing a hand over his face, a gesture so familiar it made Luke's chest ache. "I know."

Luke looked away, his jaw clenched so tight he could feel a headache blooming at his temples. The lake rippled in the gentle breeze, carrying away conversations that would never happen, apologies that might never be enough. After a long pause, they both spoke at the same time.

"How's Lexi?" Luke asked.

"How's training?" Jim said.

A brief silence as each waited for the other to continue. Then Luke answered first, relieved to talk about something—anything—that didn't scrape against old wounds. "Training is intense and way tougher than I expected. Way tougher than my last airline, for sure. In some ways, it reminds me of working in the kitchens during my hotel trainee days. A million moving parts, zero room for mistakes. The pressure is nonstop." He let out a breath that seemed to carry the weight of weeks. "But the group's solid, and there's only one more week to go. If I pass, I'll be flying out of Heathrow soon enough."

Jim smiled, a genuine one this time that reached his eyes. "Not if. When. You're more than capable, Luke."

Luke let out a short, bitter laugh that tasted of all the times he'd needed to hear those words and hadn't. "Even after all those wasted years? After Steve—" He cut himself off, but the name hung between them, a reminder of everything that had shattered in its wake.

Jim's face darkened, grief etching itself into every line. "Yes," he said, "Steve believed in you. And so do I."

Luke's throat tightened. He looked down at the bag of barbecue, focusing on the grease stains soaking through the paper rather than the emotion threatening to breach his carefully constructed walls.

"This isn't the career you imagined for me, is it?" he asked finally, voicing a question that had haunted him for years.

Jim shook his head, his eyes reflecting the sky above. "Luke, I just want you to be happy. If this is what makes you happy, then I have no right to question it."

"Funny," Luke muttered, a sharp edge creeping into his voice like frost. "Mum and you—both these bright intellectuals. And then you get me. The disappointment."

Jim's eyes flashed. "You're not a disappointment."

Luke scoffed.

"Stop selling yourself short," Jim pressed, leaning forward. "You're a kind, empathetic boy—"

"I'm not a boy, Dad." The words came out heavy with all the growing up he'd done alone.

"I know you're not," Jim said, his voice quieter now, laced with regret. "But listen to me, son. The world doesn't just need intellect. It needs people like you. If it were full of people like me and your mother, it'd be a damn boring place." He paused, his next words barely audible. "And a lonelier one."

Luke let out a small, reluctant smile, the first genuine one, feeling something loosen fractionally in his chest. "So," he said, shifting the conversation to safer ground, "how is Lexi?"

"She's good. There's a new guy in the picture. Seems serious."

"Is she working?"

Jim chuckled, the sound nostalgic and warm. "Yeah, at a magazine. Her job mostly seems to involve testing out beauty products. The house is covered in mascara and lipstick tubes."

Luke shook his head, smirking. "Sounds about right." For a moment, he could see her—his half-sister, a teenager when he'd left, now a woman with a life of her own.

The conversation faded into silence, both of them staring out at the lake. After a while, Jim sighed and stood, joints creaking audibly.

"I got a hotel nearby. If you're free later this week, we could grab dinner or something." The casual suggestion couldn't hide the note of hope beneath it.

Luke hesitated. "I don't know, Dad. It's a busy week, and I—"

Jim nodded before he could finish, accepting the rejection with practiced ease. "I get it." He paused, then reached out, pulling Luke into another hug. This time, there was no hesitation in his touch, only a quiet tremble as he held him. "Son," Jim murmured, his voice rough with emotion. "I know I screwed up. I know I should've been better. Done better. But I need you to understand that I never stopped loving you."

Luke's chest tightened. But he said nothing, the words he needed to say caught behind years of practiced silence.

Jim pulled back, searching his face for any sign of softening, any crack in the wall Luke had built between them. "You don't walk away from people you love," Luke said finally, his voice barely above a whisper, each syllable dredged from the depths of his pain.

Jim's shoulders sagged. "I was broken, Luke." His voice was raw, stripped of pretence. "After Steve, I just... I couldn't be what you needed. I made choices I have to live with. But you—you don't have to punish yourself for them too."

The truth of it cut through Luke. All these years, he'd been punishing himself. For not stopping Steve that evening, for not being enough to make his father stay, and for not being the son his father wanted.

Luke watched as his father turned and walked away, his steps slower, his shoulders heavier than before. For the first time, he saw his father not as the titan of his childhood or the villain of his teens, but simply as a man—flawed and vulnerable, trying to find his way back from his mistakes. He swallowed against the lump rising in his throat.

Then, without a backward glance, he turned and headed for the dorm. He didn't want to think about this, didn't want to unpack the emotional fallout of this meeting just yet. He just wanted sleep. Deep, dreamless sleep. The kind that would pull him under, far away from old wounds and the ghosts of what could have been.

———

Later that evening, after dinner, Luke found himself back at the same bench. The campus was quiet. Most of his classmates holed up in their rooms, revising or preparing for the next day. He should have been doing the same, but his mind refused to cooperate.

All day, he wrestled with the aftermath of his father's visit, a cyclone of unnamed and uncontrollable emotions. Why was forgiveness so damn hard? Jim had admitted his mistakes, had tried, however clumsily, to make amends. Then why did Luke still feel this gnawing resentment eating him from the inside out?

Perhaps his father leaving may not have been the only issue. Maybe it was about Luke himself—about the parts he kept hidden, locked away in the darkest corners of his consciousness. Maybe he felt unworthy of being truly seen, and it was easier to project that on to his father's absence than confront the truth that terrified him.

He exhaled, rubbing a hand over his face. Right now, though, he just felt... hollowed out. Tired of pretending. Tired of carrying the weight of a self he'd constructed so carefully that sometimes he couldn't remember who he really was beneath it all. He dropped his head into his hands, trying to summon the boy he used to be. The one who had taken his father's love and presence for granted, back when life had felt limitless, stretched out with infinite potential. When he hadn't yet learned to monitor every gesture, every inflection, every reaction that might betray him. But those days were gone. Now, there were mornings when getting out of bed felt like crossing a battlefield. When carrying on felt like a performance, one he wasn't sure he could maintain.

"Everything okay?"

Luke started as Andy dropped onto the bench beside him, the scent of his cologne cutting through the cool night air. Andy pulled out a cigarette with slender fingers, the silver ring on his thumb catching what little light there was. He offered one wordlessly. Luke shook his head, suddenly aware of how close their shoulders were, not quite touching. Andy shrugged, lighting up, then blew a perfect smoke ring into the night air. Luke watched the way Andy's lips pursed, then relaxed. For a moment, they sat in silence; the darkness settling around them like a confessional booth. The only light came from the dorms in the distance, casting a dim glow across the lawn, just enough to illuminate the sharp angles of Andy's profile.

Luke wasn't sure why, but he surprised himself by speaking. "My father showed up today, unexpectedly." His voice was rougher than he'd intended. "We, uh... we don't have the best relationship."

Andy didn't comment, just angled his body slightly toward him, his knee now centimetres away from Luke's. A silent invitation to continue.

"Actually," Luke muttered, stretching his legs out, hyper aware of the proximity, "we don't have a relationship. Haven't had one for years."

Andy took a drag from his cigarette, studying him with those piercing eyes that always seemed to see beyond Luke's carefully constructed walls. "That explains the storm cloud over your head." His voice was softer than usual, missing its usual teasing edge.

Luke let out a dry laugh. "What can I say? Some things never change."

"The fact that he showed up," Andy said, exhaling a slow stream of smoke that disappeared into the darkness, "tells me he's trying. Nobody just turns up, knowing they might get shut down, unless they care."

Luke blinked against the sudden sting behind his eyes. He clenched his jaw, determined not to let it show. Not in front of Andy, who had always seemed so remarkably himself, so unafraid of what others thought.

"You should let yourself feel something, Heathrow." Andy's voice was quiet but firm. "You walk around like you're holding your breath all the time."

The words hit Luke like a physical blow. Was it that obvious? The constant vigilance, the careful control he maintained over every aspect of himself? Luke turned to snap back at him, to defend the fortress he'd built around his heart, but before he could get the words out, Andy flicked his cigarette away and leaned in.

Luke's breath caught in his throat. Then Andy's lips were on his. For a split second, Luke froze, the world narrowing to this single point of contact. The softness of Andy's lips, the rough scrape of his stubble, the heady mix of cigarette smoke and something sweet—honey?—all of it hit him at once. His pulse roared in his ears, his body tensed, every defence mechanism screaming, but he didn't pull away.

Andy kissed him with quiet confidence, not demanding, not pushing, just sure. As if he'd always known something that Luke had been running from his entire life. And Luke, to his utter shock, found himself kissing him back. It wasn't like kissing Cindy, or Sue, or any of the other girls he'd dated—performances he'd executed with technical precision but never felt in his bones. This was different. Electric. Real. His nerves lit up, every inch of him on high alert, something unfurling in his chest that had been trapped there for as long as he could remember. This wasn't confusion. This was recognition.

When Andy finally pulled away, Luke was breathless. His world had been altered in an instant.

"I've wanted to do that since I first met you," Andy murmured, his voice laced with something tender, vulnerable in a way Luke had never allowed himself to be.

Luke shook his head, his thoughts spinning like debris in a tornado. "I don't—"

"Don't overthink it, Heathrow," Andy interrupted, standing and stretching as if nothing had happened. As if he hadn't just detonated Luke's entire understanding of himself. Then he walked away, disappearing into the shadows, leaving Luke with a truth he could no longer outrun.

Luke sat frozen, his heart hammering against his ribs, his lips still burning from the contact.

What the hell had just happened?

But even as he asked, he knew. Deep down, in a place he'd walled off for years, buried under layers of expectation and fear and denial—he knew. The kiss hadn't confused him. It had clarified something essential, something he'd been denying for so long that the denial itself had become part of his identity. Like a photograph finally coming into focus after years of deliberate blurring. His hands trembled as he pressed his fingertips to his lips, still feeling the phantom pressure of Andy's mouth against his. The rightness of it. The relief that flooded through him wasn't about Andy specifically, it was about finally, finally understanding the disconnect he'd felt his entire life. The constant sense that he was playing a role rather than living as himself.

All those relationships with girls that had felt like going through motions he'd memorised but never felt. The way his gaze had always lingered a beat too long on certain male classmates, certain actors, certain strangers, only to be ruthlessly redirected. The realisation crashed over him like a wave: he was gay. He'd always been gay.

All these years of feeling like an imposter in his own skin, of constructing a version of Luke that could navigate the world without drawing too much attention, it all made sense now. The constant vigilance, the careful self-editing, the relationships that felt like performances rather than connections. He'd been running from this truth for so long that he'd forgotten what it felt like to stand still, to breathe, to simply be.

A laugh bubbled up from somewhere deep inside him—half-terrified, half-liberated. God, he'd been so blind. Or not blind, exactly, just... deliberately not seeing. He stood on shaky legs, feeling like he might float away or collapse entirely. The campus around him looked different somehow, as if the colours had shifted and become more vibrant. Or maybe it was just that he was seeing it through unclouded eyes for the first time.

Luke wrapped his arms around himself, not against the cold but against the vastness of what lay ahead—the conversations, the reactions, the recalibration of his entire life. There would be time for fear later. For now, there was just this moment of absolute clarity, cutting through years of fog. I'm gay, he thought, testing the words in his mind. And for the first time in as long as he could remember, the weight on his chest eased just a fraction, allowing him to take a full, deep breath.

Lara (May 2000)

Plunging

"Valli, don't forget, *Sahib* needs his insulin injections in the morning and at night," Zinia reminded the maid for what felt like the hundredth time.

Lara sighed, exchanging a knowing glance with Yash. "Mummy, I think even the neighbours could recite Papa's insulin schedule by now. You've drilled it into everyone's heads."

Zinia shot her daughter a sharp look. "You don't know your father like I do. He'll forget, and then everything will spiral out of control."

From his rocking chair on the balcony, Yash chuckled. "Now, now, Zin. I'm not that absentminded."

Zinia crossed her arms. "Not absentminded, careless." Her voice was firm, but beneath the sternness, Lara detected something else. Fear.

Yash, unwilling to debate further, shifted the subject. "So, when's this taxi fellow getting here?" He had long accepted that arguing with Zinia over his health was futile. She saw herself as his guardian, the last line of defence against fate, and at the heart of it all, was her unspoken terror of losing him.

He met Lara's gaze, and in that quiet exchange, they understood each other. Lara crouched beside him, her voice softer now. "I wish you were coming with us, Papa. It won't be the same without you."

"Your papa isn't well enough to travel," Zinia interjected, peering over the balcony railing. 'Where *is* this Singh chap?"

Right on cue, a familiar taxi pulled up below. *Sardarji* stepped out, adjusting his khaki uniform, squinting up at them as if he could already sense Zinia's impatience. Over the years, he and his brother had become an integral part of her travel routine—familiar, reliable, and accustomed to the sight of her pacing the balcony before every trip. She motioned for him to come up and get their bags, then turned back to Yash, pressing a kiss to his cheek.

"I'll call every evening to check on you. And please, nap in the afternoons and turn the air conditioner on. It's getting hotter now."

Yash chuckled. "Zin, you're going to Goa, not the moon."

His tone was light, but Lara caught something in his eyes. A flicker of something indecipherable that made her chest tighten. She bent down and kissed his cheek, too. "Take care, Papa. And when I get back, we are discussing getting a car. No more objections, okay?"

Yash sighed. He had resisted this for months. Ever since he'd closed his shop and sold his beloved Bajaj scooter, they had been at the mercy of rickshaws and crowded buses. Lara had offered to take out a loan to handle everything, but he and Zinia had kept pushing back. A car was an investment, and they still viewed her as their child, not as the capable woman she had become. As she picked up her bag, Lara wondered, when would they finally treat her as an adult?

The new millennium had arrived not with a bang, but with an eerie grace. The dreaded Y2K bug hadn't ended the world—it hadn't even flickered the lights. Instead, the year 2000 slipped in quietly, almost politely, as if not to disturb the century it succeeded.

For Lara, time felt less like a river and more like a loop. Her body aged, her mind evolved, yet her life remained suspended, as if she were walking in place while the world spun forward. A woman in the number of years she had lived, yes, but she was still strangely tethered to the invisible strings of girlhood. She was in the process of becoming without actually arriving; waiting without knowing what for.

As the taxi wove through the busy streets towards the airport, Lara turned to Zinia. "Do you think Granny will want to sell the house? She spent her entire married life there. After Grandpa, surely she wants to hold on to the memories?"

Zinia exhaled, staring out of the window. "I don't think she'll have much of a choice. If we don't act now, Pedru will sell it right from under her nose. She'll be homeless before she even realises what's happening."

Four months. That's all it had been since Zinia's father had lost his battle with cancer. And already, Pedru had siphoned money from their parents' bank account. Jude had warned them that it was only a matter of time before Pedru made his move. This was why they were making this journey. First, a stop in Mumbai to stay with Jude and Roxanna. Then, they'd all drive down to Goa and take control—sell the house, divide the money fairly, and secure Granny a small flat where she could live out the rest of her days in peace.

"What will happen to Uncle Pedru?" Lara asked, though she already knew the answer.

Zinia's expression hardened. "Lara, he's in his fifties. It's time he stood on his own feet. He can't keep leeching off Ma forever."

Lara nodded. She understood all too well. Sometimes, she wondered if she was a burden too. At thirty, wasn't she supposed to be settled? There was always an unspoken judgment in people's eyes —subtle, but there. Mummy and Papa had never pressured her, never made her feel like she was failing them. But that didn't stop the gnawing guilt that crept in from time to time.

Zinia's voice broke into her thoughts. "I don't think he'll go easily."

Lara met her mother's gaze. "No. He won't."

Pedru had spent time in prison, and if anything, it had hardened him. There was no remorse for what he had done, no shame. And now, there was no pretence, either. He would fight them for control of the house, of the money, of whatever scraps he could get his hands on.

"It's good we'll have Jude and Roxy with us," Zinia continued. "Though I still don't understand why they're so insistent that we take our share now. It's Ma's to do with as she pleases." She paused, then added, almost as if speaking to herself, "I suppose they just want to make sure Pedru doesn't get his hands on any of it. Once Ma has her own place and a stipend, he won't be able to manipulate her finances anymore..."

Lara let her mother's words drift over her as her mind wandered elsewhere—back to the job she had taken two weeks off from. When she had joined the company, it had been a struggling startup. But through sheer effort, long hours, and relentless work, they had transformed it into one of the fastest-rising PR firms in the industry. And yet... now that success had come, she felt restless. The endless stream of client pitches. The same routine. The same faces. Day in and day out. She exhaled slowly. It was never the right time to quit. But if not now, then when?

Thirty. The age when she was supposed to have everything figured out. Instead, all she felt was trapped.

———

Once they had checked in and dropped off their luggage, they made their way toward security. The queue moved slowly, a dull murmur of voices filling the air. As they inched forward, Zinia's eyes followed a group of attractive young flight attendants gliding past them, effortlessly chic in their pressed uniforms as they headed to their separate security line.

She turned to Lara. "Have you given any more thought to what Luke said?"

Lara tightened her grip on the strap of her bag, her gaze fixed ahead. "Mummy, not now."

"Lara," Zinia said, her voice edged with sharpness and impatience.

Lara exhaled. "I've thought about it."

"And?"

A beat of silence. "It's not for me."

Zinia scoffed. "Nonsense! You've got everything it takes—the height, the looks, the charm. And you speak both Hindi and English fluently. What's stopping you?"

The line moved, forcing them to place their handbags onto the conveyor belt for the X-ray scan. Lara hoped the conversation would get lost in the shuffle, but she should have known better. Zinia picked up right where she had left off once they retrieved their bags. "So? What exactly is the problem?"

Lara hesitated as they walked towards the gate, her mind racing for the right words.

Luke. That name still stirred something restless in her—a quiet ache laced with memory, with wonder, with old, unspent hope. She had waited years to see him again. When the moment finally came, they approached one another like survivors of a shipwreck—cautious, reverent, uncertain of what remained from their childhood friendship.

All those years. The letters that had dwindled into silence for such a long time until they resumed their correspondence. Her yearning, vivid and persistent. His careful responses that signalled affection but never anything more. Yet, in the instant their eyes met, all of it dissolved. Time, distance, and the long corridor of waiting.

She was shy. Hesitant. When he folded her into his arms, she noticed everything: the unfamiliar scent of him, clean and woody, the soft press of his shirt against her cheek, the way a single rebellious curl slipped onto his brow, just as it had when they were young. His face had changed, sharpened by time, but his eyes, those rich, expressive eyes, held something she had known all her life.

He was, in so many ways, a stranger, yet her heart recognized him instantly.

She hadn't meant to hope. But she had. Some quiet part of her had spun a story—the kind where childhood longing becomes grown-up love, where years apart melt into a single perfect moment. But that story was not theirs. It never had been.

In time, she made peace with it. Not without heartbreak, but with the quiet strength of someone who had finally stopped asking love to be something it could never be. Luke loved her, there was no doubt about that, but not in the way she had once longed for, not in the way she had built her hopes around.

It wasn't a failure, she came to understand. It was simply the truth. Some love stories weren't meant to unfold as romance, but as something quieter, more enduring. And letting go of what might have been became, in its own way, an act of love.

Over time, she came to look forward to his layovers, to spending time with her friend, barricading her mind and heart to any other possibilities, knowing what she did now.

Luke had been so excited when he last visited, talking non-stop about his airline's new hiring initiative in India. He had practically shoved an application form into her hands, grinning, telling her she was perfect for the job. He had even promised to coach her for the interview. Now, Zinia had joined the chorus.

"I'm still waiting, Lara..." Zinia's expectant gaze bore into her.

Lara swallowed. Her voice, when it came, was barely above a whisper. "I... I can't bear the thought of leaving you and Papa."

Zinia stopped walking. The sharpness in her eyes softened instantly.

"Oh, child." She reached out, tucking a stray strand of hair behind Lara's ear. "You cannot stay tied to our apron strings forever... or in my case, my saree *pallu*." She let out a short laugh, then shook her head. "It's time, Lara. Time for you to step out into the world."

Lara looked away. "Flying? That wasn't what I'd imagined for myself."

"Maybe that's the point." Zinia's voice was gentle but insistent. "Maybe life is offering you something new, something different. A chance to do what you've always wanted—to travel, to see the world, to stay in all those beautiful places you used to dream about."

Lara let out a bitter chuckle. "A child's dreams, Mummy."

"Maybe. But they don't have to stay that way." Zinia squeezed her arm. "They can be your reality, Lara. If you let them."

They sat together in comfortable silence, the low buzz of the airport filling the space between them. Lara turned her mother's words over in her mind, tracing the edges of memories she rarely allowed herself to dwell on. On Tej. Her unofficial boyfriend with whom she had spent the last two years. All of it had been a sham, a pretence.

Tej had never promised her marriage, but she had believed— naively, foolishly—that they had an unspoken understanding. A future, if not written in stone, then at least softly sketched in pencil. That illusion had shattered the day his wedding invitations were passed around at work, like office memos. Not once had he mentioned a fiancée. Not once had he given her any sign that, to him, she had been nothing more than a passing distraction. And just like that, two years had been reduced to a footnote in his life, while she had been left questioning what any of it had even meant.

Had it broken her? No. If she was being honest, it had been disappointment more than heartbreak—a dull, numbing ache rather than a sharp, searing wound. Perhaps in some ways, it had been a relief. Tej had made the decision for her, spared her the weight of choosing.

Zinia's voice cut through her thoughts. "What do you think of Luke's new partner?"

Lara blinked, pulled abruptly from the past. "Harry?" She frowned. "I don't know. I've never even met him. He sounds nice, though. And Luke seems happy. Isn't that what matters?"

"Hmm." Zinia pursed her lips, shaking her head slightly. "I still can't believe he's a homosexual."

Lara stiffened. "Gay, Mummy," she corrected in a whisper, glancing around, hoping no one had overheard.

Zinia's brows knitted together. "Isn't that the same thing?"

Lara exhaled and looked down at her hands, shaking her head slightly. Some days the truth of his sexuality ambushed her anew. Then that old, buried longing resurfaced, whispering mockingly in the quiet corners of her heart.

Zinia studied her face, her expression softening. Then she reached over, squeezed Lara's hand, and said, "Life's too short to be stuck in one place, Lara."

"Is that the book Luke gave you?" Zinia asked, glancing at the paperback in Lara's hands. She squinted at the title. "What a strange name."

Lara traced the embossed letters on the cover. 'White Teeth' by Zadie Smith—Luke's latest gift to her. She could still picture the way he had pulled it out of his bag, a teasing smile on his lips, the book wrapped in pretty pink paper, tied with an over-the-top silver bow.

"For you, m'lady, as you step into this new decade…"

It had become their thing—this ritual of surprising each other with books, some perfectly tailored to their tastes, others so unexpected they sparked endless debates. A way to stay connected across the miles, across the years. They often discussed what the other had thought of the book, surprising each other with their insights, arguing about the messages in the book, tearing apart characters they had both disliked. She looked forward to these moments more than she cared to admit.

Zinia peered over her in-flight magazine. "Is it about a dentist?"

Lara let out an unguarded laugh. "Mummy! It's about immigration, identity, generational conflict…"

Zinia sniffed, unimpressed. "I don't see why you young people can't enjoy straightforward storytelling like Sidney Sheldon or James Hadley Chase." She shook her head and went back to her magazine.

Lara smiled, but as she tried once again to focus on the book, her mind betrayed her, drifting, inevitably, back to Luke. Three years. That's how long it had been since he had first told her. She still remembered the evening vividly—his layover in Delhi, the two of them walking in Lodhi Gardens, his voice quieter than usual, a heaviness about his person. Then, in a rush, it had all come spilling out— his confusion, his struggle, the years of guilt, the weight of his own denial. The way he had tried to be the son his mother expected, the man Sue had loved, and how, in the end, he had only betrayed himself. And Lara? She had listened. She had nodded, asked the right questions, urged him to unburden himself. But inside, she had crumbled, retreating into a quiet grief she could never let him guess at.

Now, she saw Luke more often than she had in years, his job bringing him back to her, his affection for her unchanged. But something between them had shifted. The boy she had known, the boy who had poured himself into letters, who had felt like an extension of herself, was gone. In his place was a man who looked like him, spoke like him, laughed with the same easy warmth. But one she no longer truly knew.

Luke's confession three years ago hadn't just been about his sexuality, it had been about the intricate architecture of self-deception. How did one dismantle an entire constructed identity? How many walls had to crumble before one found authentic breathing space?

She felt the weight of unsaid things pressing against her ribcage. Not just Luke's unspoken struggles, but her own carefully curated silence. The grief she'd swallowed that day in Lodhi Gardens wasn't just about Luke's revelation, it was about the gradual erosion of a shared narrative she'd taken as the truth, and the death of the tiniest ember of hope her heart had still carried within itself. With a soft sigh, Lara set the book down on her lap and closed her eyes.

"You've been so quiet since we left Delhi, Lara." Zinia's voice was gentle, probing. Lara blinked her eyes open and met her mother's gaze, the concern clear in her eyes. "Still thinking about Luke?"

Lara gave a small, wistful smile. "It's strange, isn't it? You think you know someone, and then they go and surprise you..."

Zinia nodded thoughtfully before saying, almost to herself, "Christine wasn't surprised, actually."

Lara turned to her, intrigued. "She wasn't?"

Zinia shook her head. "Not one bit. Said she'd always known... or maybe suspected. But she wanted him to reach that understanding on his own. That's the only way it truly means something."

Lara absorbed that, her mind whirring. "Did you ever suspect Mummy?"

Zinia looked genuinely taken aback. "Me? How could I? I hadn't really seen Luke since he was fourteen. And when I visited the States, I spent more time with Christine than I did with him. Besides, Lara, it's not written on someone's forehead, is it?" She gave a short laugh, then softened. "To me, Luke was always that sweet, sweet boy who pulled you out of the water and saved your life."

A silence stretched between them, deep and reflective.

Then, quietly, Zinia asked, "Can I ask you something, darling?"

Lara turned to her. "Of course, Mummy. Anything."

Zinia hesitated for just a second, then said carefully, "Have you, subconsciously, been waiting for Luke all along? Is that why no other man has ever truly stood a chance?"

Lara exhaled sharply. "There was Tej..." she protested.

Zinia's voice was soft but firm. "Apart from Tej?"

Lara parted her lips, then hesitated, pressing them shut. The truth sat like a stone in her chest, waiting to be acknowledged. But some answers were too raw to face, too deeply woven into the fabric of her being. Maybe she wasn't ready. Maybe she never would be. Before she could summon the courage to respond, the cabin crew arrived with food and drinks, breaking the fragile moment. She busied herself with selecting a drink, nodding her thanks, grateful for the brief reprieve.

Zinia waited until the crew had moved on before speaking again, her voice softer now, mindful of Lara's unspoken pain. "Just because one door has closed doesn't mean every path to Luke has vanished. He is still a part of your story. Love him for who he is, Lara. Love him for what he can give you and for what he never could. That is the only way to make peace—with him, with the past, and most of all, with yourself."

Lara swallowed hard and closed her eyes, allowing a single tear to escape. How well Zinia knew her. Was it a mother's gift, this ability to look into her child's face and see straight into her heart?

Later, as the captain announced their descent, Zinia reached over and gave Lara's hand a light squeeze. "So, tell me, why are you so against joining Luke's airline? The pay is good. You'll be based in London, and best of all, you'll fly to Delhi every week."

Lara groaned. "Oh God, not this again!"

Zinia's lips curled into the barest hint of a smile. "I'm just saying, life is about taking chances, Lara. Allow yourself the possibility of dreaming of a different future, will you? If not for yourself... then do it for Papa and me."

And in that moment, suspended between earth and sky, Lara understood that taking chances wasn't just about geographic relocations. They were about emotional migrations, about finding the courage to love beyond the predetermined borders of one's imagination.

As Lara heaved their suitcases off the luggage carousel, Zinia manoeuvred a trolley into place. As they worked in sync, loading the bags, Lara caught the faraway look in her mother's eyes.

"Everything okay, Mummy? Did we forget something?"

Zinia shook her head, but there was a hesitation to the movement. "No, no. I just had a thought..."

"What is it?" Lara asked, straightening up.

Her mother glanced around before lowering her voice. "Don't mention Luke or the airline application to Jude or Roxy."

Lara frowned. "Why not?" It wasn't like Zinia to be secretive, and what was there to hide? If anything, Uncle Jude might have useful advice.

Zinia hesitated before replying. "It's just that... Roxy is very religious, and I don't know for sure, but I think she wouldn't approve of your friendship with Luke."

Lara's confusion deepened. "Huh? What does Luke have to do with anything?"

Zinia leaned in slightly, as if sharing something conspiratorial. "She frowns upon people like that."

"Like what?"

Zinia's voice dropped to a whisper. "Gay."

Lara froze. A slow, simmering anger rose in her chest, coming from some deep and unexpected place. How dare anyone, especially someone who had never even met Luke, judge him? As if his existence, his identity, was something to be frowned upon. Being gay wasn't a phase or a flaw, it simply was.

Zinia noticed the shift in her daughter's expression and sighed. "Don't look so furious, darling. I'm just trying to spare you the agony of a sermon." Her voice had returned to its normal volume, breezy yet cautious.

Lara exhaled, shaking her head. "And the airline job?"

Zinia pursed her lips. "You know about Roxy's thwarted dreams. She wanted to carry on being an air hostess after marriage, but the airlines did not allow it at that time. Now, so much has changed. No age limit or marriage issues. She resents the fact that she had to give up that life. I don't think she'll wish you well on this. In fact, she might even try to talk you out of it."

Lara arched an eyebrow. "I haven't even been talked into it yet."

"Still," Zinia pressed, "let's keep it under our hats for now."

Lara sighed. "I was hoping to get Uncle Jude's take. He's got so much experience..."

Zinia gave her a knowing look. "Anything you tell Jude will find its way to Roxy. Best not to say anything at all. For now."

As they weaved their way through the crowd, Lara spotted a

familiar face in the distance. Jude stood waving enthusiastically, then broke into a jog toward them. The moment he reached them, he scooped Zinia off her feet in a bear hug, just as he always did, no matter how much time had passed.

Then he turned to Lara, grinning. "You're much too tall for me to do that now, Lara-lu."

Lara smirked. "And you don't want to do your back in, Uncle Jude."

Jude chuckled as she pulled him into a side hug. His warmth was still there, but something inside Lara had changed. She still loved her uncle, but the pedestal she had once placed him on was long gone. She saw him now, not as the infallible man of her childhood, but as someone deeply human—flawed, proud, deferential to his wife in ways that sometimes grated. Maybe this was what adulthood was: seeing the people you loved for who they truly were and choosing to love them, anyway. And maybe that was what Mummy had meant about loving Luke.

Jude ushered them into his spacious car, hoisting their bags into the boot with ease.

"Roxy's really looking forward to Goa this time," he said as he navigated his way out of the airport. "Last time, it was all sadness. This time, she wants to spend more time at the beach and visit a few of the far-flung churches, too."

Zinia and Lara exchanged a glance. They knew exactly what he meant by last time. Grandpa's funeral. A trip drenched in grief, in a quiet mourning, in the strange, numbing stillness of loss. And now Roxanna wanted to turn the forthcoming trip into a holiday?

Lara shifted in her seat. "Is Alex coming with us?"

She kept her tone neutral. Her relationship with her cousin had never quite recovered after the book fiasco, but she had never stopped trying.

Alex, on the other hand, had stopped everything. Stopped showing up for family events. Stopped writing. Stopped calling. Over time, he had become a ghost who lived just beyond reach. Lara knew the bare minimum—he lived close to his parents' home in Juhu, worked at a multinational company—but beyond that? Nothing. Was he happy? Was he in love? Did he ever visit his parents? There was never any news, no little anecdotes shared over tea. Roxanna kept a tight lid on her son's life, and Jude, for all his warmth, simply skimmed over the topic, as if discussing Alex too much might make him disappear entirely.

Jude nodded, swerving slightly to avoid a pothole. "Alex will meet us in Goa. He's traveling around Kerala right now with a friend."

Zinia tilted her head, inviting him to continue. "A friend?"

"Someone visiting from London. They went to school together. Best mates ever since."

So that was that. A fleeting appearance at the tail end of the trip, another excuse to keep his distance. Lara could already picture it— Alex breezing in for a day or two, always just out of reach, a familiar stranger passing through. She turned her head to the window, watching as the city unfolded outside—rickety stalls, a row of road-side eateries, swanky shops, a tide of people moving through the humid afternoon. Mumbai had its own special smell, just like Delhi did. Here, the air carried the scent of Bombay duck and saltwater. She smiled faintly, remembering the moment she had discovered that Bombay duck was, in fact, a fish.

Maybe people were like that too. Lara imagined them as ducks, and they turned out to be fish.

———

Roxanna took her time answering the door, and when she finally did, she looked dishevelled, her hair mussed, her eyes heavy with sleep. She greeted them with a nod, but there was something muted about her, as if someone had turned the volume down on her emotions.

"You okay, Roxy? You're looking a bit pale," Zinia remarked, setting her bags down in the guest room.

Roxanna waved a hand dismissively. "Just getting over a stomach bug. Nothing to worry about." She handed them towels—the ones they would be using for the duration of their stay—before asking, "Tea, or something stronger?"

"Tea." Lara and Zinia spoke in unison.

"Come to the living room once you've freshened up," Roxanna said, already turning away.

As soon as she left, Zinia frowned. "She seems a bit off. Did you think so too?"

Lara murmured in agreement as she unzipped her valise. Aunty Roxanna had always been an enigma to her. She was never overtly affectionate, never the kind of woman who wrapped you in hugs or showered you with endearments. Yet, paradoxically, she had always bought Lara the most thoughtful gifts—presents so perfectly suited to her tastes that it felt almost eerie. The prettiest frocks when she was a child, the latest Barbie doll at just the right time. Later, stylish skirts and expensive makeup. Sometimes, Lara wondered, had Roxanna secretly longed for a daughter?

After giving up flying, Roxanna had immersed herself in religion, becoming a devoted churchgoer. It was as if she had needed something to anchor herself, to fill a void. She volunteered tirelessly at the local orphanage, did countless charitable deeds within her congregation. But for all her good works, there was a distinct air of superiority about her. She carried herself as though the world was full of sinners, and she alone had found salvation.

Lara had never quite known what to make of her. There was a distance she instinctively maintained, an unspoken caution. Much as she had a degree of affection for her aunt, she felt no real attachment, no investment in the relationship. A part of her warned against getting too close. Some people, after all, were best loved from afar.

For Zinia, though, it was different. She had known Roxanna far longer and had seen the shift in her nature over the years. From the happy, carefree girl she had once been to the buttoned-up, rigid woman she had become. At first, it had baffled her. Now, she fluctuated between ignoring it completely or dissecting it endlessly. Lara had no intention of getting involved in whatever lay between her mother and her aunt. Some battles simply weren't worth getting in the middle of.

Outside, Uncle Jude uncorked a bottle of sparkling wine with a flourish.

"It's been years since you visited. That's worth celebrating, no?"

"Jude, I was making tea," Roxanna muttered, her tone edged with irritation.

"Oh, forget the tea! We have so much to celebrate—Alex's new job, the sale of Ma and Da's house..."

Roxanna set down a plate of onion *bhajis* with an audible thump. "For the love of God, Jude! I wish you wouldn't say anything until Alex has actually started."

Zinia spoke at the same time. "Aren't you counting your chickens before they've hatched? Ma hasn't agreed to anything yet."

Roxanna snorted. "He just needs an excuse to drink." With that, she turned away in a huff.

Jude ignored her, setting the bottle down and fetching glasses from the cabinet behind the dining table. "First of all, the job is practically in the bag. Second, Ma will agree. She has no choice. What would she rather—secure her future and stop worrying about that wastrel of a son, or live in constant fear of what idiotic or criminal thing he'll do next?"

From the kitchen, Roxanna's voice floated back, low and ominous. "Mothers never stop worrying about their sons, Jude."

Zinia took the glass he handed her. "Their children, Roxy. I worry too."

Roxanna emerged, holding a plate of *seekh kebabs*, her expression tight with barely concealed disdain. She took the glass Jude offered her, her fingers stiff around the stem. The toast felt forced.

"To a happy and prosperous future," Jude declared, then, as an afterthought, "and to having my favourite sister and niece in my house again."

"Your *only* sister and niece, you mean," Zinia quipped, cutting through the tension.

Later that night, as they lay in bed, Zinia whispered to Lara in the dark. "I'm telling you, something is wrong. Jude is drinking too much. Roxy is withdrawn. They barely speak of Alex. Did you notice how they didn't even elaborate on what job he's gotten?"

Lara had noticed. And there was something else—Jude's eagerness to push the sale of the property, almost as if he needed it. "Do you think they're having financial troubles?"

Zinia scoffed softly. "Financial troubles? Look at this apartment. Look at Alex—best schools, overseas education, a fancy new post. Jude has been flying for thirty years, Lara. Think of all that per diem he's saved. The conversion rate alone would have netted him a small fortune."

"Maybe you're right," Lara murmured. But the uneasy feeling in her gut remained. "We might find out on the drive to Goa," she added.

Or maybe they wouldn't. Either way, Lara wasn't about to lose sleep over it. Not tonight. The next few days would bring their own revelations, and whatever awaited them at the end of this trip, she would face it then.

Diving

They set out early Wednesday morning. Jude had insisted on 5 a.m., but by the time they packed the bags, loaded up the snacks, and Zinia dashed back inside for one last trip to the toilet, it was already 5:30.

Roxanna took the passenger seat beside Jude while Lara sat directly behind her. Zinia settled in next to Lara, humming softly as she adjusted her seatbelt. As the car rumbled to life, Lara's eyes drifted to the strands of grey peeking from beneath Roxanna's neatly pinned bun—missed spots from a rushed dye job. Then she glanced at Zinia, who had embraced the silver in her hair without hesitation. Would she do the same when the inevitable happened? Lara pushed the thought aside and tuned into the surrounding conversation.

"Does Pedru know we're coming?" Zinia asked, addressing the back of Jude's head.

"Maybe. I rang Ma yesterday to confirm our arrival," Jude replied, his voice still thick with sleep.

"I can take over some of the driving, Uncle Jude, if you need a break?" Lara offered.

Jude craned his neck to look at her. "What?"

Roxanna reached out, tapping his arm to keep his eyes on the road.

"No, no. I'm fine," he said, "NH17 is tricky—steep curves, blind turns. You're not used to these roads. Besides, I want you to enjoy the Western Ghats as we pass through. They are quite spectacular."

"And dangerous to drive through if you don't know how..." Roxanna muttered.

"Very well, then." Lara grinned. "I'll just sit back and enjoy the view."

The past two days had been filled with easy conversation once the initial awkwardness had departed. There were long hours of reminiscing and quiet moments of unease whenever Pedru's name came up. Stories of his reckless spending had resurfaced—the way he sold their parents' car without permission, shrugging off the betrayal because 'they weren't using it, anyway.'

"He's always been problematic, hasn't he, Zinia?" Jude had said over a beer the night before.

Zinia had shrugged. "You were closer in age. You probably saw it long before I did."

Jude nodded. "I did. He was always getting into trouble—disobeying teachers, skipping school. I was mischievous too, but Pedru... Pedru was different."

"Weren't Grandpa and Granny strict with him?" Lara had asked, popping a banana chip into her mouth.

"They tried. Nothing worked."

Zinia had sighed. "And then college happened. He fell in with the wrong crowd—staying out all night, smoking pot. I was only fourteen, but I remember Ma pacing the floor, waiting for him to come home."

Then Roxanna had spoken. Her voice had been steady, but her expression had darkened. "I never liked him."

Zinia frowned. "Why?"

A flicker of something unreadable passed between Jude and Roxanna. Then, almost imperceptibly, he gave her a nod. "He had this way of looking at me... as if... as if..." she hesitated, exhaling sharply. "...as if he was undressing me."

Zinia's gasp had been audible.

Now, as they exited Mumbai—grateful to have beaten the worst of the traffic—Lara replayed the moment in her mind. It was difficult, unsettling even, to imagine one's elders as young, vulnerable, and entangled in the complexities of desire and danger; to see them as the sexual beings they might have been once. Roxanna was always so buttoned-up, so rigid... yet she must have been stunning in her youth. To have been leered at by her own brother-in-law—it was pretty disgusting.

Lara turned to the window, watching the landscape shift from concrete sprawl to open road. The Western Ghats loomed in the distance, their misty peaks barely visible in the early light. The car hummed steadily beneath her, the winding road pulling her thoughts elsewhere—until Roxanna's voice cut through them.

"So, Lara," Roxanna asked, her tone light but probing. "Any beaux on the scene?"

"Bo?" Lara blinked, momentarily lost.

"She means suitors," Zinia supplied.

Lara laughed. "No, Aunty Roxanna. No one at the moment."

Roxanna raised a perfectly arched brow. "An attractive young woman like you, and you're not dating?"

Lara caught Roxanna's eye in the wing mirror and smiled. "It's not for lack of wanting. More like... a lack of choices."

Roxanna nodded sagely. "Delhi boys are quite... uncouth."

"Not all of them, Roxy!" Zinia interjected.

Roxanna sniffed. "Most of them, anyway." Then, as if struck by an idea, she added, "I could find someone here. Plenty of eligible young men at the church."

"Really, it's okay." Lara's voice was firm but amused. "I'm sure it will happen when it has to—*if* it has to."

Roxanna turned in her seat. "If?" She looked genuinely startled. "You don't want to be an old maid, do you? Thirty isn't exactly young. We'd already had our babies by then." She glanced at Zinia, who shrugged and gave Lara's hand a quick squeeze.

Before Lara could respond, Zinia smoothly redirected the conversation. "What about Alex then?" she asked. "Any girlfriends on the scene?"

Roxanna sighed dramatically. "Too many to name. It's a revolving door with him. I just want him to find a nice girl to settle down with, but does he listen to me?"

"Leave the boy alone, Roxy!" Jude chuckled from the driver's seat. "Not like he's racing against a biological clock. He could have babies well into his seventies if he wanted."

Lara felt her stomach tighten. Is that what it came down to? The ability to produce children, to be a broodmare? Where was the longing for love, the pursuit of companionship, the need for fulfilment? Was this divide between men and women, this quiet, insidious misogyny, so deeply woven into their collective consciousness that no one even noticed it? She turned back to the window, exhaling slowly as the mountains rose before them.

At the seven-hour mark, they pulled into a sleepy little town called Chiplun. The afternoon sun hung low, casting long shadows on the asphalt. As they stepped out of the car, Lara stretched, rolling the stiffness from her shoulders, while Jude leaned against the hood, lighting a cigarette with a practiced flick. The acrid scent curled into the air, mingling with the rich, earthy aroma of impending rain.

Zinia and Roxanna walked toward a small roadside eatery, their heads bent in quiet conversation. Lara hesitated, torn between lingering outside and following them in. Just as she took a step forward, a truck roared past, momentarily drowning out all sound. When the din subsided, she caught a fragment of their conversation. Something in their tone—urgent, almost desperate—made her pause. She moved closer.

"You don't know the half of it, Zinia!" Roxanna's voice trembled, frustration laced through every syllable. "Alex is drowning. And Jude? He's turned a blind eye, as usual!"

Zinia's frown deepened. "What do you mean? What's going on?"

A bitter laugh escaped Roxanna. "Loans, Zinia. Lakhs of rupees. What started as a trickle has become a flood."

Lara's stomach clenched.

Zinia inhaled sharply. "Loans? What loans?"

Roxanna let out a slow, measured breath. "Alex has always moved in wealthy circles. We wanted to give him the best, but somewhere along the way, he started believing he deserved the best. His friends flashed their designer watches, their luxury cars, their extravagant vacations. And he—he wanted the same. So, he borrowed. First from banks, then from private lenders. Now, he's in so deep, he can't claw his way out."

Zinia exhaled, shaking her head. "Oh, I see. So that's why the sale of Ma's house is so urgent."

Roxanna shivered. "I shouldn't be telling you this, but I need you to understand. I need you to talk to Jude. He has to see what's happening before it's too late."

Zinia's voice sharpened. "Talk to Jude? What about Alex? He's a grown man, Roxanna. He's made these choices!"

Roxanna bristled. "It's not his fault entirely! His so-called friends flaunt their privilege in his face, making him feel like he has to keep up. And Jude—Jude encourages it! He likes that Alex rubs shoulders with the elite, that he fits into that world. And when I ask Alex to help at the orphanage, to ground himself, Jude laughs it off. Calls me dramatic."

The boy behind the counter slid their food across, breaking the moment. Lara backed away swiftly, heart pounding.

Outside, Jude was standing at a distance from the car, looking out into the horizon. He seemed lost in his thoughts and as Lara approached, he took a final drag of his cigarette before tossing the butt to the ground, crushing it beneath his shoe. He exhaled, looking out at the mist-cloaked hills. "Beautiful, isn't it? I've seen the world, but sometimes I forget how much beauty exists in my own country."

Lara followed his gaze. The hills rose in quiet majesty, shrouded in mist, as if holding secrets they would never speak aloud. There was a stillness to them, a kind of knowing. Something stirred inside of her. A longing not just for this place, but for something unnamed. Someday, she thought, she would return. Maybe alone. Maybe with someone who truly understood her.

"Uncle Jude?"

"Hmm?"

"When is Alex joining us?"

Jude shrugged, a lazy smile playing on his lips. "Oh, I don't know... in a few days, I suppose. He's footloose and fancy-free. Living his best life, just as a boy his age should. What I would have been had I not married so young."

Lara stiffened. A boy his age? Alex was nearly thirty. Yet Jude spoke of him like he was a reckless teenager, not a man drowning in debt. And suddenly, it was clear. The problem wasn't just Alex, it was the world that had shaped him. An indulgent father, an enabling mother, an upbringing where privilege was borrowed but never truly owned. Lara stared at the horizon, trying to piece together the image of the cousin she once knew. But too many pieces were missing. And she wasn't sure she wanted to find them all.

As they made their way back to the car, Lara lingered for a moment, her gaze drifting over the rolling hills and the golden light spilling through the trees. Then, almost instinctively, she bent down, plucked the discarded cigarette butt from the ground, and slipped it into her pocket. She would get rid of it properly later. She abhorred carelessness, and had expected better from Jude. With so much beauty around them—the majestic mountains, the emerald valleys, the tranquil hush of the land—it felt almost sacrilegious to let even the tiniest trace of negligence taint it.

They arrived at the house just as the evening light was softening into twilight. As Jude pulled into the driveway, Lara glanced over to see Zinia gnawing at her lower lip, her brow furrowed in quiet contemplation. She had barely spoken all afternoon. Jude had chalked it up to fatigue, but Lara knew better. The weight of the conversation Zinia had been privy to—however unwillingly—still lingered. Was she grappling with the uneasy feeling of being entangled in something murky and unethical? Lara wished she could reassure her mother, but to do so, she would have to reveal her own eavesdropping.

The sprawling bungalow stood just as it always had, timeworn yet familiar. The paint peeled in uneven patches, and the fixtures belonged to an era long past, but to Lara, the house exuded a quiet resilience. She could still hear the echoes of laughter from childhood summers spent here, the warmth of those carefree days carved into its very walls.

The door swung open, revealing her grandmother's delighted smile. She was more stooped now, her frame smaller, her hair a cloud of white, yet something within her remained remarkably untouched by age—a quiet spark, a lightness that defied the years.

"Oh, look at you, Lara! So tall!"

Lara bent to receive her grandmother's kiss, amused by the predictability of the remark. Hadn't she been this height since she was fifteen? And yet, every visit, her grandmother reacted as though she had miraculously grown overnight.

Jude hauled their bags inside while the young houseboy hurried to bring them water.

"Where's Pedru?" Zinia asked, fanning herself with the end of her saree.

"Who knows?" Granny replied, the airiness of her tone failing to mask the sadness beneath.

"He does know we were coming, right?"

"Oh yes, I told him."

As the conversation swirled around her, Lara drifted towards the walls lined with black-and-white photographs—portraits of ancestors who had lived and died long before she had taken her first breath. This was her bloodline, her history, stretching back to heaven knew how many years. She had spent hours as a child staring at these faces, wondering about the lives they had led. Had they known great love? Had they endured heartbreak, weathered loss, and fought battles of their own? She had always meant to ask Grandpa about them, to unravel the stories behind those solemn eyes. But the questions had remained unspoken, swallowed by time. And now, she would never know.

As dinner was served, Lara scooped a generous portion of her grandmother's prawn balchão onto her plate, the fiery aroma hitting her senses with a wave of nostalgia. No shop-bought version had ever come close to this—the depth of flavour, the perfect balance of spice and tang. Each bite was a reminder of childhood meals at this very table, of sticky fingers and second helpings. She ate in silence, listening as her uncle and aunt carefully laid out their plan in front of Granny, their voices measured but insistent.

"So, we had this property dealer find a very nice apartment for you," Jude began, watching Granny closely. "It's in a safe area, with a community of like-minded people, and it's not far from the beach, either. Just like here."

Granny nodded slowly but said nothing. Lara noticed the glance Jude and Roxanna exchanged before they turned to Zinia, wordlessly urging her to step in.

"Say something, Zin..." Jude pressed, his tone edged with impatience.

Zinia hesitated, her fingers tightening around her spoon before she set it down. "I...I have a bit of a headache," she murmured. "I think I'll turn in early." Without another word, she pushed back her chair and left the room.

Granny watched her go, her weathered face creasing in thought. "When did Zinia get so old?" she murmured.

"Ma! That's your youngest you're talking about," Jude protested, but his voice lacked conviction.

Granny sighed, shaking her head. "Time flies, doesn't it? What will happen to Pedru if I move?"

"He'll get his share from the sale," Jude said smoothly. "He can buy something for himself with that."

Granny placed her fork down, her fingers tracing the rim of her plate.

"Ma," Jude pressed, his voice softening. "Are you worried about Pedru?"

She hesitated, then nodded. "He'll be furious when he finds out."

Jude let out a sharp breath. "He has no more claim over this house, Ma, than us. This, what we're suggesting, is the fairest solution. We split the money four ways, buy you that apartment, and whatever's left will be your stipend. You'll be comfortable and safe. Isn't that what matters?"

Granny's eyes clouded. "Your father wanted me to stay put here..."

"And let Pedru bleed you dry?" Roxanna's voice was low, simmering with anger. "This isn't safe for you, Ma. You know what he's like. Who knows what he's capable of?"

The air in the room suddenly felt heavy with unspoken fears. Then Granny turned, her gaze landing on Lara. "What do you think?"

Lara froze, her pulse quickening as three pairs of expectant eyes pinned her in place. She swallowed and cleared her throat. "I think... you should do whatever your gut is telling you to do."

Silence followed her remark. Jude and Roxanna's displeasure was palpable, but Lara held her ground, lowering her gaze to her plate and pretending not to notice the daggers they were glaring her way.

Maybe Jude and Roxanna felt that Zinia and Lara had betrayed their trust, but after what Zinia knew and what Lara had overheard, how could they, in good conscience, urge Granny to sell the house and leave behind everything she had ever known? And yet, the key player in this tangled drama, Pedru, remained absent in the first few days of their visit. His looming presence was like an unsprung trap, but in his absence, something unexpected happened.

At first, Jude and Roxanna withdrew, stiff with resentment over Zinia and Lara's reluctance to push for the property sale. Conversations were clipped, meals eaten in tense silence. But slowly, inevitably, Goa worked its quiet magic on them.

It began with tentative steps—all of them taking separate, solitary walks on the beach, pretending not to notice each other. Then, one afternoon, Jude cracked open a few beer bottles, the sharp hiss breaking the quiet. Later, he unearthed an old gramophone, its scratchy tunes filling the evening air. Soon, they were jiving to Neil Diamond and Frank Sinatra, their laughter mingling with the music as Granny sat beaming, tapping her feet to the rhythm. Little by little, anger melted into nostalgia. Conversations turned from repressed arguments to wistful reminiscence—tales of a Goa that once was, before the tourists came, before the beaches were overrun by hippies. They spoke of family get-togethers, of childhood pranks, of Christmases spent attending midnight mass, the joy of walking home under starry skies, their hands cold but their hearts warm with anticipation for the day ahead.

Lara listened, laughed, and watched, seeing each of them shed the weight of their city lives, slipping into versions of themselves she had never seen before.

Jude, so often the jovial showman, became boyish again, seeking his mother's approval, coaxing her to dance with him. Roxanna, usually rigid with control, let her hair fall loose over her shoulders and kicked off her sandals, walking barefoot everywhere, revealing a glimpse of the girl she once was.

But it was Zinia in whom Lara saw the most striking transformation. One evening, as they all sat outside, the air redolent with the scent of salt and earth, Zinia knelt at her mother's feet and rested her head in her lap. Granny's wrinkled fingers combed gently through her daughter's hair, their bond silent yet unbreakable. There was something achingly tender about the moment, something so pure it felt almost sacred. Lara swallowed against the lump in her throat. She had always known that love could transcend time and age, but seeing it now, so raw, so exposed, twisted something deep inside her. A realisation settled in her bones. Granny would not live forever. And perhaps Zinia had understood this truth long before she had.

Yet, beneath the laughter, the music, and the easy camaraderie, an unspoken question simmered—would Granny give in to Jude and Roxanna's wishes, or would she hold on to her marital home?

One evening, as they lounged in their usual spots—Jude nursing a drink, Roxanna flipping through a magazine, Zinia absentmindedly stroking the armrest of her chair—Granny broke the silence. "I've been thinking."

The room snapped to attention. All eyes turned to her, their breath collectively held, waiting for the verdict. She sat upright, hands folded in her lap, her voice calm but resolute. "I am getting old, and this house is getting too much to handle. Perhaps your father had hoped to pass it on to the next generation, but let's be honest, neither Alex nor Lara is going to settle here. What would they do in a place like this? There are no jobs, no prospects. I would rather see them benefit from it in my lifetime. If that means selling, so be it."

Jude shot up, punching the air in triumph. "Ma! You are amazing!"

But Granny wasn't finished. She raised a steady hand, silencing him. "There is one thing, though. I want a portion of what you and Zinia receive to be put in a trust for Alex and Lara. They are my grandchildren, and I want them to have something from me."

Jude opened his mouth to protest, but before he could speak, Zinia cut in. "Ma, you don't have to give us anything right now. Keep it. Think on it a little longer."

Granny shook her head, her gaze firm. "I have thought on it. Roxanna is right. Pedru is dangerous and unpredictable. If I don't act now, while I still have the strength, there may be nothing left to dispose of. If everyone agrees to my conditions, we will proceed with the sale."

Nonplussed, they looked at each other, too focussed on her words to notice anything else.

"Over my dead body."

The voice, low and laced with menace, sent a jolt through them all.

They turned, and there, looming in the doorway, was Pedru.

His enormous frame swayed slightly, his face slick with sweat, his clothes crumpled. The overpowering stench of alcohol and body odour clung to him. His bloodshot eyes swept over the room before landing on Lara.

A shiver ran down her spine. His gaze lingered too long, sliding over her with a slow, deliberate lecherousness that made her skin crawl. It had been years since she'd seen her uncle, but time had only sharpened the menace in him. He was the kind of man who mistook fear for respect. And Lara knew, with bone-deep certainty, that Pedru would cross any line to get what he wanted.

Granny's steady voice calmed Pedru, guiding him to his room. A single shake of her head kept the others silent. When she returned, she sighed, rubbing her temples. "He won't remember a thing tomorrow. Once he's sober, we'll talk."

Zinia hesitated. "And if he won't listen?"

"He bloody well better," Jude snapped.

"Jude." Roxanna's firm voice cut through his anger.

Granny traced patterns on her chair's armrest. "Pedru has to believe he's winning. If you push, he'll lash out. Be smart."

Lara followed Granny to her room while the others strategised. Perched on the bed, she asked softly, "Are you really okay with this?"

Granny's eyes were tired. "Not happy. Just resigned. I've seen families destroy themselves over land. I love this house, but it's just bricks and mortar. You matter more."

"And Grandpa's wishes?"

A wistful smile on her face, she said, "Your grandpa was wonderful but impractical. If he couldn't maintain this place, how will I? Better to settle this now, so I can go in peace."

By noon, Pedru finally emerged, rubbing his eyes. "Oh, hello," he greeted Zinia, moving in for a hug. She recoiled. "For God's sake, Pedru, take a shower. You stink."

He only laughed, pulling her close anyway, then spotted Lara. "Little Lara—all grown up."

Lara stepped behind Granny, her smile cool, distant.

"Someone's shy," he smirked. His gaze flicked to Jude and Roxanna. "The whole cavalry's here. What's this about?"

"I told you," Granny said. "They're visiting. Now shower. The houseboy will heat lunch."

Pedru lingered before shuffling off. As soon as he was gone, tension thickened. Granny placed a finger to her lips—a warning. Then, seamlessly, she turned to Lara. "My girl, bring me my footstool."

As Lara obeyed, Granny launched into an old family tale, her voice deliberate. A silent understanding passed through the room— Pedru was listening. And Pedru was dangerous.

Later, over cigarettes, Jude kept his tone light. "So, Pedru, we were talking about finding Ma a smaller place. Somewhere more comfortable."

Pedru exhaled smoke, eyes closed. "Hmmm."

"This house—it's too big, too expensive to maintain," Jude pressed. "Now that Ma doesn't have Pa's pension..."

Pedru's eyes snapped open, sharp and unreadable. "I'm here. I can manage it."

Jude pushed on. "The best thing is to sell. Split the money four ways."

Pedru flicked ash onto the floor, his smile slow, deliberate. "I'll burn this house, and every last one of you in it, before I let you sell."

Zinia gasped. "Pedru, what are you saying?"

His gaze swung to her, cold and taunting. "Lost your nerve now, little sister? He leaned forward, voice dripping venom. "I'll tell you what stinks—this whole situation stinks. You scheming to re-home my mother stinks. And you have the gall to tell me I stink?!" He let out a short, bitter laugh. "I promise you, none of you will get away with this. Not while I'm still breathing."

Lara shot to her feet, the air suddenly toxic. She needed to escape. To breathe. She fled outside, the cool evening air barely easing the knot in her chest.

Behind her, Pedru's mocking laughter followed. "There she goes. The first rat deserting the sinking ship."

She let the sea breeze tangle her hair, willing it to blow away the ugliness of what had just transpired. Granny had warned them this wouldn't be easy, but Lara hadn't anticipated the toxicity of it all. The menace in Pedru's words and the threat of violence that had sent a chill deep into her bones. Was this battle truly worth fighting? The thought gnawed at her until she pictured Granny, enduring his dark moods, his drunken rampages, his cruelty, day after day. If selling the house meant giving her a life of peace and safety, then yes, it was worth it.

She could only hope that Jude, Roxanna, and Zinia had come up with a solid game plan last night. But Lara wanted no part of it. She had come for Zinia, to offer support, but something about Pedru unsettled her to her core. The way he looked at her—like she was a piece of meat—made her skin crawl. Running had been instinctive, survival kicking in before reason. Maybe it was cowardly, but she didn't care.

She longed for her father. If he were here, she'd bury herself in his arms and forget that people like Pedru existed. And then her mind drifted to Luke. To his kindness, the quiet strength he carried, the deep respect he had for women. Even after things had ended with Sue, he had remained her friend. Yes, there were good men in the world. One vile man did not erase that truth. Someday, she would laugh about this with Luke, talk to him and try to understand what made people like Pedru the way they were. How they had no self-reflection, no shame and no honour.

Exhaling, she walked on, sinking her feet into the cool, damp sand, letting the rhythm of the waves soothe her. Around her, families and couples laughed, their voices mingling with the sounds of the ocean. This—this was the world she wanted to live in. A world of love, peace, and harmony. And as she let its warmth settle into her, she felt her soul beginning to mend.

She sat on the sand and traced a sad face with her finger, then, on impulse, drew a smiling one beside it.

"That's cute," a husky voice remarked with a laugh. Lara looked up to see a curly-haired woman around her age studying her sketches.

"Which one are you?" the woman asked, tilting her head.

Lara shrugged. "Both, I guess."

The woman grinned. "Makes sense. We carry happiness and sadness together in us, don't we?"

Before Lara could respond, a man approached, holding two bottles of beer.

"There you are! Took you long enough," the woman teased.

The man grinned. "They didn't have your Ultra, *jaan*. Had to go hunting for it."

She giggled. "There was a time when men hunted wild animals. Now, they hunt alcohol."

Lara laughed, the heaviness of the afternoon lifting slightly.

"Hey, I'm Mira, and this is Shyam. Fancy joining us for a drink?"

Lara hesitated for only a moment before nodding. *Why not?* She followed them to a beach shack, where conversation flowed easily, full of laughter, playful banter, and surface-level confessions. They shared anecdotes, exchanged advice, yet steered clear of anything too deep.

"How long have you two been married?" Lara asked, sipping her beer.

"Just a month," Shyam said, his gaze softening as he looked at Mira. He was clearly besotted.

"And where did you meet?"

Mira hesitated, two red spots appearing on her cheeks. "Uhh… we used to be neighbours."

There was more to that story, but Lara didn't probe.

"What about you, Lara? Married? Boyfriend? Are you from Goa?"

"No, no, and no," Lara said, laughing. "My mother grew up here, but I'm from Delhi. That's home."

"No way!" Mira exclaimed. "Shyam's from Delhi too! I grew up in Mumbai, but I studied in Delhi. Used to teach at JNU."

They compared notes, marvelling at the small-world serendipity of meeting someone from home in an unfamiliar place.

As she sat across from the couple, their laughter easy, their glances full of quiet knowing, something stirred in her again—that old, stubborn ache. When would it be her turn to be seen like that; to be chosen? When would love stop passing her by and finally find its way to her door?

By the time dusk settled in, numbers had been exchanged with well-meaning promises to stay in touch—promises they knew they likely wouldn't keep. At 7 p.m., Lara checked her watch and gasped. "Oh no! My family's probably about to send out a search party. I've got to go!"

They hugged before parting, and as Lara made her way back, the lightness of the past few hours began to recede. She wondered what chaos awaited her at home.

It was eerily quiet as Lara let herself in. The lights were on, casting long shadows against the walls, but the house felt... subdued. As if the storm had passed, leaving an unsettling stillness in its wake.

"Hello?" she called out. "Anybody home?"

A moment later, Alex emerged from the dining room, a coconut in his hands. He stopped short when he saw her. "Lara?" His brow furrowed. "Where have you been? Everyone was worried sick."

She blinked at him. This was the same Alex she hadn't seen in ten years—the one who had stolen her book as a young man and returned it in the same week, the one who was elbow-deep in debt yet somehow did not look the part. His artfully tousled hair, the deliberately faded designer T-shirt, the perfectly frayed jeans... He'd carefully managed every aspect of his appearance. A man skilled in the art of appearing effortless.

Behind him, another man stepped forward. He had a cleft chin, hair a little longer than conventionally acceptable, and a calm confidence that made him instantly likeable. "Hi! I'm Atul, Alex's friend," he said, flashing a grin.

Something electric passed between them, something that made Lara blush and look away. She stammered out a greeting before drifting toward the dining room. The table was set for eight, the rich aromas of home-cooked food filling the air. No sign of Pedru. But Jude—Jude had a black eye. Zinia was humming softly as she carried dishes from the kitchen, unbothered, as if this were just another ordinary evening.

"What... what happened?" Lara looked around, confusion lacing her voice.

"Oh, it's all been sorted, dear," Roxanna said briskly, appearing with a tray in hand, her hair wound into a tight, no-nonsense bun. "A few fisticuffs, but Pedru saw reason soon enough. The boys helped." She threw a beaming smile in Alex and Atul's direction, as if thanking them for hauling out an old sofa rather than dealing with an unpredictable menace.

Lara dropped into the chair beside her grandmother, taking in the deep fatigue etched onto the older woman's face. "And where's Uncle Pedru?" she asked.

Jude scoffed from his corner, pressing an ice pack to his eye. "Probably on a bender, celebrating the good fortune of coming into so much money at his ripe old age."

Zinia came up behind Lara, resting a warm hand on her head. "Are you okay, darling?"

Lara exhaled, shaking her head slightly. "Never better," she muttered, scanning the surreal scene before her, half-convinced she had stumbled into an episode of 'The Twilight Zone'.

So, it was done. Violence, threats, and money had been tossed into the cauldron, and somehow, an agreement had been reached. Pedru was gone—whether in surrender or temporary retreat, she wasn't sure, but the storm had passed, at least for now. And while the others had been battling it out, she had been drinking beer with strangers, pretending, for a fleeting moment, that none of this was her problem. She repeated the words under her breath, this time tinged with quiet irony. *Never better*. Across the table, Atul caught her eye and winked. Lara felt warmth rise to her cheeks as she dropped her gaze.

A subtle tingling spread through her, a quiet hum in her veins. The fight for the house was over, but something else was beginning. She felt like she was standing on the edge of a precipice, every nerve ending urging her to jump. And maybe, just maybe, someone would catch her.

When she looked up again, Atul was still watching her, his gaze steady, his smile easy. Her heart thudded in response, an unspoken acknowledgment passing between them. Pedru was the past. The house, the battle, the viciousness, it was all behind them now. Whatever lay ahead, whatever awaited beyond that cliff's edge, Lara knew she was ready to take the leap.

It was time.

Luke (May 2005)

Front Crawl

Harry slid the plates into the oven to warm while Luke stirred the sauce on the hob, the rich aroma of garlic and rosemary thickening the air.

"Penny for your thoughts?" Harry asked, coming up behind Luke and pressing a kiss to his shoulder.

Luke chuckled, shaking his head. "Just thinking how life can change overnight."

Harry arched an eyebrow. "Overnight? For who? Us?"

"No, not us. Lara."

"Ahh." Harry grabbed the table mats, setting them out with a practiced ease. "Are you worried about her?"

"Not exactly. She's strong and she's capable. But lately, she's been distant. I can't quite put my finger on it."

"Well," Harry said, adjusting the candles on the table, "you can always ask her tonight."

Luke dipped a spoon into the sauce, blew on it, and held it up to Harry. "Taste this. Tell me what you think."

Harry took the spoon, rolling the flavours on his tongue before grinning. "Mmm, perfection. You really missed your calling."

"As what? A chef, slaving away in a hotel kitchen? No, thank you." Luke smirked. "I'll take my life as it is, happily and gratefully."

Harry fluffed the cushions on the sofa. "Speaking of gratitude, why is Lara still flying? You'd think she'd have quit by now, considering she married a man who probably owns a private jet."

Luke shook his head. "That's not Lara. She's never wanted to depend on anyone—always insisted on having her own money, her own life." He set the sauce aside and began preparing the chicken. "She didn't even agree to marry Atul until three years into their relationship."

Harry nodded. "Yeah, but wasn't he the reason she took the job in the first place?"

Luke scoffed. "I'd like to think *I* was the reason."

Harry gave him a playful look. "Don't flatter yourself, babe."

Luke feigned offence. "Hey, she did live with us during those first few months of probation—"

"Yes, the little sister you never had," Harry interrupted, then hesitated, lost in thought.

Luke frowned. "What?"

"I always wondered..." Harry tapped his fingers against the table. "If she felt differently about you than you did about her."

Luke blinked. "What? What do you mean?"

"I mean that she kind of viewed you romantically, not platonically."

Luke let out a short laugh. "Oh, come on. That's not true. And even if it were, it wouldn't have mattered." He turned to Harry, wrapping his arms around him. "Because I am truly, madly, deeply in love with you."

Harry smirked. "Tell me why."

Luke hummed, pretending to consider. "Well, where do I begin? You are devastatingly handsome, wildly talented, and best of all," he lowered his voice, "exceptional in bed."

Harry burst out laughing. "Idiot!"

Luke grinned, pressing a quick kiss to Harry's lips. "Only for you."

Luke turned back toward the kitchen, rolling up his sleeves. "Right, I need to get this meal prepped, or we'll be eating at midnight."

Harry sighed and sank onto the sofa, rubbing a hand over his face. "What do you make of him, anyway? Atul Joshi?"

Luke shrugged as he reached for a knife. "He's alright, I suppose."

"You don't like him."

"I don't dislike him."

Harry tilted his head. "Then what is it about him that sets your teeth on edge?"

Luke cast him a quick glance. "Why, is it that obvious?"

"Only to me," Harry said, sounding amused.

Luke set down the knife and turned to face him. "He's just... so entitled. I understand that he's from serious money, but it's the way he wears it. With all that arrogance." He exhaled. "Honestly, he's the last person I ever imagined Lara ending up with."

Harry shrugged. "Who knows what floats another person's boat? As far as the world's concerned, she's done spectacularly well. Never has to worry about money again. Not like us plebs."

Luke snorted. "Did I ever tell you about the customs fiasco last year?"

Harry raised an eyebrow. "No. What happened?"

"Well, I heard it secondhand and never actually confirmed it with Lara, but... you know how customs randomly stop us to search our bags after a trip?"

"Yeah."

"Well, they flagged Lara and refused to believe her Rolex was real. Thought she was smuggling in a fake from Canal Street in New York." Luke laughed at the memory.

"Oh God, what did she do?"

"She had to pull up her wedding photos—actual wedding photos

—to prove the watch was real and that her ultra-wealthy husband had bought it for her."

Harry laughed. "That's brilliant. Bet they felt like right idiots."

"Egg on their faces, for sure."

Still chuckling, Harry jumped up from the sofa. "Alright, enough gossip. You go freshen up, and I'll finish up here. They'll be here in twenty minutes, and we don't want you smelling like food, do we?"

Luke rolled his eyes but grinned as Harry planted a quick kiss on his cheek. With that, he wiped his hands on the kitchen towel and headed toward the bedroom, a small smile lingering on his lips.

The doorbell rang precisely at 7 p.m. Luke opened the door to find Atul and Lara standing on the threshold, a massive bouquet in her hands, an expensive bottle of Bordeaux in his.

"Welcome!" Luke grasped Atul's hand briefly before enveloping Lara in a hug, kissing both her cheeks.

She smelled incredible—something warm and impossibly expensive. As he ushered them inside, Luke took her in discreetly. She wore her wealth effortlessly. No ostentatious designer logos, just the quiet luxury of a perfectly tailored cream outfit, a silk Hermès scarf knotted at her throat, diamond earrings catching the light. And yet, when she turned to him with that familiar, open smile, he saw the Lara he had always known—sweet, uncomplicated, lovely.

"Quite a change from the uniform," he teased, his eyes gleaming with pleasure and pride.

"I know," she laughed, "And I'm not wearing *Eau de Boeing*, either."

"Charming little place you have here," Atul commented, glancing around their flat. "Took a bit of finding—GPS sent me in the wrong direction."

"Oh yeah, it's a recent development," Harry said as he took their coats. "It doesn't always show up on the maps yet." He gestured toward the drinks. "What are we having? Wine, cocktails, soft drinks?"

"Why don't we open the bottle we brought?" Atul suggested smoothly, holding up the Bordeaux. "It's a beautiful vintage. And I have more in the car if we run out."

Luke barely contained an eye roll. "Or," he countered, "we could start with a toast. I've got a *Veuve* chilling—your favourite, Lara."

Her face lit up. "I'd love that!"

Luke ignored the flicker of irritation in Atul's expression as he grabbed the champagne flutes.

As Harry poured, Atul said, "You must let Lara and me host next time. We'll take you to this Michelin place near our place in Mayfair. Just opened. Supposed to be extraordinary."

"Sounds great," Harry said easily, handing Atul a glass. "But tonight, you get to experience Luke's cooking. And I may be biased, but I promise you—it's Michelin-worthy too."

Luke grinned, then suddenly remembered something. "Hang on. Before I forget..."

He disappeared into the next room, returning with a small, wrapped package, which he handed to Lara. "Happy Birthday, Lara, belated though it might be!"

"Let me guess," she said, laughing as she unwrapped it. "'Never Let Me Go' by Kazuo Ishiguro." She turned the book over, reading the blurb. "This looks so interesting."

"Only the best for you, my Lara." Luke grinned.

Atul's smile tightened. "Is there some kind of message in that title?"

Luke met his gaze with practiced nonchalance. "Message? No. It's a tradition of ours—picking books to push each other out of our reading comfort zones. Lara got me 'Cloud Atlas' last year, which, by the way, I really enjoyed."

Atul stifled a yawn. "I don't read books. Waste of time."

Lara turned to him, eyes flashing. "Not true, Atul. I'll tell you what is a waste of time—all those ridiculous video games you play into the night."

Atul shrugged, unbothered. "Each to their own."

Harry, sensing the mood, quickly passed around the snacks while Luke stepped into the kitchen to check on the chicken.

"So," Atul asked, turning to Harry, "what is it you do?"

"I teach at a local primary school. That's why we moved here."

Atul gave a polite but disinterested nod. "A teacher and a flight attendant. That's an interesting setup. How do you make it work?"

Harry's expression remained pleasant, but there was an unmistakable steel beneath it. "Like any other relationship, I suppose. Built on love and trust."

"But you're not from here, are you?"

"No, I'm from Wales, as you can probably tell from my accent." Harry smiled.

Lara jumped in, eager to lighten the mood. "Oh, tell Atul how you met Luke."

Harry exchanged a look with Luke, then smiled. "We met at the local pool we both used to frequent. I'd watch this dark-haired Adonis slicing through the water and I'd wonder—is he single?" He winked at Luke playfully. "Then one day, I was busy minding my business, putting my shoes on, and he came right up to me and asked me out."

"And the rest," Lara chimed in, "is history."

She turned to Luke, eyes twinkling. "If I know you at all, it must have taken you weeks to work up the courage. You're a real 'fraidy cat with that kind of thing. So something about *you*, Harry, had to be special."

Luke smirked and tossed a piece of cucumber at her head playfully, which missed and landed by their cat, Shakespeare. The feline sniffed it, unimpressed.

"Remember Arthur Conan Doyle, Luke?" Lara picked up the cucumber and lobbed it back at him.

Laughter filled the space, the conversation flowing effortlessly from childhood memories to work stories. Luke watched Lara in the middle of it all. She seemed happy. And even if he would never quite like Atul, that didn't matter. What mattered was that she was happy. That, he supposed, was all he had ever wanted for her.

In the kitchen, Lara leaned against the counter, cradling her wine glass as Luke plated the food. She took a slow sip before asking, "How's Christine doing?"

"She's great. Frank has been wonderful to her, and even though she won't let him move in, it's nice that he's just a doorstep away."

"I'm so glad she found love again."

Luke paused, mid-scoop, his expression thoughtful. "I don't know if it's love, exactly. But it's companionship. And I'm happy for her."

Lara nodded. "Companionship is underrated."

A beat of silence stretched between them before Luke cleared his throat. "And your folks? How are they?"

"They're doing okay. Honestly, the money from the Goa house sale helped more than I ever thought it would. Mummy's finally ready to retire, and Papa—well, he can't wait to have her home. Even if they fight like cat and dog."

Luke smirked, shaking his head. "Your parents. To anyone else, they'd seem like the most mismatched couple on the planet, but somehow, they make it work. They really do love each other."

Lara's smile softened, her eyes misting slightly. "As do the two of you. Harry is perfect for you, Luke. After all those non-starter boyfriends."

"Beginning with Andy..."

Lara made a face, rolling her eyes. "Ugh. What ever happened to him?"

"Last I heard, he was shacked up with some guy from corporate headquarters."

"Climbing the greasy pole, is he?"

Luke let out a short laugh, though something flickered across his face—the memory of an old, faintly aching wound. "Something like that."

Back at the table, Atul took another bite and let out a satisfied sigh. "This is fantastic, Luke. Lara's always raved about your cooking, and I have to say she wasn't exaggerating."

Luke smiled, reaching for the wine bottle. "More?"

"Yes, why not?"

Lara shot Atul a look. "You're not driving if you drink that."

"We'll take a taxi," Atul dismissed, swirling the wine in his glass. "Our Audi will be fine here in visitor's parking, won't it?"

Harry, clearing plates, gave a good-natured shrug. "Yeah, it's safe here. This is a sleepy little village, not central London."

Atul scoffed, setting his fork down. "You two are wasting your lives out here. You're young and you should be in London, where things are happening." His eyes flickered between them, assessing. "I could find you an apartment. A prime spot. You'd love it."

Luke and Harry exchanged a glance, but before they could respond, Lara cut in smoothly.

"Atul, they're not clients for your next real estate venture," she said lightly, though there was an unmistakable firmness in her tone. "Besides, Harry's work is here, and Luke needs to be close to the airport. And," she turned to Luke with a knowing smile, "someone enjoys having his mum nearby."

Atul groaned. "Mothers. I wish mine didn't live so close. She never stops interfering."

Lara's jaw tightened just slightly. "It's only because she cares."

Atul let out a short, humourless laugh. "You're sweet, honey, especially after the colossal bitch she's been to you."

Luke stiffened. A fleeting shadow crossed Lara's face before she masked it with a small smile. Without a word, Luke pushed back his chair and went to help Harry in the kitchen.

"Should I say something?" he murmured under his breath.

"Why?" Harry kept his voice even, stacking plates by the sink. "Lara seems to have it under control."

"It's just... he gets combative when he drinks."

Harry arched a brow. "He's drunk?"

Luke sighed. "Not yet."

But he knew the night wasn't over yet.

At ten past midnight, they finally called it a night. Harry rang for a taxi, repeating the exorbitant fare he'd just been quoted, his eyebrows raised in question. Atul just shrugged, as if money was an afterthought.

Lara took her jacket from Luke, wrapping him in a tight hug. "This has truly been a lovely evening. Thank you."

"Well, it was long overdue. Ever since the wedding, pinning you down has been impossible."

She winced. "You know how it is..."

Atul strode over and pumped Luke's hand, his earlier animosity forgotten. "Hey, is it alright if Lara picks up the car sometime next week?" He slurred the last few words, but Luke pretended not to notice.

"No problem," Luke said, shooting Lara a glance. "But don't you need it before then?"

"Nah. I'll just use the Land Rover." Atul waved dismissively. "Besides, the TT is more Lara's car now, anyway."

Lara smiled, an unreadable expression on her face. "I'll text before dropping by, okay?" She hugged Harry, then stepped out into the cool night.

The door clicked shut behind them.

Harry exhaled, stretching his arms over his head. "Well. What did you make of that?"

Luke ran a hand through his hair, the events of the evening still lingering in his mind. "I don't know. He's not awful, exactly, just... something about him."

"I'll tell you what it is."

"Mmm?"

"He's used to getting his way all the time. That can come across as obnoxious." Harry grinned. "But Lara? She's no pushover. She's a challenge, that one. She doesn't fall at his feet or cater to his every demand. He likes that. That's why he fought so hard to marry her. He'd probably never met anyone like her before." Harry poured the last of the wine into two glasses and handed one to Luke.

Luke accepted it gratefully. "I just hope the charm of it doesn't wear off."

"Why would it? They dated long enough for him to know she will not change."

Luke swirled his glass absently. "That mother-in-law, though. You saw her face at the wedding—thunderous. And tonight, when Atul made that comment..." He exhaled. "I just hope Lara is strong enough to withstand the resentment she's facing there."

Harry scoffed. "Strong enough? She's Lara. Stop worrying about her." He patted the seat beside him. "Come here."

Luke curled up next to him, letting the warmth of Harry's body seep into his own. "I think once she has their babies, she'll cement her place in that family," Harry murmured. "Then no jealous mother-in-law will upstage her."

"I hope you're right," Luke said, nuzzling closer.

And this—this was the part of the night he cherished the most. These quiet moments, when they dissected the evening, when they analysed people with a mix of amusement and concern. When they sat together, completely at ease, safe in their love for each other. How had he gotten so lucky?

He thought back to all the false starts, the missteps, the heartbreaks. Navigating the gay world had been a minefield. In those early years, when he had finally embraced his truth, he'd swung wildly between extremes—dazzled one moment by ultra-effeminate queens who sparkled with sharp wit and high drama, then drawn the next to butch gym rats with sculpted bodies and stunted emotions. All he had ever wanted was someone real. Someone who shared his values, his vision of life.

Then came Harry. And after eight years together, after love weathered through fights and laughter and an adopted cat who ruled their home, Luke knew—Harry was *The One*.

"Are you planning to go to Swansea for the summer holidays?" Luke asked casually, but the moment the words left his mouth, he knew he'd ruined the moment. It was the way Harry stiffened, the shift in his posture.

"Why?"

"Well, I thought I could come with you this time. Meet your family, finally."

"Luke..."

"Oh, come now, Harry. After all these years?" Luke leaned back, searching Harry's face, reading the resistance in his guarded expression.

"My dad..." Harry started, then stopped, his face tightening.

"Must surely suspect?" Luke pressed, gentler this time. "I mean, you've never brought home a girlfriend. Never even mentioned one."

"You don't know him." Harry shuddered, as if the mere thought of his father conjured something dark and dangerous.

"But I want to." Luke's voice softened. "I want to know him. And your mum. And your sisters. If this is for life, shouldn't we at least try? You've met my mum countless times."

"Christine is different."

"But have you even tried with them?"

Harry stood abruptly, turning his back to him. He yanked open the dishwasher and began loading it, the clang of plates sharp and deliberate. A clear signal. Conversation over. Luke exhaled, watching the tense line of Harry's shoulders. This was the only fly in the ointment, the one thing Harry refused to face. Every time Luke reached for that locked door, Harry slammed it shut. But how could they move forward—truly move forward—if this was always standing between them?

———

"It's only a quiche," Lara said, holding up a Waitrose bag with a wry smile. "Thought we could have lunch together."

Luke smiled as he let her in. She'd called an hour earlier, asking if she could swing by to pick up the car. He knew Lara well enough to recognise the real reason for the short notice—she didn't want to give him time to cook or go to any trouble for her.

"How did you get here?" he asked, taking the quiche and salad from her and setting them on the counter.

"Train from Waterloo, then walked."

"I could've picked you up."

"What? And miss this glorious day? It's such a lovely walk anyway, and so green around here."

"What will you drink?"

"A coffee, please."

As he busied himself with the cafetière, Lara wandered over to the framed photographs, running her fingers lightly over the glass. Then she picked up one particular photo—the two of them as children, standing by the pool, grinning cheekily into the camera. "I remember this exact moment!" she exclaimed. "Jim took this photo, didn't he?"

Luke nodded. "Yeah. Milk? Sugar?"

"Just black."

"How's Jim?" she asked, setting her mug down, her gaze still on the photo.

"He's fine, I guess. We don't talk much, but we email occasionally."

"Did he ever meet anyone?"

"My dad?" Luke laughed. "No. He was too busy mopping up Lexi's messes to focus on his own love life."

Lara turned sharply. "What's she done now?"

"Third divorce. And she's back with Dad again. I think part of the problem is he coddles her too much. He's never really let her grow up or deal with the consequences of her own choices."

Lara sighed. "Maybe I should introduce her to Alex. They'd be perfect for each other."

"Alex? Your cousin?" Luke arched an eyebrow. "The debt-ridden one?"

"Yeah. Also Atul's best friend."

Luke let out a low whistle. "Now that's a disaster waiting to happen."

"Oh, tell me about it." Lara waved a hand dismissively. "Suffice to say, I'll have Alex tied around my neck like an albatross for the rest of my life."

"Rime of the Ancient Mariner," Luke grinned, catching the reference immediately. "So, what are your sins, lovely Lara?"

"Falling in love, I suppose," she admitted with a sheepish smile. "But enough about me. Tell me what's going on with you. Why don't I ever see you on my flights? We really need to buddy bid!"

"I've been saying that for ages, but since you barely work, that's an impossibility."

"I *do* work, Luke!" Lara countered. "I just happen to be lucky enough to have gone part time. Even so, wouldn't it be nice to get a layover together at least once in a while?"

The oven beeped, and Luke pulled out the quiche, setting it aside as he tossed a fresh green salad. They sat across from each other, eating in comfortable silence, the only sound being the occasional chirp of a bird on the tree outside.

"I miss you, Lara," Luke said suddenly, his voice quieter than before.

Lara paused mid-bite, then set her fork down, pulling a face. "I miss you too, Luke. Remember all the fun we had when I lived with you in that tiny flat?"

Luke grinned, nostalgia lighting up his face. "How could I forget? Those were the best days."

He put down his fork, his expression turning serious. "I have a confession to make, though. At first, I was worried about how it would work—living together, after all those years apart. I mean, beyond our childhood, all those letters, and my quick trips to Delhi, we hadn't really spent much time together."

Lara raised an eyebrow. "And?"

"It was perfect. From day one. So effortless, the way you fit into our home, into our lives. Even Harry was gutted when you moved out."

A soft smile played on Lara's lips. "I have so many wonderful memories from that time. But I needed to explore my relationship with Atul on my own terms—without opinions, without judgment."

"I get that."

"The thing is," she hesitated, "Mummy and Papa didn't really take to him. And if you had said the same, I...I might not have gone through with it."

Luke studied her carefully. "Regrets, Lara?" His voice was gentle, inviting honesty.

She shook her head vigorously. "No. Not a single one. He treats me like a queen, pampers me no end. His family still hasn't fully accepted me, but they will. It takes time. I'm from such a different world."

She leaned back, laughing. "You know, the women in his family don't work? It's been a battle and a half just to hold on to my job."

"Don't you dare give it up," Luke warned.

"I won't," she said, her voice firm. "I remember your words when I got engaged, and I promise I'll always remain financially independent."

"Zinia must be proud."

Lara sighed. "I don't know what Mummy really thinks of it all, but for once, she's holding her tongue." She took the last bite of her quiche, then shot him a knowing smile. "And how goes it with Monsieur Harry?"

Luke's grin was immediate, effortless. "*Très, très bien*. In fact..." He hesitated for only a beat before saying it aloud. "If I could, I'd marry him tomorrow. No question."

Lara's eyes sparkled. "I knew it!"

He chuckled. "I've actually been thinking about a civil partnership for a while now."

She clapped her hands together, delighted. "Yes! Make an honest man of that Harry." Then, with a gentler smile, she added, "But Luke, you don't need a piece of paper to prove you belong together. It's enough that you feel it in your heart."

Later, as they lounged on the sofa, her laughter filling the room, Luke watched her with quiet affection. And in that moment, he realised—one part of his heart would always belong to Lara. Not in the way of a man loving a woman, not in the way the world expected. But in the way that mattered most. Loyally, unquestionably, eternally.

Back Stroke

"Why do we have all this stuff, Mum?" Luke groaned, eyeing the overflowing trolley. "We were just supposed to get your chest of drawers!"

Going to IKEA was never high on his list of enjoyable activities, but since Frank didn't drive, Luke had promised Christine he'd help her pick up the furniture and assemble it. Now, staring at the mountain of miscellaneous items—candles, picture frames, a throw blanket, and what looked suspiciously like a set of salad tongs—he wondered if all of it would even fit in the boot of his car.

"Oh, it's just a few bits and bobs," Christine said breezily as they headed to the till.

"Right. Like going to Costco for loo roll and coming out with a flippin' television."

Christine widened her eyes in mock innocence. "And has that ever happened to you, darling?"

Luke chuckled. "Alright, alright, let's get a move on before you start eyeing the Christmas decorations."

Once they'd paid, they made their way to the cafeteria for their usual Swedish meatballs and potatoes. It was tradition—one of those unspoken rituals they never questioned.

"So, Lara's already thinking of having a baby?" Christine asked, tucking her hair behind her ear. "They haven't even been married that long, have they?"

"Coming up to six months. And like she said, she's not getting any younger."

Christine stabbed at a meatball thoughtfully. "To me, she'll always be Zinia's little girl." She took a moment, then added, "I suppose she's right, though. The later you leave it, the harder it can be... although—"

Luke narrowed his eyes. "Although what?"

Christine hesitated, then sighed. "Her husband. He doesn't strike me as the responsible type. I have a feeling that when it comes to raising that child, it'll all fall on Lara."

"Mum, they have more money than they know what to do with. There'll be an army of nannies and staff."

"Maybe. But money doesn't change character." Christine dabbed her mouth with a napkin, then softened. "I wish her well. She looked so beautiful on her wedding day in that cream saree. So simple, so elegant."

Luke nodded. "I was surprised by her choice. I thought she'd go for something brighter."

"I think it was an homage to Zinia, to her roots." Christine paused, then added, "Although, I heard Yash grumbled privately that only widows wear white."

Luke rolled his eyes. "Mum, it was *cream*, embroidered with pearls and Swarovski crystals."

"I know that. But her in-laws weren't thrilled either, were they?"

"By that stage, I don't think she cared. She's been fighting an uphill battle with them since day one."

Christine studied him for a moment, as if weighing her next words. Then, just as quickly, she pushed her empty plate aside and smiled.

"Pudding?"

Later, as they drove home, Luke shifted uncomfortably in his seat, regretting the extra helping of meatballs.

Christine, as if reading his mind, patted his arm. "We don't do this all the time, love. A little indulgence won't kill you."

Luke shot her a quick smile, then changed the subject. "How's Frank?"

"He's fine. You'll probably see him later—he's eager to help with the assembly. But for the love of God, don't let him." Christine sighed theatrically. "The man has no patience for instructions. He'll put the whole thing together backwards and then wonder why there are left-over screws."

Luke chuckled. "He's a nice chap, Mum."

"I know," Christine said, her voice quieter now. "I suppose I've been lucky, finding someone at my age."

Luke stole a glance at her. "But you won't move in together?"

Christine scoffed. "What for? I'm perfectly happy living on my own. And I'm not about to play housekeeper and nursemaid to any man—not after Jim. With him, that was part of the vows. But now?" She shook her head. "Now, I owe nothing to anyone. Except you, of course, my sweet boy."

Luke grimaced. "Mum, I'm thirty-seven."

Christine grinned. "And still my sweet boy."

Luke groaned, but she just laughed.

"And what about lovely Harry? When do I get to see him next?"

"Soon. Actually, I was thinking—why don't you and Frank come over for Sunday roast?"

Christine brightened. "Now, that is a splendid idea." Then, as if something had just occurred to her, she hesitated.

Luke caught it immediately. "What?"

"I... I was wondering if you could get us a discount on flights to India." She hesitated again, then rushed on. "I wouldn't ask, but with our pensions, it does add up, and since you're with the airlines..."

"Mum!" Luke gave her a mock-exasperated look. "I've been

telling you for years to use my passes, and now you finally ask? Of course it's fine. Just tell me when, and I'll sort it straight away."

Christine let out a breath, her shoulders relaxing. "That's a load off my mind."

Luke glanced at her. "Mum, I want to help in whatever way I can. Let me absorb the cost, at least."

Christine's jaw tightened. "Not a chance. If that's the case, I simply won't accept them."

They argued about it all the way home—Luke insisting, Christine refusing. But deep down, he knew how it would end. Her independence was hard-earned, and he wouldn't presume to take that away from her.

"I've never been to India," Frank said, patting the newly assembled chest of drawers like a proud craftsman.

Luke suppressed a grin. Keeping him away from the assembly process had been a task in itself—Christine had sent him on all kinds of fake errands around town, just to prevent him from turning the whole thing into a disaster.

"When Christine said she wanted to visit Shimla, I thought— why not?"

Luke's head swung toward his mother. "Shimla? I thought you were going to see Zinia in Delhi."

Christine hesitated for half a second before answering. "We are. To start with. But then, I'd like to go to Shimla."

Luke frowned. "Shimla," he repeated, tasting the unfamiliar name. "Why? Where even is that?"

"In the foothills of the Himalayas," Christine said vaguely.

"Okay... but why there? What's in Shimla?"

Frank looked at Christine, then at the floor, then back at her again. "I think you should tell him," he said.

Christine exhaled, as if bracing herself. "There's nothing much to tell, really," she began, then paused before continuing. "After Mama died, I found an old photograph of hers as a baby. On the back, there was a date, and a place inscribed: Simla, 1917. She spoke so little of her past, of where she came from, that I thought... maybe I'd go and see if there was something left to find."

Luke studied his mother, his concern flickering into something deeper. "Why, Mum?"

Christine's gaze softened as she looked at him. "There's always been a missing piece in me, Luke. A part of my history I never really understood. I was raised British, travelled all over the world, even lived in America, but I never knew what lay behind my mother's mysterious nature. She was always such a closed book. Beautiful but remote." She gave him a small, wistful smile. "You look so much like her, you know. Sometimes, when I see you, I imagine what she might have looked like as a young girl."

Luke said nothing. He didn't quite understand the sudden urgency of her search, but he knew better than to talk her out of it.

Christine straightened her shoulders. "It's the last big journey I'll ever take. If I don't do it now, I never will."

Luke sighed but nodded. "Alright. When were you planning to go?"

"How long will it take to sort the tickets?"

"A day. Two at the most."

"Then as soon as possible." Christine smoothed her trousers with one hand. "Zinia and Yash might come to London in July, and I'd like to be back by then."

Luke raised an eyebrow. "Mum, have you forgotten how hot it gets in Delhi in May and June?"

"We'll only be there a few days before heading to Shimla. It'll be cooler there—or so I've been told."

"And visas?"

Christine gave him a sly smile. "Already done."

Luke let out a low whistle. "Wow. You really got a head start on this."

"Why wait? We're not getting any younger." She said it simply, echoing Lara's words from just days ago.

As Luke made a mental note to book the flights, he couldn't shake the thought—was this what people meant by second childhood? When parents, once so measured and practical, suddenly became impulsive and started chasing dreams from decades past? A restlessness stirred within him. He made another mental note: keep a closer eye on Mum and Frank.

As he stepped outside, Christine followed him to his car, the late afternoon breeze ruffling her hair. "Don't worry, Luke. I am more than capable of taking care of myself."

"Promise me you'll stay safe?"

"Of course." She kissed his cheek, her touch warm and reassuring. "But I'll have to take a rain check on the Sunday roast."

"That's fine, Mum." Luke opened the car door, then hesitated, turning back to her. "Actually, I wanted your opinion on something."

Christine raised an eyebrow. "Tell me."

Luke hesitated, then took a breath. "I've been thinking about a civil partnership with Harry..."

Christine's face lit up. "Yes?"

"The problem is... I've never met his family. Not once. I don't even know if they know I exist. Or..."

"...or that Harry is gay?" Christine finished softly.

Luke sighed, looking down at the ground. "Yeah. I want to celebrate our partnership, throw a big party, invite everyone we love... but how can I, when the people who should mean the most to him don't even know about me?"

Christine exhaled, considering her words. "Luke, you can't force someone to acknowledge you. He has to want to. And if he hasn't told them by now, he must have his reasons."

"But how long is he going to keep me hidden, Mum? It's been eight years."

"And you've tried talking to him?"

"So many times. It always ends the same way—he clams up."

Christine placed a gentle hand on his arm. "Give him a little more time. But Luke... no long-term relationship can be built on secrecy. Before you take this step, he needs to make peace with himself. And with them. Otherwise..." She didn't need to finish the sentence.

As Luke pulled away, he caught sight of his mother in the rearview mirror, waving until he turned the corner. His chest tightened. How was he supposed to convince the man he loved to confront his truth and the deceptions of his past, when that was exactly what Harry seemed to be running from?

———

Luke carried the plated meal over to 12A with his signature easy smile.

"I hope this one is more to your liking, Miss Collins. Apologies about the special meal—it wasn't very special, was it?"

Miss Collins looked up, her previous irritation melting into a sweet smile. "Oh, this looks much better," she said, before tucking into the chicken with gusto.

Back in the galley, Maria was waiting, arms crossed. "Well?"

Luke leaned against the counter. "Crisis averted. She's happy now."

Maria snorted. "So, Miss 'Strict Vegetarian' has miraculously converted?"

"To be fair, that special meal did look like slop, didn't it?" Luke admitted, grinning.

Neil bustled in, stacking trays. "Has he charmed her, then? Always so smooth with the ladies..."

"And the men," Maria added pointedly. "You could take a leaf out of his book."

"Hey, schmoozing isn't part of my job description. I'm just here to fling meals at people and mumble 'goodbye' a couple of times a quarter to keep my qualification intact," Neil said with a smirk.

Maria shot him a teasing look. "Yeah, and judging by the enthusiasm in your 'goodbyes,' you're better off staying buried in union paperwork."

Luke chuckled, leaving them to their bickering as he made his way through the cabin, topping up wine glasses and engaging in brief, effortless conversations with passengers. It was second nature by now—reading their moods, knowing when to linger and when to move on. He caught smiles as he passed, some warm, some flirtatious, others simply grateful.

This job had been his life for ten years. He could do it in his sleep. The closest thing to a real crisis had been a diversion to Reykjavik once—some odd electrical smell in the cabin that turned into an expensive layover rather than a disaster. And yet lately, something gnawed at him.

He loved his colleagues, the freedom of his schedule, the thrill of a different city every few nights. But at nearly forty, was this all there was? A decade of perfectly executed service, of charming passengers and smoothing over minor hiccups?

Christine had once told him, "Your job doesn't define you." And he didn't think he was above this career—it had given him so much. But it didn't fulfil him anymore. He craved a challenge. Something that tested him, stretched him. Something beyond routine. He just didn't know what that was yet.

Minutes later, the inter-phone buzzed sharply, summoning Luke to the back. An altercation had broken out between two passengers, and from the raised voices, it was already getting heated.

"He won't bloody sit still!" the tall, burly man in the aisle seat growled, arms crossed like a disgruntled nightclub bouncer. "Like a bloody jack-in-the-box. Up and down, up and down! I've been trying to sleep, and he's climbing over me every five damn minutes!"

"I can't help it if I need the toilet," the smaller man shot back, his face flushed. "I have a medical condition, alright?"

Luke took in the scene quickly. The smaller man's hands trembled slightly, his expression defensive. The taller one looked ready to throw a punch.

"Alright, gentlemen," Luke interjected, voice calm but firm. "Let's take a breath, yeah? No need to escalate this."

The big man huffed. "I just want some peace!"

"And I just want access to the loo!"

"Okay," Luke said smoothly, positioning himself between them, "here's what we'll do. Sir," he turned to the smaller man, "I'll move you to the aisle seat so you have easier access to the restroom. And you," he looked at the taller man, "there's an open seat a few rows up. I'll get you settled somewhere quieter so you can get some rest. Fair?"

A tense pause. Then, begrudging nods.

Once the seating shuffle was complete, Andrea, hands on her hips, let out a low whistle. "A storm in a teacup," she mused. "Thought I was gonna have to break out the handcuffs."

"Not on my watch," Luke grinned. "Keep an eye on them, though. We've got six more hours to go—let's not turn this into 'Fight Club'."

Andrea smirked. "As if we have a choice. You cram a few hundred people into a flying tin can for ten hours. Some of them are bound to lose their minds."

"And it's our job to keep the peace," Luke said, giving her a wink. "Now, let's hope that's the worst of it."

Famous last words.

As he made his way up the aisle, Luke's trained eye caught an elderly man leaning against the bulkhead, his face pale and clammy. Alarm bells rang instantly.

"Sir? Are you alright?"

The man gave a weak shake of his head. "I'm feeling... faint..." His voice was barely above a whisper.

Luke didn't hesitate. He called for assistance, gently guided the man into a seat, and handed him a glass of orange juice. "Here, sip this slowly. Help is on the way."

Within moments, Andrea arrived with the emergency oxygen bottle. Luke kept a steady hand on the man's shoulder as he took a few deep breaths through the mask. Slowly, some colour returned to his cheeks.

"Are you traveling alone, sir?"

The man blinked up at him, his breathing steadier now. "No... my granddaughter is in 36E."

"Alright. I'll go get her."

Luke strode through the cabin, quickly spotting the young woman. He crouched beside her seat and spoke in a low, reassuring voice. "Your grandfather wasn't feeling well, but he's stable now. He's getting oxygen and being looked after. Would you like to come check on him?"

Her eyes widened in alarm, but Luke's calm demeanour seemed to ground her. "Yes, please."

After reuniting them, Luke returned to the galley, where Maria gave him an appraising look. "Well, you've had quite the eventful stretch."

"A clusterfuck is what we call it," Neil muttered, stacking trays.

Luke exhaled, rolling his shoulders. "Let's just hope the rest of the flight is uneventful." He grabbed a clipboard. "Now, if you'll excuse me, I have some reports to fill out before the next crisis hits."

After landing in Singapore, once most of the passengers had deplaned, Luke spotted the tall, burly guy from earlier wandering aimlessly around the economy cabin, looking thoroughly bewildered. Luke approached, already bracing for whatever fresh chaos was about to unfold.

"Can I help you with something, sir?" he asked, keeping his tone polite but wary.

The man turned to him, his brow furrowed in deep confusion. "Yeah... I think I've lost my shoes."

Luke blinked. "Your... shoes?"

"Yes." The man looked down at his sock-clad feet as if noticing them for the first time. "I definitely had them when I got on the plane."

Luke bit back a laugh. "Right. And at what point do you recall not having them?"

The man scratched his head. "I took them off to get comfortable, but now—" He spun in a slow circle, scanning the cabin as if his shoes might magically materialise. "They've just vanished."

———

"Turns out," Luke said with a chuckle, swirling the ice in his glass, "the little guy took them at some point during the flight and stashed them in an overhead bin."

Maria nearly spat out her drink. "No way!"

Neil let out a low whistle. "That's some next-level pettiness. I respect it."

"Revenge," Maria said, wiping her eyes, "is a dish best served hidden."

Luke grinned. "I say kudos to him. Imagine spending your whole life getting elbowed out of the way by bigger blokes. This was his moment."

"Poetic justice," Neil agreed. "And there you all were, tearing apart the economy cabin for half an hour, looking for those bloody shoes."

"By which time," Maria smirked, "the little guy was probably already through immigration, whistling his way to baggage claim."

They were lounging on the rooftop bar, enjoying the warm Singapore night, the city skyline glittering like scattered diamonds. This was what Luke loved about the job—the camaraderie, the adventure, the sheer unpredictability of it all.

As they moved on to their second round of gin and tonics, Neil leaned in, his expression turning serious. "Luke, have you ever thought about joining the union?"

Luke snorted. "Me? Involved in airline politics? No thanks, mate."

"I'm serious," Neil pressed. "You're great with people. The crew respects you. You understand how management works, and more importantly, you give a damn. That's exactly what we need."

Luke waved him off. "I don't do politics, Neil."

Maria shrugged. "Nor do I."

Neil sighed. "It's not politics, it's survival. Management tightens the screws every year—longer hours, lower pay, impossible rosters. And don't even get me started on benefits vanishing before our eyes. We need strong voices at the table."

Maria smirked at Neil, then turned to Luke. "Why am I a part of this proposal, hey? It's Luke you want, not me. My hands are full with my kids and my insane dogs."

Neil ignored her and leaned forward. "Okay, no names, but just last week we got someone's job back. Crew member was unfairly dismissed after a medical leave issue. Some stupid paperwork that wasn't filed on time."

Luke's interest piqued.

"They weren't even given a chance to fight it," Neil continued. "One day, they were flying, the next, out on the street. If we hadn't stepped in, that would've been it. That's what we do, Luke. We fight for the people who don't have a voice."

The conversation moved on, but Neil's words stuck with Luke. He'd always been the one to step up for his colleagues, to smooth things over, to make sure people felt heard. But officially getting involved? That was a different beast altogether.

Later, as they walked back to the hotel, Neil gave him a pat on the shoulder. "Just think about it, mate. You've got what it takes to make a real difference."

Back in his room, Luke stared at his reflection as he brushed his teeth. Was this it? The challenge he'd been searching for? A way to stay in the airline world he loved, but on a different level?

He collapsed onto the bed, drained, but his mind refused to slow down. Possibilities whirled through his head, each more insistent than the last. He told himself he'd think about it tomorrow, that a good night's sleep would bring clarity, but deep down, he knew. If life was nudging him in a new direction, maybe this wasn't just an opportunity. Maybe this was the answer he hadn't even realised he was searching for.

———

It was late May, a crisp morning dappled with sunlight, and the air was rich with cut grass and the redolent promise of an early summer.

Luke pushed open the doors to the local pool, the familiar scent of chlorine and damp tiles wrapping around him like an old friend. He changed quickly, tugging his goggles into place, and strode to the pool's edge. With a practiced ease, he slid into the water; the coolness rushing over his skin like a reset button.

Stroke. Breathe. Stroke. Repeat.

The world outside faded, leaving only the rhythmic splash of his arms cutting through the water. This was his meditation—weightless, thoughtless, free. The only place where his body worked and his mind untangled. But today, his thoughts refused to stay quiet.

Was union work really for him? It was one thing to be a listening ear for his colleagues, but this would mean longer hours in meetings, fewer flights, and on the plus side, no more jet lagged nights in far-flung cities. Was he ready for that move?

His mind flicked to a memory from years ago. A new recruit, wide-eyed and petrified, had panicked and blown the emergency slide upon landing in Chicago. A mistake that could have cost her everything. But the union head had been on that very flight. He had stepped in, fought for her, saved her job. Luke had flown with her years later. She was a purser now—calm, in control, excellent at what she did. Had the union not fought for her back then, she would never have become the leader she was meant to be.

And now, he was being offered the same chance to make a difference. Could he do it? Would he even be good at it?

His arms powered through the water, and his thoughts drifted to Harry now.

With Harry, he felt seen, safe, loved. But was that enough? He wanted more. The ring in his bedside drawer had been there for far too long. He had picked it out with care, imagined the moment he'd slip it onto Harry's finger. Maybe it was time to push forward on the dream he harboured. Maybe a proposal would give Harry the final nudge he needed to come clean to his family.

Luke didn't want a big spectacle. No grand declarations—just the two of them, promising forever. A simple moment, a quiet truth: I choose you. Always. Would Harry say yes to a vision of the future he imagined for them? No deceit or subterfuge. Just love and transparency. A relationship that was steady, secure and real.

By the time Luke finished his laps, his mind was buzzing with possibilities. As he drove home, the smell of the chlorine still clinging to his skin, the weight of his choices pressed down on him.

Union work. Civil Partnership. The unknown.

Back at home, he made himself a coffee, flipping open his book, trying to lose himself in fiction. Then, his phone buzzed. Sue. He hadn't heard from her in ages. Curious, he picked up straight away.

"Luke," she said, her voice warm and familiar.

"How are you, darling?" Luke answered with a warm smile, leaning back in his chair.

Sue had long since transitioned from ex-girlfriend to lifelong friend. He had been there for her wedding to Matt, had visited them shortly after Alan was born, had held her hand when Alan was diagnosed with autism, and had offered support and advice when she finally gave up flying to focus on her family. Life had pulled them in different directions over the years, but never apart.

"I'm fine, lovely! You? How's Harry?"

They chatted for a while, the usual catch-up dance of old friends, before Sue finally got to the point. "We're moving to the New Forest,

Luke, and I have this incredible business opportunity. I thought I'd run it past you and see if you'd be interested... as a business partner?"

Luke sat up a little. "A business partner?" That was new. Sue had never been entrepreneurial, or even ambitious in that way. He was intrigued. "What kind of opportunity?"

"We're buying a house with an attached cattery. It makes sense—I'm home anyway, and when Alan is at school, I have all this free time. Matt's happy that I've found something for myself. It's just that..." She hesitated.

"Just that...?"

Sue took a breath. "We can't afford the down payment."

She rushed on before he could respond. "If you wanted to invest as a sleeping partner, I'd run the business, and we could split the profits. Everything would be done legally, of course... It's just an idea. No pressure at all!"

Luke was silent for a beat longer than usual, turning it over in his mind.

Sue sighed. "Luke, really, you can say no. I don't want you to feel obligated. I just thought... maybe it could be extra income for you. And if it worked out, maybe you could even cut back on flying?"

That last part struck a nerve. Cut back on flying. Between the union offer, the proposal to Harry, and now this—why did life always throw everything at him all at once?

He exhaled. "Can I have some time to think about it?"

"Of course! No rush. Just let me know by the end of June?"

They chatted a little longer before hanging up, but Luke's mind was already spinning. Union work. A business venture. A proposal to plan. Opportunities were like buses—nothing for ages, and then suddenly, they all arrived at once.

It was Tuesday, May 31st. Harry had warned Luke he'd be late. The Parent-Teacher meetings would drain him, like always. Luke had planned everything perfectly. Soft jazz played. The lasagne baked in the oven, timed to perfection. A chilled bottle of white wine waited. Tea lights flickered, casting a warm glow over the dining table set for two.

When Harry finally walked in, he sighed, dropped his bag, and collapsed onto the sofa. Luke handed him a glass of wine. "Tough evening?"

Harry exhaled. "Manic. Same troubled kid, every parent complained. He needs a special school, but his parents won't listen. We don't have the resources. It's frustrating as hell."

Luke listened, offering quiet sympathy, just as Harry did after his long-haul flights. Then, Harry sniffed the air. "Is that...don't tell me. You've made lasagne?"

Luke grinned, pulling the dish from the oven. "New recipe. Lara sent it."

Harry raised a brow. "Lara? She cooks?"

"She used to. Still loves experimenting. This was one of her ideas."

Harry leaned in, inhaling deeply. "Okay, what is it? Smells incredible."

Luke smirked. "Butter Chicken Lasagne."

Harry's eyes widened. "Are you serious? That sounds amazing."

They ate, laughing between bites, Harry devouring every last bit, mopping up the sauce with garlic bread. When he finally sat back, satiated, Luke whisked away the plates and returned with two bowls of homemade tiramisu.

Harry groaned. "I'm stuffed. But I can't say no to this. Another of Lara's?"

Luke shook his head. "No. This one's all me."

Harry dug in. He took a bite, then another. Then—stillness. A small clink. He frowned and reached into his mouth, pulling something out between his fingers. A ring. A gold ring with a delicate Celtic design on it, lightly encrusted in cocoa.

His gaze shifted to Luke, who was already kneeling, steadying his breath, readying himself to deliver the words he had carefully chosen. "My darling Harry, would you do me the great honour of sharing my life, officially, as my partner?"

Silence.

Harry's mouth opened, but no words came. His breath turned shallow. Hands trembled. Eyes darted, searching for escape. Then, suddenly, he shoved his chair back, its legs screeching against the floor. "I...I can't..." His voice just above a whisper, thick with panic. He placed the ring on the table—carefully, reverently—then bolted for the door.

Luke barely had time to react before he was gone. Stunned, he sank to the floor. Candlelight flickered. The ring lay abandoned. The tiramisu sat half-eaten. His mind reeled. Where had Harry gone? Had it been too soon? Too much?

His phone rang, stopped, rang again. Insistently this time. At first, he ignored it. Then it occurred to him that maybe it was Harry. Calling with an explanation or an apology. He snatched it up. "Hello?"

A woman's voice. High, frantic, and barely holding together. "Luke?"

His stomach clenched. A voice he knew but couldn't immediately place. "Yes?"

"Where's Christine? I've been trying to call her. She's not answering..."

He blinked, trying to push through the fog in his brain. "Mum's in India."

The woman gasped sharply. "Then you have to come! I don't know what to do. I don't know who to call—"

Luke sat up straighter. "Wait, come where? Who is this? What are you talking about?"

"It's Dad!" The voice cracked. "He's had a stroke. I called 911—they're on their way—but I need someone... anyone... Please, come..."

His heart slammed against his ribs. Lexi. His half-sister. And Jim. His father. For a second, the world blurred. A single memory flashed in his mind: Jim walking away from him at the training centre, his shoulders slumped in defeat. The last time they had seen each other. A lifetime ago.

Luke gripped the phone tighter. "I... I'm on my way." His voice came out hoarse, barely above a whisper.

All thoughts of Harry vanished. The only thing that mattered now was getting to Jim before it was too late.

Lara (May 2010)

Currents

Lara (May 2010)

Currents

"Look at us," Lara said with a dry laugh, pulling her jacket tighter against the sea breeze. "Two heartbreak survivors in our forties, single and slightly jaded. Who'd have thought?"

Luke nudged a pebble with his foot. "At least we can laugh about it now."

"Barely." Different heartbreaks, different timelines, same ache. But they had held each other up when everything else collapsed. She glanced at him. "Any news from Harry?"

Luke's smile faltered. "Nothing." He skimmed a stone into the waves. "Probably for the best. I pushed too hard."

Lara sighed. "Luke, eight years isn't too soon. If he couldn't decide then, maybe he never will."

Luke exhaled, forcing a grin. "Well, we still look good in our forties. There's hope for us yet."

She saw through him. The charm, the jokes were just scaffolding around a broken heart. Harry had been his once-in-a-lifetime. No fling could fill that void. She shifted the conversation. "How's Lexi?"

Luke's jaw tightened. "Not great. Dad's death gutted her. I think she finally realised that no man will ever love her like he did."

"Poor thing."

"She's barely herself anymore. Oversized T-shirts, daytime TV, junk food. She's just... given up."

"How often do you visit?"

"Once a year, at least." He hesitated. "Funny, isn't it? I couldn't stand her as a kid. Now, all I feel is pity."

They turned toward the sun-drenched stretch of Manhattan Beach, where a ribbon of restaurants and cafés pulsed with the easy glamour of Los Angeles. The air carried the tang of salt and grilled seafood, laughter rising above the hum of clinking glasses and crashing waves. This was the coveted layover they'd managed to wrangle—a brief, golden interlude—and they intended to savour every moment of it together, as if time itself might be coaxed into slowing.

"Brunch?" Luke asked.

Lara nodded.

As they scanned the menu, Luke glanced up. "This one's on me. A belated birthday treat."

She exhaled dramatically. "Fine. But for the record, I was fully prepared to go Dutch."

Luke smiled. "Please. This LA trip wouldn't have happened if you hadn't worked your magic to get me on the crew. Besides, I forgot to get you a book for your birthday, so let's call this atonement."

Lara gasped in mock horror. "You forgot?" Then, grinning, "Kidding. I know you've been swamped with union work. Still enjoying it?"

Luke leaned back, considering. "It's rewarding in ways I never expected. Frustrating in ways I should have." He shrugged. "But if I can make a difference, even a small one, I sleep better at night."

Lara smiled. "Christine must be so proud."

The waiter arrived with their poached eggs and orange juice. Lara caught his attention. "Could I get some Tabasco, please?"

"Cholula okay, miss?"

Luke winked. "Anything spicy will do." The waiter chuckled as he walked away.

Lara shook her head. "Stop flirting with the poor boy."

Luke grinned. Then his expression shifted. "How's Yash?"

Lara's smile faded. "Still devastated. He keeps saying it should've been him instead of Mummy." Her voice wavered. A single tear slipped free. She wiped it away. "I still can't believe she's gone, Luke. She was so full of life. And to go that quickly..."

"I know, honey." He reached for her hand. "But at least Zinia knew how much you loved her. My dad... he died thinking I hated him."

Lara squeezed his hand. "No, I'm sure that's not true."

Luke exhaled, eyes dark with regret. "Oh, but I think it is. Our relationship was... transactional at best." A bitter chuckle. "Lesson learned. Tell the people you love that you love them, before it's too damn late."

They sat in silence, hands clasped, lost in thought. Then, as if on cue, they withdrew, returning to their food.

On the walk back to the hotel, Luke nudged her. "Planning a nap before checkout?"

"I'd love to, but I need to check the loads on the Delhi flight for Wednesday."

Luke frowned. "Didn't realise you were leaving so soon."

She nodded. "Mummy's *barsi*...errr, her one year death anniversary, is on Saturday. I want to get there early to help with the arrangements."

"That makes sense." He hesitated. "How's Yash managing?"

Lara sighed. "Valli's still with him, but she keeps talking about going back to her village. And my *bua*, his sister, has come to help. For now, he's not alone. But I worry, Luke. Papa's old and frail. The fact that he's outlived Mummy... it makes no sense to him. Or to me."

Luke's voice was quiet but firm. "Zinia was lucky."

Lara turned to him, surprised.

"If I could choose how to go," he continued, "I'd want to go in my sleep too."

She knew he wasn't being flippant. He was reminding her that Zinia hadn't suffered. Despite the pain, despite the grief, there had been mercy in the suddenness.

She didn't reply. She didn't need to. Instead, they walked in silence, the ghosts of their respective losses walking between them—shadowy, familiar, unspoken.

The night flight from LA was packed, every seat in First Class occupied. The three of them—Lara, Luke, and Andrea—moved in quiet synchronicity, their years of experience turning the demanding service into a well-rehearsed dance. Lara plated the meals with practiced precision while Luke and Andrea served the passengers with effortless charm.

"You've become quite the gallerina," Luke teased, watching her deftly drizzle hot fudge into a tiny silver jug and place it on the dessert cart, her movements smooth and assured.

"Practice, sweetie," Lara murmured with a knowing grin.

"Been flying this position a lot?"

"A fair bit."

"Flying a lot in general?"

Lara's response was a nonchalant shrug, but Luke didn't miss the flicker of something in her eyes as she arranged the cart.

"Money?" he pressed.

Lara shot him a fleeting glance before her eyes darted to Andrea.

Then she gave a small, almost imperceptible nod. Luke understood. *Not now.* They fell back into the rhythm of the service.

It was only later, when most of the cabin had dimmed for the night and Andrea was on her break, that Luke picked up the thread again. Seated side by side on the jumpseat, picking at their crew meals, he turned to her. "Alright, go on. Why are you flying so much? I thought the divorce settlement was more than generous."

"It was." Lara speared a potato with her fork and chewed it slowly. "And I'm not flying so much. I'm just... getting it out of my system."

Luke frowned. "What does that mean?"

She exhaled, staring at the meal tray as if the answer lay somewhere between the rice and the wilted green beans. Then, finally, she looked up at him. "I'm thinking of quitting."

His fork paused mid-air. "What?"

"I need to go back to Delhi."

Luke's surprise turned to concern. "Lara... why?"

"Papa." Her voice was small. "I can't leave him alone forever, Luke. He's old. He's not well. He's lost Mummy, and he has no one else."

Luke leaned in. "Then bring him to London."

"And do what?" Her voice trembled slightly. "Move a seventy-year-old man to a country where he knows nobody? Where he'll be a prisoner in the house? And who's going to look after him when I'm away on trips?"

"But quitting your job? Lara, the perks alone—"

"You've stepped back too."

"Stepped back, not walked away completely. I'm still accruing seniority. That's worth its weight in gold."

"I know, Luke," she said, her tone softer now. "But honestly... apart from you, there's nothing keeping me in England. And you can always visit me in Delhi. That won't change, will it?"

"Of course not." He sighed, rubbing the back of his neck. "But please, don't rush into this. You don't have to work a day in your life if you don't want to, but what are you going to do in Delhi? You'll go mad with boredom."

Lara gave a small, tired smile. "I've thought of that. I reached out to my old PR agency. Asked if they'd let me freelance. I could take on the occasional project, stay connected to work."

Luke studied her. "You really think you're ready to leave all this behind?"

She hesitated just a fraction too long before saying, "I have to do what I have to do."

Luke sighed. "Just promise me one thing—give it a little more thought. Don't make a decision you can't take back."

Lara didn't answer right away. She just stared out at the sleeping cabin, at the dim glow of the galley lights. "I'll think about it," she said at last.

Lying in her bunk on break, Lara squeezed her eyes shut, willing her restless mind to quiet. Sleep wouldn't come. Memories surged instead—of airports and layovers, of friendships forged at 35,000 feet, of the sheer, intoxicating freedom that flying had given her. She hadn't chosen this life. Not at first. Luke and Zinia had nudged her toward it, and she had fallen—hard. Even Atul, with all his wealth and promises of an opulent, grounded life, hadn't been able to lure her away. But now... now, the choice was stark. Keep flying, or go home to Yash. And there was no real choice at all.

Zinia's sudden death had been a brutal wake-up call. 4,000 miles had separated her from her mother in the end, and Lara couldn't shake the ache of that distance or the cruel truth of how little time they had actually spent together in those final years. She wouldn't make the same mistake with Papa. He needed her. And, though she hadn't admitted it until this very moment, she needed him too. His warmth, his quiet wisdom, his unwavering love.

Turning onto her side, she pressed her hands together, whispering the old prayer he had taught her as a child.

Ma Gayatri, give me the strength and courage to make the right decision.

The words circled her mind, steady and soothing. Eventually, exhaustion won over, and she finally drifted off to sleep.

———

They hugged tightly after stepping off the crew bus, reluctant to let go.

"When will I see you next, Lara?" Luke's voice was light, but his eyes—those kind, knowing eyes—were filled with concern.

"I'll call you once I'm back from Delhi. We'll plan something then," she promised. Then, with a small smile, "Why don't you come to London this time? We'll catch a show, and you can crash at mine."

"Deal."

They hugged again, a silent understanding passing between them. This moment felt different. Like the end of an era. As Lara walked toward her car, an ache settled in her chest. Was this the last time they would fly together? She glanced back. Luke was still watching her. He blew her a kiss. She caught it, pressed it to her heart, and waved.

The drive into Central London was its usual nightmare— anywhere from forty-five minutes to two soul-crushing hours. But she never took the tube after a long-haul. Lugging bags up escalators? Squeezing into sweaty carriages on the tube? No, thanks. This was her one indulgence, and it wasn't like she had anyone waiting at home.

She sipped her espresso, cranked up the music, and let the familiar rhythm of post-flight exhaustion settle in. Then, her car's speaker crackled to life with her voicemail messages. "Lara, this is Atul. I've been trying to reach you. Guess you're on a trip. Alex is in town and we're grabbing dinner at *Dishoom*. Wanna join?"

Lara sighed. Atul. She tapped his name and dialled.

"Lara!" His voice was warm, familiar. "How are you?"

"Tired," she admitted, letting the weariness seep into her tone. "Just got back from LA."

"Hmm," he murmured distractedly. "So, listen, Alex is here, and we were wondering if you're free for dinner?"

"Not tonight, Atul. I'm wrecked."

"How about tomorrow?"

"I leave for Delhi the day after."

"Then let's make it early."

She hesitated, then relented. "Fine. Which *Dishoom*?"

"Covent Garden. Six?"

"I'll be there."

As the call ended, silence filled the car, but not her mind. It drifted, unbidden, to the slow unravelling of her marriage. Atul had never hurt her. No violence, no betrayal. Just a slow erosion, a quiet crumbling of something that had never been strong to begin with. Her parents had seen it before she had. The fundamental incompatibility. The polite, empty affection that had never held any real depth of love. And then, of course, there had been the one thing she could not give—an heir.

Her in-laws had never hidden their disapproval. She had been an outsider from the very beginning, a wife they tolerated, not one they embraced. When the doctors confirmed her infertility, they wielded it like a crowbar, prying her and Atul apart.

Ironically, it hadn't even mattered in the end. Because deep down, she had already known. Atul was fond of her—would always be—but it had never been the all-consuming, soul-deep love she had witnessed between her own parents.

Now, he had remarried. A perfect, suitable wife, handpicked by his mother. A woman who had already given him one heir and was carrying a second. And yet... he still called. Still reached for her. Did his mother know? She smirked. *Not a chance.*

But there was no bitterness in her heart. No resentment. That chapter of her life had served its purpose. It had taught her the most valuable lesson of all: she would never again settle for simply being chosen. She would demand to be seen. To be valued, not for what she could produce, but for who she was. Not a trophy wife. Not a symbol of lineage. Just Lara. An empowered woman who knew her worth.

———

At home, Lara unpacked swiftly, tossing her laundry into the washing machine without ceremony. The rhythmic hum of the cycle filled the silence as she stepped into a hot shower, letting the steam and water wash away the exhaustion of travel.

Afterward, wrapped in a fresh robe, she made herself tea and toast, comfort in its purest form. She checked her mail, sorting through the bills and putting them into the wooden bowl she had won years ago in school, a memory that still brought a smile to her face. Then she curled up in her armchair, iPad in hand, scrolling absently through the news.

Her small but perfect home in Marylebone was nothing like the lavish house she had once shared with Atul, but it was hers. Every inch, every curtain, every appliance, every carefully chosen shade of cream and blush pink, reflected her. She had decorated without compromise, knowing there would be no grubby little hands smudging the walls, no scattered toys cluttering the floors.

The thought stung. No children. No pets. Just her. She allowed herself a flicker of sorrow, the dull ache of absence, before shifting her focus. There was freedom here, too. The kind she had never known in her old life. Her gaze fell on the bouquet of pink peonies she had bought a week ago, in full bloom now, their scent thick in the air. A silent indulgence. She made a mental note to discard them before leaving for Delhi. She hated coming home to wilting things.

Then her eyes landed on the photograph. Zinia. Radiant. Laughing. Captured in a stolen moment, oblivious to the camera. Lara rose slowly, walked over, and lifted the frame with careful hands. She carried it back to her armchair, settling in as her fingers traced the contours of her mother's face.

The tears came, unbidden, an outpouring of grief that still

ambushed her unexpectedly. Zinia's loss was an unhealed wound that time had not filled. She had been the life force of their home—the sun around which they had all revolved. And now, without her, they were lost. Adrift. Unmoored.

Oh, Mummy... why did you leave so soon?

When the sobs finally subsided, Lara pressed the photograph to her chest, holding it close like a child clinging to its blanket. She closed her eyes, her breath slowing. No one knows how much time they have. Wasn't it better to live by one's own truth? To choose joy, as Zinia had done for most of her life?

Later, when she woke from her nap, she noticed a new voicemail. Christine. "Lara, Luke told me you're going to Delhi soon. Please give my best to Yash and tell him that anytime he wishes to visit, he will always have a home with Frank and me. Our trip to Shimla with Zinia and him is one of our fondest memories of the past few years. If not for him, I would never have tracked down my mother's antecedents or made sense of my lineage. Your parents are very special people, Lara, and I know that wherever Zinia is now, she is looking down on you with pride and love."

Lara inhaled deeply, Christine's words settling somewhere deep inside her. She wouldn't call back right away. Not today. Not yet. But someday, when the weight in her chest felt lighter, she would. And when she did, she would tell Christine just how much those words had meant to her.

———

Alex had aged. The thinning hair, the balding patch on his pate—poorly disguised by a desperate comb-over—only accentuated the passage of time. The boyish good looks he had once owned had faded, replaced by something more hollow, more strained.

"I keep telling him to go to Turkey for a hair transplant," Atul teased, nudging Alex, "but he claims he doesn't have the time."

Lara responded with a polite smile, her indifference carefully veiled. Once, Alex had been her favourite cousin—a confidant, a play-mate, someone she had enjoyed spending time with. But life had chipped away at that fondness. Now, she met him out of duty rather than desire, out of politeness rather than affection.

"How are Uncle Jude and Aunty Roxanna?" she asked, effort-lessly steering the conversation away from Alex's hair woes.

"They're fine," he said with a casual shrug. "Funny, isn't it? After all these years, they ended up in Granny's old flat."

It was ironic. After Granny had passed, after Uncle Pedru had been found dead from an overdose, Jude and Roxanna had made the unexpected decision to sell everything in Mumbai and retreat to Goa. Granny's flat, once a decision made in Lara's presence, had become their last refuge.

"They miss Aunty Zinia, though. They wanted to come for her... umm, cremation. But Mum wasn't well, so they couldn't."

Lara knew the truth. Roxanna had never approved of the crema-tion. She had wanted a burial, as per her beliefs, and when the family honoured Zinia's wishes instead, Roxanna had chosen silence as her protest. A quiet, pointed absence. Lara didn't press. Some things weren't worth revisiting. "And how's your business?" she asked, watching Alex closely. His transformation from a withdrawn teenager into a garrulous, slightly overcompensating middle-aged man fascinated her.

Rumours swirled around him—whispers that Jude and Roxanna had sold their Mumbai home to bail him out of debt. Now, without them cushioning his failures, how was he managing?

"Great!" Alex flashed a too-wide smile, his eyes darting away. Lara recognised the evasion but chose not to chase it.

As the conversation meandered through the usual topics—old friends, the latest hotspots, the trendy bars where they had racked up *huge* bills—she felt a familiar pang of resignation. Nothing had changed. Alex had always wanted to keep up with the Joneses. And he would never stop trying, no matter how many business ventures collapsed, no matter how many lifelines he exhausted. One failed relationship after another. Women who had entered his life, dazzled by his charm, only to realise that hitching their wagon to him meant careening toward disaster. Lara felt a flicker of pity. But beneath that, an undeniable frustration. This didn't have to be his fate. Had his parents grounded him instead of feeding his delusions of grandeur, had they encouraged him to value his middle-class roots rather than chase an unattainable high-society dream, maybe he wouldn't be sitting here, spinning the same tired stories, evading the same uncomfortable truths. But some people never learned.

The evening ended early, and as Lara stepped into the quiet sanctuary of her home, she felt an overwhelming sense of relief. No forced conversations. No lingering obligations. Just her, alone, in the space she had carved out for herself.

She booked a taxi for the airport and, while waiting for the confirmation, let her mind drift. She had told Luke that nothing was holding her back in London. That had been a lie. Despite the wreckage of her marriage, she had built a life here that she loved. A life of independence, of choice. Lara worked because she wanted to, not because she needed to. She was the mistress of her own time, free to do as she pleased. She had Luke. And in an odd, complicated way, she also had Atul. Two men who, despite everything, would drop everything for her if she truly needed them.

Then there was London itself—a city that pulsed with possibility. Galleries that fed her mind. Museums steeped in history. West End shows that transported her to another world. She never lacked for friends, even if none of them came close to the bond she shared with Luke.

And she had herself. That, too, was enough. She enjoyed her own company, often taking herself out for lunch or catching a matinee. She was content. But not always. If she was honest, she missed companionship. Someone to share the mundane with, to curl up on the sofa and watch Graham Norton, to book last-minute city breaks with, to have someone's warmth beside her in bed. And if she was brutally honest? She missed sex. The intimacy, the sheer, human closeness of it.

So what was waiting for her in Delhi? Besides Yash, nothing. The air was thick with pollution. The government was a mess. The friends she had once cherished had long since scattered. And the freedoms she held so dearly in London? They would shrink too, caged by culture, by expectation, by society. Yet, duty outweighed desire.

She could always come back. London would wait. Her home could be rented out, her life placed on pause. But Yash needed her now. And maybe, just maybe, this trip would bring her the clarity she needed. Or, at the very least, help her decide where she truly belonged.

Undercurrents

The *havan* was a simple one. Yash had found a priest willing to come home and perform the sacred rites, guiding Zinia's soul on its journey to the afterlife.

On the balcony, where she had once sat laughing over tea, sharing stories that were woven into the fabric of their family, the fire now burned in a small metal container. As the priest's chants filled the air, Lara blinked through her tears, overwhelmed by how fleeting the time with her mother had been. Once, this space had been filled with Zinia's presence, her voice, her unshakable spirit. Now, they sat in the same place, bound by grief, longing for the life force that had held them all together.

Yet, in the flickering light of the fire, among the family, friends, and neighbours who had come to pay their respects, Lara saw something undeniable—Zinia had left her mark. Even those who had once opposed her, like the aunt who had disapproved of Yash marrying a Goan Christian, had come, as if finally conceding that what truly mattered was not convention, but character. Zinia had never fit into the mould of a typical housewife. She had been fiery, defiant, intolerant of prejudice, but above all, she had been good. And in the end, goodness left an imprint. The people gathered here were proof of that. Zinia had departed the physical realm, but in stories, in laughter, in love, she was still very much alive.

Later, as Lara served lunch to those who had stayed behind, they spoke of her mother with reverence, with humour, with the sort of warmth that softened even the sharpest edges of grief. When she came upon *Sardarji*, one of the taxi driver brothers (she still didn't know which one)—old and frail now, pressing his hands together in a trembling *namaste*, chuckling as he recalled memsahib's legendary temper—Lara felt her chest tighten, tears pricking at her eyes once again.

But it was Yash who surprised her the most. Grief had etched deep furrows into his face, yet he remained composed. One by one, people approached him, their voices softened by memory. "Remember when she...?" "That time Zinia said..." Each recollection a small flame, illuminating the life of a woman who had burned so brightly. A marriage built on defiance, a family stitched together with love. A tapestry of moments—some cruel, some beautiful. Vivid in the telling, yet already slipping into the haze of the past.

Later, after the last guest had left and the remnants of the *havan* cleared away, Lara and Yash sat together, nursing cups of tea. The house was still, except for the soft clatter of dishes as Valli washed up in the kitchen. *Bua* had retreated for her siesta.

Lara glanced at her father. Dressed in his white *kurta-pyjama*, a thin shawl draped over his shoulders, he looked smaller somehow. More fragile. "Papa, I've been thinking..."

Yash looked up, his lined face briefly lighting with amusement. "You think too?"

She groaned, laughing despite herself. How many times had he teased her like this when she was a child? When had that easy playfulness between them begun to fade? Had it been when she left for London to start flying? When she married Atul? Or was it later, when he and Zinia had visited her in a home grander than any five-star hotel they had ever stayed in, watching her navigate a life they could no longer guide?

Somewhere along the way, he had stepped back, retreating into quiet observation, withholding opinions on her choices—the marriage, the divorce, the life she had built for herself. As if accepting that she was now on a journey he no longer had a role in.

Zinia had never been like that. She had been vocal, both in her praise and her disapproval—never hesitating to say the hard thing, the necessary thing. When Lara had told her she was filing for divorce, Zinia had merely muttered, "About time."

But now, sitting here, it felt as if the past decade was dissolving, as if they were reaching back through time to rediscover what had once nourished them. "No, listen, Papa... seriously... "

He leaned forward, tapping her knee lightly. "I've been thinking too, Lara."

She stilled.

"This house," he said, his voice quiet, "is too full of memories for me. Your *bua* has asked me to move to Indore. There's a small flat near their home that I can rent. I'll be close to family, and Valli can finally go back to her village, as she's wanted to for so long. And you —" He met her gaze. "You, my dear girl, won't have to worry about your Papa quite so much."

Lara's breath caught. She had not seen this coming. Not once, in all these years, had he ever spoken of leaving Delhi, let alone going to Indore.

"Papa..." she began once again.

He shook his head gently. "No, *beta*. It's time for me to return to my roots. Some of my happiest memories are of my childhood there. And besides..." He exhaled, his voice steady, resolved. "That life—the one before—did not have Zinia in it. I can be happy there again. Or at least, as happy as life will allow after losing your mother." He stood up slowly, steadying himself with his walking stick. "Let me go."

And with that, he turned and walked inside, leaving Lara sitting in the silence, wondering at life's constant capacity to surprise her.

"Lara?" A voice, familiar yet distant, rang out. "Lara Seth?"

She turned, scanning the crowded marketplace, until her eyes landed on a face from another lifetime. Renu.

"I knew it was you!" Renu beamed, nudging the teenager beside her. "I told Monty it was you."

Monty, presumably, was the lanky boy shifting uncomfortably at her side, flanked by a girl just a few years older. Lara took them in quickly before turning her attention back to Renu. Without hesitation, she swooped in for a hug. It had been years—since Renu's wedding, to be precise. The two had drifted apart, life pulling them in opposite directions. Yet now, here they were, in the middle of Greater Kailash, M Block Market, as if no time had passed.

Renu pulled back, eyes shining. "You haven't changed! Still as beautiful as ever."

Lara laughed, waving off the compliment. "Of all places, I never expected to bump into you here."

"Why not?" Renu asked.

"I thought you'd moved to Panipat."

"Oh, we did," Renu nodded, distracted as her daughter tugged at her hand, whispering something urgently. She sighed. "Fine, go." Without so much as a glance at Lara, both kids hurried off.

"That was Sonu, my daughter," Renu said belatedly. "They're off to McDonald's."

Lara watched them disappear into the crowd, a flicker of something unnameable passing through her. Had Renu not thought to introduce them? Or had it simply not occurred to her?

"Come on," Renu said, linking her arm through Lara's. "Let's grab a drink."

They ended up at Moti Mahal, a landmark in the area. As the rich aroma of butter chicken filled the air, Lara idly wondered what the chefs here would think of her butter chicken lasagne back in London.

"So," Renu leaned in, eyes twinkling. "Last I heard, you were in London. Are you back for good?"

Lara hesitated. "Just for a bit. I'm here for Mummy's *barsi*."

Renu's expression shifted instantly, her smile faltering. "Oh, no... not Zinia Aunty." She reached for Lara's hand. "I'm so sorry. What happened?"

And just like that, they fell into the old rhythm of conversation—catching up on lost years, offering congratulations for the wins, condolences for the losses. But as they spoke, Lara felt something subtle yet undeniable—an awareness of the vast distance between them now. Renu's world revolved around school pickups, family functions, and tiffin boxes. Lara's was one of airports, independence, and solitude.

This was the same girl she'd once promised to take a trip with, back when friendship felt eternal and the future was a blank canvas. How different they were now—shaped by years, by silences, by lives that had pulled them in opposite directions. Could they ever reclaim that bright, unfiltered intimacy, that wide-eyed belief in each other and the world?

"Remember how we used to play hopscotch in the back lane?" Renu said suddenly, a wistful smile on her lips. "We had no idea where life would take us."

"No one ever does," Lara mused. "But you... you got your happily ever after. Prince Charming and all."

Renu snorted. "Prince Charming is a myth. Marriage cured me of all that nonsense." She grinned. "I mean, my husband's a good man. He takes care of us, but he's no Salman Khan."

"Thank God for that," Lara teased. "I don't think any sane woman would want to be married to him."

They both laughed, the moment stretching comfortably between them. Then Renu's eyes gleamed mischievously. "And what about you? Did you ever marry that guy you used to moon over?"

"Who... Luke?" Lara nearly choked on her Coca Cola. "Luke and I? No, no, we're just really good friends."

Renu smirked. "Two good-looking people, best friends for years, and nothing ever happened? I don't buy it."

Lara shook her head, smiling. "Renu, you claim to be a cynic, but you're still a romantic at heart. Luke and I... what we have is special, but not in *that* way." She paused. "Besides, marriage cured me of any romantic notions, too."

Renu's brows lifted. "Wait—you're married?" Her gaze flickered to Lara's bare ring finger.

"Happily divorced," Lara confirmed.

Something changed. It was subtle, but Lara saw it. The slight shift in Renu's expression, the minuscule step back, as if divorce was something contagious. Lara wasn't offended. She understood. In India, divorce still carried a whisper of shame, an air of quiet failure. For her, though, it had been liberation.

The rest of their conversation felt... perfunctory. The exchange of numbers, the vague promise to meet again, both knowing they wouldn't. When Renu's phone rang, her son informing her they were done at McDonald's, she rose with barely concealed relief.

Lara reached for the bill. "This one's on me. You can get the next."

Renu hesitated, then nodded. "Take care, Lara." And just like that, she was gone.

Lara sat there long after, absently playing with the salt and pepper shakers. Some friendships faded gently over time. Others you didn't even realise were over until you were sitting alone at a restaurant, staring at the empty seat across from you.

With just a few days left before her return to London, Lara found herself buried in logistics. The hours were spent ironing out the details of Yash's move to Indore—figuring out the best way to apportion his pension so he could live comfortably, discussing how to pension off Valli, deciding what to do with Zinia's things that Lara couldn't take and had no space for. It was exhausting. Necessary, but exhausting.

On Sunday afternoon, they finally allowed themselves a breather. Yash, in an unusually light mood, pulled out the old gramophone. "Let's listen to some music," he said, carefully placing the worn vinyl on the turntable. Moments later, the crackling strains of K.L. Saigal's voice filled the room.

Lara groaned. "Oh, come *on*, Papa."

Rohini, her *bua*, grinned. "This is the one thing we never understood about Yash. The rest of us were dancing to Kishore Kumar, Mohammad Rafi, and all the peppy sixties music, but there he was—an old man before his time—lost in K.L. Saigal and Pankaj Mullick." She shook her head fondly. "Believe me, Lara, we used to groan exactly like you."

Lara rolled onto her stomach, propping her chin on her hands. "Tell me more, *bua*."

The air grew warmer, softer, as they all lounged together on the same bed, the strains of Saigal's melancholic melodies drifting around them like mist from another era. Rohini leaned back, eyes twinkling. "Well, your father was always a naughty boy—completely disinterested in school. Except for Maths, which he could ace without opening a book."

Valli walked in, balancing a tray of tea and snacks. She handed them out, then settled on the floor with her own cup, her eyes alight with curiosity.

"He used to run away from school to watch movies at the theatre," Rohini continued, laughing. "We called him 'First Day, First Show' because he *had* to see every new film the moment it was released."

Lara sat up, scandalised. "Papa! You gave me so many lectures about skipping school. And you—" She pointed an accusatory finger at him.

Yash had the grace to look sheepish.

"Oh, that's not even the best part," Rohini smirked. "He once set off firecrackers in the school toilet. The entire building was evacuated—an unplanned holiday for all the kids."

Lara gasped. "No!"

"He was a hero that day," Rohini said. "Not for the teachers, of course. For them, he was a menace."

Yash sighed dramatically and looked up at the ceiling. "Rohini, if you give up all my secrets, they'll have no respect for me at all."

Valli chuckled from her spot on the floor. "Only person who could handle *sahib* was *memsahib*."

A hush fell over the room. Zinia. She wasn't there, and yet, suddenly, she was everywhere. The soft hum of the record player, the scent of old books, the worn bedspread beneath their hands—everything seemed to hold a whisper of her.

"Yes," Rohini said gently. "It's true. It was only after Zinia entered his life that Yash got serious about making something of himself. Before that, he was content to while away his days playing cricket and watching movies."

Lara hesitated before asking, "But *dada dadi*—your parents—they didn't want Papa to marry Mummy, did they?"

She saw Rohini glance at Yash, waiting for his approval before answering. When he gave a slight nod, she said, "No, they didn't. Not at first." She took a slow sip of tea, choosing her words. "They were small-town people, Lara. They believed in familiarity—the same house, the same neighbours, the same routines. It was their version of peace, of stability. And then Yash fell in love with a Goan Christian girl. That was more upheaval than they knew how to handle."

Lara's jaw tightened. "They thought she'd make him convert, didn't they?"

Rohini smiled sadly. "They thought she'd change him. That he'd start going to church, eating beef... that he'd stop being theirs."

"Mummy never did that," Lara said fiercely.

"Exactly." Rohini's gaze softened. "In so many ways, their marriage was something I admired. They let each other be. Even when they argued, even when they disagreed, they never tried to change the other. My parents came to see that over time. And when they did..." She exhaled, a small smile playing at her lips. "They loved her, in their own way."

Lara swallowed past the lump in her throat. Zinia had been the force that shaped their family, the quiet anchor who had held them together with no one truly realising it. And now, without her, everything was shifting—Yash moving to Indore, the house being emptied; the memories being packed away or discarded. She looked over at her father, his eyes half-closed, listening to the music. Saigal's voice trembled through the room, singing of love lost and time slipping away. Lara reached for her father's hand and squeezed it. Some things would change. Some things had to. But not this. Not the stories. Not the memories. Not her.

But today wasn't about loss. It was about discovery. About peeling back the layers of Yash—the boy he had been before he became the father she knew and loved. As *bua* regaled them with stories of his many escapades, laughing as she recounted the chaos he once thrived in, Lara found herself watching him differently. Really seeing him.

It was so easy to see parents as static figures, their identities fixed within the roles they played—mother, father, protector, provider. But they were more than that. Before her, they had lived entire lives—had dreamed recklessly, loved fiercely, lost painfully, and dared in ways she would never fully know. Their histories weren't just stories. They were inheritances, stitched into the fabric of who she was in ways deeper than blood. What had she carried forward?

Did Yash's quiet resilience pulse within her, his mischief flickering in the edges of her laughter? Did Zinia's fire run through her veins, her unshakable convictions shaping the woman Lara had become? And if they did—what did any of it matter, if it all ended with her?

A hollow ache pressed against her ribs. A lineage lived on through children, through names whispered into the future. But her bloodline would end with her. Was that how legacy was measured?

By what was left in flesh and bone? If she could not pass them forward, did that mean they would fade, as if they had never existed at all? Lara closed her eyes, letting the weight of it settle, the quiet sorrow of what would never be pressing into the lonely corners of her soul.

And then, softly, like the echo of a lullaby carried on the wind, her mother's face surfaced in her mind. Zinia was smiling. A warm, knowing smile. As if to say, things only end if we let them. As if to remind her that time was not a straight line but a vast, unbroken tapestry, where nothing—no love, no memory, no trace of those who came before—ever truly vanished.

Saigal's music swelled around her, rich with longing, steeped in history. And in that moment, Lara sensed it—that mystical confluence of past, present, and future, a tide, surging and receding, folding into itself in an endless, fluid embrace.

The ache inside her didn't vanish, but the music wove around it, softened its corners, turned it into something almost tender. A quiet benediction. And so she let go. Let the bittersweetness of her reality seep into her bones. Let herself dissolve into it, and it into her, until what remained was something softer, something beautiful, something achingly, imperfectly whole.

***

"I always thought you'd become a journalist or something, not an air hostess," Shweta said, sipping her cocktail.

"Flight attendant," Lara murmured, not bothering to correct her tone, just the words.

Shweta waved it off with a laugh. "Same thing! It's impossibly glamorous, just like you. Honestly, I should have seen it coming. With your height and looks, you could've been a movie star or a model, but flying is just as fabulous!" She paused as the waiter set down their pizza. "At least you didn't get stuck in some dull 9-to-5 job. Anyway, where's Madhuri? She's always late."

Reaching out to her college friends had been a small act of defiance. A challenge to herself, to see if any part of the girl she had once been still existed in the city that had shaped her. Renu's quiet disapproval had left a bruise she wasn't willing to acknowledge, but something in her had needed to prove that she still belonged, that she wasn't a stranger to herself or to the people who had once known her. And here was Shweta, eager to fold her back into old memories, ready to place her once again at the centre of a story they had all lived together.

"Sandy still carries a torch for you, you know," Shweta said, grinning as she ordered another round of drinks. "Of course, the fact that you live in London now just adds to the mystique."

"Mystique?" Lara spluttered. "I am the least mysterious person on the planet. All this 'glamour' you're imagining, it's just surface-level. The reality is jet lag, sore feet, and anonymous hotel rooms that all blur together. What I actually love is the flexibility and the travel perks. But the glamour? Pah!"

"No matter what you say, it suits you," Shweta said, studying her with something like nostalgia. "You still look just like you did in college."

Lara smiled, knowing it was just kindness. Neither of them were the fresh-faced twenty-year-olds they had once been. Life had settled onto them, in the softness of their bodies, the faint lines marking their foreheads. And yet, some part of them remained frozen in time. When she thought of Shweta and Madhuri, she still pictured them as the girls they had once been, not the women they had since become.

"Here she is! *Late Latif*, as always," Shweta griped as Madhuri finally arrived.

The hugs were warm, the pleasantries effortless, but Lara couldn't help but take a step back and observe. Madhuri, the quiet, unassuming girl she remembered, had sharpened into someone striking. A sleek bob, a knowing smile, and a confidence that hadn't been there before.

"Tell me about the divorce," Madhuri said, getting straight to the point. "What an idiot to have let you go."

Lara hesitated, choosing her words carefully. She wouldn't turn Atul into a villain. Not because she owed him anything, but because that wasn't the truth. "It wasn't like that," she said finally. "There was no drama, no catastrophe. Some things just run their course, and you realise you're holding onto something that no longer fits. We let go before it turned to resentment."

Madhuri tilted her head, considering her answer. Shweta frowned, as if trying to comprehend a love story that didn't end in fire and ashes.

"Maybe it's payback," Madhuri laughed, swirling the last of her wine. "For all the hearts you broke in college."

Lara raised an eyebrow. "Payback?"

"Oh, don't look so stunned," Madhuri teased. "If we announced you were back in town, there'd be a line a mile long waiting to snap you up." She turned to Shweta, ignoring Lara's exaggerated shudder. "Did you tell her about Sandy?"

Shweta grinned. "Still listens to ghazals and mourns the fact that you never took his love seriously. No idea what his wife makes of it."

"Shut up, both of you!" Lara groaned. "Tell me about yourselves. That's what I'm interested in. Not all this ancient history you're dredging up."

As the conversation shifted, Lara found herself relaxing, falling into the easy rhythm of their banter. Why had she waited so long to call them? Here they were—women who had built their own lives, who had grown into versions of themselves that their college selves could never have imagined.

Madhuri, the once-timid girl, had found confidence in an arranged marriage that had turned into a partnership. Her husband had encouraged her to step out of her shell, to carve a career in teaching, to find her voice. And Shweta, forever the rebellious one, had married for love, defying her parents, only to watch them begrudgingly embrace her husband and eventually weave him into their family business, while she, ironically, still felt like an outsider.

They laughed, reminiscing about the past, marvelling at the strange paths life had taken them on. And for the first time in a long while, Lara felt something shift within her, a kind of lightness she hadn't even realised she had lost. In their company, she felt the echo of the girl she had once been. The Lara who had left college brimming with ambition, desperate to see the world, to lose herself in five-star hotels and foreign cities, not knowing how she'd get there but certain she would.

Hadn't she done exactly that? Maybe it hadn't looked the way she had once imagined it would. Maybe the dream had rougher edges and more tangled realities. But did that really matter? From the outside looking in, she had carved out a life on her own terms. And maybe, just maybe, that was enough.

Madhuri, now on her third glass of wine, leaned in conspiratorially. "Did I ever tell you," she slurred slightly, "I bumped into Mrs. Girdhar a few years ago?"

Shweta and Lara both turned to her, intrigued.

"She looked so much older, way less terrifying. Or maybe I'd just grown up by then." Madhuri smirked. "Anyway, I had to remind her who I was. Mousy little me probably didn't leave much of an impression. But guess who she did remember?"

Lara tensed slightly, waiting.

"She was very interested in what you were up to." Madhuri paused for effect, eyes glinting with mischief. "And when I told her you'd joined the airlines, she just shook her head and went, 'What a waste.'" A beat of silence. Then Madhuri set her glass down with a dramatic sigh and burped gently. "Don't let it bother you. She was a crazy old bat, anyway."

Lara laughed, but something inside her twisted, just a little. A waste. The word lingered, uninvited. But as the night carried on, she let it slip away, dissolving into the music, the laughter, the warmth of old friends who knew her beyond what anyone else thought she should have been.

———

"I've been wondering how it's going?" Luke's voice was warm, familiar, reaching out on the phone, covering the distance between them. "Any decisions been made yet?"

"Some," Lara admitted, momentarily thrown off guard. His call had come out of the blue, just as she was folding the last of her clothes into her suitcase, preparing to head back to London.

"And?"

"Oh." Realisation dawned. "No, I'm not quitting just yet. Papa doesn't want me to." And then, as if a dam had burst, the words came spilling out—the whirlwind of the past few weeks, Yash's decision to move to Indore, his insistence on selling the house. "He won't take any financial help from me, Luke. He says he doesn't need it, but I know his pension is barely enough. And even after selling the house, how long will he be able to live off the proceeds? He's being so stubborn, so—" she sighed, pressing a hand to her forehead. "So proud."

"Let him," Luke said gently. "If holding on to his self-respect is important to him, let him."

"But—"

"Listen," he cut in. "Here's what you do. Open a joint account with him. Tell him it's for your expenses whenever you come to India. Then, slowly, transfer as much money as you want—small amounts, nothing that will make him suspicious. That way, if he ever needs it, the money is there."

Lara was silent for a beat. Then she whispered, "Sneaky." A slow smile spread across her face. "I like it."

"I'll tell you what I like," Luke teased. "I like that you're not leaving."

"Yet."

"I'll take yet." His voice was rich with satisfaction. "I told you not to make any hasty decisions. And look, life took the decision out of your hands."

Lara exhaled, realising he was right.

"The reason I called," Luke added, his tone shifting slightly, "is that Mum wants to speak to Yash. She's been wanting to for a while, but when I came over to see her, we figured it was the right time."

"Hold on," Lara said, a flicker of guilt passing through her that she hadn't returned Christine's call.

Yash took the phone from her, brow furrowed in mild confusion as she mouthed Christine. Then recognition dawned. She watched as his face softened, lit up by a warmth that had nothing to do with the present and everything to do with the past. As Christine's voice carried across years and distance, she saw the quiet tremor of emotion flicker through him—the bittersweet dance of sorrow and joy as they reminisced, patching together fragments of old memories, shared laughter, and an understanding that time could never erode. And in that moment, as Lara observed him, it struck her—her mother's friendship with Christine had never been just theirs. It had quietly expanded, embracing Yash, enveloping Lara, binding their families together in ways that neither time nor circumstance had unravelled. It was no accident that she and Luke had remained in each other's lives. It had been the quiet, persistent work of two women who had understood the power of connection, of love that transcended borders, of friendships that refused to fade.

When Yash finally hung up, he exhaled, as if releasing something long held inside.

Lara hesitated before asking, "Are you okay, Papa?"

He looked at her, his expression weary yet full of something deeper, something akin to acceptance. "Yes, my sweet girl," he said, his voice laced with fatigue. Then, after a pause, he added, almost to himself, "There was a time I thought it wasn't a good idea for your mother to be friends with Christine." He shook his head, a faint, wistful smile on his lips. "What a fool I was."

On the flight back to London, Lara sat in quiet anticipation, waiting for her name to be called. As a standby passenger, she was always among the last to be assigned a seat, a silent observer, as paying customers were accommodated first.

Finally, they called her name. 9K. A Business Class seat. Relief flooded her—she hadn't been looking forward to spending the overnight flight crammed in economy. With the newly introduced lie-flat beds, she could actually get some rest.

Boarding last, she made her way to her seat, pausing only to exchange a quick hello with a flight attendant she recognised from a previous trip. When she reached her row, she found the man in the aisle seat sprawled out comfortably, his legs stretched across the space, his book lying open on her seat.

"Excuse me," she said, her tone neutral, though irritation flickered beneath the surface.

He looked up, startled, then yanked his legs back, snatching his book as he muttered a quick apology. Perhaps he'd assumed the seat would remain empty, that he'd have the luxury of solitude. Well, she wasn't sorry to disrupt that illusion. She belonged here just as much as anyone else. These were the perks of staff travel, and she wasn't about to start feeling guilty about it.

Tucking her handbag neatly under the footrest, she fastened her seatbelt and settled in. She had barely adjusted her seat when Jason appeared from the galley, weaving through the cabin with a glass of champagne in hand.

"Lara!" he called out, grinning. "Luke messaged me you're on our flight tonight! Bubbles for the journey."

Heat rose to her cheeks as she accepted the glass, murmuring her thanks. Trust Luke, she thought, smiling to herself. "I'll come down and say hi after the service," she promised. As Jason disappeared down the aisle, she took a sip, savouring the crispness of the champagne.

"You're popular," a voice drawled beside her.

Something in the deep baritone sent a strange ripple down her spine. She turned to her seatmate, finally taking a proper look at him. And then—a jolt. Recognition flickered at the edges of her mind, just out of reach. She knew him. From somewhere, somehow. Just how she wasn't sure yet.

He caught her lingering gaze and frowned. "I'd really like to fly under the radar tonight, so if you don't mind, no autographs."

Lara blinked, caught off guard. Then, just as quickly, irritation flared. *Who the hell does he think he is?* If she weren't flying on an airline pass, she might have given him a piece of her mind. Instead, she dropped her gaze, shoved in her headset, and ignored him for the entire taxi and takeoff.

When Jason came around to take her meal order, he leaned in apologetically. "Lara, I'm so sorry, there's no more chicken left. Pasta okay?"

She shrugged. "I'm not really hungry. Just a glass of wine. I'll head to bed after that."

A few minutes later, with warm nuts and drinks in front of them, her seatmate turned to her again. "Look, I'm sorry about earlier," he said, his voice quieter now. "It's been a long day. I just wanted to relax."

Lara gave him her sweetest, most insincere smile. "Oh, please, don't let me stop you. Relax all you want."

He laughed, low and rich. "I'm guessing I'm not forgiven, but let's at least try to be friends for the next ten hours."

She glanced at the hand he extended toward her and deliberately ignored it. "Fellow passengers," she corrected.

She could feel his gaze lingering on her.

"You look familiar," he mused. "Have we met before?"

With a sigh, Lara pulled off her headset and turned to face him, impatience flickering in her dark eyes. "Why do you think I was staring earlier?" she shot back. "You looked familiar, too. I just couldn't place you. And if you're someone famous, let me assure you,

I have no idea who you are, and I definitely don't want your autograph!"

"Whoa." He held up his hands, mock wounded. "The lady has sharp claws."

Despite herself, a laugh escaped her. There was something about the way he said it, like she was a genuine threat, like she could maul him on the spot if she wanted to. As if she wouldn't lose her job in an instant if she did.

"Alright." She gave a grudging nod. "Truce."

He grinned. "Now, let's figure out where we know each other from."

With a sigh, she paused her movie and turned to him again. "School?" Could he have been in one of her neighbouring schools?

He named his, and she shook her head.

"College?"

"St. Thomas," he said.

The memory hit her like a jolt of electricity. The competition. The tall, gorgeous boy who had stopped her in the corridor, complimented her on her elocution, then walked away, straight into the arms of his waiting girlfriend. His dark eyes searched her face, sensing the shift in her expression. He knew she'd figured it out. He waited. Instead, she smirked, slid her headset back on, and pretended to restart her movie.

"Hey! No fair," he grumbled. "Now I won't be able to sleep, racking my brain trying to place you."

She slipped off her headset again, and this time, she took him in properly. The years had sharpened him. The once boyish handsomeness had matured into something more rugged. There was silver dusting his temples now, a gauntness to his features that only added to his appeal. What had once been beautiful was now something far more dangerous. And just like that, the attraction she had felt all those years ago came rushing back. Every instinct in her screamed a warning. *Danger ahead. Proceed with caution.* But the moment their eyes met, she knew it was already too late. His pupils widened. He was feeling it, too. The magnetic pull between them was undeniable.

Lara's gaze flickered to his left hand. No ring. The alarm bells quietened, just a little. Coincidence? Maybe. But something about this felt too deliberate, too perfectly timed. As if the universe had been waiting for the right moment to bring him back into her orbit.

What lay ahead? A slow, reckless smile curved her lips. She had a feeling she was about to find out.

Luke (May 2015)

Plunging

"Mum, how are you enjoying the Algarve?"

"It's wonderful, absolutely wonderful." Christine's voice brimmed with enthusiasm, her happiness practically spilling over through the phone. Clearly, Frank had hit the jackpot with this trip.

"When are you back again?"

"Oh, not for another ten days," she lowered her voice conspiratorially. "Just between you and me, Luke, I think Frank wants us to settle here. He's been making a few enquiries about buying a property."

Luke sat up straighter. "Settle? As in... move permanently?"

"He seems quite keen," Christine admitted. "And honestly, the weather is a dream compared to back home. There's a thriving expat community, good healthcare, a slower pace of life... I'm not averse to the idea."

Luke forced out a chuckle. "What happened to 'I love my independence'?"

"Oh, don't be daft, Luke. Independence doesn't mean I want to spend my golden years in a freezing flat complaining about the price of heating." Her words were lighthearted, but something in them sent a pang through him.

After they hung up, he sat still for a long moment, staring absently out the window. The idea of Christine moving abroad had never crossed his mind—not really. Frank's arthritis had been getting worse, and the warm climate would be good for him. That much was clear. But Christine? His mother, who had always insisted she would live out her final years in England, who had spent decades fiercely protecting her autonomy?

And yet, maybe that was just it. Over the years, he had watched them become so intertwined, their lives so seamlessly woven together, that it was hard to distinguish where one ended and the other began. Like all long-term couples, they had absorbed each other's quirks, picked up each other's mannerisms. And if Frank needed this, Christine, Luke's pragmatic, unsentimental, fiercely loyal mother, wouldn't hesitate to follow.

He was happy for her. He really was. But where did that leave him? With Christine gone, who did he have?

Lara was still in London, of course. And Sue, with whom he shared both a business and a deep, uncomplicated friendship. They were his 3 a.m. people, should he ever need them. But Christine... Christine had always been his safe harbour. The one person in the world who had been there, through every triumph and every failure. At forty-seven, was he being ridiculous, childish, even, to want to hold on to that? Or was it just that, for the first time in his life, he was feeling truly, terrifyingly alone?

Then he shook his head and strode to the kettle. Time for a cuppa, and to stop all this pointless worrying. If there was one thing life had taught him, it was that it didn't care for careful planning. It would toss surprises his way, some pleasant, others brutal, and all he could do was brace himself and handle whatever came next.

He picked up his phone again, hesitating only for a moment before dialling the one person he knew for certain was lonelier than him. She answered on the first ring, her breathless voice carrying the unmistakable edge of someone who had been waiting.

"Luke," Lexi gasped. "You didn't call yesterday."

Guilt pricked at him. "I'm sorry. Work's been mad. I'm knee-deep in contract negotiations. You know how it is."

"How long are you going to keep doing this union work?" Her voice was petulant, sulky, the way it had always been when she felt abandoned. "I haven't seen you in months."

Luke sighed. He knew why she clung to him the way she did. When Jim died, something inside her had broken, and in his absence, she had latched onto Luke, replacing him as the mainstay in her rudderless life. She had retreated from the world, becoming a recluse, burying herself in solitude, living like a ghost in a house full of memories. It was sad. He didn't mind being her anchor. Not really. But there were limits.

Softly, he said, "It's my job, Lexi. And I'm good at it. I promise, as soon as I get a break, I'll come and see you."

She was silent for a beat, then said, "How's your girlfriend?"

Luke frowned, nonplussed. "Girlfriend?"

"Lara." Her voice sharpened, turning brittle.

Ah. So that was where this was going. "Lara's fine," he said, keeping his tone deliberately even. "I'm seeing her tomorrow, actually." The moment the words left his mouth, he knew they had been a mistake. Because this—this—was always the problem. It wasn't just that Lexi disliked Lara, a lingering shadow of some long-buried childhood grudge. It was that Lara mattered. That she was still very much a part of Luke's life, still someone he turned to, still the friend and confidante that Lexi could never be.

How could he possibly explain that his love for Lara wasn't a threat? That it wasn't the same as what he felt for Sue, or even for Lexi herself? That there was no hierarchy, no contest. Only different kinds of love, each occupying their own space within him. But Lexi had never seen it that way. And she never would. Luke exhaled slowly. Some battles weren't worth fighting. Lara and Lexi would never cross paths again. And that, he had long since accepted, was for the best.

"Phantom again?" Luke mock-complained, though he already knew why Lara had chosen it. Again. It was *their* musical—the first one they had seen together at the theatre, back when she had stayed with him and Harry. He could still picture her face from that night, wide-eyed and spellbound as the chandelier swung wildly above them. Later, he had gifted her the soundtrack, and he'd loved catching her humming the songs as she dusted or cooked, mouthing the lyrics with gay abandon. It wasn't about 'Phantom of the Opera' anymore. It was about them, about the memories woven into its melodies.

Inside the theatre, as the curtain lifted, Luke allowed himself to sink into the familiar story—the phantom lurking in the shadows, taking a young ingénue under his wing, sowing chaos but never harming her, even as she fell in love with another. A tale of devotion, obsession, and heartbreak. A tale as old as time, and yet, every single time, it gave him goosebumps.

Later, as they strolled toward a bar for a drink, Lara was still buzzing with excitement. "I wish I could have seen the original with Sarah Brightman. Remember the CD you gave me? That was her voice! She was incredible..."

Luke watched her, taking in her animated expression, the way her whole face lit up when she spoke about something she loved. How many years had he known this woman? How much had she changed? And yet, tonight, for the first time, he hesitated to bring up the one topic that had been weighing on him for months.

"Alright, come on," she teased, nudging him playfully. "Give it up! Which book is it this year?"

Luke grinned and pulled the gift-wrapped book from his bag. "Here you go. Happy Birthday, lovely Lara."

She tore off the paper, curiosity flickering in her eyes before turning into delight. "'All the Light We Cannot See'. What an intriguing title! I can't wait to start this." She chuckled, tucking the book into her bag before blowing him a kiss. "You, my darling Luke, never fail to surprise or delight."

For a moment, everything felt easy. Just as it had always been. But then, casually, carefully, he asked the question that had been circling his mind. "So, what plans for your actual birthday? Is Loverboy visiting?" He said it lightly, making sure his tone was breezy and inoffensive. But he saw it instantly—the shift. The way her shoulders stiffened, the way the light in her eyes dimmed just a fraction.

"Yes," she said, her voice clipped. And just like that, the moment passed.

Luke let it go, steering the conversation toward safer ground. He watched as she relaxed again, slipping back into the Lara he had always known. But in the corners of his mind, he couldn't ignore the other Lara—the one who had surfaced in recent years. The guarded, defensive Lara. The one who took offence too easily, who shut him out whenever he asked about Sushil Nair. The man he had never met. The man who stayed in the shadows, mysterious and impenetrable.

London shimmered in the aftermath of theatre lights, its streets damp with recent rain and aglow with the hush of midnight. As they walked back to her flat, their fingers entwined with the ease of long familiarity, their laughter rose and fell like a shared memory. There was comfort in the cadence of it—the kind that came from knowing each other for so long, from having nothing to prove.

"Why haven't you met anyone else, Luke?" Lara asked suddenly, her voice soft but insistent. "Surely you're not still pining over Harry?"

"Not pining, no," Luke said with a small smile. "But wary. Wary of giving my heart away again."

"Hasn't there been anyone?"

"Oh, plenty." He shrugged. "Dalliances, mostly. Fun, fleeting things. But nothing lasting. No one noteworthy. Besides, Lara, I feel I'm a little too old for the game now. Maybe I come across as that pathetic old perv leering at young men in clubs."

"Stop it, Luke!" She halted mid-step, turning to him with fire in her eyes. "You're not old, and you're definitely not a perv. Anyone would be lucky to have you. You're just too scared to put yourself out there."

Her conviction startled him. He chuckled, squeezing her hand. "Oh, darling, if only everyone saw me through the same rose-tinted glasses as you."

She rolled her eyes but linked her arm through his, pulling him close as they continued toward her flat. Luke was staying the night, and he knew how this would go. They'd talk for hours, their voices growing hushed as the night deepened. They'd share stories, secrets, and a bottle of wine, just as they had for years. He couldn't wait.

The soft strains of jazz drifted through the dimly lit living room, wrapping around them like a sensuous memory. The air was thick with reminisces aided with bottles of Pinot Noir. They sat cross-legged on the couch, both in worn pyjamas, their bodies slouched with the easy familiarity of people who had known each other forever. The outside world felt far away, all their worries forgotten, just for now.

But by the second bottle, Luke could see it—that hazy gleam in Lara's eyes that always came when she was teetering on the edge of holding it together and falling apart. Without warning, she tossed her head back and launched into a loud, off-key, theatrical rendition of The Phantom of the Opera.

"The Phantom of the Opera is heeere... inside my mind!" she trilled, twirling on the spot, nearly sloshing deep red wine onto her pristine cream rug.

Luke leaned back, watching her with a half-smile, half-prayer that her glass wouldn't become collateral damage. But as suddenly as she had started, she stopped, placing the glass down with a surprising tenderness, like it was the only thing she could control. She turned to him then, eyes glassy, voice softer now but thick with something deeper. "Can I tell you something, Luke?"

He straightened, instantly alert. "All ears, Lara."

Her smile wobbled. "If you had been straight," she said, a tremor in her voice, "I would have married you and never let you go."

The words hit him like a blow. Somewhere within him, the suspicion that had lingered resurfaced. *Oh, Lara!* Luke stared at her, torn between laughing it off and reaching for her hand. Before he could decide, her face crumpled, her body folding in on itself as tears filled her eyes, spilling over faster than she could stop them.

"Hey, hey, hey—Lara." He was off the couch and on the floor beside her in a heartbeat, wrapping an arm around her shoulders as she shook against him. "Talk to me, love. What's this really about?"

Her breath shuddered, her fingers clawing at her own sleeves like she could hold herself together if she just held on tight enough. "Why?" she whispered, voice raw. "Why do I always pick the wrong ones, Luke?"

His heart twisted. "Wrong ones?" he echoed carefully.

"First you. Then Atul. And now... Sushil." His name fell from her lips like a confession.

Luke's stomach clenched. She buried her face in her knees, her words breaking apart into sobs. Luke rubbed a hand down his face, willing himself to stay calm. He stood, moved to the kitchen, and returned with a glass of water and a box of tissues. Whatever storm was coming, he was here for it.

She was staring into her empty wine glass when he sat back down. Her face was pale, her hands trembling. He gently took the glass from her and set it aside. "Here, drink some water for me, yeah?" His voice was soft, coaxing, like he was talking her back from a ledge. She obeyed, her hand brushing his as she took it. Luke sat beside her, close enough that their shoulders touched.

"You know," he said, "we may not be married, but you've always been my person, Lara. My favourite human, after Mum, of course." A weak chuckle escaped her, but it didn't reach her eyes. He turned to her, gentler now. "Atul was a disaster, and you know it. You walked away from that, Lara and you survived it. Look at what you've made for yourself. You've built this life, this home. All of it. Without him. You found your strength." Her head sagged against his shoulder, her breath unsteady. "But this chap, Sushil? I don't know him. You've never let me meet him. Which tells me something." She stiffened, but he pressed on, softly. "Love shouldn't make you feel like this, Lara. Like you're breaking apart. It shouldn't be a secret you have to guard so tightly that it's eating you alive."

Her voice was a whisper, barely there. "But I love him, Luke. I love him so much it hurts."

Luke's jaw locked, but he forced himself to stay still, stay present. "Then why are you here, crying on the floor, my lovely?" he asked, voice gentle but firm. "If he loves you back, truly, why this?"

Lara was silent, her hands twisting in her lap. Finally, she whispered, "Promise me you won't judge?"

Luke's heart ached at the fragility in her voice. "Never," he said. "Tell me."

She swallowed, the words scraping out of her. "He's married."

The silence that followed was thick and brutal. Luke inhaled sharply, but didn't move away.

"Unhappily married," she rushed on, desperate now. "They don't live like husband and wife. But because of his career, his kids—he can't leave."

Luke shut his eyes for a long second. "Can't? Or won't?" he said finally, and his voice was quieter now, but it carried an edge she couldn't miss.

Lara recoiled like he'd slapped her. "See?" she snapped, standing on shaky legs. "This is why I didn't tell anyone. Not you, not Papa, not *bua*. Because of that look—that tone. Like I'm some pathetic, home-wrecking idiot."

Luke stood too, but slower, holding his hands out as though to calm her. "Lara, no one thinks you're pathetic—"

"Don't they?" she bit out. "You don't know what it's like to love someone and never be able to have them, Luke."

He flinched. "Maybe not. But I know what it's like to lose yourself in someone who will never choose you back."

That gave her pause. "I just want something that's mine," she whispered. "Something real."

Luke's voice dropped to a whisper, his eyes searching hers like he was trying to reach the part of her that still trusted him. "Then why are you settling for crumbs, Lara?"

Her lips trembled before she broke, tears spilling down her cheeks unchecked. "Because crumbs are better than nothing." Her voice cracked.

Something in Luke's chest twisted painfully. "No, Lara." He took a step toward her, as if sheer proximity could make her believe it. "You deserve the whole damn cake. You deserve to be chosen—loudly, proudly. Not hidden away like you're something to be ashamed of."

She flinched as though his words had struck her, arms wrapping around herself. "You don't understand," she whispered, shaking her head.

"Then help me. Help me understand," he pleaded, reaching out, but she was already pulling back, swiping at her tears with angry hands.

"There's no point," she rasped, her voice raw. "You've already made up your mind, haven't you?"

"Lara—"

But she cut him off with a sharp shake of her head, swallowing down a sob. "I'm going to bed."

The words felt like a slammed door, final and cold. Luke stood frozen in the wreckage of their perfect evening. What had he done? Hadn't he promised not to judge and then done exactly that? Hadn't he promised to be a safe space and then gone and betrayed that trust? *What had he done?*

The next morning, they played pretend. Pretending that nothing had happened the night before. That no words had been spoken that couldn't be taken back. No revelations that had unleashed a tsunami of sorts.

Lara stood at the stove, flipping pancakes with mechanical precision, her back to him. Her voice was too bright, too brittle when she asked, "Lemon and sugar, or Nutella?"

Luke sat at the table, watching her, feeling like a stranger in a place that had once felt like home. "Whatever you're having," he said lightly, as though the right choice of topping might patch over what had broken.

They moved through the motions, pouring coffee, passing plates, like actors stuck in a scene neither of them wanted to be in. Luke filled the silence with shop talk, his voice steady as he recited the dry details of union life. But he kept to the surface, never letting her see the undercurrents swirling beneath.

It couldn't last. When their plates were empty, Lara set her fork down with a deliberate clink and looked at him, all false brightness gone. "So," she said, her voice cool and sharp-edged, "how are the contract negotiations going? From what I hear... not so great."

Luke stilled. There was something in her tone—something that cut. "That's not true," he said, carefully neutral. "You know how long these things take. It's complicated, Lara. And people love to speculate when they don't know the whole picture."

Her smile was tight, humourless. "Right. Speculate. Like the rumours that the union's going to fold. Again. That you've already made a deal behind closed doors."

Luke set down his coffee cup with precision, as though focusing on that tiny task would keep him steady. "Where are you hearing this?"

She gave a casual shrug, but her eyes didn't leave his. "I fly more than you do, Luke. I hear things."

For a long moment, he didn't speak. When he did, his voice was low. "People are angry. I get that. But turning on each other isn't the answer. The company wants us divided. You know that."

Lara leaned forward, her gaze sharp enough to cut through glass. "Or maybe," she said softly, "people are tired of trusting leaders who've forgotten what it's like out there."

Luke swallowed, the accusation hitting harder than he expected. "Is that what you think? That I've forgotten?"

Her eyes flickered, just for a second, but she held his gaze. "I think anyone can be bought, Luke."

Silence followed.

He stared at her, something dark unfurling in his chest. "Bought." The word tasted bitter on his tongue. "That's what you think of me?"

She didn't flinch. Didn't look away. "Corruption exists every-where," she said. "Even in places you think are safe."

And there it was—the line they had never crossed now drawn thick between them.

Luke pushed back his chair, standing slowly, carefully, as though afraid anything faster would shatter what was left. "I think I should go," he said, voice tight. He gathered their plates, rinsing them with clinical detachment, avoiding her eyes. Moving around her kitchen like a stranger. She didn't stop him. Didn't say a word as he grabbed his coat and bag.

At the door, he hesitated, hand on the knob, but she stayed rooted to the spot, arms crossed over her chest like armour. When he stepped outside, the cold air hit him like a slap, but it still didn't shake the weight pressing on his chest. Is this what she really believed? That he could be bought? That everything he stood for—the fights, the sacrifices—meant nothing?

The drive home felt endless, but not long enough to unravel the knot inside him. Was this about last night? About Sushil? About her own guilt? Luke gripped the wheel tighter as memories tumbled over each other—years of friendship, of trust built and rebuilt—and now, what? Reduced to this?

He had known Lara for most of his life. Known every version of her. But this woman, the one who had sat across from him and questioned the very core of who he was, felt like a stranger. Was it independence that had turned her brittle? Or heartbreak? Or something worse—fear?

But even now, even angry, he couldn't turn away from her completely. She had stood by him when he had nothing left to give, when he was at his lowest ebb. Letter after letter confirming that someone still cared and would always care. And though everything inside him screamed to walk away, to protect himself from the hurt, he knew he wouldn't. Not really. Not yet. He would give her space. Let her lash out if she needed to. But he wasn't done. Lara might have given up on herself, but he never would.

As for Sushil Nair, Luke would find out who he really was. If Lara couldn't protect herself, he damn well would. Because love—true love—wasn't about walking away when things got hard. It was about staying. Fighting. Even when the other person didn't want you to. Even when it hurt. And for Lara, he would fight to the end of time.

"I think you're due a break. And don't you want to visit all the cats we've got right now? Check out the business you've invested in, hey?" Sue's voice was warm and grounding, an antidote to the strange, combative weekend he'd just had with Lara.

Luke exhaled, pressing the phone closer to his ear. "You just want me there for your debauched anniversary weekend, don't you?"

Sue laughed. "Truer words were never spoken. Matt and Alan can't wait to see you. It's been way too long, Luke."

And it had.

In the early days, after his breakup with Harry, he had visited Sue and her family often, watching as their little bungalow and cattery took shape after the refurbishments. He had loved seeing Sue find her purpose, loved the quiet rhythm of the place, the cats winding themselves around his ankles. It had reminded him of Shakespeare, the cat Harry had taken when he'd left, citing Luke's job as a flight attendant as the reason.

Investing in the cattery had been a smart financial move, bringing in a small side income, but that wasn't why he had done it. He had done it to give Sue a leg up, to help the girl who had never once resented his change of heart. Which was why Lara's words still stung, long after she had said them. Did she really think so little of him?

He shook his head, pushing the thought aside. "I'll be there, with bells on. And tell Alan I've got a new jigsaw puzzle for him. He's going to love this one."

Later, at the union office, buried in casework, he let the noise of the job drown out the noise in his head. Work had become his refuge. The one place where the loneliness of his life couldn't touch him. Despite everything, flying kept his social side alive. The union work gave him purpose—a sense of service, of fighting for something bigger than himself. But there were still too many evenings when the weight of his life pressed down on him.

No partner. No siblings. His mother planning to move abroad. And now, a rift with his closest friend. No matter how much he tried to fill his time—with work, books, television, swimming—the loneliness remained. It sat at the core of him, a constant ache. A longing for someone to share his life with. Someone to love and protect. Someone who would love and care for him in return.

But people like that were scarce. Workplace relationships were out of the question—his position made that impossible. And the few men he had met? None were interested in anything lasting. So much was written about women struggling to find love, but the irony was that, as a man, he was just as lonely as any middle-aged single woman.

His thoughts drifted to Lara. She hadn't reached out, and he didn't expect her to. Lara was stubborn. She saw him as the opposition now, and she would dig her heels in. He still planned to message her on her birthday, but he doubted she'd respond.

With a sigh, he turned back to the case in front of him—a flight attendant accused of being rude to a premium passenger. A classic case of "he said, she said," where the only defence was an unblemished work record and a desperate attempt to fight off yet another character assassination of the accused.

He rubbed his temples. Lately, this job drained him in a way it never used to before. The lines between right and wrong had blurred. There was ugliness on both sides of the board—greed replacing integrity, viciousness replacing humility, forgiveness and compassion long since forgotten. What was he in all of this? A cog in the machine? The very people he fought for thought little of him, quick to believe the worst, to spread rumours that undermined everything he had worked for tirelessly. And then there was the nagging suspicion—the one he had pushed away for far too long.

Neil had left not long after recruiting him, moving on to a cushy position higher in the union hierarchy. Had Luke been pulled into this just to make way for Neil's departure? A convenient replacement? The thought had lingered in the back of his mind for years, but lately, it had been resurfacing more and more. Now he wondered, if he walked away, would someone else already be waiting in the wings to take his place?

He shook his head again. It didn't matter. Right now, there was work to do. And so, with the weariness of a man who had long stopped expecting gratitude, Luke buried himself in the case and got back to it.

Diving

On his day off, Luke craved the rhythm of water, the solitude only swimming could offer. He had spent the morning deep in an internet spiral, scouring every detail on Sushil Nair. Now, he needed to clear his head. Stroke after stroke, he cut through the shimmering blue, but his thoughts refused to settle.

Sushil Nair wasn't just anyone. A former investigative journalist turned media mogul, a man who built his career exposing corruption. On paper, his reputation was impeccable. In photos, he was the kind of sharp-suited, intense-eyed handsome that attracted both admiration and scandal. Married to his college sweetheart, Kalyani, a respected academic, with two children. Their dignified magazine spreads painted the picture of a perfect life. So where did Lara fit into it?

Luke had sensed something was off for years—casual mentions of Sushil, unfinished sentences that left ripples which never quite settled. This wasn't just an old friend. Lara had been invested in this man long before she admitted it. But until last night, it had never even crossed Luke's mind that Sushil was still married. He had assumed, wrongly, that Lara wouldn't entangle herself in something so obviously doomed.

Reaching the end of the pool, Luke gripped the edge, chest heaving. Had she known? Of course she had. Lara wasn't naïve. She'd seen the same articles, the same photos. So why walk into something bound to hurt?

He felt for her. He knew how deeply she longed for love, for someone to choose her. Didn't he long for the same? But surely she was smart enough to know that, to a married man, she'd only ever be the bit on the side.

He hauled himself out of the water, feet skimming the surface as he sat at the edge. Love was blind. God, he knew that better than anyone. Hadn't he let Harry string him along for years—hidden away like an afterthought, waiting for a future that never arrived? Maybe this was Lara's version of that same helpless waiting.

The truth was, it wasn't just concern driving him. It was fear. Fear of losing her. Of watching her waste herself on someone who would never choose her the way she deserved. He stood, rolled his shoulders, as if that might shake the thoughts loose. But they followed him to the showers, thick and clinging, like the steam in the air.

Had she really chosen this of her own free will? And if she had, how was he supposed to stand by and watch her drown?

On his way out of the gym, he nearly walked past Anne, Christine's neighbour, before her cheerful voice broke through his haze. "Luke! Do you know when Christine and Frank are back? I think I killed one of her plants!"

He forced a polite smile. "In a few days, Anne."

As she rambled about wilted leaves and watering schedules, Luke barely absorbed a word. His mind was elsewhere, circling the same relentless question: Was it even his place to interfere? And yet, what kind of friend did nothing while someone they loved ran headlong into heartbreak?

Exhaustion hit him in a fresh wave. God, he needed to get away.

Not just to Lexi's or Sue's cottage, but far, far away. Somewhere untouched, where the weight of other people's lives wasn't his to carry. A place where he could breathe, where silence wasn't filled with worry.

As Anne's voice faded behind him, the ache inside him deepened. He thought of the time after Steve's death, when the world had lost all colour, when days had blurred into endless, sleepless nights.

This was different. Not just emptiness, but a mind caught in a vice—restless and unyielding. A storm without pause. The same questions, the same names, the same ghosts circling like vultures: Lara, Jim, Christine, Harry.

When would his thoughts stop devouring him from the inside? When would the noise let go?

On Lara's birthday, Luke sat staring at his phone longer than he cared to admit, before finally typing out the message he'd sent every year without fail.

Happy Birthday, Lara! Hope you have a lovely day. x

Short. Light. No drama. A message a friend would send. A friend trying to pretend nothing had fractured between them. He hit send, exhaled slowly, and waited, though he already knew there'd be nothing coming back.

As expected, silence. Still, he checked her roster anyway, a ridiculous habit he couldn't shake. She wasn't flying. So, she was in town, ignoring him. Luke sighed, his chest tightening in that now-familiar way. Shoving the phone face-down on his desk, he turned back to his case files, willing himself to concentrate.

At noon, Lisa, his second-in-command, breezed into the office, sharp-eyed as ever. She took one look at him, really looked, and tossed her bag onto a chair.

"Right," she announced, hands on hips. "We're going out for lunch. Now. And you're leaving that damn phone behind."

Luke blinked, startled. "I'm fine—"

"Liar," she cut him off smoothly. "Come on, Brown. I've got tuna sarnies from Marks, and you're going to sit in the sun and pretend to enjoy them. Doctor's orders."

With a reluctant smile, he gave in, following her out into the unexpected warmth of a May afternoon. Even as they unwrapped their sandwiches and sipped on the coffee Lisa had brought, Luke had to admit that this was a good idea. There was something about the breeze on his face and the quiet hum of life around them that made the world feel a little less heavy.

Lisa soon had him laughing as she regaled him with stories of her wild, mischievous son and the chaos he left in his wake. For a little while, Luke let himself forget—forget about Lara, forget about everything weighing on him.

As they finished, Lisa pulled out a cigarette, lighting up with a contented sigh. She leaned back, watching him through narrowed eyes. "So," she said, exhaling a trail of smoke, "when's your next flight?"

Luke stretched, glancing up at the sky. "Not till June."

"Where to?"

"Sydney."

Her eyes lit up. "Ooh, jackpot. Ka-ching!"

He smirked. Sydney was the big money trip, one everyone fought to get on the roster. He knew Lisa, still climbing the seniority ladder, rarely got a shot at one. "What are you flying next month?" he asked casually.

She rolled her eyes. "The usual. Washingtons."

He hesitated for a beat, then said lightly, "Want to trade?"

Lisa blinked. "What? My Washington for your Sydney? Are you mad? You'll lose a fortune in per diem!"

Luke shrugged, forcing a grin. "I don't mind. Done enough of them over the years. And honestly, I don't envy you the jet lag."

For a moment, she stared at him, cigarette halfway to her lips. Studying him. Then she smiled, soft and a little sad. "You know, Brown, you're one of the good guys. Don't let anyone tell you differently."

Luke looked away, blinked hard and pretended to be distracted by a bird on the fence nearby. "Thanks, Lis," Luke chuckled, gathering up their empty sandwich wrappers and coffee cups before walking over to the nearest bin. As he tossed everything in, he added with a wry smile, "Come on, back to the grind."

By the time the office clock crept toward five p.m., Luke rubbed his eyes and glanced at his phone out of sheer habit. And there it was. A message from Lara.

Thanks, Luke. Sorry about the other day. Are you free to come to dinner tomorrow? Sushil is in town and I'd really like you to meet him. xx

For a moment, his heart stopped, then thudded heavily in his chest. Of all the things she could have said, this was not what he had expected. This casual invitation, the equally casual dismissal of what had happened. He stared at the screen, reading it twice, three times, as if the words would rearrange themselves into something else. Something easier to comprehend. Carefully, he set the phone down on the table beside him, rubbing his jaw, thinking.

She'd sent it at 2:15 p.m. and it was nearly three hours later. Knowing Lara, she'd probably been agonising over his silence, checking her phone a dozen times, wondering if she had pushed him too far to come back. He ran a hand through his hair, exhaling slowly, torn between relief and fresh confusion.

So she wanted him to meet this man, this Sushil Nair. The man they had fought over not so long ago, the man that he had done a background check on just a few days ago. Luke wasn't sure what twisted in his gut—curiosity, jealousy, or protectiveness. He stared at the message a moment longer, weighing his response like it was a live grenade in his hand. Finally, he typed, fingers slower than usual, as though each word carried a thousand things unsaid:

Can't wait. x

And the thing was, he really couldn't wait. Because behind all his calm politeness, questions burned. Questions he'd been harbouring for a long, long time. What was it about this man that had made Lara abandon reason, doubt herself, and risk everything? What had made her pull away from him, from the one person who had always stood by her? And most of all, was this Sushil really worth it?

Luke leaned back in his chair, staring out the window at the darkening sky, knowing tomorrow might give him those answers, but not knowing if he was ready to hear them. Still, he'd be there. Because when it came to Lara, he always showed up.

———————

Luke stood outside the little Italian restaurant Lara had chosen, brushing invisible lint from his jacket, stalling for time. When he finally stepped inside, he spotted them immediately. Lara was laughing. Laughing in the way she used to, full and bright, her face alight in a way Luke hadn't seen for months. And across from her, a man who could only be Sushil Nair, watching her like she was the only thing that mattered in the world.

He was better-looking in person than in the carefully curated photos online. Salt-and-pepper hair, sharp dark eyes, but softened by a lazy, warm smile, the kind that made people want to confide, to trust, to believe. Luke hesitated. This was what Lara looked like when she was genuinely happy, like the unguarded, radiant girl he used to know before life had bruised her in places no one could see. Then she spotted him, and her face lit up with pleasure and a smidgen of relief. Had she thought he wouldn't show up?

"Luke!" she called, rising to embrace him. There was a question in her hug: *Do you forgive me?*

"Hey, beautiful," he murmured, pulling her close in a brief, tight squeeze, holding on just long enough to let her know: *Yes. Of course I do.* But forgiveness, he knew, was a complicated currency. And tonight, they were spending it recklessly.

When he pulled away, Sushil was already on his feet, extending a hand. "You must be the famous Luke," Sushil said, his smile disarming, genuine. "I've heard so much about you."

"All lies, I'm sure," Luke replied, gripping his hand firmly, measuring, calculating. *Who are you really?*

They sat. Menus arrived, but Lara barely looked at hers, too busy leaning into Sushil, too busy smiling like the world was right again. Sushil's eyes rarely left her.

"Lara tells me you've travelled the world," Sushil said, settling back with an effortless, almost feline grace. "I envy that. These days, I barely get out of Delhi unless it's to do with work."

"Perks of the job, I guess," Luke said with a faint smile. "Though now you're more likely to find me buried in union paperwork than on a jumpseat."

"You still fly, though?" Sushil pressed. "There's something liberating about flying, isn't there?"

Luke chuckled. "Half the time it's just hotels and airports. Less glamorous than it looks."

Sushil smiled, thoughtful. "Still. There's something about moving through different worlds. I think it makes people wiser, more aware, you know?" His eyes rested on Luke, steady and searching. "You strike me as someone who's seen way more than you'll ever say."

Something in the way he said it, soft and perceptive, unnerved

Luke more than he wanted to admit. Lara was watching them closely, anxiety flickering behind her smile. Luke caught her gaze and gave a small, reassuring nod.

As the evening unfolded, Luke found himself reluctantly charmed. Sushil was everything he wanted to resent—articulate, witty, thoughtful—but he never dominated, never bragged. He asked Luke about his work, actually listened, and didn't once mention his own awards or reputation, though Luke knew of them. Against his will, Luke found himself laughing over ravioli and red wine, drawn in by Sushil's sharp humour and easy way with words. But even as he laughed, his eyes kept catching the small moments—the way Sushil's hand brushed over Lara's, the way she leaned in too close, how her eyes clung to him like he was her everything. God, she was in deep. Really deep.

Throughout dinner, Luke watched. Not just with his eyes, but with every instinct honed by years of witnessing human complexity. Sushil was dangerous not because he was malicious, but because he was magnetic. At one point, Sushil stepped away to take a call, and Lara leaned in, eyes searching his.

"So?" she whispered.

Luke took a breath, feeling that familiar weight in his chest. "He's... impressive," he said finally. "I can see why you—" he caught himself, softening it, "—why anyone would be drawn to him."

A small smile touched her lips, but it didn't reach her eyes. "I know what you're thinking," she murmured.

"Do you?" he asked, gently.

She didn't answer.

Before he could say more, Sushil returned, apologising with that same warm smile, sliding back into place as if he belonged there, as if he belonged to her.

Later, Sushil shared stories from his reporting days: near misses, exposed scandals, hard-won victories. Even Luke leaned in, caught up in the tales of facing danger and corruption with nothing but words, research and truth. But beneath it all, Luke couldn't stop wondering: where does Lara fit in all this? Where is there room for her?

When the bill came, Sushil waved away Luke's attempt to split it. "Next time, you can get it," Sushil grinned. Next time. As if this were the start of something.

Outside, under the cool night sky, Sushil clasped Luke's shoulder warmly. "I'm really glad to have met you," he said, meaning it. "Lara's always said you're the one who knows her best."

Luke smiled back, but something inside him twisted. "Likewise," he said. But the word felt false in his mouth.

As Sushil turned to say something soft to Lara, Luke watched them. The way she leaned into him, the way Sushil's gaze lingered too long, too tender. And just like that, the night felt colder. Luke had known men like Sushil. Men caught between two worlds, wanting both, but unable or unwilling to commit to either. And Lara was right there in the middle, hoping for a miracle.

As they walked to their cars, Lara brushed Luke's arm. "Thank you for coming," she murmured.

Luke smiled, though it tugged at something deep inside him. "Anytime, love."

And he meant it. He would always be there. Whether it was to pick up the pieces when it all came crashing down or to celebrate her joy *if* it all came together. For all her brave smiles, he knew that tonight, this whole dinner, had been about showing him he still mattered. That his opinion mattered to her. Greatly.

As he drove home, her words echoed in his head: "I know what you're thinking."

Maybe they were both thinking the same thing. Because no matter how much Luke liked Sushil, the truth gnawed at him incessantly: this was going to end in heartbreak. And deep down, maybe Lara knew it, too.

The next Friday, Luke drove down to the New Forest, a familiar longing tugging at him as the trees thickened around the road. He was eager to see Sue, Matt, and Alan, the family he wished he'd been blessed with. Though they always insisted he was part of them, he knew the truth: their life was a kind of normal he could only visit but never truly belong to.

Still, whenever the world felt heavy, this was where he ran to. They had never once let him down. There was always a bed made up, a place set at the table. He had lost count of how many times Sue had called, saying, "Just get in the car and come."

As he pulled into their driveway, Luke took in the life they'd built —a cozy three-bedroom bungalow with an attached cattery and a little granny annexe they let out as an Airbnb. Simple, sturdy, and full of love. Between their small businesses and Matt's work as a care home nurse, they had carved out something real, something lasting.

Sue had walked away from flying without a backward glance, content to sink roots deep into this quiet corner of England—roots Luke had never quite put down for himself.

The front door flung open before he'd even switched off the engine. Sue barrelled toward him, arms wide, her face glowing with that familiar mischief. She'd softened around the edges—a little rounder, a little slower—but the peace in her eyes suited her. She looked like a woman who had fought some battles and finally gotten to the other side.

"Luke!" she squealed, pulling him into a fierce hug. "Will you stop getting more handsome? Honestly, it's rude at this point."

He laughed, holding her tight, allowing himself to relax. "You're not looking too bad yourself, pumpkin," he teased, ruffling her hair as they headed inside.

"Matt and Alan are picking up the last bits for tomorrow's party. Thank God," she grinned over her shoulder. "Means I get you all to myself for a bit. G&T?"

"Tea first," he grinned, handing her a bag of gifts. "But let me get this lot out of the way." He set the packages on the kitchen table, ticking them off like a list: "Cotton pyjamas from India, as ordered. Czech crystal vase for your anniversary—don't argue. A puzzle for Alan. I want to give that to him myself. And a bottle of whisky for Matt."

Sue put her hands on her hips, mock glaring at him. "Luke. I asked for pyjamas, not half a suitcase. You could've just brought a bunch of flowers."

"Well, now you've got a nice vase to put them in." He smirked. "Come on, put the kettle on, love. I'm parched from that drive."

An hour later, they sat in the warm kitchen, a space that smelled of tea and toast and home. They caught up on the months they hadn't seen each other, filling the air with uninhibited laughter and conversation that didn't need effort.

Luke dipped a biscuit in his tea and gave her a pointed look. "You know, you could come see me sometime."

Sue snorted. "And leave all my babies? No chance. Speaking of which—" she stood abruptly, her grin widening. "Come on. I want you to see them." He swallowed the last of his tea and followed her out the back door.

The garden was already dressed for the next day's celebration. Streamers were dancing in the breeze and balloons nodding on their strings. They walked along a narrow path that curved around the house, leading toward the cattery. Luke paused for a moment, taking it all in—this life she had built, filled with love and small joys. A life that felt like a balm to the chaos inside him.

There were six cats in their various pens, and as Sue opened the mesh doors and coaxed each one out, murmuring soft words and stroking their fur, Luke stood back and watched, a slow warmth seeping into him. She moved with such care, her hands gentle, her voice full of affection. Watching her like this, completely in her element, made him happy for her. When she finally turned and deposited a scruffy old tabby into his arms, he chuckled as its whiskers brushed his cheek.

"Well, aren't you a handsome old boy," he murmured, letting the cat nestle against him.

Sue beamed, as if he'd just paid her the compliment. "That he is. Took me a week to win him over."

They lingered there for a while, making sure each cat had been fed and fussed over, until finally Sue said, "Come on, let's get back inside."

As they walked through the garden, past the bobbing balloons and streamers, Luke glanced sideways at her, a smile tugging at his lips. "You love this, don't you?"

Sue's grin was easy and full of joy. "Completely. I've found my calling, Luke. If it wasn't for the husband and kid, I'd be that crazy cat lady without a second thought."

Luke laughed. "Who'd have thought, eh? When I first met you—all wild hair, leather jacket, cigarettes—this is not where I pictured you ending up."

Sue grinned, bumping her shoulder into his. "Yeah, well. Life has a funny way of sorting itself out. Speaking of which..." She turned to eye him carefully. "What about you? How's work? Anyone on the horizon, love-wise?"

Luke bent down to pry a leaf from his shoe, avoiding her gaze. "Work is... draining. And love?" He straightened up, exhaling hard. "Non-existent. Honestly, Sue? I feel lost."

Her brow furrowed. "Lost?"

He gave a small, helpless laugh, but there was no humour in it. "I'm nearly fifty, Sue. And some days I feel like I'm still wandering around in the dark, searching for something that makes all of this make sense. Like I've lived all these years and still... haven't figured out where I belong. Or what I'm for."

Sue stopped walking. He felt her eyes on him, sharp and clear. "Luke," she said quietly, "don't you dare think like that."

He swallowed, but stayed silent.

She stepped closer, her voice firm but kind. "Listen to me. You don't see what the rest of us see. You never have. You think because you don't have some picture-perfect life—a house, a partner, all of that—that it means you don't matter. But, babe, you matter so much. You are one of the kindest, most generous people I've ever known. You show up for people. You listen. You love, without asking for anything in return. And that's rare, Luke. It's precious. More precious than you'll ever realise."

Her words hit something raw inside him. He blinked against the sting in his eyes, unsure how to respond.

Sue smiled gently, softening her tone. "You're you, Luke. And if you don't know what you bring to the table, let me be the one to remind you—it's more than enough."

For a moment, neither of them spoke. The only sound was the distant purr of a cat in the cattery behind them and the breeze catching the streamers overhead. Luke took a shaky breath, finally meeting her gaze. "Thank you," he whispered, his voice hoarse.

She looped her arm through his and squeezed. "Come on. Let's go make those G&Ts now."

Much later, long after the last slices of pizza were gone and the wine bottle stood empty on the table, after Luke had spent an hour bent over the jigsaw puzzle with Alan while Matt and Sue sat curled together by the fire, after Alan had trudged off to bed saying goodnight in his usual clipped way, and Matt had followed with a yawn and a stretch, Luke found himself alone on the couch with Sue, each cradling a glass of brandy.

The fire cracked and spat softly, casting golden shadows on the walls.

"I hope I don't wake up with a hangover," Luke said, swirling the amber liquid. "I rarely drink this much."

Sue grinned over the rim of her glass. "Don't worry. I'll make you the biggest fry-up known to man. It'll soak it all up."

Luke chuckled, leaning back, letting the warmth of the fire penetrate his bones. "You're terrible for my figure. And my arteries, you wicked moo."

She laughed, but he caught her watching him. He glanced back at the fire. "Alan seemed... easier with me tonight. I thought he might be a bit more standoffish, given how long it's been."

Sue's face softened. "He remembers you, Luke. He's sharp as a tack, you know that. And he's always been clear about who gets in and who doesn't." She smiled. "You're in."

Luke swallowed, something tightening in his throat. "And school?" he asked quietly, not quite meeting her eyes. "Still okay?"

For a moment, she stared into the fire, her fingers absently tracing the rim of her glass. "It's better," she said finally. "Much better. He's calmer now. Settling in. But God, in the beginning..." She exhaled, shaking her head. "It nearly broke us, Luke. You know how it was. Trying to find a place that would take him as he is, not try to force him into something he's not."

Luke nodded, the memory of those desperate phone calls still sharp in his mind.

"The cats help," Sue added, her face softening with a smile. "He loves them—feeding them, talking to them. It's like they speak his language in a way people don't. That's part of why I wanted this life. This house, the cattery, all of it. For him." She turned to him, her eyes suddenly bright with emotion. "And you made that possible, Luke. Don't shrug it off. You helped us when we couldn't see a way through. I'll never forget that."

Luke shifted uncomfortably. "It wasn't a big deal."

"It was everything," she said firmly, reaching over to squeeze his hand.

He looked down at her hand on his, swallowing hard. "More brandy?" he offered, voice a little too light, reaching for distraction.

Sue leaned back, watching him over the rim of her glass, eyes thoughtful. Then, casually, she asked, "Any news of Lara?"

Luke turned to her, surprised. "Lara? Why do you ask?"

Sue gave a small shrug, her eyes narrowing slightly, a smile playing on her lips. "Oh, you know... I like to keep tabs on the competition."

He let out a soft laugh. "Competition? Come on, Sue. What are you talking about?"

She gave him a look, half teasing, half serious, and reached over to tap his arm. "Don't play dumb. She was always your girl, Luke. Long before me, and long after too, if we're being honest. Not that I mind. As long as Matt keeps me at the top of his list, I'm not too hard done by."

Luke shook his head, a hollow laugh escaping him. "She was never *my* girl, Sue. You know that."

Sue tilted her head, watching him like she could see right through him. "Maybe not on paper. But in your heart? Whole different story."

He looked away, staring into the fire.

Sue leaned forward, softer now. "I liked her, you know. That one time I met her. Beautiful, in a quiet way. Like she didn't even know it."

Luke smiled faintly. "She's not a girl anymore, Sue. She's... a woman now. With her own life and her own mind."

Sue sipped her drink, studying him over the glass. "I see her on Facebook sometimes. She doesn't look all that different to me. Still has that glow about her. That Indian skin doesn't age, does it?"

Luke laughed again, but there was a sadness in it. "Did you know I've got Indian blood too?"

Sue blinked, surprised. "No! You've never told me that."

He leaned back, swirling the brandy, a ghost of a smile on his lips. "Yeah... My grandmother was Anglo-Indian. A fact no one in the family talked about much until my mum went digging. Years ago, she took off to India on what I thought was a wild goose chase, but she came back with stories that shook up everything we thought we knew."

"Gosh! Want to spill?" Sue rubbed his hand between both of hers, waiting for him to go on.

Luke took a slow sip of his brandy, the firelight catching the shadows on his face. "You know... my grandmother never talked about her past. Not a word. And now I know why."

Sue leaned in, her brow furrowed. "Why?"

Luke exhaled, a heavy sound. "Because she felt... unwanted. She was abandoned as a baby—left on the steps of an orphanage in Shimla. She was just a few weeks old when a childless English couple adopted her. Raised her like their own. But I think," he paused, "I think that part of her always believed she was never good enough to be wanted."

Sue's eyes softened, her grip tightening on his hand. "Christ, Luke..." she whispered. "That's heartbreaking."

He nodded, staring into the middle distance. "It was Mum who went digging. Traced old records at the orphanage. And that's when she found something, well, a rumour, really. The story was that my grandmother was the illegitimate child of a British soldier and the daughter of some important town planner. Scandalous back then. Apparently, the girl's family forced her to give up the baby."

Sue's eyes were wide now. She was utterly absorbed. "And that's why she was left at the orphanage?"

Luke gave a grim smile. "Yeah. But the saddest part? Years later, long after my grandmother had already been taken to England, her mother, the birth mother, came looking for her. But by then, it was too late. The trail ends there. An entire lifetime of searching for each other, and they never reconnected."

Sue let out a slow breath, shaking her head in disbelief. "Wow. That's... that's something else, Luke." She sat back, watching him, almost as if seeing him through fresh eyes. "And to think, all this time, that story was sitting in your veins."

Luke gave a soft, wry laugh. "Yeah. Funny, isn't it? A whole secret life under my skin and I never really thought much of it until recently. Now, I'm trying to fit all my pieces together like a jigsaw puzzle. Trying to figure out who I am, really."

Sue smiled, though her eyes were still shining with emotion. "You know what? I wish I had skeletons like that in my cupboard. Something exciting. Makes me feel like my lot's painfully ordinary."

Luke looked over at her, warmth in his eyes. "Ordinary? You? You're the most extraordinary person I know, darling."

She laughed, swatting his arm lightly, though her cheeks flushed. "Oh, shut up, you charmer. You always did know how to make a girl feel special."

The next day was a flurry of activity as they set up for the barbecue. Matt manned the grill, and Luke found himself roped into stringing up the last of the streamers while Alan meticulously arranged chairs and tables with such surgical precision that Luke couldn't help glancing at Sue, eyebrows raised. She caught his look and grinned, giving a helpless shrug that said, *Yep, that's just how he is!*

By the time the first guests trickled in, the garden looked stunning. Streamers swayed in the soft breeze, balloons bobbed like lazy clouds, and strings of fairy lights twinkled even in the afternoon sun. A banner stretched between two trees—'Fifteen Years'—fluttering proudly above the scene. Tea lights in little jars sat ready to be lit when dusk fell, and bright tablecloths brought bursts of colour to every corner.

Luke handed out flutes of Prosecco as people arrived, watching the ease with which neighbours greeted each other, laughter already spilling into the air. There was something about their warmth, their simplicity, that tugged at him—a life lived without the constant weight of overthinking, without the ache of never quite belonging. Why couldn't he be like that? Why couldn't life be that easy?

As he topped up a glass, a young man wandered into the garden, looking like he'd taken a wrong turn. He stood awkwardly near the entrance, scanning the crowd.

"Um, excuse me," the man said, his voice uncertain. "Is Sue around?"

Luke paused, eyeing him curiously. He was younger than everyone else there by at least a decade, if not two, his uncertainty marking him as an outsider.

"Yeah, over there." Luke nodded toward Sue, still wondering who he was and why he seemed so out of place.

But before he could dwell on it, one of Sue's regular clients, a jovial woman who always boarded her pampered Persian, pulled him into an animated conversation about her cat's latest antics. Still, as he laughed along, something about that young man's lost expression lingered at the edge of Luke's mind, like a puzzle piece that didn't quite fit.

Later, Luke found himself wedged between an elderly man fiddling absently with a hearing aid and the young stranger, who sat quietly, nursing his drink and avoiding eye contact. After several failed attempts to chat with his older neighbour, who only responded with polite but distracted nods, Luke turned to the young man on his left. "So," Luke ventured, offering a casual smile, "how do you know Sue and Matt?"

The young man shifted uncomfortably, fingers tugging at the corner of his napkin. "I don't. Not really." His voice was soft, hesitant, with a slight stammer that caught Luke off guard. "I'm just... staying at their Airbnb for a bit. Sue was kind enough to invite me."

Something about his quiet, uncertain manner, so different from the loud, confident people Luke was used to, made Luke pause. It was disarming. Refreshing, even. He studied the man discreetly: sandy hair that flopped into pale blue eyes, a sharp collarbone peeking out from an over-washed T-shirt. Easy to overlook, but there was a gentleness about him, something raw and unpolished.

"I'm Luke," he offered, extending a hand. "One of Sue's oldest friends, way back from when she was flying the skies as cabin crew."

The man looked at him then, properly, a flicker of surprise lighting up his face. "She was cabin crew?" His gaze wandered back to Sue as if seeing her for the first time in a new light. Then he caught himself and turned hurriedly back. "Sorry, I should've—um—I'm Ben. Ben Wallace." He reached out to shake Luke's hand, his grip tentative, his palm soft in a way that made Luke hesitate for half a second longer than necessary.

"What do you do, Ben?" Luke asked, curious despite himself.

Ben gave a half-hearted shrug, eyes darting away. "I'm an IT consultant. Or I was. Out of work right now. Looking for... something. Anything, really." His voice wavered slightly, and Luke caught the weight in those simple words. This was a man adrift. "My mum booked me into the Airbnb. Thought maybe getting away, being in nature, would help."

Luke's expression softened. "She wasn't wrong. Nature can work minor miracles when you let it."

Ben offered a faint smile, but it faltered before it reached his eyes. There was something shuttered behind it—a quiet damage, carefully concealed. Luke didn't press. He knew that look. He'd worn it once himself: wary, uncertain, always braced for the world to disappoint. It wasn't just empathy he felt, it was recognition. This was someone who moved through life at the edges, not because he liked the shadows, but because he'd learned the cost of the light. Someone who kept his pain folded neatly inside, where no one could touch it.

They sat in a kind of easy silence for a moment, a delicate thread of connection hanging between them. Luke found himself unexpectedly moved by Ben's presence. The vulnerability, the quiet courage it must've taken to show up to a stranger's party, to sit there while everyone else laughed and joked like old friends. Still, when Matt called him over to help at the barbecue, Luke rose, giving Ben a parting smile. But as he crossed the garden, he caught something that made his pulse falter—a quick glance from Ben, eyes lingering a second too long, before darting away. Was that interest?

Luke shook his head, laughing softly to himself as he skewered another piece of chicken. Don't be ridiculous, he chided himself. You're old enough to be his... well, not quite father, but close enough.

Still, every so often, as the evening wore on and the sky turned pink with dusk, Luke would look up and catch Ben watching him again. And every time, that unfamiliar tug in his chest grew just a little stronger. Was it real? Or was he simply seeing a reflection of his own loneliness in a stranger's eyes? Luke didn't know.

Was he brave enough to find out?

Lara (May 2020)

Sinking

Lara stood by the window, forehead resting against the cold glass, staring at a world that had once been alive. The street, once filled with children, laughter, and life, now lay silent. Parked cars like abandoned relics. The sky was clear, the air deceptively pure, but an invisible predator roamed—silent, merciless, slipping into lungs, reducing lives to numbers on a screen.

She hugged herself, as if that could ward off the fear. Too many were gone. Every news report was another tally of loss. Not just faceless statistics—mothers, fathers, friends. The world whispered the same command: Stay inside. Stay safe. Wait. But waiting meant loneliness, an emptiness pressing into her bones.

She flicked on the television, only to be met with exhausted doctors, overcrowded hospitals, elderly patients dying alone. Her stomach twisted. She shut it off. Was this how the world ended? Not with fire and fury, but with silence and separation?

Reaching for her iPad, she breathed in relief as Yash's face appeared—tired, older, but still warm with love.

"How are you, *beta*?"

"I'm fine, Papa," she lied.

He smiled, waving a trembling hand. "Rohini won't let me out. So I sit on the *barsati* and talk to the birds. A little *bulbul* visits every morning. I think it's Zin," he added softly. "Your mother comes back to see me."

Lara swallowed hard, forcing a smile. "That's beautiful, Papa." She didn't dare break his illusion. If it brought him comfort, who was she to take it away?

"Any word from the airline?"

She shook her head. "Still nothing. Just... waiting."

He studied her, then said quietly, "It will pass. The world is healing, *beta*. Finding a way to renew itself."

After they hung up, his words lingered. Was this renewal? Or was this some kind of reckoning? A silent storm rising against all the ways humanity had ravaged the earth?

She picked up her phone, scrolling through the messages she wished she hadn't sent. Twenty-three unanswered texts to Sushil. Each one more desperate than the last. She had called him once, just once. He had cut the call within two rings.

At first, she had reasoned with herself—he was trapped with his wife and children, what could he say? But as the silence stretched into weeks, it started to feel like abandonment. Had she been so easy to erase? A decade of stolen moments, of whispered promises, and all it took was a couple of months for him to disappear.

Her phone buzzed. Her breath caught. Sushil?

No. It was Luke.

> Morning, you. Just checking in. Hope you're hanging in there. Call me if you need to rant. x

A wry laugh slipped from her lips. Luke, faithful, kind Luke, who had messaged her every single day. The only person still reaching across to hold her steady. Beneath the comfort, though, she knew what he was thinking. *I told you, Lara. I told you he'd never choose you.*

She wiped at her eyes, swallowing the lump in her throat. She knew. She had always known. But knowing didn't make it hurt any less.

———————

The rain tapped against the window, tracing patterns down the glass like tears Lara was too numb to shed. She sat motionless, watching puddles swell, the grey sky pressing down. Once, she would have ignored a day like this—gym, coffee, idle chats. Now, the world was shuttered, and even her own voice felt unfamiliar.

She tugged at the frayed sleeve of the jumper she had worn for days. It smelled of stale perfume and pasta sauce. Her hair, limp and unbrushed, hung like a curtain she hadn't bothered to part. Only Papa and Luke saw her like this, their silent concern reflected in their eyes. Still, apathy clung to her like fog. *Move. Shower. Eat.* She told herself, but she remained anchored to the stillness.

Her phone flashed—a Zoom call with Shweta and Madhuri. The thought of feigning interest in homemade *rasmalai* and yoga made her cringe. What could she contribute when her life had ground to a halt? While they juggled kids, husbands, and lockdown woes, she sat in silence, a ghost in her own home. Yet, guilt nudged her. With a sigh, she dragged herself to the bathroom.

The mirror revealed a stranger with shadowed eyes, sallow skin, hair greasy and tangled. She had wasted away, appetite swallowed by indifference. She pressed trembling fingers to her cheekbone, splashed water on her face, and swiped on lipstick, a feeble attempt at normalcy. It wasn't much, but it would have to do.

Logging into Zoom, she forced a smile as their voices filled the room, bright and full of life.

"Oh my God, Lara! How are you holding up?"

"Lockdown might be extended!"

"I swear, if I have to homeschool my kids one more day—you're so lucky, Lara. Just you, your space!"

Lucky. The word twisted inside her. They had love, noise, people to care for. And she? She was drowning in silence. Forgotten by the man who had sworn he loved her. Too proud to lean entirely on the one friend who still reached for her.

When the call ended, relief flooded her, followed by an unbearable emptiness. She picked up her phone, scrolling out of habit. Nothing. No messages. No "thinking of you." No Sushil.

Her chest ached with the sharp sting of disappointment. It had been months. Yet, she kept hoping, as if staring at the screen long enough might summon him back. But the truth was clear: he wasn't coming. No heart emojis lighting up her nights, no secret whispers of "I miss you." The realisation hit like a slap. If he had wanted to reach her, he would have. If he had loved her, he would have found a way.

Shame crept in. The memory of a desperate night spent scouring the internet for traces of him. Hospitalised? Dead? No, he was fine. His Facebook still bore that moody black-and-white photo. His WhatsApp still said "busy". Life had never stopped for him. As if she had never existed.

Her fingers trembled as she set the phone down, throat tight with unshed tears. Why did she always choose the ones who put her last? What was broken within her that she kept sabotaging her own happiness?

Then, a ping. Her heart leapt, traitorous and desperate. But of course, it wasn't him.

Luke.

> Survived another day of staring at my walls.
> How about you? Wine o'clock yet? x

A watery smile tugged at her lips. Luke. The only one who hadn't disappeared. The only one who checked in, day after day. Blinking away tears, she stood, walked to the fridge, and pulled out a bottle of Sauvignon Blanc. Pouring herself a glass, she picked up her phone and typed:

> It is now. xx

She hit send, watching the message disappear into the ether. Then she took a sip of the wine and leaned her head back against the kitchen cupboard, the glass cool against her fingertips.

It was nearly two in the morning when Lara finally closed her iPad with a soft sigh. The screen went black, but her mind still whirred.

Luke had been urging her for weeks to watch 'Schitt's Creek'. "Watch it, Lara," he had insisted. "It's funny, silly, and heart-warming. It'll help you switch off from all this madness, even if just for a little while."

She had resisted for ages, telling herself she wasn't in the mood for comedy, but tonight she had finally given in, and to her surprise, she had devoured an entire season in one sitting.

At first, the characters had seemed ridiculous, like caricatures drawn too broad to care for. But as the episodes rolled on, their eccentricities, their brokenness wrapped in bravado, seeped under her skin.

She found herself smiling, even laughing aloud, an alien sound in the silence of her flat. For a brief, shimmering moment, she had remembered what it was like to feel light again.

But now, as she lay in the dark, her head against the pillow, the glow of that borrowed joy was already fading. She closed her eyes and clung to the feeling, as if she could summon those quirky, loving misfits back to hold the emptiness at bay.

Then her phone rang. Her heart shot straight to her throat. She snatched it off the bedside table, her breath already shallow as her eyes focused on the screen.

Atul. The name stopped her cold. She blinked, sure she must be imagining it. Atul hadn't called her in months, years even, family commitments taking their inevitable toll on their already tenuous bond. Save for the dutiful exchange of Christmas cards that felt more like habit than connection, she rarely heard from him these days. What on earth was he doing calling her at this hour?

Dread prickled her skin. "H...hello?" she answered.

There was a pause, and when Atul spoke, his voice was strange — distant and cracked. "Lara?"

"Yes, Atul, it's me. What's wrong? Are you okay?" Her body was already tense, her hands gripping the phone tight as worry surged through her. Despite everything that had transpired between them, there was still a part of her that cared for her ex-husband.

"It's Alex..." Atul's voice faltered, breaking on the name. "He... he died last night."

The words landed like a physical blow. "What?" Lara sat bolt upright, the iPad sliding off her lap and thudding to the floor. "What are you saying? What do you mean, he died?"

"They all got Covid, Lara... Uncle, Aunty, and Alex. They were all taken into hospital. ICU. The doctors tried everything. Uncle and Aunty pulled through somehow, but Alex... he didn't make it."

The room spun. "No, no, that's not—" Her words tumbled out in fragments. "He was... he was fine. He was young! He was healthy! How... how could this happen?"

"I don't know," Atul whispered. And then, in a voice so small it broke her heart, "I didn't know who else to call. You're the first person I thought of. He... he was always so fond of you, Lara. He always said..."

A sharp pang of guilt tore through her. Fond of her? She had spent years brushing Alex aside, dismissing him as a wannabe, someone who existed on the periphery of her life, someone she was connected to by blood, but not much else. And now, he was gone.

She swallowed hard, forcing herself to focus on Atul, to be steady for him when everything inside her was shaking. "Atul, I'm so, so sorry," she murmured, her voice thick with unshed tears. "I can't believe this. I... I don't know what to say. Are Uncle and Aunty... are they okay? I mean, as okay as they can be?"

"They're alive," Atul said quietly. "But broken. Their only son, Lara... gone."

A sob slipped from him, and Lara blinked furiously to keep her own tears at bay. She stayed on the line for as long as he needed, whispering words of comfort that felt hollow in the face of such staggering loss. When the call finally ended, she sat in bed, frozen, her hands clutching the phone. The duvet was pulled up to her chin, but she felt cold. So cold.

Alex. Dead.

The boy she had known since childhood. The boy she had chased around her grandmother's vast bungalow in Goa—gone. The grumpy teenager who had barely exchanged two words with her—gone. The man who had become the third wheel in her marriage with Atul— gone. How was this possible?

Her chest ached as she realised she couldn't even remember the last time she had spoken to him. A year? Longer? She leaned her head back against the wall, closing her eyes, and in the darkness, her thoughts became a tangled mess of sorrow and regret. She prayed for Alex's soul, for Uncle Jude and Aunty Roxanna, for anyone and everyone trying to survive this relentless storm. And as she lay there, one awful truth pressed down on her, heavier than the night itself:

nothing in this world was certain. Nothing was safe. And the people you thought would always be there could be snatched away in an instant.

———

"Happy BIG Birthday, Lara!" Luke's face filled the screen, cheerful and bright, a jarring contrast to the heavy fog in her chest. It was barely 7 a.m., and already her head throbbed from lack of sleep. "Your book should be arriving today. It's 'Girl, Woman, Other'. I've read it. Bloody brilliant. I think you'll love it."

Lara managed a smile, though she knew she looked a mess—eyes swollen, hair tangled like a bird's nest. But she didn't care enough to fix it, and part of her was sure Luke would see straight through her façade, anyway. And, of course, he did.

Luke's brow furrowed, concern seeping into his voice. "What's happened? Something's happened, hasn't it?"

There was no use pretending. The tears she had been holding back since dawn threatened to spill over. "I heard last night..." Her throat tightened around the words. "Alex died."

Luke's face froze, his eyes darkening with shock. "Alex? Your cousin? In India? How? Was it Covid?"

Lara nodded, unable to speak for a moment, biting her lip so hard she tasted blood.

"Oh, Lara..." Luke exhaled, shaking his head. "God, I'm so sorry. I don't even know what to say. Is there anything I can do? Anyone you need to call? Anywhere you need to get to?"

She shook her head, then said, "I have to start phoning everyone now. Papa first." She rubbed her temples, as if she could ease the pounding inside her skull. "It's just... horrible, Luke. I've been so wrapped up in my own misery these past months. So... so blind to what's happening outside of it. And now this. God, I should have called Alex, written to Uncle and Aunty. Something. Anything. Why didn't I?" Her voice cracked.

"Hey, hey—hush now, Lara," Luke's tone softened, but there was an insistent edge to it. "Don't do this to yourself. We're all just... trying to survive. You had no way of knowing. None of us did. And even if you had reached out — even if — this wasn't something you could have stopped from happening."

Lara swiped at her cheeks, her fingers trembling.

"Listen to me," Luke pressed on, his voice steady now, grounding her. "Make your calls. Talk to your dad. Then I want you to take a shower, get outside, even if it's just for ten minutes. The sun is shining, and I swear, Lara, even a bit of air will help. You can't stay locked up inside your head all day."

She nodded, swallowing down the lump in her throat.

"I'll call you this evening, alright?" he added gently. "We'll talk properly then. But for now, just breathe. One thing at a time."

"Okay," she whispered. "Okay."

Later, long after she had made the calls, Lara sat in silence, her phone still clutched in her hand. She had listened to Papa wish her a hollow happy birthday, his voice thick with grief, his eyes filled with helplessness. She had tried to console Uncle Jude, her own voice shaking as he broke down, his sobs raw and jagged. And in the background, Aunty Roxanna's wails had cut through the conversation, the sound of a mother's heartbreak so visceral that it had sent a deep chill through Lara.

It was only much later, when there were no more words to say, no tears left to shed, that Lara forced herself to move. Slowly, as though her limbs no longer belonged to her, she walked to the bathroom and turned on the shower. As the warm water sluiced her body, she leaned against the cold tiles and let it all come—wave after wave of grief, guilt, fear. Memories and regrets mingling together. She stayed there, letting the water hit her skin, her breath ragged in the steam. And slowly, as if the water were drawing the poison out of her, something inside began to shift. The emotions that had ambushed her, crippled her, now ran down her body along with the rivulets of water, circling the drain and disappearing, at least for now. She stayed under the shower until her skin began to prune, until the tension in her shoulders eased a fraction. When she stepped out, it felt like she had shed a part of the weight pressing down on her.

She dried off carefully, then she reached for a bright peach jumper, the boldest colour she had dared to wear in months, and slid it over her head. A pair of jeans followed, and sunglasses to shield her still-puffy eyes from the world. With a deep, deliberate breath, Lara stepped out of her apartment. The air hit her like a balm—crisp, cool, and alive. She inhaled deeply, filling her lungs, anchoring herself in the sensation of simply breathing. Then she slipped her mask on.

For one moment, she let her mind be empty. No thoughts of Sushil, of Alex, of anything beyond the sun on her skin and the feel of solid ground under her feet. Because today, she was alive. And in a world where so many had been snatched away without warning, she owed it to herself, and to them, to at least step outside, to feel the sky, to remember what it meant to be here.

Lara was surprised by how many people were out walking in the park. After months of solitude, it felt surreal, as if she'd stumbled into a different world. She vaguely remembered hearing that restrictions had been eased to allow outdoor recreation, but having been shut away in her own cocoon of grief and apathy, the sight of masked strangers cautiously weaving around one another to maintain distance still jarred her. It was a reminder that life, no matter how fragmented, was still pulsing on.

From the corner of her eye, she spotted a neighbour from two doors down, someone she hadn't spoken to in months, who lifted a hand and offered her a thumbs-up, a silent check-in across the distance. Lara returned the gesture, a small flicker of relief warming her chest. The world hadn't completely stopped.

She found a bench under a tree and sank into it. Above her, birds chattered in the branches, and she closed her eyes, tilting her face to the pale spring sun. Fifty. She had turned fifty today. Half a century of living, and yet she felt as though she had been sleepwalking through so much of it. This was the first birthday she had ever spent alone. No hugs, no cake, no clinking glasses. But after the devastation of hearing about Alex, she couldn't summon the energy to feel sorry for herself. Not anymore. Not when life had been so cruelly snatched from him.

Her phone had been buzzing relentlessly since morning, a strange, almost grotesque mix of birthday wishes and condolences, tangled together as though the universe itself was playing some bitter joke. She let the phone rest on her lap, her hands limp at her sides, as she gazed across the park.

A toddler wobbled on unsteady feet in front of her, falling down hard on his nappy-padded bottom. He blinked in surprise before bursting into tears, and his mother swept him up, cradling him close, soothing away his momentary heartbreak. Nearby, three young women laid down a picnic blanket, laughter spilling from them as they uncorked a bottle of Cava, sunlight catching on the sparkling wine. Lara watched them, unsure whether they were bending the rules. Unsure, and for once, uncaring. There was something comforting in their careless joy, something human in a way she had almost forgotten. For a moment, she let herself share in their warmth, if only as a spectator.

Eventually, her fingers drifted to her phone again, scrolling absentmindedly through messages. A tap here, a swipe there, until, without quite meaning to, she found herself staring at Kalyani Nair's Facebook page. The latest picture hit her like a punch. Kalyani, beaming beside her children. And Sushil. His face, too familiar, too intimate, smiling broadly, an arm around his family. "Glad for this time together," read the caption.

Lara's breath caught. Her fingers trembled as she set the phone down on the bench beside her, the ground suddenly tilting beneath her feet. So that was her answer. Without a word, with no explanation, Sushil had gone back to his life. The life she had never really belonged to. Whether guilt had finally caught up with him, or whether she had only ever been a pleasant diversion from his real world, Lara would never know. And for the first time, she realised it didn't matter anymore. What mattered was that she found her way back to herself. That she salvaged what remained of her pride, her dignity.

With a strange calm that surprised her, Lara picked up the phone again. Slowly, deliberately, she began deleting every trace of him. Old messages, photos, his number. One by one, like exorcising a ghost. She blocked him on social media. Erased the digital footprints of a love that had never really been hers to hold. By the time she finished, her hands no longer shook.

This is my gift to myself, she thought. Freedom.

Later that evening, as dusk painted the sky in soft lilacs and gold, she opened a bottle of champagne and poured herself a flute. The bubbles caught the light like tiny stars as she dialled Luke. His face appeared on the screen almost immediately, slightly flushed, his hair tousled as though he'd rushed to answer.

"Darling!" he exclaimed, a wide grin lighting up his face. "I was just about to call you. Ah! I see the bubbles are ready. Wait, wait, I need to get my glass."

She watched him disappear off screen for a moment, chuckling to herself despite everything. When he returned, holding his own glass aloft, he grinned.

"To the fabulous birthday girl," he said, raising his glass. "And listen, when all this craziness is over, I'm taking you to a beach somewhere. Proper celebration, no excuses. Deal?"

Lara smiled, a genuine smile this time. "Deal," she murmured. She lifted her glass, her voice warm but steady. "I want to raise a glass. To Alex, to memories, to surviving another year. And to you, Luke. You have no idea how much you mean to me."

His eyes softened. "And you to me, sweetheart. More than you'll ever know."

As they drank, something—a movement, a shadow—flickered in

the background of Luke's screen, and Lara tensed. Her eyes sharpened, focusing. "Is someone there with you?" she asked, trying to keep her voice light.

Luke hesitated, just a beat. "No," he said quickly, shifting in his seat. "Why do you ask?"

She hesitated. "I... I thought I saw someone. A shadow, maybe."

He laughed, a little too brightly. "Oh darling, that imagination of yours... always working overtime." She smiled faintly, but the unease gnawed at her. He was alone, wasn't he? Hadn't he always said he was?

As they ended the call, and Luke blew kisses at her with his usual flourish, Lara watched the now-dark screen, her reflection faintly visible in the glass. Maybe it was just her imagination, but then again, why did it feel like he hadn't been entirely honest with her? This was Luke. Her Luke. She was his Lara. The one person who knew every crack, every scar he carried, and he, hers. Hadn't they always prided themselves on that? On the fact that there were no secrets between them? Not after all these years and all they'd been through?

And yet, tonight, something had felt off. Like a window she hadn't known existed had suddenly cracked open, and for a fleeting second, she had glimpsed something, or someone, hidden beyond it.

Floating

May had been a month of contradictions. Sunshine and sadness, solitude and unexpected sparks of hope. Turning fifty had felt like an epiphany. Not a slow dawning realisation, but a sudden jolt, as though life had tapped her firmly on the shoulder and said: *You can do more. You can be more.* And now, as she sat at her kitchen table, shafts of morning light cutting through the half-open blinds, Lara scribbled furiously in her notebook—ideas, feelings, fragments of thoughts—doodles in the margins where her mind spun faster than her pen could keep up.

When the phone rang, she glanced at it, smiling as Luke's name flashed on the screen.

"Morning, gorgeous! How are we today?" His voice, cheerful and familiar, washed over her.

"Hey you," she greeted, flipping the notebook around so the camera could catch a glimpse of her chaotic brainstorming.

Luke squinted. "And what's all this madness? Planning a heist? A secret novel?"

She laughed. "No! I... I'm thinking of starting a podcast." The words tumbled out, half-terrified, half-thrilled to give voice to the idea that had been exploding in her head since the early hours of the morning.

Lara had always been a devoted listener of podcasts—some about wellness, others about mindfulness, all small rituals that made her feel anchored. Sushil used to chuckle at her habit of queuing one up before she cooked, calling it her "kitchen sermon." But now, something had shifted. An idea had risen from the quiet corners of her mind—unexpected, insistent. And for the first time in a long while, she felt it had weight. Purpose. Maybe even possibility.

Luke's brows shot up. "A podcast? Well, now you have my attention. What's it about?"

"Everything," she said, leaning forward, her eyes glowing. "Me. My life. The loneliness. The menopause rollercoaster. My heartbreaks, and how I've been navigating lockdown. And books. Travel— even if only in my mind right now. I was thinking of calling it 'Lockdown Life with Lara'. You know, like... a snapshot of this time."

Luke tilted his head, thoughtful. "Hmm. I like it, but..." He paused, as if tasting the idea. "I think you should call it 'Living Life with Lara'. Because, darling, the lockdown will end. But you? You're just getting started. Your voice is bigger than this moment."

Lara blinked, surprised by his quiet wisdom and the faith he placed in her. "You think I can do this?" she asked, her voice a little softer now, a sliver of doubt creeping in.

Luke didn't hesitate. "Lara, you absolutely can. This is gold. You know why? Because people are desperate for honesty. For authentic stories. You have both. You'll make them feel seen, like you always do for me. So yes, you must do this."

She smiled, warmth blooming in her chest. "God, Luke, when you say it like that, it feels possible."

"It is possible." He grinned. "And when you're a big podcast star, I'll be your loudest cheerleader."

"Whoa, whoa," she laughed, holding up her hands. "There's a ton to do first. I've been looking up online courses, podcast equipment, how to set up a home studio. It's a lot."

Luke waved a hand dismissively. "Mere semantics, love. You'll figure it out. I know you. And I'll be here, clapping and popping champagne when your first episode drops."

"Thank you, Luke," she whispered, the gratitude deep and real.

He beamed at her. "So, guess what? I've got news, too."

"Oh?" she leaned in, curious.

"They're talking about us flying again. Maybe by autumn!" His voice brimmed with hope. "It's not official, but... there's movement. It's happening."

"Luke! That's amazing!" Her heart swelled at the thought of things returning to normal. "God, I can't wait to get on a plane again. I want to go see Papa. And you and I—we have to do that holiday we've been dreaming about."

Luke chuckled. "Easy, tiger. Let's get through the next few months first. But yes, there's light at the end of this long, dark tunnel."

They shared a quiet moment, both thinking of the loved ones they longed to see.

"You know," Lara said, her voice softer, "I've been so wrapped up in my mess that I never asked—how have you been coping? I know books and TV help, but what about swimming? You've always said that was your meditation."

Luke's smile faltered just a touch. "No swimming. And yeah, I miss it like hell. But this whole thing has put life into perspective. First thing I'll do when I can? Head to Algarve and see Mum. She's not getting any younger. I miss her, Lara. I really do."

"I know, honey. I miss Papa, too. And you're right. We get so caught up in life that we forget how little time we might have left with them."

Luke nodded, his expression shadowed, and for a moment his eyes drifted off the screen, gaze fixed on something to his left.

"Luke?" Lara frowned, observing him.

He blinked, quickly turning back. "Yeah? Sorry, thought I saw something outside." He smiled as he deflected her question. But before she could probe further, he changed the subject, his tone guarded. "Any news from Sushil?"

Lara shook her head. "No," she said firmly, her voice steady in a way that surprised even her. "And I don't want to know. That chapter's closed. I've wasted enough time looking back. It's time to face forward, to live again."

For a beat, Luke said nothing, just watched her with something close to pride in his eyes and a softness that made her throat tighten. Then, with a quiet smile, he lifted his coffee cup in salute, the gesture simple but powerful, like a silent vow. "To that," he said, his voice soft. "To living again." He held her gaze as he took a sip, and in that small, wordless moment, Lara felt it. His quiet approval, his unwavering presence, and a reminder that she was never truly alone. Whatever lay ahead, she would face it. And Luke—steady, loyal Luke —would be right beside her.

Lara threw herself into every online podcasting course she could find, devouring YouTube videos and online courses like a woman starved. She started with the free ones, thinking they'd be enough, but soon realised they only scratched the surface, offering her just a taste when what she craved was a full feast.

So, on a quiet afternoon, with the sunlight slanting across her kitchen table, Lara did something she hadn't done for herself in years —she invested. An expensive, full-fledged course on podcasting, sound production, and content creation. A birthday gift to herself. A gift that said: *I am worth this.*

Still, she hadn't quite expected how hard it would be to get her brain firing on all cylinders again. The years had rusted her learning abilities, and though technology had changed, her insecurities hadn't. There were no dog-eared books to flip through this time, just endless tabs and videos that demanded focus, and skills that didn't come easily. But with every new challenge, there was a piece of herself coming back to life.

One evening, with notes sprawled in front of her and her laptop humming in the background, she video-called Yash to show off her progress. "Look, Papa!" she beamed, turning her screen to display a mess of scribbled ideas, flowcharts, and highlighted takeaways.

Yash's face softened, his eyes crinkling with quiet pride as he shook his head, amused. "Ah, Lara, *beta*... It's so good to see you like this," he said, a chuckle in his voice. "I don't think I could have studied this much at your age!"

She laughed, her heart warming at his words. "I'm trying to explain podcasting to him," she narrated to an imaginary audience, as though already hosting her show.

"And it's like... radio?" Yash asked, sceptical but engaged.

"Sort of," Lara grinned. "Like a radio talk show. But no music, just me rambling about life—books, travels, lockdown... the works."

Yash raised his brows, clearly still trying to wrap his head around it."And people want to listen to this?"

Lara shrugged, though there was a spark of mischief in her eyes. "Well, if I can make it interesting enough, why not?"

Yash smiled, leaning closer to the screen. "You've always had the voice for it. All those elocution competitions are finally coming in handy, huh?"

For a flicker of a second, Mrs. Girdhar's stern but kind face floated in her mind: "Stand straight, Lara. E-n-u-n-c-i-a-t-e!" Would she have been proud of this older Lara, fighting her way back to herself? Lara hoped so. But she shook the thought away. There was still too much to do.

And so, the days that had once stretched endlessly, thick with loneliness, now raced by in a blur of learning and discovery. Her notebooks filled up fast—diagrams of soundproofing hacks, lists of microphone options, marketing notes, and raw, unfiltered reflections she might one day share on air. She joined an online community of newbie podcasters. Strangers who quickly became a source of inspiration, advice, and camaraderie. They swapped tips and shared triumphs, and for the first time in months, Lara felt part of something again—a tribe, a movement, a new beginning.

The day her podcasting microphone arrived, Lara cradled it like a rare treasure, dancing around her apartment as though she'd already made it to the top of the charts. That's when Luke's message pinged on her phone, a simple link to an editing tool that even a beginner could master.

You've got this, love! x

She stared at those words, a grin spreading across her face. For once, she allowed herself to believe that maybe, just maybe, she did.

Lara had begun waking earlier than she had in years, dragging herself out of bed with a resolve that felt sharper than the morning chill. Gone were the days of lying in, lost in thought and regret. Now, as the coffee hissed and frothed in her cafetière, filling the apartment with its rich aroma, she moved with purpose—tidying up, wiping surfaces, opening windows to let in the pale sunlight that filtered through like a quiet promise.

By the time she sat down by her window, her favourite mug warm in her hands, the world outside was just beginning to stir. It was her sacred moment, a few precious minutes to breathe, to gather herself, to map out her day. And unlike before, there was clarity now, a vision of what she wanted her life to become, even if she was still figuring out how to get there.

First on her list was always Papa. Their morning calls had become a ritual, grounding them both in a world still spinning wildly beyond their control. They exchanged news, shared small jokes, and when his voice wavered with uncertainty, Lara bolstered him with gentle reassurance. Though half the time, she was doing it as much for herself as for him. Afterwards, a quick text to Luke, setting up their evening chat, had become another ritual. A simple message, but one that reminded her she was not alone, that there were people who saw her, who cared.

In another life, the life she had lived not so long ago, this might have seemed boring, even suffocating. The predictability of it. But now? Now, it soothed her like a salve. The very monotony she might have once despised had become her shield, her quiet rebellion against the chaos of her own heart.

But it wasn't just about coping anymore, it was about becoming.

She signed up for online yoga classes, determined to connect with her body in a way she never had before. And as she stumbled through sun salutations and toppled over during tree pose, she laughed, a real, unrestrained laugh that filled the empty spaces of her home. Beneath that laughter was a silent vow: I will get better. I will get stronger. This was her fight back, against the years of letting life simply happen to her, against the heartbreak that had made her question her worth.

Her podcasting course was already pushing her mind to grow, to think differently. Yoga, she decided, would be her way of grounding her body and spirit, stitching herself back together, piece by piece. And beneath all this determination, there was Zinia's voice—not in reality, but in memory. Zinia, who would have looked her straight in the eye and said, "Don't you dare settle for being an afterthought, Lara. You were never made for second best." So Lara rose. Day by day, breath by breath, she rose. For herself, and for the fierce, unrelenting love Zinia would have demanded she give to her soul.

On their weekly Zoom call, Shweta and Madhuri stared at Lara, wide-eyed, as if they were seeing her for the first time in months. Really seeing her.

"Gosh, Lara, the colour's back in your cheeks!" Shweta exclaimed, leaning closer to the screen.

"You look amazing! What's going on? Yoga? New skincare? New man?" Madhuri teased, her eyes twinkling.

Lara laughed, a full, throaty laugh. Their teasing felt like college days all over again. It was only then she realised she was still in her yoga clothes, her hair tied up messily, not a smudge of her usual lipstick or mascara in sight. For once, she hadn't bothered to put on the armour she used to think she needed, and yet, here they were, telling her she looked better than she had in ages.

"Well, yes, yoga, kind of, if you can call me flopping around like a fish yoga," she grinned, "but honestly, I think it's also just... I don't know... finally choosing to do something for myself." She sat back, a little breathless from her own admission, as if saying it out loud made it more real. "And you guys, you simply have to watch 'Schitt's Creek'!" she added, leaning forward again, eyes sparkling. "It's hilarious. I've already binged it once, and now I'm rewatching it. That's how good it is. It's like a warm hug that I didn't know I needed."

They asked her questions, spoke of their own daily trials, laughed about their children, complained about their husbands, and in all of that Lara felt something she hadn't felt in a long, long time—a sense of belonging. She wasn't sitting there pretending to be okay, nodding along while feeling like an imposter in her own life. No. She was present. Whole. Bringing herself to the table, not just fragments and shadows of a pretend person.

When there was a lull in the conversation, Lara took a deep breath. "Also... I've signed up for a podcasting course." She let the words hang there for a moment, as if testing how they sounded in the air.

"Seriously? That's incredible!" Shweta beamed.

"Oh my God, that's so cool! You're actually doing it?" Madhuri gasped.

"Yep. Watch this space. I'll be harassing you guys to listen the moment I get my first episode out," Lara laughed, her cheeks glowing.

The two women whooped and hollered, clapping and cheering like she had just announced she'd won an award.

"You're going to smash it!"

"We'll be your first listeners, your biggest fans!"

With every word of encouragement, Lara felt taller, stronger, like she could take on the world and win. And a small voice inside her whispered, *You're not broken. You never were.*

A few evenings later, Lara poured herself a glass of wine, a small reward after a week that had drained her dry. It was Friday, and she had promised herself she would save her drinking for weekends only, a quiet truce with her own demons. She felt that delicious mix of exhaustion and exhilaration, coupled with the satisfying knowledge that she had been doing her best all week long. All she wanted now was to curl up in her favourite armchair, legs tucked beneath her, and disappear into the book Luke had sent her, one she had yet to begin reading. But she had barely made it past the second page when her body betrayed her, slipping into that half-world between waking and sleep, a dusky space where memories, like ghosts, rose unbidden.

And there it was. The memory she had buried deepest now clawing its way to the surface. The night she had first learned Sushil was married.

They had been together for eight months then. Eight months of believing his carefully constructed lies, of seeing only what she wanted to see. That evening, he had arrived as usual on one of his lightning trips to London. He had handed her his jacket and disappeared into the bathroom, leaving his phone unattended, she realised later, for the first time in her presence. When his jacket had started vibrating, his phone buzzing, urgent and insistent, as though it were alive, she had reached into his pocket, telling herself she was only going to pass it to him. A harmless gesture. But as she had pulled it free, the screen had lit up before she could turn away, and there, staring back at her, was a photo she would never unsee. His wife, lounging in silk, smiling seductively, with a message that burned itself into her brain:

Can't wait for you to tear this off me. xxx

In that moment, something inside her had shattered. When he'd emerged, casual and unsuspecting, she had flung the phone at him, and with it, all her hurt and rage. But he was ready. A master of stories and subterfuge. He had given her every excuse he could muster.

"I'm staying for the kids."

"She's unstable."

"She's obsessed with me, won't let me go."

"You're the only one I truly love."

And like a fool, like a woman starving for love, she had let herself believe. Because believing was easier than breaking her own heart.

Now, in this liminal space between sleep and wakefulness, her heart thudded against her ribcage as the truth, raw and merciless, stared her down. Wasn't she complicit, too? Hadn't she chosen to look away when she knew, deep down, that the man she loved belonged to someone else? Hadn't she willingly stepped into a story that wasn't hers to live? *Hadn't she taken something that didn't belong to her?* As she hovered in that fragile twilight moment, wine glass trembling slightly in her hand, Lara realised that taking charge of her life now also meant owning her mistakes. All of them. Not as punishment, but as a reckoning, as a path to healing.

She had crossed a line, clung to the scraps of affection thrown her way, knowing deep down they were never fully hers to hold. And in doing so, she had not only betrayed another woman and attempted to break a family, but had betrayed herself most of all. Her values, her upbringing, her principles and all that she believed she was made of.

Maybe the loneliness that had wrapped itself around her like a shroud all these years wasn't just grief, but her penance. A silent, gnawing atonement she had carried without ever naming it. But if she was ever going to step out of that darkness, if she was ever going to claim the life she still had left, she needed to face her shadow—fully and fiercely. She needed to forgive herself, to stop being at war with her own heart, and vow never again to betray her worth or the worth of another woman.

Setting her glass down with a soft but decisive thud, she let out a long, trembling breath. No more lies, she whispered into the dim light of the room. No more chasing what was never mine to begin with. Then, as if moved by a sudden clarity, she picked up her journal, the leather soft and worn beneath her fingers, and began writing, words pouring out of her as though they had been waiting for years to be uncorked. Words that would become her first podcast episode:

I am as human, as flawed, as vulnerable, and as full of regrets as any other woman. Maybe more. But if there's one thing I've learned, it's that we carry so much of our pain in silence, thinking we are alone. We are not. My journey may not mirror yours, but somewhere in these words, I hope you'll find a piece of yourself. That quiet yearning we all share: for love, for belonging, for a place in the world that feels like home.

My name is Lara. I'm fifty years old, standing at the edge of what I hope will be the most fearless, most honest chapter of my life. A chapter I didn't think I had the right to write until now. But here I am, ready to meet life as it is—wild, wonderful, and unpredictable.

So, if you're willing, I hope you'll walk this road with me. I'll be talking about all of it—love, heartbreak, loneliness, menopause, and the strange, invisible ways lockdown has messed with all our minds. I'll be real. I'll be raw. And I'll be here, hoping that by sharing my story, you'll find a little courage to face your own.

As May drew to a close, Lara felt a strange, steady warmth settle in her chest, a feeling she hadn't known in years. Maybe it was because, for the first time in forever, she had something to look forward to. Or maybe, she thought, it was because she had finally laid something to rest.

The days were growing longer, drenched in honeyed sunlight that lingered well past supper. Windows stood flung open, birdsong mingling with the occasional sound of laughter from behind garden fences, proof that even in lockdown, life was quietly pushing forward. And yet, beneath the stillness, there was a restlessness in the air. A subtle hum, like the world itself was longing to stretch out and breathe again. People were tired of being cooped up, Lara knew. After all, human beings were social creatures. Keeping them caged and away from one another felt wrong, however right it was in the moment. If Luke lived close by, she mused, they would have found a way, sitting at opposite ends of a bench, coffees in hand, talking till sunset.

One afternoon, as she sat on her tiny front step, sipping lemonade and watching clouds drift lazily across the sky, a voice called out, cutting gently through her thoughts.

"Lovely day, isn't it?"

Lara looked up to see Mrs. Jensen standing across the street in her garden, watering can poised mid-air, her wide sun hat casting a soft shadow over her smiling face.

"It really is," Lara called back, her lips curving into a smile that felt natural, unforced. "Your flowers look stunning."

Mrs. Jensen beamed, adjusting her hat. "Thank you, dear! They've been my company through all this madness. But if I talk to them much longer, I fear they'll start answering back."

Lara laughed, surprising herself with how easily the sound bubbled up. "I've been chatting to my kettle like it's my roommate, so no judgement from me."

Mrs. Jensen let out a delighted chuckle that carried across the quiet street. "If it gives you any backchat, you send it my way. I've tamed worse."

Lara stood, brushing off her hands, and walked to the edge of her step, careful to keep her distance but feeling, for the first time, like maybe that gap between her and the world was shrinking.

"You know," Mrs. Jensen said, leaning on her fence, her eyes twinkling, "we're having a little 'doorstep chat' on Saturday. Nothing fancy. Just a few of us sitting out in our gardens or standing on our doorsteps, cups of tea in hand, yelling at each other across the street like proper eccentrics."

The old Lara, the one who had spent years hiding behind polite smiles and excuses, would have mumbled something vague, retreating behind the safety of her door. But this new Lara, the one rising from the ashes of heartbreak and hard lessons, surprised even herself.

"I'd love that," she said. "As long as we're not breaking any rules."

Mrs. Jensen's face lit up as though Lara had just handed her a bouquet. "Oh, don't you worry, luvvie. Sitting in our own gardens is permissible. I checked." She winked. "Saturday, then. Weather gods permitting."

"Saturday," Lara echoed, feeling a small bloom of excitement take root.

Just then, a woman stepped out two doors down, baby monitor in one hand, a rubbish bag in the other. Lara had seen her before. Chloe, she thought her name was, but they'd never spoken.

Chloe glanced up and caught Lara's eye. "Hi! You're Lara, right?" she called with a smile. "Mrs. Jensen tells me you make an amazing lemon drizzle cake!"

Lara felt her cheeks flush, but laughed easily. "Guilty. If you ever want some, just say the word."

Chloe's grin widened. "I always want cake. Maybe we can swap? I make killer brownies."

A laugh slipped out of Lara before she could help it. "Deal."

As Chloe disappeared inside, waving over her shoulder, Lara

turned back to Mrs. Jensen, who gave her a smile so knowing, so quietly triumphant, that Lara couldn't help but laugh again.

It was a smile that said, 'Welcome back to the land of the living.'

As she sat back down on her step, the breeze playing with the loose strands of her hair, Lara realised with a jolt that this, this easy connection, these small kindnesses, was what she had been starved of. Not just love, but community. A place to belong. People who saw her.

Her phone buzzed in her lap, a message lighting up the screen. It was Luke.

> You okay? Thinking of you. x

She smiled, fingers moving swiftly over the screen.

> I'm good. Better than I've been in ages.
> Remind me to tell you about my cake-for-
> brownie deal. xx

A moment later, Luke's reply popped up.

> Ha ha! Look at you go, mafioso! Can't wait
> to hear all about it. Talk in an hour? x

Lara laughed softly, her heart lighter than it had been in months.

As the sun dipped low, casting long golden rays across the street, she leaned her head back against the door, a smile lingering on her lips.

———————

Maybe it was because it was the last day of May, or maybe it was simply because it was a Sunday, but Lara allowed herself the rare indulgence of a lie-in. When she finally stirred, sunlight pouring insistently through the cracks in the curtains, the bedside clock blinked 10:07 a.m. She blinked at it, disorientated, her body heavy with the unfamiliar weight of deep sleep. Reaching for her phone with a lazy stretch, her stomach tightened as she saw three missed calls from an unknown number.

Her heart stumbled. Sushil. The name slid, unbidden and unwelcome, into her mind. But she crushed the thought as quickly as it rose, her fingers curling into her palm as if to physically squeeze it out of her system. No. Not again. Not today.

But then, a voicemail. Her thumb hovered over the screen. A beat passed, then another. With a breath she didn't realise she was holding, she pressed play.

"Lara, it's me, Sue. I don't know if you remember me, but we met a long time ago at Luke's place... when...umm... he was with Harry. I — I used to date Luke, back in the day."

(A nervous laugh)

"Anyway, please call me whenever you can. It's about Luke. And it's... it's urgent."

Lara sat bolt upright, the phone still clutched in her hand.

Sue?

The name echoed in her head, dredging up half-formed memories. A blonde woman, warm and easy to talk to, years ago, at one of Luke's casual get-togethers. Lara had registered her presence only in passing, curious at first because Luke had mentioned her once or twice, in the way one speaks of people who matter but aren't really in the other's orbit. Then she had realised that this was Sue. Luke's Sue. But, they'd never stayed in touch, never even crossed paths again. So why was she calling now? And urgent, what did that mean?

A sharp prickle of unease crept up her spine as she tossed the covers back and got out of bed. Pulling her robe tighter around her, Lara padded to the bathroom and splashed cold water on her face, willing herself to wake up properly. As she brushed her teeth, her mind whirled. Why hadn't Luke mentioned anything? They spoke almost every day, sometimes about nothing, sometimes about every-thing. What could be so urgent that Sue, of all people, had to reach out?

By the time Lara made it to the kitchen, her pulse was a steady thrum beneath her skin. She filled the kettle and stood by the window as it boiled, the comforting rumble of it at odds with the churning in her gut. She leaned her forehead lightly against the glass, watching the morning unfold outside. Mrs Jensen pottering in her garden. Cecil from next door, standing in his doorway with a mug in his hand, nodding at the child on the tricycle, someone's dog barking at a bird in a tree, the neighbour's wind chimes catching a soft breeze. Ordinary life. But nothing about this felt ordinary. How had Sue even gotten her number? Had Luke given it to her? Or had she gone looking, and if so, why?

The kettle clicked off, but Lara didn't move. She stood frozen, one hand resting on the counter, eyes fixed on nothing, a slow dread rising inside of her. Something was wrong. Terribly, unmistakably wrong. And she needed to know what. Her hand hovered over her phone. Before she could decide whether to call back, the phone rang again; the noise slicing through the stillness. Without thinking, she snatched it up.

"Hello?"

A pause. Then a voice, soft and tentative, said, "Hello... is that Lara?"

"Yes, this is Lara." Her throat was dry, her voice sharp with tension. "Is that Sue?"

A rush of relief on the other end. "Yes, yes... thank God. I wasn't sure I had the right number. I'm so sorry to reach out like this, out of nowhere..."

"Sue, has something happened to Luke?" The question burst from her before she could stop it, a wave of panic cresting in her chest.

"Oh! No, no, he's okay. He's fine..." Sue rushed to say, but there was a hesitation, a crack in her voice. "But..."

Lara gripped the phone tighter. "But what?"

There was a pause. "I'm afraid Luke's gotten involved with someone... someone who isn't who he seems to be."

Lara's heart thudded painfully in her chest. "Involved? What do you mean 'involved'?"

The next thirty minutes unravelled like a slow nightmare. By the time Lara ended the call, she felt as though the ground beneath her feet had shifted. She sank heavily onto a chair by the window, her head in her hands, her mind a tangled mess of disbelief, anger, and fear. Why hadn't Luke told her? What was he hiding? Had he known she would not approve? Had he kept her in the dark because he knew that something was off?

Sue's words echoed in her head, sharp and raw. "He met Ben years ago, at my place. I never knew they'd stayed in touch, not until recently when everything started falling apart."

Apparently, Sue had only discovered the connection when a woman, an older lady, came looking for Ben. A woman who, Ben had claimed to Sue previously, was his mother, but was in fact his lover. A woman he had bled dry of thousands of pounds, promising love, promising forever. All lies. "She's been trying to track him down because he disappeared again," Sue had said. "And she mentioned Ben kept talking about a friend, someone he met through me, someone he said was helping him get back on his feet. He called him a lifeline. It didn't take much to guess it was Luke."

A deep ache gripped Lara's chest. Luke, her Luke, who always led with his heart, always saw the birds with the broken wings and tried to heal them. "What makes you think they're still in touch?" Lara had whispered, though some part of her already knew the answer.

Sue had hesitated for a long moment. Then, her voice soft but laced with something akin to sadness, said, "Because the last time Ben stayed at my Airbnb, he left in a rush. And when I was cleaning up... I found a book. One of Luke's books. And inside there was an inscription to Ben. You know the kind of thing Luke writes, don't you? Like he's baring his soul on paper."

Lara had closed her eyes then, as though she could somehow block out the ache that bloomed in her chest. Of course she knew. She had dozens of those books on her shelves, each one bearing a little fragment of Luke, a quiet intimacy, a simple sign of his love for the recipient. Luke didn't give away books casually. And if he inscribed one, it meant something.

Now, as Lara sat unmoving by the window, staring blankly at the quiet street outside, the weight of it all pressed down on her. The sun caught on the metal of parked cars, sending sharp flashes of light into her eyes, but she barely noticed. Her mind was racing, a thousand thoughts colliding all at once. How could she even begin to confront him? What could she say that wouldn't push him away? How do you tell someone that the thing they believe is saving them is the very thing that's going to destroy them?

Sue's voice, shaking but insistent, echoed in her ears. "I didn't know who else to turn to, Lara. I'm scared for him. This man, Ben, he'll take everything Luke has to give. His kindness, his trust, his love. All of it. And when there's nothing left, he'll throw him away like a pile of rubbish, like he did with that woman."

Lara felt her hands curl into fists on her lap, her nails digging into her palms.

"You know what Luke's like," Sue had gone on, her voice thickening, as though she were holding back tears. "He'd give the shirt off his back if someone asked for it. He wants to believe people can be good, that he can fix them. But Lara... he's vulnerable. And lonely. God, he's so lonely. And Ben knows that. He's using that. We have to do something before it's too late."

Lara blinked hard, fighting the tears that had come unbidden. Because everything Sue had said, every word, was true. She knew Luke. Knew how he carried his wounds quietly, how he poured love and care into everyone else as though that could patch over the cracks inside himself. And she knew, too, that if Ben was the predator Sue described, Luke would never see it coming. He would believe in him. He would try to save him. And Ben would take everything. Then, when Luke was emptied out, he would walk away without a second glance.

Sue had tried and failed. Luke had shut her out, pushed her away because she had dared to tell him the truth.

But Lara couldn't let it end there. She had to do something. Say something. Even if Luke didn't want to hear it. Even if it tore apart their friendship. Because if she stayed silent, if she stood by and watched him willingly self-destruct, and he ended up broken in a way no one could fix, she would never forgive herself. Never.

As she stared out at the street, her reflection pale in the glass, Lara felt something cold and sharp crystallise inside her, a resolve that cut through the fear. She would reach him. She had to reach him. Even if she had to pull him back from the brink with her bare hands. Whatever it took, she would do it.

Luke (May 2025)

Drifting

It was nearly dusk by the time Luke sealed the last box, pressing the tape down with a finality that matched the hollowness in his chest. The flat was filled with neatly labelled stacks, each destined for the charity shops Christine had so carefully listed in her will—her final act of meticulous care for possessions she would never touch again.

Luke collapsed onto the couch, exhaustion washing over him. His hands hung uselessly between his knees as shadows lengthened across the room. The last rays of daylight filtered through the blinds, painting golden stripes that seemed to mock the darkness inside him.

April had made it a year. A whole year since Frank's voice had come through the phone, frantic, panic-stricken: "Luke, it's your mum. Christine's had a heart attack."

The memory wasn't just sharp, it was serrated, cutting fresh with each recall. How his body had frozen before instinct took over. The mechanical motions of booking flights, throwing clothes into a bag with hands that wouldn't stop trembling. The desperate prayers muttered to a God he wasn't sure he believed in anymore. But by the time his plane touched down in Portugal, she was already slipping

323

away, her body thin and pale against the stark white of the hospital sheets.

He could still taste the antiseptic air of that sterile hallway, feel the cold linoleum beneath his feet as he paced, trying to breathe past the vise tightening around his lungs. All while trying to hold Frank together when he himself was shattering on the inside.

He had sat by her bed, holding her hand so gently, afraid the IV needles might shift, might hurt her when nothing should hurt anymore. Her fingers were delicate and paper-thin in his, blue veins visible beneath translucent skin. Wires snaked from her wrists to machines that reduced her life to electronic pulses, the cold metrics of a heart faltering.

"Don't go, Mum," he had whispered, his voice breaking on each syllable. "Please. I still need you. I need you so much."

But she had gone anyway. Gone while those words were still warm on his lips, as though she had held on just long enough to hear her son's voice one last time before surrendering.

"She waited for you," Frank had said later, tears trickling down his weathered face as Luke held him. "She knew you were here. That gave her permission to let go."

As he wrapped his arms around Frank's trembling shoulders, Luke had swallowed his own keening grief, forcing himself to be the stable one for the man who had loved Christine with such complete devotion. He reminded himself that she had found real joy in her final years, with someone who adored her in a way she had always deserved. What more could he have wished for his mother?

And yet, the child in him raged against the injustice of it all. Because with her gone, the foundations of his world had crumbled. The one person who had always been his refuge had vanished. Now, there would be no one left to gather him close, to brush back his hair with those gentle hands, and say with absolute conviction, "It's okay, my darling boy. You'll see. One day, it will all make sense." The truth was, nothing made sense. Nothing had for a long time.

As he had run his fingers over her scarves, still carrying the faint trace of her perfume, over her books with their cracked spines and pages marked with her neat handwriting, over all her little treasures lovingly collected across decades, he kept asking why. Why now? Why like this? Why leave him alone in a world that had already taken so much? But of course, the answer wasn't there. It wasn't in the silk of her scarves or the margins of her favourite novels or the delicate porcelain figurines that had once made her smile.

With a heavy sigh, Luke poured himself a glass of wine—her favourite Rioja—and stood in the middle of his living room, looking around at the life he had constructed. A life that suddenly felt like a house of cards, precarious and meaningless.

Years ago, after Steve's death, he had stood in a similar void, staring down the dark tunnel of grief, questioning everything. Life, death, love, his own purpose. But back then, he was young, still raw and unformed, gathering the fragments of his identity. Now, after everything, after living through loss and love, through decades of soaring triumphs and crushing failures, through friendships that saved him and betrayals that nearly broke him, he stood in that emptiness again, asking the same questions. Did any of it matter? Did *he* matter? What were they all but fragile creatures—muscle, sinew, blood—destined to return to dust? Whether they were good or evil, whether they had loved fiercely or lived selfishly, whether they had given everything or taken until there was nothing left. The end was always the same.

Yes. The end was always the same.

Luke tipped his head back and drained his glass of wine in one defiant swallow, feeling the sharp burn trace a path down his throat. For a moment, he kept his eyes closed, as if shutting out the world could silence the maelstrom inside him. He didn't want to be that man, that bitter, broken man who kept asking, "Why me?"

Everyone suffered. Loss, grief, sickness, death. These were the universal currencies of human existence. People across the world carried burdens that would crush him, walked through fires that would incinerate his complaints to ash. So why should the universe make an exception for him?

No.

What he needed now wasn't pity, from others or from himself. He needed strength. The strength to stand up every morning when everything inside him wanted to fall apart. The strength to keep loving, even when love had betrayed him time and again. The strength to live, fully, honestly, on his terms. To be able to look at himself in the mirror daily and know, without question, that he had done right. By himself. By those who loved him. By those he had loved and lost.

———

"Mum left you a few pieces of jewellery she thought you might like," Luke said, his voice softer than usual.

Lexi blinked, her brows knitting in surprise. "Christine? Left me jewellery?"

He nodded, watching her carefully on the iPad screen. "It's not much, Lex. Just a couple of bracelets and a small Tiffany necklace. Dad had bought it for her when they were married. She thought you should have it. Said you'd want it because... because it was from him. Gifts from Jim."

Lexi's mouth fell open slightly, her eyes wide and unguarded. "Oh..."

Luke took in her reaction quietly. It was still strange, seeing her like this, larger than he remembered, but softer in other ways, too. Softer in spirit. There was a lightness about her, something he hadn't seen in years. And though a part of him worried about Miguel, about how much she might be leaning on him, another part felt a flicker of peace. She was, for once, at ease in her own skin.

"I'll send it over to you soon, alright?" he added gently, managing a small smile.

Lexi's eyes filled with something like wonder, or maybe guilt.

"Oh, Luke... I haven't even asked how you are." Her voice cracked slightly. "How are you? I've been so busy here..."

Luke shook his head, giving her a quiet look. "I'm glad you're happy, Lex. Really. You've met someone who brings you peace, and that's all I ever wanted for you. Means I don't have to worry so much anymore."

She gave a small, teary laugh. "My younger brother, who's always been more of an older brother to me."

They exchanged a smile, one of those rare, unspoken moments where old wounds and shared battles were acknowledged without words. A hard-won sibling bond, grown from chaos and pain into something real.

Luke hesitated, then said, "I'm also going to send some old photographs. From when we were kids. Pictures Dad took. I don't think you have copies."

Lexi's face softened even more. "Don't you want to keep them? They're your memories too."

He looked away for a moment, his jaw tightening. "I'm clearing things out, Lex. Minimising. After Mum... I realised how much we leave behind. Rooms full of things that mean nothing to anyone except the people we loved. I want you to have what matters. The rest... it's time to let it go."

Lexi studied him closely now, her eyes narrowing just a little. "Luke, are you sure you're okay? You seem... different."

He opened his mouth, but before he could answer, a sudden burst of energy filled the screen as Miguel appeared, grinning broadly, a large Alsatian bounding in behind him.

"¡Hola, Luke!" Miguel beamed, waving at him like an old friend. "When are you coming to visit again? You promised!"

The spell broke, and Luke smiled automatically and said, "Soon, I hope."

After he hung up, Luke sat for a long while, staring at the darkened screen, thinking about the strange turns life took. The irony wasn't lost on him. Lexi, who had spent so much of her life chasing impossible dreams, had finally found love in the arms of a man she would never have looked twice at in her younger years. Miguel, with his gentle eyes and easy laugh, was nothing like the men she used to chase. And yet, here she was, glowing with the sort of peace and contentment Luke had never seen in her, not in all the years they had known each other.

A small smile tugged at his lips. Life could be funny like that. And then the smile faded. Because here he was, still standing in the ruins of everything he had ever wanted. He had searched for love all his life. And what had he found? Heartbreak. Betrayal. Emptiness.

Maybe for some people, waiting for love was like standing alone on a forgotten train platform, suitcase in hand, watching train after train arrive and depart, none of them stopping for you. You could stand there for years, watching the sky change, watching others come and go, hoping that one day, the right train, *your* train, would finally arrive and take you where you were meant to go. But deep down, you knew. You knew that the train wasn't coming. And still, you waited. Because what else was there to do, when all you'd ever wanted was to be loved and to love in return?

He dragged a hand through his hair, exhaling slowly. Maybe it was time to stop waiting. Time to stop watching for a train that was never coming. Maybe the love he had spent a lifetime chasing, that fierce, all-consuming love, was never meant for him. And maybe, just maybe, that was something he could make peace with. Because if he was brutally honest, what he did have was more than most people ever held onto.

Friendships that had walked with him through fire. Love that had taken other shapes—in laughter, in loyalty, in the quiet understanding of those who knew him best. Memories, etched into his bones, of the people who had made him who he was.

He closed his eyes for a long moment. Perhaps it was time to stop longing for what was never going to be his, and instead, to gather up all that he had been given and call it enough.

Packing up a life was never easy. It wasn't just about sorting through objects; it was about sifting through memories, each one dragging you down winding corridors of the past, whispering, *remember when?*

Luke sat on the floor, surrounded by the photo albums Christine had so carefully preserved. The same albums they used to pore over together, side by side, laughing, remembering, bonding over every shared story. Now, they felt like relics from another lifetime. As he turned the pages, searching for some trace of the boy he used to be, the boy before loss, before disillusionment, he let himself drift backward. For once, he didn't fight the memories.

There he was, a baby perched precariously on a camel, Christine's arm wrapped tight around him, her smile wide and fearless. The pyramids rose in the background, ghostly and immense. A small, sepia-toned square, but within its faded edges lived a world bursting with adventure and hope, a time when the future had been a wide-open sky. He traced his finger over his mother's youthful face, trying to remember her like that, vibrant and unburdened. Turning the page, he found another: Christine again, her scarf knotted at the nape, laughing as she cradled a red-faced, scowling toddler, his cheeks still flushed from a tantrum, eyes squinting at the camera as if the world had done him some great, unspeakable injustice. A breath escaped him, half a laugh, half a sigh.

Further along, there was a photo of him standing by a pool, wedged between Steve and Lexi. All three sunburned, squinting against the sun. Where was this photo taken? He frowned, carefully sliding the photo from its sleeve and turning it over.

Florida, 1978, read Christine's neat handwriting.

Florida. They had been to Florida. And yet, his mind was a blank slate, scrubbed clean of that trip, like so much else that had slipped through his grasp over the years.

As Luke flipped through the pages, moving from one album to the next, he traced the arc of his life in pictures, a silent testament to the years he had lived. There he was: a beaming little boy, wild and fearless, caught mid-run on some sun-drenched lawn. Then, as the pages turned, the boy became a quiet, introspective teenager, his gaze shifting from the camera to something just beyond its lens, already searching for a place to belong, for a future he couldn't yet see. His hand paused over a photograph of Steve with Christine. Steve's arm was slung loosely around her shoulders, his eyes warm with a fondness that was no illusion. Steve had loved Christine with a steady devotion, as much as Lexi had despised her back then. Funny, the opposites life held in such fragile balance.

Luke kept flipping through the albums, mentally noting the pictures he would send to Lexi, wanting to get it done, wanting to finish, and yet, something in those photographs held him captive. *Look at us,* they seemed to whisper. *Look at what you've forgotten. Look at the portal we offer to all that was, and all that can never be again.*

His fingers lingered on a photo of himself in a hot kitchen, chef's hat askew, his face flushed with sweat and effort, focused on the plate in front of him. Who had taken that picture? He couldn't remember. Another of him and Sue in bright blue uniforms, smiling at each other, their faces alive with excitement as they headed out on a flight together. Had he sent that to Christine? He turned another page. A photo of his entire batch at graduation, standing tall in a formation determined by the photographer. Andy stood near the centre, grinning cockily at the camera. How many of them were still flying? How many had let go of those dreams to chase new ones, or because life had forced them to?

His hand stilled over an image of Christine, Frank, Zinia, and Yash, standing against the misty hills of Shimla, arms linked, laughing. Older, yes, but content, happily content to be travelling together, in the company of friends, unfettered from their youthful responsibilities. Then, Lara, radiant in a cream saree on her wedding day, eyes shining and slightly glassy, caught in that strange moment between joy and loss. Behind her stood Luke and Harry, both watching her with quiet pride.

Luke sat back heavily, the album open in his lap. How many moments of happiness had been lost to time? How many pieces of himself had been left in those frozen frames? How different was he now from the man he'd been back then?

Packing up a life wasn't just hard, it was brutal. It was a slow, relentless confrontation with every version of yourself you had outgrown or left behind. It was facing the echoes of who you used to be, and realising, with sudden clarity, that there was no way back.

———

"I'm glad you're taking this break," Sue said gently over the phone. "You owe it to yourself."

"Mmm-hmm," Luke murmured, dragging the suitcase out from under the bed, his phone set to speaker as he moved around the room. He had only just returned from mailing the package he'd finally put together for Lexi.

There was a pause, and then Sue asked, "But... why Brighton? I mean, of all the places in the world you could have chosen?"

Luke paused, running a hand over the dusty case before reaching for the vacuum cleaner. "Brighton has some happy memories," he said. "Recent ones."

"Oh," Sue murmured. "You mean after..."

"Yes."

Another pause, heavier this time. Then Sue's voice shifted, cautious but firm. "Luke... about that. Wendy's decided to prosecute."

Luke froze, his hand on the case handle.

"What about you?" Sue asked carefully.

"Wendy is the woman who...?"

"Yes. The one Ben scammed for years."

"Ah." Luke sat down heavily on the edge of the bed, the suitcase resting at his feet like. "No, Sue. I'm not doing that."

Her frustration was immediate, palpable even through the line. "Luke, he took nearly ten thousand pounds from you! Why aren't you furious? I'm furious on your behalf!"

Luke exhaled, leaning forward, elbows on his knees. "It's only money."

"Your hard-earned money!" she shot back. "Thank God he didn't get his hands on anything Christine left you. Can you imagine if—"

"I know," Luke interrupted softly, rubbing his face with both hands.

There was a long silence. Then, quieter, "Luke, I still don't think you understand how much he hurt you. How much he used you."

"I do," Luke said, his voice low. "Believe me, I do." He let out a long breath. "Sue, I still haven't thanked you properly, have I? If it hadn't been for you—"

"And Lara."

"And Lara," he agreed, smiling faintly. "If it wasn't for you both, I'd probably still be trapped in that mess. I'm sorry I pushed you away at first."

"Oh, Luke," she sighed. "You were in his thrall. I get it. But... if you let this go, he'll just move on to someone else. Someone more vulnerable, maybe."

Luke closed his eyes, leaning his head back. "Sue, I know. I know you're right. But I can't go there. I just don't have the fight in me. Not now. I hope Wendy wins. I hope she gets justice. But I can't drag myself through that all over again. I'm just... done."

There was a beat of silence before she said, softer now, "Okay. Alright. I'm sorry. I didn't mean to push."

He smiled faintly. "I know."

"Let's talk about Brighton then," she said, her voice lighter, though he could still hear the worry beneath. "Tell me what you've booked. Where are you staying?"

As he described the little Airbnb near the beach, the sound of seagulls in the distance, the memory of the sun on his face during his last visit, he wondered if Sue felt left out. If, now that Alan was older and more independent, she felt adrift. Matt's promotion meant longer hours, more responsibility, more absence from home. Did she wish Luke had asked her to come along?

For a moment, he almost offered. But then he caught himself. No. That wasn't where Sue was needed. She had her own life, her own responsibilities. She needed to be home, surrounded by her "babies", the cats she loved so fiercely.

After he hung up, Luke stood by the window, gazing out at the garden he had tended with such care over the years. The peonies and roses, the alliums and irises, all in glorious, defiant bloom, jostling for space like guests at a grand party, each trying to outshine the other. Yet as they swayed gently in the soft breeze, he knew he loved them all equally. For their wild beauty, for their colour, for the quiet joy they gave to anyone who looked.

Finally, he turned away and crossed back to the bed, spreading a sheet over it before laying the suitcase down. The case had layers of dust on it. He ran the vacuum carefully over its top and sides, watching the months of settled stillness get sucked away.

Then, slowly, methodically, he began to pack. The action was familiar, muscle memory kicking in, but it felt different now, more sad somehow. It reminded him of all those times he had packed for flights, checking weather apps on his phone, trying to decide whether to bring jeans or shorts, long johns or a bathing costume. Little rituals that had once filled him with excitement, with purpose.

What a life it had been.

Leaving flying had been harder than he ever admitted, harder than he'd let anyone see. To walk away from a world where the sky was his second home, where in just a matter of hours he could be in a new country, drinking cocktails by some turquoise sea, laughing with a crew who had become like family, that had carved a hollow space inside him. And leaving the union... That had been its own kind of heartbreak. For all the years he thought he was just a cog in the machine, nothing special, nothing central, and then, at the farewell, when people had stood up to speak, when cards and emails had poured in, telling him what he had meant to them, what his kindness and steady presence had given, he had felt his heart clench, and he'd blinked back tears, unable to meet anyone's eyes.

He crossed the room to the wardrobe and slowly opened its door. His uniform still hung there, crisp and pressed, the wings gleaming softly on the jacket, a quiet symbol of a life that had once been his entire world. He reached out and ran his fingers gently over the wings, tracing their familiar lines. Ah, yes, he thought, a small smile tugging at his lips. It had been a good life. A rich life. And for that, he had no regrets.

"So, I truly believe love can come to us in any form. It can be the love of a pet or a sibling, the love of a child or a friend. The love of someone who knows your darkest corners and still chooses to stay. The source doesn't matter. What matters is that we learn to recognise it when it arrives—often quietly, without fanfare—to hold it close like a precious stone warmed by the sun, to let it shape us into something better than we were before. Because love, in its purest form, isn't just something we feel, it's something that transforms us."

Lara's voice was smooth, steady, imbued with the kind of quiet conviction that made people lean in, made them listen, made them feel seen in a world that so often looked past them. Her words flowed through the recording studio, resonating with a truth that felt both universal and intensely personal. 'Living Life with Lara' had started as a small niche podcast recorded in her spare bedroom, something born out of curiosity and catharsis during the darkest period of her life, but it had since grown into a phenomenon. A word-of-mouth success that had catapulted her into the mainstream, where her raw honesty and hard-won wisdom made her not just heard, but believed.

Lara.

The pride he felt seeing her like this—confident, purposeful, entirely herself—was almost overwhelming. How bittersweet it had been to watch her leave flying behind to chase something bigger, something that would let her touch more lives than she ever could at thirty thousand feet. At the time, he hadn't realised how soon he, too, would walk away from the skies, drawn back to earth by circumstances neither of them could have predicted.

And yet, as he listened to her now, he marvelled at how well she had done for herself. Conversations with celebrities who dropped their carefully constructed personas in her presence, deep dives with thought leaders who revealed more than they'd initially intended, raw and real discussions that resonated with thousands, perhaps millions, across the globe. People listened to her because she was unfiltered, because her wisdom didn't come from a place of superiority, but from lived experience, from every battle and every wound she had endured, from every betrayal and every loss, from every time that she had fallen and somehow found the strength to rise again.

Lara.

The same Lara who had fought for him when he wouldn't fight for himself. The Lara who had dug up evidence on Ben when Luke was too blinded by love to see the truth, who had forced him to confront what he hadn't wanted to. The Lara who had stormed into his home, eyes blazing with righteous fury, and faced Ben head-on while Luke stood frozen in disbelief. Fiercely protective. Unrelenting. With the sort of loyalty that didn't waver, no matter how much you tried to push away, no matter how many times you insisted you were fine when you were anything but.

Now, as he closed his suitcase with a sharp snap, locking its contents away, he wondered if he was being entirely fair to her. He needed her, but did she need this?

Brighton had been her idea the first time. Fresh out of COVID, still raw from wounds both seen and unseen—him from Ben's betrayal, her from Sushil's abandonment—she had insisted they escape. Somewhere by the sea, somewhere they could breathe salty air and lick their wounds, scream into the wind and rage at their own stupidity for falling for men who had seemed, at first, to be everything they had ever wanted.

"We need a place where we can be broken without explaining ourselves," she had said, half-joking, half-serious.

Brighton had been a gift. A city that pulsed with life, where the well-heeled mingled with the beautifully strange. Where rainbow flags snapped in the sea breeze, where indie music drifted from tiny bars and laughter spilled from open terraces. The scent of salt and fish and chips clung to the air, and the Lanes glittered with the promise of hidden treasures—vintage shops, quirky cafés, old bookstores where they had lost themselves for hours. And beyond the city, the South Downs rolled toward the horizon, a sanctuary of green, vast and unbothered.

That trip had cleared out cobwebs, reminding him of everything he still had in his life. Lara, most of all. The friend who had known him longer than anyone, who had seen him at his best and his worst and loved him through all of it. The one constant in a life that had so often felt like shifting sand beneath his feet.

Was that what he was trying to replicate? That moment of clarity, of connection?

Her fifty-fifth birthday was approaching, and he wondered, not for the first time, if it was selfish to ask her to come again. But when he had hesitantly suggested it, voice careful, she'd laughed, that deep, throaty laugh that seemed to start at her toes and work its way up.

"Luke, I can't think of a better place, or a better person, to spend my birthday with. Besides," she had added, eyes gleaming with mischief, "we're not getting any younger. We might as well enjoy the seaside while we can still walk along it without assistance."

And so it was decided.

Now, as he picked up his case and cast one last look around his home, nostalgia brushed against him, light but insistent. This house had been his sanctuary for years—a place of solitude, of mourning, of reckoning. The place where he had licked his wounds after Ben, where he had grieved Christine in private, where he had come to terms with his future. But he reminded himself that he was leaving one sanctuary for another.

Lara would soon be at London Bridge Station, waiting for him to arrive, nursing a coffee, people-watching as she loved to do. Together, they would take the train to Brighton, just as they had before. Only this time, the journey would be heavier, weighted with unspoken words and truths not yet revealed.

Tucked inside his case was his birthday gift to her. A book. Always a book. It had become their tradition, this exchange of stories, of worlds to get lost in. And inside the book, he would put in a letter. A letter that told her how much he loved her, and how very sorry he was.

Drowning

Lara took his hand and began swinging it playfully as they walked along the sandy foreshore, their feet sinking into sliver of sand revealed by the low tide. The waves murmured at their heels, the salty breeze ruffling their hair. Seagulls wheeled overhead, their cries occasionally piercing through the steady rhythm of the surf. The late afternoon sun cast long shadows across the beach, gilding everything in a honeyed light.

"I know we look ridiculous," she said, still swinging his hand with childlike abandon. "But I don't care. Do you?"

Luke glanced at their entwined hands, then at her mischievous grin, the same one that had first captivated him decades ago, now etched with fine lines that spoke of years of laughter and pain. With a sheepish smile, he shook his head. This lightness in her, this refusal to take life so seriously, was new. Or maybe it had always been there, buried beneath responsibilities and heartbreak, finally breaking free. Whatever it was, it nourished something inside him he hadn't even realised was starving—a hunger for simplicity, for joy untethered from expectation.

"Can you believe we're back in Brighton? Same Airbnb, four years later. How the hell did you manage that?"

"Easy, Lara," Luke chuckled, his voice carrying the familiar teasing tone they'd perfected over four decades. "It's called the internet. You should try it sometime."

She laughed, a full-throated sound, but then, just as suddenly, she stopped and turned to face him. Her expression shifted, the playfulness giving way to something deeper, more searching. The wind lifted strands of her hair, which she tucked behind her ear with an unconscious grace. "How are you, Luke? Really. After everything? After Christine?"

He let his gaze drift out over the water, where the horizon blurred into the sky in a seamless gradient of blues. A boat crawled along the distant edge, a tiny dark smudge against the vastness. "How am I? I have no idea. I don't even know *who* I am anymore." His voice broke slightly on the last word, the admission costing him more than he'd imagined.

She squeezed his hand, her palm warm against his. "You're you, Luke. The same loving and giving person you've always been. Don't lose sight of that, okay?"

They walked in silence for a moment. A young couple ran past, laughing as they chased a kite dancing erratically in the wind.

"And you, Lara?" he finally asked, watching her profile as she gazed ahead.

She exhaled, a quiet chuckle escaping her lips. "Me? Never better. I'm happy. More settled." She picked up a smooth, flat pebble, turning it over in her palm before skimming it across the water. They both watched as it bounced three times before disappearing beneath the surface.

"Do you miss Yash?"

She stilled for a moment, then turned to him, her eyes shining with unshed tears. "Every single day, Luke. Just like I miss Mummy. But you know what keeps me going? Knowing they're together now.

That he left this world peacefully, surrounded by birdsong." She closed her eyes briefly.

Luke nodded, swallowing past the tightness in his throat. "That is a blessing."

"I don't think any of our parents would want us to stop living," Lara continued, her voice growing stronger. "That would go against everything they taught us." She bent down to collect a small shell at the edge of the water, before slipping it into her pocket—a small treasure to remember this day.

He watched her then, the passion in her voice, the gratitude she carried even in her grief. There was a strength in her now that hadn't always been there. She would be alright. She didn't need saving. In fact, she was the kind of person who did the saving.

The waves whispered their secrets to the shore as they walked on, speaking of careers and failures, love and loss, the wounds that never quite healed but had scarred over with time. They passed a group of children playing with the shingles on the beach.

"Do you realise," Lara said suddenly, her voice full of wonder, "in a few days, it'll be exactly forty-five years since we met?"

Luke smiled, warmth spreading through him. "A lifetime."

She looped her arm through his, leaning slightly against his shoulder. "A lifetime of love, Luke. You are the bestest friend I've ever had." Her deliberate use of the childish superlative—a running joke between them—brought back echoes of countless shared moments.

Luke chuckled, the sound mingling with the crash of waves. "And now we sound like a pair of mushy pre-teens."

But in a quiet corner of his heart, a thought lingered, unspoken. How different might life have been if he had been wired another way? If he had loved her the way she had once loved him? The question hung in the air between them before dissolving into the salt spray and shifting sand, like so many possibilities that life presented and then reclaimed.

As the sun began its final descent toward the horizon, casting long amber rays across the water, they turned back toward their accommodation, their shadows stretching behind them like elongated versions of their younger selves—still joined, still walking forward together, regardless of what paths they had chosen.

The next morning, Luke rapped his knuckles against her door. "Come on, sleepyhead, wake up! I'm coming in with coffee."

A muffled groan came from within, followed by the sound of Lara burrowing herself deeper under the covers. "Aaaargh, do I have to wake up?"

"Well, you could stay in bed and miss the most glorious day outside," Luke countered, stepping inside and setting the coffee down beside her. The scent of roasted beans curled into the air, rich and inviting.

Lara groaned again but reluctantly pushed herself upright, hair wild, eyes still laced with sleep. She wrapped her hands around the warm mug, inhaling deeply before taking a slow, luxurious sip. "It's been a mad few months," she murmured. "I feel like I haven't slept in years."

"I know," Luke said, sitting on the edge of the bed. "But I also know you'll kick yourself if you waste the day hiding under the covers."

She sighed, stretching out like a cat before pushing her hair back from her face. "Damn you for knowing me so well." Then, as she took another sip, her expression shifted. "One thing I need to clarify, though."

"Hmmm?"

Her gaze locked onto his, suddenly sharp. "Why did you really give up the job?"

The question hit him like a gut punch. He hadn't seen it coming —not from her, not now. He had never explained it, never given a proper reason. Just walked away and let the world assume what it wanted. But Lara wasn't the world. She was Lara. And she was watching him now, her dark eyes steady, peeling back his silence layer by layer. He swallowed, forcing a smile. "I had my reasons, Lara. I'll tell you one day. But not today." He reached over and nudged her knee. "Now, get up and get ready, or the day will just vanish before we know it."

She held his gaze for a moment longer, as if debating whether to press him further. Then, with a sigh, she nodded.

When he left her room, he leaned his head back against the hallway wall and exhaled. God, how he hated keeping things from her. He had hidden Ben from her for months, and look how that had ended.

Now, as he absently flipped through a local magazine while she got dressed, a question gnawed at him. Could she already sense it? Did her instincts, so damn sharp when it came to him, pick up on his distress? Or was he still managing to hide it?

Later, as they sat at a weathered wooden table overlooking the water, the scent of salt and vinegar mixed with the crisp sea air. The breeze whipped through their hair, tangling it in unruly waves. Every so often, a brazen seagull swooped down, snatching a chip from Lara's plate. She laughed, unbothered, tossing another one their way like an offering. When she finished eating, she pushed her plate forward, letting the scavengers feast on the remains.

"The owner's not best pleased," Luke warned, watching as a nearby staff member shot them a disapproving glance.

Lara shrugged, stretching lazily before rising to her feet. "Are you done? Come on, let's walk."

They wandered side by side, their steps in sync, their silence comfortable. Around them, Brighton thrived with life. The delighted shrieks of children echoed as they chased the tide. The chatter of tourists blended with the calls of street performers, their voices rising and falling like the waves crashing against the pebbled shore.

The scent of glazed donuts and hot sausage rolls curled through the salt-heavy air, mingling with the briny tang of seaweed and the distant smokiness of charred fish from the pier's bustling food stalls.

Seagulls wheeled above, their sharp cries slicing through the breeze, ever watchful for an unguarded cone of chips.

The sea stretched before them, endless and glinting under the afternoon sun, its restless waves kissing the shore with a rhythmic hush. Wooden groynes jutted out into the water like weathered sentinels, their surfaces rough with salt and time. Nearby, a couple sat on striped deckchairs, their laughter swallowed by the wind as they sipped cider from plastic cups.

Lara paused, inhaling deeply, letting the crisp air fill her lungs. "God, I've missed this," she murmured.

Luke smiled, tilting his face toward the breeze, the taste of salt lingering on his lips. "Yeah," he said softly, "Me too."

Then, suddenly, Lara spoke, her voice laced with reflection. "Did you know Sushil got in touch with me a few years ago?"

Luke's stomach clenched. Sushil. His name alone stirred old resentments, old regrets. Why hadn't he seen through him earlier? Why had he not protected Lara when he should have?

"Really?" His voice was measured, but the tension curled tight in his chest. "Why didn't you tell me?"

Lara exhaled, kicking at a stray pebble. "Because, honestly, by then, I didn't even care. Talking about him would have given him more space in my head than he deserved. Besides," she glanced up at him, "you were still picking up the pieces after Ben. I didn't want to dump another mess at your feet."

Luke stopped walking. "Lara, your problems are never a mess to me." His voice was firm, his brow creased. "So, what did he want?"

"Oh, the usual," she said, rolling her eyes. "Crap apologies wrapped in self-justifications. I listened for all of five minutes and wondered what I'd ever seen in him. That's when I knew I was over him. Completely and utterly." She reached for Luke's hand and squeezed it. "It was a relief," she admitted. "And you know what? That old saying—'Time is a great healer'? It's true. Give it time, Luke. One day, Ben will be a footnote too."

Luke stumbled slightly, then caught himself. "Can we sit for a while?" he asked. Before she could respond, he sank down on the pebbles. Lara settled beside him. He stared out at the sea, at the endless horizon where the sky met water, where everything blurred into something vast and unknowable. "What Ben did…" Luke stopped, swallowed. "What Ben did just proved, again, what a poor judge of character I am. A fool. An idiot when it comes to love. No wonder I keep getting duped."

Lara's head snapped toward him, her eyes flashing. "Don't you dare," she said, voice sharp with anger. "You are no fool, Luke. You're all heart. And it's them, the ones who used you, betrayed you, and let you go, who are the fools. They are the ones who should live with regret, not you."

Luke smiled, but it barely touched his eyes. He turned back to the water, watching as the late afternoon sun cast golden ribbons across the surface, making it shimmer like scattered sapphires. "The thing is, Lara," he said, voice barely above a whisper, "if Ben or Harry ever came back, if they apologised, like Sushil did, I wonder if I'd have the strength to walk away. Or would I just let them in? Let them step all over me once again?"

Lara scoffed, gripping his arm. "Not a bloody chance I would let that happen." Her voice was fierce now. "Just because you don't have a wicked bone in your body doesn't mean I wouldn't break a few bones on your behalf."

They looked at each other for a long moment, picturing Lara as an avenging goon, and then, suddenly, uncontrollably, they burst into laughter. "Oh, Lara," Luke gasped between chuckles, wiping a tear from his eye, "if only your podcast listeners could hear you now."

"I try to keep things apolitical, but by Jove, has the world gone to hell in a hand-basket!" Lara lay on her stomach, lazily flicking through the same magazine Luke had browsed earlier. A half-empty bottle of wine sat in the chiller beside them, condensation glistening on the glass. Every so often, without a word, she would reach over and refill his glass, then hers. Luke swirled the wine in his glass, watching the liquid catch the dim light. Lara sat up abruptly, running her fingers through her hair, frustration lacing her voice. "You know, Mummy and Papa were on completely opposite ends politically for most of their lives, but it never once affected their love or respect for each other. They debated, disagreed, even argued, but it was never ugly. Never personal." She exhaled, shaking her head. "I don't get it, Luke. Political parties change. Allegiances shift. Promises are broken. Are we really supposed to destroy friendships and families over something so fickle? Isn't that ridiculous?"

Luke nodded. He had always admired this side of her—the Lara who could eviscerate an argument with razor-sharp clarity but never wielded her intellect as a weapon. She wasn't interested in silencing people, she wanted discourse. Lara welcomed opposing views, as long as they came from a place of reason and truth, and she approached everything with empathy and curiosity.

"Anyway," she continued, her voice charged with conviction, "I want to write a book about this. A book that explores why we must step out of our echo chambers, why we must listen, really listen, to what's being said. Even if it's uncomfortable. Even if it goes against everything we believe in. Without conflict, we don't grow. We don't learn." She turned to him, eyes gleaming. "What do you think?"

"I think it's brilliant," Luke answered, but there was caution in his tone. "Just... be careful. You know the trolls will come after you."

Lara let out a bark of laughter. "Ha! They already have. Remember when I did that podcast on internalised misogyny? I got death threats from women. Imagine that—women threatening me for pointing out how we're conditioned to undermine ourselves."

Luke smiled, shaking his head. "Unbelievable."

As the night stretched on, Lara spoke animatedly about her ideas, her hands slicing through the air as she laid out her vision. She was on fire, electric with passion. Luke listened, nodding, throwing in the occasional quip, but mostly, he remained silent.

Lara was too sharp not to notice. "Okay, what's going on with you?" Lara pushed the magazine aside and looked him square in the face. Her eyes bore into him, pinning him against the sofa. "You've been so quiet this entire trip. Tell me. I want to know."

Luke exhaled, forcing a smile. "Nothing much, Lara. I'm just tired. And honestly? I have nothing exciting going on in my life right now. Nothing worth mentioning, anyway."

She frowned, scrutinising him. "That's ridiculous, Luke. Life doesn't have to be thrilling every second of every day for us to talk about it." Her voice softened. "Really. What's up?"

Before she could press further, Luke sprang up from the sofa. "Oh, before I forget!" He disappeared into his room and returned moments later with a small bag in hand. "Something from Mum."

Lara took the bag hesitantly, her eyes widening. "Christine left me something?"

She reached inside and pulled out a silk scarf—cream, adorned with delicate pink peonies. The moment she saw it, she gasped. "I remember this," she whispered, running her fingers reverently over the fabric. "She wore it to my wedding. I told her it was beautiful. She... she remembered." Her voice quivered, and before she could stop them, tears welled up in her eyes.

Luke swallowed hard. "Mum always remembered the little things. It was her favourite pastime, giving people exactly what they wanted, even when they didn't realise it themselves. When I was a child, I thought it was some kind of superpower."

Lara let out a watery chuckle. "Oh, but Luke, it is."

Slowly, she draped the scarf around her shoulders, then brought it to her nose and inhaled. "I can still smell her perfume on it."

"Sorry, I didn't have time to dry-clean it."

"Don't be silly," she murmured. "I love it. It makes me feel closer to her."

Bit by bit, the memories unfurled between them. The first time they'd had lunch together at The Centre. Their mutual love for vanilla ice cream drowned in hot fudge sauce. The way their mothers' bond had spilled over into their own lives. Lara reached for her phone, scrolling through old photos—some crisp, some grainy, some nearly unrecognisable.

Luke squinted at one. "What is this?"

Lara burst out laughing. "It's us, dressed up. Me as a village belle, you as an Indian dacoit."

Luke stared at it in disbelief. "I have zero memory of this moment."

"Oh, this was during my mad dress-up phase that I somehow roped you into." She smirked. "I think you look quite dashing."

Luke shook his head with a laugh. "You have got to be joking."

But then she stilled, her expression softening as she looked at him, really looked at him. "You know... this might have been when I first fell in love with you."

Luke's breath caught, but before he could react, she smiled, a slow, sweet, knowing smile.

"I still love you, Luke," she said, her voice soft. "You know that, don't you? You don't have to hide anything from me. Please... believe me when I say that."

She rested her head on his shoulder, and he let her. Words would only ruin the moment. So, instead, he pressed a kiss to the top of her head and let his silence speak for him.

———

Luke lay in bed, staring at the ceiling. The clock had long since crept past midnight, yet sleep remained stubbornly elusive. The unfamiliar shadows of the Airbnb room shifted and danced as headlights from occasional passing cars swept across the walls. Outside, the distant rush of waves provided a constant backdrop to his tumultuous thoughts. Nature's indifferent lullaby failing to soothe him.

Over an hour ago, Lara had stumbled into her room, laughter still lingering on her lips, her body swaying slightly from the wine they'd shared. The scent of salt air and that perfume she'd worn for decades clung to her as she'd leaned against her doorframe. She had thrown him a drowsy warning: "Don't wake me too early."

He had grinned, falling easily into their familiar rhythm. "Not even to wish you Happy Birthday?"

For a moment, her face had stilled, eyes widening as if she had only just remembered. Then, with a small, decisive shake of her head, hair brushing across her shoulders, she had said, "No. Not even for that."

Now, as he lay in the dark, replaying the evening over and over, a gnawing thought took root in his mind. Had he done the right thing? The fair thing? Bringing her here to Brighton, unearthing memories that perhaps should have remained buried. He fingered the edge of the bedsheet, his knuckles white with tension. He had spent his whole life trying not to hurt people. Moving through the world with careful, measured steps, mediating conflicts rather than causing them, offering comfort rather than demanding it. And yet, here he was.

Then, without warning, the tears came. Hot. Relentless. Wrenching through him, shaking him from the inside out. They caught him by surprise—these emotions he thought he'd carefully compartmentalised, now breaking free like water through a crumbling dam. He buried his face in the pillow, muffling the sobs as they tore through him. He cried for Steve, his brother, who died much too young. For Jim, his father, who he never made peace with. For Harry, who had chosen his own exit. For Christine, whose love he missed every single day. For Lara.

He cried for the boy he had once been. The boy who had been so full of dreams, of love, of hope. The boy who had believed in happy endings, in redemption, in the fundamental goodness of the world.

And now? Now he was just tired. So very tired. A weariness that seeped into his bones, that lived beneath his skin. A soul-deep exhaustion that no amount of sleep could ever replenish.

He stared at the moonlight filtering through the thin curtains, creating patches of silver on the worn carpet. If a life could be measured in moments of happiness, then he had no right to complain.

He had seen joy—bright, dazzling, almost too much to bear. He had lived with freedom, chased adventure across continents, loved with an open heart, and endured the ruinous aftermath of heartbreak. He had danced until dawn in Barcelona, hiked the misty heights of Machu Picchu, slept under desert stars, and swum in waters so blue they seemed otherworldly.

But what he had never done, and would never do, was wither into dependence. The thought of becoming feeble, of needing love, care, and kindness from strangers filled him with a quiet horror.

Luke turned onto his side, watching the digital clock tick over to 2:47. His mouth was dry, his eyes swollen. In the next room, he could hear Lara's soft, rhythmic breathing through the thin wall. How peaceful she sounded.

By 3 a.m., he surrendered. Swinging his legs over the edge of the bed, he rose and padded to the bathroom, his bare feet silent on the cool tile floor. The harsh fluorescent light made him wince as he flicked the switch.

Luke splashed cool water against his face, allowing it to shock him into momentary clarity. Droplets clung to his eyelashes, ran down his neck, soaked the collar of his t-shirt. He lifted his gaze to the mirror and studied himself—the gauntness of his face, the pallor of his skin, the quiet defeat etched in his eyes. The lines that fanned from their corners speaking of laughter as much as sorrow. Then he gave his reflection a wan smile, a private acknowledgment between present self and past selves. He turned and walked back to his room; the decision crystallising with each step.

Inside, he pulled out a sheet of paper from his case, ready for this very purpose. He uncapped the pen, settled himself into the little chair, bending over the desk, and began writing. The words came slowly at first, then in a rush, as if released from a lifetime of restraint. His breath steadied as he wrote, each sentence a step toward the forgiveness he was seeking. Outside, the first hints of dawn began to lighten the sky, the darkness gradually yielding to the inevitable.

My Dearest Lara,

By the time you read this, I will be gone.

This may be the most selfish thing I have ever done. Perhaps the most unforgivable. And yet, if there is anyone in this world who might understand, who might, one day, find it in their heart to forgive me, it is you.

Lara, I never wanted to hurt you. Never. When you told me yesterday that you love me, I believed you with every fibre of my being. I felt it in your arms around me, in the way your voice wrapped itself around my name. You have fought for me and beside me. For my happiness. My sanity. My very existence. But, my love, there are battles you cannot fight. Wars waged in silence, in solitude, long before anyone else even knows they have begun.

Mine began a year ago. Or maybe, if I'm honest, it was always there, waiting beneath the surface. The fatigue I dismissed, the numbness in my fingers I blamed on long flights, the unsteadiness I chalked up to exhaustion. But the truth, Lara, is that I have multiple sclerosis. The primary progressive kind. The kind that does not pause, does not relent, does not offer the illusion of remission. Slowly, inexorably, my body will fail me—my movement, my mind, my very sense of self, slipping away piece by piece. The tremor in my left hand that I have hidden from you. The growing difficulty with stairs. The sudden, suffocating fog in my brain. The changes have already begun. Small, insidious but irreversible.

You asked why I left my job. This is why. I knew I couldn't keep flying. The medical evaluations confirmed what I already suspected. And without the flying, the union—our union—had no place for me either. I couldn't bear to tell you then—to watch the realisation dawn in your eyes, to witness your confusion transform into pity. I've seen that metamorphosis before, in doctors' faces, in nurses' eyes. I couldn't bear to see it in yours.

I have spent months trying to make peace with this. Nights drowning in research, days weighing the unbearable. I have consulted every specialist, chased every flicker of hope, only to reach the same, inevitable truth: there is no cure. Only a slow, merciless decline.

And so, I have chosen to leave while I am still myself. While I can still walk, think, remember. While I can still look at you and see love, not loss. I refuse to let this disease strip me down to an echo of the man you knew. I will not let it take my dignity, my agency, my choice. I want to go on my terms, Lara. Not the disease's.

My affairs are in order. Almost everything I have, I leave to you—my house, the vintage records you always teased me about, the money Mum left me. The cattery belongs to Sue; that's my gift to her. And Lexi—she already has what she would cherish most. I have written to her separately.

And now, the hardest part.

I know calling you here was selfish. Maybe even cruel. But Lara, I was afraid. What I am about to do is not bravery; it is fear. Fear of what my life will become if I stay—the indignities, the dependence, the slow erosion of self. But I am just as afraid of what lies beyond. The great, unknowable vastness that awaits us all.

I needed you. One last time. Your strength, your light, your unshakable love. I needed to be held and to be reminded that I mattered. That my life, for all its flaws and failings, meant something. That I was more than a diagnosis, more than a prognosis, more than a timeline of deterioration. And you gave me that, Lara. As you always have. From the very beginning, right up until last night.

Please, please forgive me. For the pain I know this will cause. For the questions that will never have satisfying answers. Forgive me for my weakness, my fear, my final act of defiance. And know this: my love for you was the truest thing I have ever known. It alone has made this life—this imperfect, fleeting life—worthwhile.

All my love, always and beyond,
Luke x

P.S. This year's gift for you is 'Orbital'. Its depth, its aching beauty, left me breathless. I hope it does the same for you. And, Lara, know this: in some way, in some form, I will always orbit you. Even after I am gone. In the music that moves you. In the sunset that takes your breath away. In the quiet moments when memory embraces you like an old friend. Look for me there. And know that I am at peace.

Before dawn, Luke placed the book outside Lara's door, the letter carefully folded between its pages. His fingers lingered on the cover, his touch featherlight, tracing the title of 'Orbital' one last time. A silent farewell.

He stood there, breathing deeply, listening to the soft rise and fall of her breath on the other side of the door. For a moment, his resolve wavered. His hand lifted, hovering inches from the door's surface, trembling slightly—whether from emotion or the early symptoms of his disease, he couldn't tell anymore.

But no. The decision was made. The path chosen.

He withdrew his hand, stepped back. His heart constricted

painfully in his chest, a physical manifestation of his emotional torment. This was mercy, he reminded himself. Then he turned away.

The door shut behind him with a soft click. Outside, the air was sharp with the scent of salt and damp earth, the distant murmur of waves curling against the shore. The sky stretched above him in inky darkness, the dregs of the night reluctant to let go. But on the horizon, the first slivers of light were creeping in. Orange flames licking at the edges of the deep blue, the sun stirring from its slumber. How fitting, he thought, to leave as the world awakens.

He started walking.

The streets were empty, the world hushed, as if it, too, held its breath. His flip-flops smacked softly against the pavement, an oddly mundane sound, until he reached the shingle beach. There, he slipped them off, allowing his bare feet to touch the cool pebbles. A jolt of sensation travelled up his legs—he catalogued it carefully, this simple pleasure of feeling, knowing soon it would be gone forever, one way or another. The waves whispered their lullaby, lapping gently at the shore, beckoning him closer with foamy fingers that reached up the beach before retreating, only to reach out again.

He hesitated.

With his toe, he tried to trace a pattern in the stones, an unconscious movement. A nudge to separate. A swirl. A question mark. He tried and failed, the pebbles barely shifting under the pressure. It didn't matter. Nothing really mattered now.

A gull cried overhead, its lonely call piercing the pre-dawn silence. Luke looked up, watching its silhouette glide against the lightening sky. Free. Untethered. He envied it with a sudden, fierce ache.

He exhaled. Took a step forward. Then another.

The first kiss of water sent a shiver through him. It was colder than he'd expected, colder than the morning air, seeping into his skin, curling around his ankles, swirling and foaming, teasingly inviting him in. The shock of it cleared his mind, bringing everything into sharp focus. He waded deeper, the water rising, wrapping around his calves, his thighs. His clothes—a simple white t-shirt, cotton shorts—grew heavy as they absorbed the sea, clinging to his frame. He hadn't bothered changing. What was the point?

Each step was a surrender. The rocks beneath him felt smooth and slippery, eroded by time and tide. He kept wading, his balance wavering, his feet losing their grip now and again, until he no longer felt the bottom.

He closed his eyes.

A memory rose, unbidden. Him as a boy, sleek and brown under the sun, arms slicing through the sea, cutting through the waves like this was his natural habitat. His father's voice calling from the shore, proud and strong: "Look at my boy go!" Water had once been his playground. A place of meditation and recalibration. His muscles twitched with instinct. Swim, they urged. Breathe. Move. But he didn't. Not this time. He'd spent the past year fighting—fighting his diagnosis, fighting the progression, fighting the inevitability of it all. He was tired of fighting.

The water lapped at his chin, cool, steady, welcoming. It whispered to him, gentle and insistent. *Come deeper. Let go.* And for the first time in a long time, he felt calm. A strange peace settled over him, the kind that comes when the fight is over, when there's nothing left to hold on to. The fear dissolved, numbed by the cold. He thought of his mother's womb—warm, weightless, endless. This was just another transition, another threshold to cross.

Here, in the arms of the sea, he was returning to something primal, something vast and eternal. A place with no past and no future. Only the quiet pull of the tide and the gentle pull of the depths. The water reached his lips now, tasting of salt and minerals and ancient things. His body wanted to rise, but he willed himself down, down into the embrace of the ocean.

Then, a sound. Faint. Distant. A voice. His name?

"Luke!"

A trick of the mind. A final illusion before the end. The voices in his head, multiplying, growing frantic—his father, his doctor, Lara.

Lara.

He ignored it. He had to. The letter explained everything. She would understand, eventually. She would forgive him, eventually. He just needed to complete this final act.

The water rose higher. His body wanted to float, to resist, but he forced himself to be still. He was almost there. Almost at peace. His lungs burned, sending urgent signals to his brain that he deliberately silenced. His consciousness began to fray at the edges, darkness encroaching on his vision. It wasn't so bad, this letting go. Not as frightening as he'd imagined.

Then, hands.

No.

Strong arms. Grabbing. Yanking. Dragging.

No, no, no!

The intrusion was violent, jarring him from his surrendered state. Fingers dug into his flesh, desperate in their grip. His chest seized, his body convulsed. A violent cough tore through him, burning salt into his throat. He fought weakly, but it was useless. His limbs were uncoordinated, his body betraying him even in this final desire.

More hands. More voices.

"I've got him! Help me!"

"Luke! God, Luke!"

"Someone call 999!"

A body against his. Pulling. Holding. He felt himself being dragged through the shallows, his back scraping against the pebbles and shell fragments. The indignity of it cut through his fog—to be saved like this, to be denied even this choice.

The sea fell away, retreating, retreating, leaving him sprawled on the beach, shaking, gasping, his breath ragged and raw. The world blurred around him, his limbs heavy, unresponsive. His vision swam with black spots and bursts of light. Morning had broken fully now, the sun cresting the horizon, casting long shadows across the beach, illuminating the small crowd that had gathered.

And just before the darkness claimed him, he saw her.

Lara.

Her silhouette backlit by the rising sun, dripping wet, her clothes plastered to her body. She must have followed him. Her face was wet—was it from the sea or from tears? Her hair clung to her cheeks and her eyes were wild with terror, with fury. Her mouth moved, forming words he couldn't quite catch. He tried to listen, strained to make them out. But all he heard was—

"No, Luke, no. Don't you dare!"

His consciousness flickered, dimming. The last thing he felt was her hand gripping his, anchoring him to the earth, to life, to her. And in that moment, he wasn't sure if he felt gratitude or resentment that she'd pulled him back from the brink. The darkness enveloped him completely, but her voice followed him down, crying, "I won't let you go. Do you hear me? I won't let you go."

Lara

Present Day

Lara watched him doze in the armchair, chin resting on his chest, a book open on his lap. Its pages lifted and fell with each shallow breath, like waves on a distant shore. His face, once full of life, was pale and drawn, etched with the cartography of exhaustion that had become their new landscape.

She had spent a lifetime memorising him. The sharp angles of his face, the way his lips curled slightly when something in a book amused him, the rebellious lock of hair that always fell forward on his forehead, refusing to be tamed even now. But as she sat across from him, watching the way his fingers lay slack over the pages, she saw not just the man he had become, but every version of him she had ever loved—the boy with the nut-brown skin, the young man with the kind eyes, the staunch friend whose hand had never left hers through decades of storms.

Luke had once pulled her from the shallows into the deep, his grip steady, his voice sure. *I won't let go, Lara. I promise.*

But he had let go.

Not then. Not in that shimmering blue pool all those years ago, but here, in this fragile aching purgatory between what was and what

359

would be. He had let go of her, of himself, of hope. He had tried to slip away in silence.

She had read once that when someone saved your life, they became responsible for it forever. Back then, it had seemed like nothing more than poetic sentiment, an idea to be considered and forgotten. But now, looking at him—the man who had given her everything, his loyalty, his love, his unwavering presence—she understood. Luke had been her compass. The one steady point in a life that had drifted so often into chaos. Through distances that ached like physical pain, through heartbreak that threatened to unmake her, through the quiet treachery of those who should have stayed—he had remained. Her friend. Her family. Her heart. The brightest star in her sky. Her North Star. The one she had always searched for when lost. The one she had always trusted to guide her home.

Now it was her turn to be the light.

When she had dragged him from the sea that morning, muscles screaming in protest, lungs burning, his body a deadweight against hers, there had been no room for hesitation. No space for doubt. Only one truth that crashed through her like a tidal wave: *I won't let go. I can't let go.*

She had gripped him as if sheer will could keep him tethered to this world. And when strangers had dragged his body to shore, she had fought the terror rising inside her like a scream. *Was I too late? Have I lost him?*

But she hadn't. Not yet.

Luke had saved her once—not just once, but in countless moments scattered across decades, in ways he never even recognised. He had stood witness to her worst self and still chosen to stay, even when she had given him every reason to walk away. Now, it was her turn.

Later, sitting outside his hospital room, hands trembling in her lap, she had opened the book he had left her. There was a letter, folded neatly between the pages, waiting. She had read it in silence, and then she had wept. Not just for him, but for herself. Had he really believed she wouldn't fight for him? That she wouldn't walk through fire? Had he not known or felt that she would go to the ends of the earth, to the darkest depths, just to keep him safe?

A click of the latch. That tiny, fateful sound that had pulled her from sleep. That soft creak of the door and the ghost of his silhouette slipping through the breaking dawn. The way she had stumbled out of bed, heart pounding with a fear she hadn't yet understood, watching Luke disappear toward the beach. Grabbing her dressing gown. Following him. Instinct? Or something else? A whisper in the dark. A force she couldn't see, couldn't touch, but had understood in her bones.

Go. Find him. Don't let him go.

So she had.

Now in the hush of her living room, she watched the slow, steady rise and fall of his chest. He was still here. That was all that mattered. His eyes fluttered open, finding hers across the space between them. A moment passed between them, silent and electric, holding all they had been and all they were yet to be.

"You're still here," he whispered, voice rough with sleep and something else. Wonder, maybe.

"Always." The word was both a promise and a reminder. She moved to him, kneeling before his chair, taking his hands in hers. "I told you once I wouldn't let go. I meant it then and I mean it now."

His eyes, those eyes that had witnessed her at her most broken and loved her anyway, filled with tears. "I was trying to spare you."

"You can't," she said, her grip strong. "Because we're not separate things, you and I. We haven't been for a very long time."

Lara loved him fiercely. Not with conditions, not with expectations, but with quiet, steadfast devotion. She would be his support when his body failed him in ways they couldn't yet understand. She would steady him when he faltered, lift him when exhaustion set in. Lara would remind him, over and over, that he was not alone. That he was wanted, and that he was loved. He was woven into the fabric of her soul. The last person who truly saw her. The one constant in a life of variables and the one heart she could not survive losing.

Not now. Not yet.

She would learn, adapt, fight alongside him. And when the weight of it all became too much, when grief and frustration threatened to pull him under, she would be his safe harbour. She would hold him through the long nights, the pain, the moments when hope felt impossibly far away.

His fingers curled weakly around hers. "I'm scared," he admitted, barely audible.

"I know," she said, her voice steady despite the trembling in her chest. "So am I. But we've always been braver together, haven't we?"

A ghost of his former smile. "Yes. I suppose we have."

She rose then, sliding beside him in the chair that was too small for both of them but somehow contained them, anyway. His head found the hollow of her shoulder, that space that seemed carved by the universe specifically for him. She pressed her lips to his temple, pouring decades of unspoken devotion into that single point of contact.

"Thank you, Lara," he murmured against her skin. "I love you."

"I know," she whispered.

Once, she had ached for those words, believing they would somehow make her whole. Now she realised those words had always been there, written in a thousand different languages: in coffee brought to her bedside, in arguments where he fought fair, in the way he remembered minor details of stories she had told years ago.

As the setting sun cast golden fingers through the window, painting them in the light of a day ending but another yet to come, she knew with absolute certainty that whatever time they had left—years, months, moments—it would be enough. It had to be enough. They had discovered in each other what most spent lifetimes searching for and never found: a love that defied explanation, that remained steadfast when every other foundation crumbled.

When the darkness rose, when the sea threatened to claim them, they would fight. Together. Side by side. His battle was hers now; her strength was his. No matter how vast the ocean, no matter how merciless the tide, they had always found their way back to each other. And they always would.

Always.

THE END

Afterword

Did you know there are four other books in 'The Friendship Collection'? You can check them out here:

The Intimacy of Loss
A Quiet Dissonance
Intersections - A Novel
Our Liminal Spaces

Please do remember to rate and/or review this book on your preferred site. It helps other readers discover this novel. Thank you!

If you enjoyed this book, you can sign up to hear more about my new releases and any special offers.

Do visit www.poornimamanco.com to keep abreast of all my news.

Acknowledgments

This book was written under extraordinary circumstances. Midway through the writing process, I experienced a medical emergency known as Sudden Sensorineural Hearing Loss (SSNHL). It was initially misdiagnosed, and I missed the critical 72-hour window during which steroid treatment might have saved my hearing.

By the time the correct diagnosis was made—three weeks later—I began a course of steroids and Hyperbaric Oxygen Therapy in a last attempt to restore what had been lost.

It wasn't enough. As I write this, I have lost 80% of the hearing in my right ear. I will be wearing a hearing aid, a reality that has taken time to accept.

In the midst of fear, uncertainty, and grief, I found solace in Luke and Lara's world. Their story became my refuge, offering escape when I needed it most.

I could not have navigated this journey alone. I am deeply grateful to my family, my friends, my brilliant editor Charulatha Dasappa, and the community of fellow authors who stood by me with unwavering encouragement.

No one walks through life untouched by hardship. I did retreat for a time, but I have returned with hope in my heart and the comfort of knowing I am loved and valued for who I am.

I wish the same for you.

About the Author

Poornima is an award-winning novelist whose short stories have been published in The Guardian and The Telegraph newspapers in the UK. Born and raised in India, she still retains a deep connection to her motherland, which reflects in all her stories and books. Poornima lives in the UK with her family.

Also by Poornima Manco

Parvathy's Well & other stories

Damage & other stories

Holi Moly! & other stories

Parvathy's Well & Other Stories: The India Collection

Twelve - stories from around the world

Eight - Fantastical Tales From Here, There & Everywhere

Six - Strange Stories of Love

Around the World in Twenty-Seven Tales

The Intimacy of Loss

A Quiet Dissonance

Intersections - A Novel

Our Liminal Spaces